BOOK THREE OF THE REFORGED TRILOGY

HAMMER OF TIME

ERICA LINDQUIST & ARON CHRISTENSEN

LOOSE LEAF STORIES

Cover art by Rowena Wang
Edited by Andie Letourneau, Amber Presley, Lacey Waymire,
Mara Joya, Mitzie Renville, Cedar LaBrie, Kathy Lindquist and Sean Emerson

This is a work of fiction.
All characters, organizations, places and events portrayed in this book
are either the product of the authors' imagination or are used fictitiously.

Find more of our books at LLStories.com

For Chris and Elaine Christensen
You taught us to build cities from sand

[1]

GLORIOUS

Xartasia stood in front of the window, her arms folded into her white sleeves. Her feathered wings moved restlessly and filled the Oslain'ii's small observation deck with a faint rustling sound.

"Do you not wish you were out there, commander?" she asked. "With your soldiers? Surely you hunger."

Xartasia could see his reflection in the smoothly curved glass. The oil-slick black nanite armor curled up from his skin, rippling in the ship's recycled air like smoke and momentarily obscuring his shape. A moment later, the swarm of microscopic machines settled once more onto Dhozo's knotted, hugely muscular body. The Devourer bared his wide mouthful of sharp white teeth.

"My soldiers will bring the best of the kill to me when it's done," the alien commander rasped. "They know better than to lie to me."

That wasn't really his voice, Xartasia knew. Dhozo's own voice was that deep growl almost outside hearing that sounded like the rumble of thunder. The snapping, grating voice was the Devourer's nanite swarm computer translating his words.

"Why not take it for yourself?" she asked.

"I trust my people, aerad. I don't trust you."

Xartasia shrugged at his reflection. She didn't trust Dhozo and his Devourers, either.

Xartasia returned her attention to the scene outside. She had to squint to see much of anything. The Oslain'ii maintained a safe distance from the silvery oblong enormity of Koji Far-Orbit Station 144. Another gout of searing, blinding white flame flashed from one of the station's large airlocks. The huge fibersteel door folded across the middle like a discarded mycolar wrapper, crumpled and then vanished, yanked inside by an unseen force. Unseen, but not unknown. Dhozo had dispatched seven Devourers to take the station run and protected by over a thousand Alliance personnel.

KFO Station 144 was tearing in half. Of the twelve starfighters that protected the installation, only two remained. Another Devourer crested the station's humped back. Xartasia knew the aliens' names, but she couldn't tell them apart, not at this distance.

The Devourer fired a pair of particle beams that seared black lines of char across one of the fighter's engines. The thruster flared and then went dark. A long barbed chain as thick as Xartasia's waist lashed out from the Devourer and wrapped around the cockpit before the fighter could spiral further into the void. Hooks tore through the canopy as the Devourer pulled the fighter down. They required metal and minerals, but what the Devourers truly craved was meat.

"You have earned your name," Xartasia said quietly.

Her words weren't meant for Dhozo, but his smoky black cloud of nanites heard her and sent the audio signal straight to the huge commander's brain.

"Devourers?" Dhozo filled the observation deck with a grating sound like scraping metal. He was laughing. "That's not our name."

A burst of static echoed from the direction of Oslain'ii's cockpit and controls.

"Sections eight through twelve have lost pressure!" cried a voice in Aver. "What the hells happened to the airlocks?"

The frightened voice on the com was distorted. Security guards and researchers shouted over the Alliance frequencies.

"Something's cutting through the bulkhead!"

"I can't raise operations–"

"Where's the fire? The core is full of smoke, but I can't see any fire. Fire suppression–"

"There's something in the smoke!"

Screams echoed through the Oslain'ii.

"You are ensuring that those will not be received, yes?" Xartasia asked. "Jamming them?"

Dhozo nodded. He didn't look at the Arcadian.

Somewhere deep inside the Alliance outpost, a vital support gave way. The station's blunt nose twisted and tore, collapsing in on itself. Bulkheads blackened as though burned and crumbled. A long-limbed shadow moved through KFO Station 144. It seemed small, but only from this distance. The Devourer was almost twice Xartasia's height, she knew, and five times her weight.

Hooked black tendrils tore through the ruined metal that used to protect the space station. The flames guttered and died as their oxygen vented into space. But even the swiftly freezing gas wasn't wasted. Barbed nanite nets flared out like wings from the indistinct black shape of the Devourer and raked through the pale cloud of frozen gas.

"Calling any CWAAF forces, please respond. Please!"

The voices from the Oslain'ii's cockpit overlapped and blurred together.

"–But we'll breach the hull!"

"Those things are tearing right through! Return fire!"

"Please respond!"

"I've put two batteries worth of laser into that thing–!"

"–eating them! Oh God, they're eating them!"

Perhaps it was the static, but Xartasia thought that she could hear the thick wet sounds of tearing flesh. The screaming didn't stop.

"Any vessel... we need assistance. Help us! Oslain'ii, do you read me? Are you out there? Please dock on level two! We have to evacuate! Get to level two–!"

Xartasia stepped into the cockpit and flipped a switch on one console with a slender white-gloved hand. The terrified cries finally went silent.

"Now we feed," Dhozo said.

"And then?" Xartasia asked.

"We will build your ships, little aerad. We have made our deal. The station should have metal and minerals enough to begin."

Dhozo's gaze remained fixed on the twisting, shattering Alliance space station. One of the remaining portholes was smeared in red and stared back at the Oslain'ii like a bloodshot eye. The Devourers were monsters. But Xartasia would make her alliance with them worth the blood and horrors to come. For her people, for her fallen kingdom.

All would be as it should have been.

"You said *Devourers* is not your name," Xartasia said at last. "Or not your only name, at least, as I have adopted *Xartasia*... And as you call the Arcadians by their old names, *aerads*. So what do the Devourers call themselves?"

Dhozo finally turned away from the devastation outside to regard the fairy. He towered over her and had to bend at the waist to avoid hitting his slick, bald head on the ship's fibersteel ceiling. Dhozo bared his multitude of long fangs again.

"Us? We are the Glorious."

[2]
MIR

"Needing advice doesn't make you a fool, but ignoring that advice does."

- XIA (233 PA)

Tiberius Myles hummed the fragment of song to himself. He couldn't remember the whole thing, just that single line. And even that didn't sound right. Was that really how Bristler's Call *was supposed to go?*

His off-key song bounced and echoed through the Phoenix's cockpit. Orphia lifted her gray-feathered head from under one wing and fixed a cloudy eye on Tiberius. The old hawk squawked at him — a squeaking, rusty-sounding noise. Tiberius wasn't sure if she was joining in or reproaching her master. Either way, he fell silent.

The last echoes faded away and silence fell over the empty Phoenix. Tiberius flew on. Orphia went back to sleep, leaving the old Prian captain very much alone.

———— ● ● ● ————

"You can't be serious!" Duaal shouted. "We *saw* them!"

"We have only your word for that," Ralison said.

The CWAAF submajor sat back and inspected a datadex in his hands. His office was as impeccably clean as his own dark green uniform. The room smelled sharply of soap and harsher disinfectants. Maeve couldn't look anywhere in the room without facing her own angry reflection.

"No, you don't!" Duaal pounded his fist on the polished black tabletop. "You have reports from the Prian police, too."

"Not very many of those," Submajor Ralison said He wrinkled his nose as though he could smell something unclean in his perfect office. "There are... three reports in total? That's not very much to go on."

"Because everyone else is dead!" Maeve cried. She tried to keep her voice quiet and civil, but fury tightened her throat and her words were a strangled cry. "The Devourers tore them apart and left not even remains enough to mourn."

Ralison put his datadex aside and avoided Maeve's eye. Instead, he looked out one of his windows. The office was located on the two hundred eighty-seventh floor, halfway up the starscraper where thousands of offices maintained the Alliance apparatus on Mir.

"That's convenient, isn't it? These Devourer things are supposed to have been gone for a hundred years." Ralison said. He risked a brief glance at Maeve. "*If* they ever existed at all. Why would they return?"

"We have already been through all of this with the authorities on Tynerion," Maeve said. Her head throbbed and her voice was rising again.

"Where are these Devourers, then?" Ralison asked in a tone that made it clear he didn't expect an answer. He ran a finger along the gleaming surface of his desk and inspected the results with a frown. "CWAAF has received no reports of anything like your smoke monsters anywhere in the galaxy. Surely somebody would have noticed something like that."

"I already told you, I don't know where they went," Duaal said.

"Yes, you *banished* them," Ralison sighed. "Using a Waygate of which there is no record. And using magic that cannot be scientifically verified."

"Kemmer kept the discovery a secret while he studied the Pylos Waygate," Maeve protested. "It–!"

"And the Prian police buried it in the mountain," Ralison interrupted with a wave of his striped hand. He glanced over at Duaal. "And you used this conveniently undocumented device – of which none have ever been seen in the core – to send the Devourers away. By your own report, you don't know where, but you are somehow *certain* that they're still a danger."

"They are!" Duaal insisted. He jumped to his feet beside Maeve, cheeks darkened.

Ralison gazed impassively at Maeve and Duaal.

"And they're allied with this–" The officer checked his datadex. "–Xartasia, an Arcadian princess. Why exactly would she work with the creatures that supposedly destroyed her own civilization?"

"We do not know," Maeve answered. "But my cousin sacrificed many lives in the pursuit of her unknown goals. Whatever use she has for the Devourers will cost us all in blood. Why will you not listen to us?"

"He is listening," Logan Coldhand said. He leaned against the wall next to the door. He fixed ice-blue eyes on the submajor. "He just doesn't want to believe us."

Ralison's lips pressed together into a thin line, but he didn't look at all embarrassed. Outside the perfectly clear window, pale wisps of cloud raced across the blue sky. Far, far below, the city gleamed, almost as clean as the submajor's office.

"No, I don't believe any of this," Ralison said. The tall Mirran submajor checked the time on his computer and stood. "I've wasted enough time with this. Look, Miss Cavainna, we have plenty of real problems to deal with. My loyalty is to the citizens of the Alliance, not to some wandering fairy princess making a plea for attention at best, and a grab for power at worst."

"Power?" Maeve asked. "What power do you think I could seize by this... this madness?"

Logan stepped closer to Maeve and put his hands on her shoulders. The cybernetic fingers of his left hand were cold and heavy.

"See? Even *you* call it madness," Ralison said with satisfaction, then looked at Logan. "But you're the one with credentials on file. You arranged this meeting. You haven't said much, though, Mister Centra. Surely no one with a background in proper law believes any of these fairy tales."

"I do. I've seen the Devourers," Logan answered. "I was at Pylos. Which you would know if you had actually read the reports. But even if I hadn't encountered them myself and even if I didn't believe Maeve about it, I would listen."

"Wait, what exactly–?" Ralison began.

Logan didn't wait. "Maeve is warning you about a threat to the entire Alliance. Even if she was wrong about it – which she isn't – you should take every threat seriously."

Ralison stood up and crossed his long arms over his chest. The mask of stripes around his eyes contorted as he scowled at Logan. "An E3 license grants you many privileges, Mister Centra. Privileges and freedoms that depend upon you maintaining a good standing with the Central World Alliance Armed Forces. CWAAF trusted your past experience and training would guide you in execution of Alliance law."

"Trust*ed?*" Logan repeated, emphasizing the last syllable.

"You've clearly been compromised," Ralison said. "CWAAF can't have its own employees inciting panic, Mister Centra. I'm revoking your bounty hunter's license."

"I am *not* compromised," Logan said in a voice like cracking ice. "You can't revoke my permits unless I've committed a felony offense or failed a psychological evaluation."

The submajor snatched up his datadex, tapped the screen a couple of times and then threw it back on the table. "Which you just did. Now get the hells out of my office."

"Why are you–?" Maeve asked, but Duaal grabbed her arm and towed the fairy away.

"Don't make things any worse, Maeve," he hissed. "The Alliance doesn't want to listen. We're on our own."

Duaal led Maeve out through the open door of Ralison's office. Logan followed a step behind.

Gripper, Panna and Xia waited for them at the Hanjirrah library, just a few blocks away from the huge CWAAF starscraper. They sat on the steps of the polished blue dome, in the shade of a colorfully striped awning. Panna set down the datadex she had been reading and Gripper jumped to his huge feet.

"How did it go, Glass?" he asked, calling Maeve by her newest nickname. "What did they say?"

Maeve waited for a middle-aged human in a smooth brown suit to brush past – primly ignoring the Arcadian – and then sank down on the steps beside Xia.

"You're back early," the Ixthian said. "I doubt that bodes well for your success."

Duaal threw his hands into the air. "They won't listen! CWAAF thinks we're crazy, or else that we're trying to start a panic."

"Submajor Ralison suggested that this was all some sort of ploy for attention," Maeve added miserably. "Though even he could not say how."

"And then that idiot revoked Logan's license," Duaal finished. "I didn't even know he could do that."

Every last eye turned toward the bounty hunter. The *ex*-bounty hunter. Logan Coldhand stood on the edge of the tiled sidewalk, arms crossed. He met each shocked gaze in turn until the others looked away. Except Maeve. Logan didn't look at her.

Panna picked up her datadex and turned it over in her hands without reading the screen. "What now? We came to Mir because it had the largest military presence in the core. Except for Axis, of course."

"We can just try again, right?" Gripper said, his plaintive voice ridiculously belying his huge, ogreish appearance. "We can talk to someone else. Someone in another city? Or maybe on Hyzaar?"

"We cannot," Maeve said more sharply than she meant to. She hated to upset the young Arboran, but what else could she tell him? "Without Logan's authority, we cannot make our words heard! Submajor Ralison met with us this morning based only on Logan's rank."

"But... but..."

Gripper had no other ideas, but obviously didn't want to give up. Maeve shared his painful frustration. They had been through all the same arguments and fights on Tynerion, first with the local board of Poes Nor University and then with the global regents.

No one believed them. No one *wanted* to believe the Devourers could ever come to the core. The huge, smoky monsters were a century-old story from a race of people the coreworlders ignored as a matter of course. A hundred years was a long time to the Alliance, Maeve reminded herself as she stared down at her hands. Generations. There were still some alive who remembered the first appearance of the Arcadians, their flight from the Devourers, but they were few now. And even those had only heard stories of the Devourers. Only the Arcadians had seen them.

Only we remember, Maeve thought. But what did that matter? It wasn't her own people that she was trying to convince.

"We should get back to the Blue Phoenix," Xia said. "Staying in Hanjirrah has been expensive and we can't afford to be here longer than it's useful."

"But we don't know where to go next," Panna protested.

"Wherever it is, we can figure it out and get there in the Blue Phoenix," Duaal said. "Let's get the hells off Mir."

No one had any new objections, so Gripper keyed up the mainstream from a dented and claw-scarred computer he carried in one oversized pocket and ordered a large taxivan. It took almost an hour to arrive at the domed library and then for all six to squeeze inside. Gripper's weight made the vehicle bob a little on its orange-tinted null-field. The stripe-skinned driver looked over her shoulder at the strange alien, but said nothing.

No Mirrans had commented on Gripper, Maeve thought. Not where she had been able to overhear, at least. When Maeve whispered her observation to Panna, the wingless Arcadian girl nodded.

"Mir has a greater number of predator species capable of taking down humanoids than any other core world," she answered in the same hushed tone. "The ancient Mirrans survived because they hid from their predators, and they still have that prey mentality. I doubt any Mirran will go out of their way to attract attention from anyone as big as Gripper."

The driver darted another look over her shoulder at Maeve and Panna. Xia's compound eyes turned an amused blue-green color. She smiled at the Arcadian women with shiny silver lips.

"And they retain their ancestor's sharp ears," Xia said. She didn't bother to whisper.

Maeve's face went hot and she quickly turned her attention to the window. They were driving through an older part of Hanjirrah that looked nothing like the glassteel needle rising up into the clouds where they had met with Submajor Ralison. Most of Hanjirrah looked like shelves of pottery. The endless plains of Mir contained little stone large or strong enough to quarry and even less in the way of useful metals. As a result, other than the Alliance starscrapers, almost everything on Mir was built from brick, ceramic and tile.

Maeve's view was of arches and domes in a hundred sizes and colors, all covered in tile mosaics or painted with depictions of plants and animals that Maeve didn't recognize. Most of the people in the doors, on the sidewalks or driving past were Mirran, all tall and long-limbed. Their green and brown stripes reminded Maeve of grass. As they were supposed to, she guessed.

A wall loomed ahead as the taxivan glided over the crest of a hill toward the edge of Hanjirrah. It towered over the city. Not as high as the Alliance starscraper, but the wall had probably been the tallest thing in Hanjirrah until its construction. Maeve craned her neck. She assumed that the gigantic wall encircled the whole city. Some of Hanjirrah had spread beyond the wall, but most of that was the skyport, landing fields like the one where the Blue Phoenix was now, and not many Mirrans lived there.

The wall was old, tall and very thick. Its patterned surface was mottled by centuries of repairs. At a huge gate, a customs officer asked a few questions – there were a number of substances legal on Mir that were not on most other Alliance worlds – but no one had bought any of them and the taxivan slid quickly through the checkpoint.

Unlike the relatively uniform inner surface of the wall, Hanjirrah's towering edifice was painted with vast murals of strange serpentine creatures, all covered in impressive spines as long as Maeve was tall. Looking back over her shoulder as they drove through, she could make out the huge, dark-hued scales painted in meticulous detail. Not loving or artful, she thought, but as though perfectly depicting the great lizard was of the utmost importance to Mirran artists. But no wall – even if the monsters painted on them came somehow to life – would be enough to keep Hanjirrah safe from Xartasia and the Devourers.

"What are those?" Maeve asked, pointing to the paintings.

She only wanted to think of something other than her cousin, but Panna's pretty face lit up. She had been an ardent student of archeology and anthropology before all this began. Even Gripper and Xia looked up, curious.

"There are similar walls around most Mirran cities," Panna said. "They predate the Central World Alliance by hundreds of years. Traditionally, they serve to keep out wildlife, predators that hunted primitive Mirrans for millions of years."

The taxivan was close to the landing field now. A great, flat sea of pale green grass rippled all the way to the horizon, broken only by the angular silhouettes of grounded starships. As if to punctuate Panna's lecture, a snarling howl echoed across the landing field, just audible over voices and the distant grind of ship engines.

Gripper shifted his impressive weight uncomfortably, making the seat creak in protest. He came from a race of herbivores, of prey, too. The Arborans lived high in the trees of their homeworld. It wasn't so different from building great walls to hide behind, Maeve supposed.

"The paintings vary by city and local mythology, but I believe that these big guys–" Panna twisted in her seat to point to the train-length monster in the mural. "–are called *sosurrians*. They're a sort of dragon. The pictures are supposed to scare predators away. In some stories, Mir itself is a sosurrian egg. The Mirrans say that the world will end when the great wyrm inside finally hatches. Later, in Union of Light texts, the sosurrian became one of the forms of the devil."

Ripples of pale cloud reflected the bright Mirran sunlight and Maeve squinted at the sosurrian. Despite the hot and humid day, she shivered. Panna followed the princess' gaze and bit her lower lip in a frown.

"It *does* look a bit like a Devourer, I guess," she said. "With all the black scales and spikes and such."

Maeve's stomach knotted until she wondered if she would be sick right there in the taxivan. The Devourers were terrible enough in nightmares, as monsters of myth and history. But they were back.

And Xartasia had made some kind of alliance with them.

Ralison was an idiot, but the man was right about one thing. Why would *any* Arcadian ally with the Devourers? It made absolutely no sense, but Xartasia had done just that. Summoning the deadly aliens seemed to have been her entire purpose in joining Gavriel and his Nihilists.

But why? Xartasia couldn't plan to use the Devourers simply to wreak destruction on an unjust galaxy. That was what Gavriel had wanted. If she had wanted the same thing, why kill her one-time student at all? He would have done Xartasia's work for her.

Was it pride, then? Was her victory only worthwhile if she led the suicidal charge herself? Maeve didn't think so. Xartasia lacked that sort of mad hubris. Something was badly broken inside her cousin, Maeve knew, but she didn't think that Princess Titania had lost her mind. No, Xartasia had some careful and probably clever plan. What it was, however, Maeve had no idea.

She didn't realize that the taxi had stopped until Gripper was rocking the entire van as he squeezed out the door. Logan offered Maeve his hand. He hadn't said a word since leaving Ralison's office. As the tall Prian helped her down, Maeve searched his face for any sign of what he was thinking, but found nothing. Logan Coldhand felt passionately and deeply – as they had both discovered – but whether he wanted to or even *could* express all those emotions remained to be seen.

The Blue Phoenix squatted on top of a sun-bleached concrete pad, sensor spars bristling out in every direction. Many of them were bent and several were broken. Gripper had repaired them as best he could, but the old freighter needed replacement parts. Parts that cost money its new young captain didn't have. It was expensive enough just to keep the Blue Phoenix flying and its crew fed... A crew that no longer included Maeve, she reminded herself. She and Logan were passengers aboard Duaal's ship, dependent upon his friendship and generosity in their battle against Xartasia.

"Let's get some lunch," Duaal said as he unlocked the streaked gray airlock. The door thunked heavily and swung open. "Maybe we'll be smarter on a full stomach."

Xia, Gripper and Panna followed him into the starship. Maeve lingered in the pale sunlight. Logan stopped beside her, his pale blue eyes fixed on Maeve.

"You want to talk to me," he said.

"I do," Maeve admitted.

She couldn't help smiling at her hunter. Even if he was hard to gauge, Logan had no difficulty reading her. He always seemed to know what Maeve was thinking. But this time he was wrong.

"Without my bounty hunter's license, I'm doing you no good," Logan said. "I can probably challenge Ralison's decision, but that will to take time. More time than we have. I can't help you anymore, Maeve."

It had been a long day. A long year... And a long century before that. Maeve was tired and had trouble following what Logan was saying. But when she finally did, she scowled up at her hunter.

"You think that you have failed me," Maeve said.

"I have," Logan answered, expression blank. "Now I'm just another mouth to fill and you don't have much money."

"And so you will... What? Remain here on Mir while I fly away?" Maeve asked.

"If you want me to," Logan said. His tone was flat and pragmatic. "There's not much point in me going with you."

How could he think that? Maeve took both of Logan's hands in hers. The left one was as steady as ever, but the right one shook. Not much, but she felt the delicate tremor like a heartbeat.

"You are not some tool to me," Maeve said. "You have not served some purpose after which I would discard you."

Logan went very still and said nothing. Maeve strained up onto the tips of her toes, stretching her wings out behind her for balance, and still couldn't quite reach the human's stony face.

"I am not a queen," she said, "and you are not my vassal. You are my lover and I would not be parted from you."

"But–"

"As to the cost of your food and lodging aboard the Phoenix," Maeve interrupted. She smiled at Logan. "You share my room and Duaal will gladly suffer the loss of food in exchange for keeping me out of his way."

Logan Coldhand actually blushed at that and lifted Maeve into his arms, finally giving her the kiss that she had been reaching for. His illonium fingers were cold against her back, even in the warm Mirran sun. Maeve shivered and smiled. There was no touch quite like her hunter's.

"But I... we *did* fail today," Logan said when he had breath again. "Xartasia and the Devourers are still out there."

Maeve shook her head and kissed Logan again. She had no answers for him, and no idea what to do next.

[3]

DISHES

"No kingdom is built in a day."

- PANNA SUL (234 PA)

After lunch, Xia was the first to bring up Axis again.

Maeve poked a blob of greenish goo around her plate and made a face. The coreworlds were full of technological marvels: engines that propelled ships between the stars faster than light and the null-inertia fields that made it possible, laser weapons that could fire thousands of shots on a single charge, cloned and – though far less popular – cybernetic replacements for lost limbs and organs, janitorial and medical nanites that eliminated the need to clean dishes or sharpen blades, even the phennomethylln that coated the Blue Phoenix hull that allowed it to fly into a star's searing corona.

And yet the protein and vitamin paste that made up most meals on the Blue Phoenix felt and tasted like glue. Still, it was far better than nothing... Maeve had been hungry before, starving on the streets of one of Hyzaar's arcologies. Maeve heaped her spoon and swallowed as quickly as she could. *Nutritious* was about the best praise she could lavish on her meal, but that was enough.

When they were done eating, Logan helped Maeve collect the dishes and then carry them to the sink. Duaal's spoon flew toward her with a thought. Gravity was apparently an easy force to manipulate with his new power. In small amounts, at least.

Maeve dodged aside just in time to avoid the spoon dripping on her wing. Logan caught the dirty little missile and dropped it into the soapy water. Maeve rolled up her sleeves and began scrubbing. The sorts of nanites that made it unnecessary to wash dishes may have been amazing pieces of technology, but they were also costly and so it was Maeve's job to scrub away their congealed dinner remains.

"I believe there is still dessert," Maeve told him.

Logan smiled and the expression was still strange on his serious face. Clumsy, somehow.

"I'd rather watch you," he said, and hesitated and before adding: "You're sweeter than any dessert."

"You could help me with the dishes."

Logan raised his left hand. The illonium was as unreflective as a gray shadow. "It's manufactured to be waterproof, but I've cracked the casing too often. Not a good idea to submerge it."

Maeve went quiet, trying to figure out if Logan Coldhand was making a joke. She decided that she couldn't be sure and gave him a kiss instead. His lips were slightly cool to the touch, as though the cracked casing of his cybernetic hand had leaked cold metal out into the rest of his body.

"You could dry them," she suggested.

"I could."

Logan searched around until he found a threadbare dish towel. Panna had been thumbing through something on a datadex – the same one she had been reading earlier that day, Maeve suspected – but now looked up with a frown.

"Are you... doing dishes?" she asked.

"Sort of," Maeve admitted. "Logan was distracting me."

"I bet," Panna said. But she was still frowning. "You shouldn't be washing things, princess."

"Why not?" Maeve asked.

She hoped that Panna didn't think she was unequal to the task. It was just dishes... But the other Arcadian got up and plucked the sponge from the sideboard.

"You're a *princess*," she said, emphasizing the title. "You're above this kind of scullery work!"

"But she does it all the time," Gripper objected. He didn't look at Panna, but was eyeing Logan as though afraid the Prian might kill him with the towel he held.

"And what else is a princess supposed to do while on a ship?" Maeve asked.

Panna shook her head and didn't answer that. Gripper fidgeted and Maeve reached for the sponge. Panna was visibly torn between wanting to keep it away and reluctance to fight with her princess. It made Maeve uncomfortable, but she could at least take a moment's advantage of Panna's indecision. Logan held out the towel to Panna.

"You can dry them," he offered.

Panna sighed and took the towel. Maeve squeezed some bright green soap into the water and got to work. Tiny iridescent bubbles sifted up from the sink and landed on her skin, smelling of artificial pine.

"Our landing fees are only paid up through tomorrow night," Duaal said. He smoothed down thick, curly brown hair. Ever since Prianus, he had stopped bleaching it. "Should I renew them? Or are we going somewhere?"

"What about Axis?" Xia asked. "There's got to be someone who will listen to us about the Devourers."

"We can't go back there," Duaal answered. "We're dead to the Axis police. And if we come back to life in their records, we're criminals, remember? We'll have to go through a trial and pay fines before we could talk to anyone."

"You don't have enough information to make your case about the Devourers," Logan said. He leaned against the counter next to Maeve as she scrubbed a dented pan. "We need to be able to tell them where to look and what to look for."

"But we don't *know* that," Gripper objected in a squeaky voice.

No one on the Blue Phoenix had quite adjusted to Logan's presence, but it was hardest for Gripper. The huge brown alien was still terrified of Coldhand.

"So we need to find out," Logan answered evenly. "We need to find Xartasia."

"How, exactly?" Duaal asked.

He leaned back in his chair and kicked his feet onto the table. His leather boots filled the mess with the slightly chemical smell of polish and left black smudges on the tabletop.

"I don't know yet," Logan said.

Duaal looked at Maeve, who had paused in washing dishes to listen. "And this is the man who always managed to find you?"

"She was trying to get caught," Logan pointed out. "The galaxy is vast. Trying to find any one person in it is next to impossible. So I usually find out where my prey likes to be. I go there myself and then wait. Or else I let it be known that I have what they want and they come to me."

"Can we do that with *her*?" Gripper asked.

He had no nickname for Xartasia and seemed reluctant to give her one.

"I have no idea what my cousin wants or what she intends to do," Maeve said.

"But whatever it is, Xartasia must be leaving some kind of trail," Logan said. "Everyone leaves their marks. We just need to find and then follow it. Gripper, I'll need you to come into Hanjirrah with me tomorrow."

"What?" Gripper jumped up and banged his head on the mess ceiling. "Me? Why me?"

"I'll need mainstream access and there's no significant signal outside the city," Logan said. "There's going to be a lot of information and I need an extra set of eyes. Yours work, right?"

"Yeah," Gripper answered skeptically, apparently not quite sure about this fact. "I guess..."

"What about me?" Maeve asked, a bit stung that her lover hadn't asked for her help.

"You don't like computers," Logan reminded her.

"Oh... yes," Maeve agreed sheepishly. "Is there something else that I can do?"

"I was going to go find where the Arcadians live around here," Panna said. She finished drying the pan and replaced it in a cupboard. She closed and latched the door with a click.

"To find out if they've heard anything about Xartasia's plans?" Xia asked.

"Uh... no," Panna answered, flushing. "I just wanted to talk to them, actually. Maybe see if any of them have some glass armor from the old kingdom to go with the princess' spear. But I can find out if they've heard anything about Xartasia."

Panna glanced over at Maeve. "Do you want to come? I'm sure it would mean a lot to see their princess alive. Everyone thought the whole royal family was dead."

Maeve scrubbed hard at a bowl to conceal her hesitation. She didn't like to advertise herself. It was Maeve, after all, who had accidentally summoned the Devourers into the White Kingdom, where they decimated her people. Even before that, she had been only a cousin to the royal family, in no danger of ascending to the throne or doing anything important.

Maeve had meant what she told Logan – she was no princess. Not really. Not anymore.

"I will stay," Maeve told the sink full of soapy water. "I am sure I will be of more use here."

"Sure," Duaal said. "There are plenty more dishes to do."

Maeve darted a look back over her shoulder at the new captain. Was he taunting her again?

No. Maeve saw a teasing twinkle in his dark green eyes, but it didn't seem malicious. Maybe Duaal even thought he was offering Maeve a legitimate excuse to remain behind.

"Yes," she answered in an admittedly brittle tone. "I have dishes to do."

Panna's face fell, but she nodded.

"How about you, Xia?" she asked.

The silver-skinned Ixthian nodded. "Sure, I would be happy to go with you."

"What about me?" Duaal asked. "Don't I get an invitation?"

Panna actually stuck out her tongue at him.

"I'm sure you have plenty of work here on the Phoenix," she told Duaal. "Overseeing the dish washing and such."

Anger flashed in Duaal's eyes and a red ember of fire kindled in his palm. The proud young mage had never liked being teased. But then the flame snuffed out and Duaal laughed.

"I guess I do," he agreed. "I should put in for supplies in case we figure out where in the three hundred hells we're going."

"Want to trade jobs?" Gripper mumbled. He was chewing on one of his thick climbing claws and spoke awkwardly around it. "I can do dishes."

"I think Maeve and I can manage," Duaal said with a smirk. "You enjoy your trip with Coldhand."

Gripper looked at Logan again and whimpered.

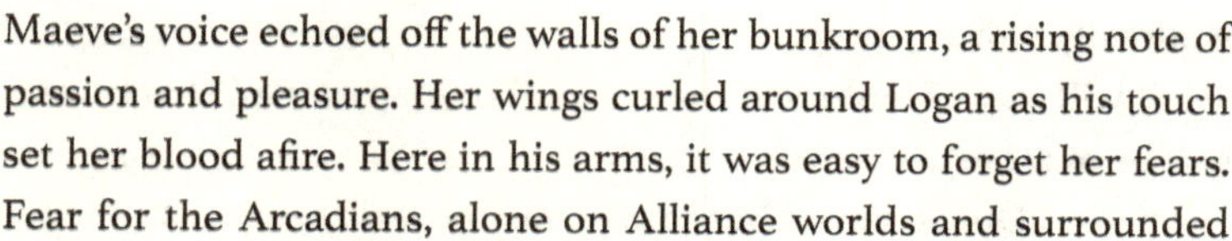

Maeve's voice echoed off the walls of her bunkroom, a rising note of passion and pleasure. Her wings curled around Logan as his touch set her blood afire. Here in his arms, it was easy to forget her fears. Fear for the Arcadians, alone on Alliance worlds and surrounded by aliens who didn't care if they lived or died. Fear of Xartasia and whatever she intended.

And terror of the Devourers.

But not here, not now... Now there was only the hot-cold presence of Logan within her, the feeling of his sweat-damp skin against hers and the musical sounds of her joy. Logan kissed her, never silencing Maeve, but tasting her song.

● ● ●

Maeve lay in Orthain's arms. Her eyes were closed and Aes' golden light caressed her skin with smooth, warm fingers. Birds chirped in the well-tended trees and a nearby stream burbled as cheerfully as a happy child. Orthain stroked Maeve's long black hair as he sang.

"To you I give my love,
My heart and life,
The heart and life we share."

Maeve looked up into Orthain's exquisite golden-green eyes. She lifted her hand and caressed his smooth cheek. Orthain caught her wrist and kissed her fingertips.

"Will you share in my oathsong, enarri?" he asked.

His voice shook. His glass armor could not protect his heart from the woman he loved. Maeve sat up and brushed back Orthain's hair.

"To you I give my love," she sang.
"My heart and life,
The heart and life we share."

Her lover's eyes lit up. Orthain spread his long wings and vaulted into the air, pulling Maeve with him. He twirled her around above the garden, singing in pure delight.

"I must have missed something lovely," said a voice from below.

Maeve looked down. Another winged shape stood in the grass, waving and wearing a simple white robe that rippled in the warm breeze. His tightly bound hair was the black of a raven's wing. Maeve slipped from Orthain's arms and landed in the garden.

"Caith!" she cried and hugged her brother tightly. "Orthain has asked me to marry him!"

"And what was your answer?"

Orthain landed beside a blooming rose tree. He picked a pink blossom and tucked it into Maeve's ebony hair. The knight kissed her brow.

"Maeve has agreed," he said with a grin. "You will be my brother, too. And then you will have to share her with me."

———— ● ● ●

Maeve woke alone, but the mattress beside her was still warm and full of Logan's strange, salty human smell. She gathered his pillow to her chest and hummed happily.

There was a knock at the door. Maeve wrapped a sheet around her chest and unlocked the door with a swipe of her fingers across the control panel. Panna stood outside, still dressed very much like a Poes Nor student, like a human woman with her shirt concealing her back, to cover the scars of her wing removal.

To think that any Arcadian would cut off her wings... Panna's sacrifice made Maeve feel guilty for refusing to go with her today.

"Good morning," Maeve greeted the younger Arcadian. "Do you need anything?"

Panna had inclined her head and raised it now, blushing a brilliant pink at the sight of Maeve's undress.

"I'm sorry," Panna stammered, blinking rapidly. "I didn't mean to interrupt."

"Logan is not here."

Panna was still blushing, but a small, sly smirk spread across her face.

"Humans are much larger than Arcadians," she noted. "That must be a challenge at night."

Maeve refused to be abashed, but her cheeks went quite hot.

"Logan and I are more or less compatible in the bedroom," she answered. "And I was a knight of Arcadia. I am not so fragile."

"I'm sure you can handle any weapon Coldhand carries," Panna agreed with a giggle. She covered her mouth to stifle the laugh and then cleared her throat self-consciously. "I was hoping you would reconsider coming with me today, Highness."

Maeve didn't feel *that* guilty. She shook her head.

"I am no hero for our people," she said. Panna at least deserved honesty. "I have no hope to give them."

Panna stood in the narrow fibersteel corridor, her hands thrust into her pockets and shoulders hunched. She was disappointed, but the blonde girl nodded.

"Alright," Panna said. "Just Xia and me, I guess. Where's Coldhand? Did he leave already?"

"Yes. Though not long ago, I think," Maeve answered.

Panna nodded and turned away.

"Did it... hurt to have your wings removed?" Maeve asked.

Panna turned to face Maeve again and stepped back until she stood pressed against the opposite wall, rubbing her palms over her chocolate-colored pants. She chewed her lip before answering.

"Not much. The anesthetic and pain blockers were very effective. The surgeon did a good job and I healed quickly."

"But you did it in order to attend an Alliance university," Maeve said. She loosened the sheet wrapped under her wings. "Which you have left to help me. Do you regret the decision? Would you take it back if you could?"

Panna clasped her hands in front of her.

"No," she said. "If I had my wings, I would still be on Cyrus. I would never have known Professor Xen or you, princess."

Maeve didn't know what to say. Panna bowed to her and before the princess could ask her not to do that, Panna had turned away and retreated down the hall. Maeve sighed and went to find some clothes. Maybe there were actually some dishes to wash.

[4]

SILENCED SONGS

"Don't go looking for stuff you don't want to find."

- ANANDROU "GRIPPER" (233 PA)

Logan and Gripper hired a ride into Hanjirrah. It was a waste of time and money to drive to the city just for mainstream access, but necessary. On most planets, the worldwide computer network was accessible from orbit, but Mir didn't bother investing precious cenmarks in extending the mainstream.

Modern Mirran culture was still centered on family and tribal bonds, Logan noted as they passed through the huge, painted city wall, and tended to focus solely on local problems and ties. Mir spent more into global defense than any world but Axis, the CWA capital. There was a military network accessible from anywhere on Mir, but without his bounty hunter's license, Logan couldn't use it. So that meant going into Hanjirrah.

Domes and arches in Mirran browns, greens and blues flickered past outside the taxi windows. It was another hovering van, since they were the only rental vehicles large enough to carry Gripper. The lanky young alien sat as far away from Logan as he could...

which wasn't far. Even in the large taxivan, Gripper was just too big to make much space. He checked his computer. The device looked tiny in his rough brown paws.

"I've got a signal," he said in a shaking voice.

"Good."

Logan stopped the taxi driver and paid with a handful of white plastic cenmark chips. The bald Mirran's striped forehead furrowed as he counted the meager tip, but he didn't argue. The locks all snapped shut behind Gripper and Logan, then the driver swerved hastily back into the street, cutting off a lumbering Starwind hauler and a bus with flashing green lights. No one honked or shouted at each other.

It had been a mistake to come to Mir, Logan thought, not for the first time that day. He had hoped that the Mirran's natural caution would work in their favor, but...

There was no point in dwelling on past mistakes. Vorus had reminded Logan painfully of that particular lesson back on Prianus. All he could do now was move forward. Logan led Gripper toward the station the bus had just left. There was a sandwich shop wedged between a luggage store and an Ixthian redprinter. Gripper perched precariously on a stool at one of the patio tables.

Logan took a seat beside Gripper and waited while the Arboran opened up his folding displays. The view from the shop was uninspiring. The road rose up four tiers high, cars and trucks and street trains racing by on null-fields. Logan could see across the road only in splintered fragments between one vehicle and the next. There was a starport depot, the sort of large warehouse that catered to starships, supplying ducting and fuel, food and water and spools of wire and tape – the things that held ships and their crews together.

The sort of crew Logan now found himself a part of. It had been only six years since Hallax – one of Gavriel's red-robed Emberguard – ran Logan Centra through, killing a young cop and creating a bounty hunter in his stead. Six years since Logan had worked with a partner, been a part of the Prian police force. Since he left Jess, the woman he had every intention of marrying.

With the exception of Logan's bounty marks – all of which he quickly turned over to the Alliance military or local police – he had been more or less alone for six years. But now everything was so different... Logan raked his fingers through his hair, still damp from the shower. A drop of water tickled down the back of his neck.

"I'm all set up. So... what exactly am I supposed to look for?" Gripper asked.

"Anything strange in local or Alliance news," Logan answered. "Probably violent. Xartasia means to use those Devourers for something and I don't think it's planting a garden. We only need to look back nine weeks."

"Nine weeks? How come?"

"That's how long ago Gavriel summoned the Devourers."

"Oh," Gripper said unhappily. "Right."

The Arboran set to work using the parameters Logan had given him, typing delicately with his huge claws and muttering to himself. Gripper shook the computer as his mainstream link froze.

"Um, this is going to take a while. That's a lot of data," he said. "There's no search term for *strange*. Sorry."

Gripper delivered his apology with a cringe, like he was afraid of being shot for the delay. Logan's right hand crept down to the Talon-9 on his hip. Without his license, there were many places he could no longer legally carry the weapon. Logan's jaw clenched so hard that his teeth throbbed.

"Fine," he said in a tight voice. "Just get the information. Download half of it to a datadex so I can look through it, too."

Gripper cringed again, failing to understand Logan's anger. He fumbled a datadex – nearly as claw-scarred as his computer – from a huge, oil-stained pocket and began sending information to it. A tiny indicator light flashed green as the datadex received Gripper's data.

A waitress in a very short skirt that showed off a great deal of slim, striped leg veered away from their table when she saw Logan and Gripper. Fine. Logan didn't want anything. He drummed impatient illonium fingertips on the table. The thick gray metal clanked loudly.

The Mirrans built their walls to keep danger out, but trapped other, more subtle dangers inside. Mir was a coreworld. Last night, outside Maeve's window on the Blue Phoenix, Logan had seen a sky as full of stars as sand on a beach. On Axis, they shone brilliantly even in the middle of the day, filling the heavens from horizon to horizon with twinkling silver points. But Hanjirrah's morning sky was a uniform and flat yellowish green. Mirran city walls trapped pollutants inside, making the air thick and fetid. It seemed to cling to his skin and made Logan want another shower. Mir was far warmer than his native Prianus, and more stable, less prone to icy storms and tectonic upheaval. But Logan suddenly missed the mountains and black skies of his homeworld with an aching intensity.

Logan wondered if this was how Maeve felt. If Xartasia did, too.

The Mirran waitress was whispering nervously to her manager, a Lyran with patchwork black and white fur. His yellow eyes and then muzzle turned toward Logan. The short wolfin man nodded to his waitress and then stalked across the patio, ears lying flat against his skull. Logan stood up as the Lyran approached, cybernetic hand clenched.

"Is there a problem here?" he asked.

"I hope not," said the manager. "But your friend needs to leave."

"Gripper?" Logan asked.

He was used to being the problem and Logan looked over at the Arboran, who finally lifted his huge nose up out of his work.

"Why?" Logan asked.

"He's frightening my customers," said the Lyran. "I don't know what he is and I don't care, but I want him gone."

"Oh," Gripper said. His tone was that of a child all too accustomed to being reprimanded for someone else's petty crimes. "Yeah, sure. Just let me get my stuff–"

"You're not going anywhere," Logan interrupted. "You haven't done anything wrong, Gripper. You don't have to go anywhere."

The Lyran didn't actually snarl, but his furry chops peeled back from curved white fangs. The Lyrans were *not* prey animals and never had been. The manager's eyes went to Logan's cybernetic left hand and narrowed.

"Look, you mutts," he growled low in his throat, "I want you out of my shop right now. You haven't even ordered, so just leave without a fuss."

"Come on, Coldhand," Gripper said. "Let's just go."

Logan pulled out his wallet and threw one of his few remaining red hundred-cenmark chips down on the tabletop. "Bring us something to eat. No meat for Gripper."

"Mister, I think..." But the Lyran didn't finish his objection. He scooped up the money and hurried away. Gripper exhaled loudly as the manager left.

"That was a lot of money," he said. "I... I could have just gone, you know."

"Why? He was being a xenophobic idiot. What did you find?"

"I'm not really sure," Gripper said.

He handed over the datadex. The light on the bottom had gone from green to blue, indicating that the memory was full.

"There's been loads of news over the past few weeks," Gripper said. "I couldn't even narrow it down by planet."

Logan nodded and then began thumbing through news stories: unrest and rebellions on Arrideen when the CWA withdrew some funding, a mine collapse on high-gravity Orsin and another police raid on the Sipho underground that left seventeen dead. People died every day throughout the Alliance. Three weeks ago, there had been an outbreak of rughalla on Andris Gia with twenty-nine dead.

A high-speed null-inertia commuter train had derailed on Varnum. Eighty-three dead.

The shop's Lyran manager returned with a pair of large sandwiches and two tall glasses of lemonade. Gripper finished his food in three huge mouthfuls and downed the lemonade with a single swallow. Logan pushed his glass across the table and Gripper drank it gratefully. The Lyran store manager hastily brought more.

Mir's thick air was heavy inside Logan's lungs and sweat dripped in crooked, itching tracks down the back of his neck. He kept reading. There was an industrial accident on Vii. Fifty-nine dead, more than three hundred injured. Seventeen crates of experimental fuel rods stolen from the nearby planet of Vii-Xa, where Starwind Enterprises kept and shipped most of their products.

Logan scanned the Vii-Xa story a second time and frowned.

"Why did you include this one?" he asked, turning the datadex to face Gripper. "No one died or was even injured."

"Oh. Um," Gripper said. He looked embarrassed and Logan had to wait for him to go on. "Well, I thought the Devourers might... you know... need stuff. They don't just eat people, right?"

That was true. Logan wolfed down a few bites of sandwich and returned his attention to the news. Gripper's idea was a good one. Whatever Xartasia and her Devourers had planned, they probably needed equipment or supplies. It was not much of a lead and actually expanded their search instead of restricting it, but Logan was determined not to fail Maeve again.

Reports of an unknown attack on one of Harukin's deep-space observatories. Logan scanned the headline again and brought up the story. Four weeks ago, the Sanford-Belson Observation Platform had gone silent. When authorities went to investigate, they found only a few pieces of debris. Of the rest of the satellite and its two hundred personnel, there was no sign.

Logan reread the account. It didn't contain very many details, but there was a list of related stories at the bottom. Seven of them.

Logan had Gripper pull each of them down from the mainstream. All seven were about missing space stations or starships located in deep space. There had been no recorded attacks, only sudden and absolute silence from their staff. In each case, there were few – if any – remains left behind to investigate.

"Sounds like the Devourers' style," Gripper said. "No leftovers. Do you think it's them?"

"There aren't many who could make entire space stations disappear," Logan agreed. "The ships, maybe, but the Harukin and Koji stations weren't small installations."

Demolishing them was within the Devourers' power. Logan remembered the brutal efficiency with which they brought down his well-armed and armored Raptor. And he had been prepared. Space stations taken by surprise didn't stand any chance at all against the Devourers' superior weaponry and ruthless aggression.

"What do we do now?" Gripper asked. "Do you know where to go yet?"

"No, not yet," Logan answered. "I usually know more about my mark than this, about their crimes and goals."

"But Xartasia was a Nihilist," Gripper protested. "You know all about them!"

"Xartasia was never really a Nihilist. She used Gavriel and his people to get what she wanted. Gavriel never truly knew her, and neither do we."

Logan pushed his plate away and kept reading. Gripper gulped hard and did the same.

Xartasia sat on her black throne, white skirts spread around her like the petals of a flower. The points of her glass crown glittered with brilliant rainbows under the lights. Dhozo stood behind her, arms crossed over his huge chest. His nanite armor swirled and billowed like smoke, deceptively delicate as the tiny machines gathered and transmitted a constant stream of information.

A group of Arcadians knelt at the foot of the dais. The knight in front of them wore shining glass armor. Calathan had long, braided blond hair and dark, intelligent blue eyes, and reminded Xartasia just enough of her beloved Anthem to make her rather fond of him.

Calathan's otherwise handsome face was marred by angry red scars left by a raging Lyran. The coreworlder was long dead, but the mark of his claws remained. And the anger of that attack drove Calathan still. He had been a Nihilist, one of Gavriel's oldest converts from the cult's early days on Prianus. Even now, Calathan wore black and red scarves wrapped beneath the glass armor that Xartasia had given him.

"We have the Devourers now, Your Majesty," Calathan said. "Yet we have passed by a dozen Alliance planets, attacking only the outlying fringes! You have at your wingtips the very definition of destruction, my queen. Why do you use it with such restraint?"

The scarred knight's tone was respectful, though there was a current of true need beneath. Xartasia looked up at Dhozo, but the Devourer's face was hidden behind his swarming black armor. Still, she knew that the hulking monster felt much the same as Calathan. Maybe more... It was only by Xartasia's orders that the Devourers didn't begin their feast with the growing number of Arcadians who followed her.

"I am not Gavriel," Xartasia said. "Our design is far greater than simple destruction. Restrain yourself, Sir Calathan."

The knight in black conferred quietly with the other Arcadians. When he turned back to Xartasia, his eyes were fever-bright. "But why, Your Majesty? What can there be for us anymore? Is death not all that remains?"

"Your glass-shelled morsel has a point, little queen," Dhozo said. His voice rasped unpleasantly. "We can consume any of these planets in a matter of days."

Xartasia rose gracefully to her feet and spread her long white wings.

"No," she told Calathan and Dhozo both. "What we have lost, we will yet regain. You want the secrets that your people have lost, Dhozo, the secrets of magic and the Waygates. And *we* shall have the White Kingdom, our home and heart, once again."

There was a rising scale of surprise from the knights. Calathan's scarred face lit up with almost childish delight.

"The White Kingdom, my queen?" he asked. "We will return?"

"When our work is finished," Xartasia said. "When *your* work is finished, Sir Calathan."

He swept one trembling wing across his chest. ""Yes, Your Highness. What are your orders?"

"Well, it sure looks like it could be them," Duaal agreed. He slid the datadex back across the table to Logan with a thought, without touching it. "But it's still not actual proof. I doubt we can take it to the Alliance."

"Unless we can figure out where they are going next," Maeve said. She sat beside Logan – distractingly close – and smelled good. "Perhaps we can warn their next target and convince the CWAAF to intervene."

"We can't convince CWAAF to do anything," Logan said.

Gripper nodded. "We've been trying since we got back to Tynerion two months ago. We need proof."

"But if we can get to Xartasia's next target before her, we may be able to warn the local law enforcement," Logan said. He found himself unexpectedly nervous, hoping that Maeve would approve of the admittedly tenuous plan.

"Then, if we're at all lucky – which I wouldn't bet on – we'll have some witnesses that we can take to CWAAF," Duaal said. "Right?"

Logan nodded. "Yes. That's the plan. If we can figure out the Devourers' next hit."

"That's kind of where the plan falls apart," Gripper admitted. "We don't know where they're going."

"We might be able to help with that," Xia said from the door.

She walked into the mess with Panna close on her heels. Xia sat, but Panna bit her lip and paced. Maeve looked at the girl with concern plain on her face. Was there something wrong with the Arcadians on Mir?

"What happened?" Maeve asked.

"We found some Arcadians just outside Hanjirrah," Xia said. "They can't afford to live inside the wall, of course. They're cheap labor on the roads and electrical lines that run between the cities."

"But they left!" Panna interrupted breathlessly. "Not all, but a lot of them."

"Left?" Duaal asked, his dark brows furrowed. "To go where?"

"They're going to join the queen of the White Kingdom, apparently," Panna said. "She's offered a home and a purpose to all Arcadians who will join her. A lot of them don't believe it, but enough do that almost half of the Arcadians in Hanjirrah are gone!"

Maeve recoiled as though physically struck by the news.

"Xartasia?" she gasped. "She...? I would never deny our people a home, but..."

"How did they intend to reach Xartasia?" Logan asked. "They don't have ships or colour, so the Arcadians must have some other plan. Is she on Mir?"

"I don't think so. They said that Xartasia arranged a ship," Xia reported, shaking her head and making her antennae wave. "The pickup was two days ago in Lameaux. Those who went to Lameaux haven't returned, so the Hanjirrah fairies think that they got away... Or that it was all a trick and now they're dead."

"Either way," Panna finished darkly, "they're all eagerly awaiting the next chance to flock to the White Queen."

"The White Queen?" Maeve asked.

"That's what they're calling her," Xia said. "The next pickup is supposed to be on Sunjarrah. I'm not sure when... Most of the Arcadians can't afford passage off Mir, so they don't really care when the Sunjarrah pickup is supposed to happen."

"Sunjarrah?" Logan asked. "That's a Mirran colony. It's not far from here, but Sunjarrah isn't one of the planets where the Arcadians appeared a hundred years ago. Not many will have emigrated. Xartasia won't need to stop for long to collect them."

"What about the ship and deep space station attacks?" Gripper asked. He brought up the news stories they had found that morning on his computer. "Where does that fit in?"

"I don't know," Logan answered. "But if we can get to Sunjarrah and catch Xartasia in the act – whatever it is – we can find out."

"Now hold on just a minute," Duaal said. He was on his feet and frowning. "I want to stop that bitch and her big freaky friends, but if we *do* catch up to them, then what? Your plan to help Xartasia's next targets and then use them as witnesses is great and all, but first we have to be able to help. How? The Blue Phoenix is a cargo ship, Logan. We're unarmed and not even that fast."

"I'm not sure yet," Logan admitted. "But what else can we do?"

He looked at Maeve. She sat unmoving in her seat, her silver eyes still wide in shock. Duaal put his hands on his hips and sighed.

"You're right," he said. "I hate it, but I guess we better get up into the black. Sunjarrah's not far, but Xartasia's got a head start on us. Everyone buckle the hells up and get ready to fly."

[5]

SUNJARRAH

"The journey begins not when you step onto one of our ships, but the moment you book your flight."

- XOS, SILVERSTAR CRUISES REPRESENTATIVE (103 PA)

"Not that I am displeased to have you so close, but you must miss your Raptor," Maeve said. She sat on top of an orange plastic crate, legs folded beneath her.

Logan shrugged. "It was only a ship. But we might all be missing its weapons before long. Why doesn't the Blue Phoenix have any?"

"This is a cargo ship," Maeve pointed out. The spear Panna had repaired lay across her lap. She inspected the glass blade for nicks or smudges. "The work here does not often call for violence."

Logan stood next to another crate with his Talon-9 scattered in pieces across the top. He picked up a rough cloth pad and scrubbed at the contacts inside where the battery connected to the weapon.

"I only hunted you for a year, dove," Logan said. "I couldn't have been the first dangerous thing that Tiberius ever encountered. I've heard he was the one who got the original sample of phenno from the Nnyth hive."

"He was. Duaal and I accompanied him," Maeve answered. She could find nothing wrong with her spear and set it down, then slid off her crate. "Tiberius hired me as a guide to take him out to the Tower. All he had were outdated maps from a survey many years ago. But the White Kingdom had a long history of respect for the Nnyth. They taught us to use the Waygates. None know their operation better than the wasps of the Tower."

"So you knew the way. Useful bit of data," Logan said. "And you negotiated with the Nnyth to get some of their secretions?"

Maeve didn't look at Logan. Her face was hot.

"No. We... took it," she admitted. "And fought one of the Nnyth to get away with what we had stolen."

There was a cold, heavy weight against Maeve's shoulder, just above her right wing, and she lifted her head. Logan had set down his gun and rested his metal hand on her back. He didn't stroke or squeeze, unable to trust his indelicate cybernetics not to hurt the small Arcadian woman.

"That was a long time ago," Logan said.

Maeve guessed that was meant to be reassuring. Logan wasn't good at comfort, but that he would even try made Maeve's heart flutter. Infiltrating the Nnyth Tower with Tiberius and Duaal really wasn't so long ago, Maeve knew – not even by human standards – but she had been a different woman then, and Logan Coldhand a different man...

The hunter pulled Maeve into his arms and kissed her. She held Logan close, raking her fingers down the hard muscles of his back.

"Hey, Glass," called a loud voice. "Are you down here? Do you know where Shimmer put the–?"

Maeve leapt back from Logan, blushing furiously. Gripper filled the narrow catwalk above with his rough brown bulk, and his wide mouth hung open.

"Great Green, I...!" he gasped, grabbing at the front of his oversized shirt. "Oh, I'm so sorry. I'll just um..."

"What's going on?" asked another voice. "Move over!"

"It's nothing, Silver!" Gripper announced far too loudly. "We should go away. Like *right now*."

"Come down here," Logan said.

Sighing, Gripper slunk down the stairs. Xia followed him with curiosity on her silver face. Logan returned his attention to the impromptu tabletop and began reassembling his Talon-9.

"What do you need?" Maeve asked.

"Duaal says he ordered up some more keline," Xia said. "But it's not up in the medbay."

Maeve nodded. "I believe I saw it recently."

She flew up over a stack of water barrels and searched the other side until she found the box that Xia needed. It was too heavy to fly with, but Gripper tucked it easily under one long arm and carried it back to Xia.

"Got it, Silver," he announced proudly.

"Thanks," Xia told him. "Can you take that up to the medbay for me?"

Gripper climbed the stairs and then vanished deeper into the Blue Phoenix. Maeve looked at Xia.

"Do you think you will need it?" she asked.

"I used gallons of keline when Coldhand was chasing you," Xia said. She glanced sidelong at Logan.

"The medical expenses were considerable," he agreed.

"They are going to be much worse when the Devourers attack an inhabited Alliance planet," Maeve said. She leaned against the water barrels. The plastic net covering them was rough between her wings. "Far beyond payment..."

"We're not going to let that happen," Xia answered. "We should be on Sunjarrah tonight."

Xia left and Maeve heard the Ixthian retreat back up the stairs, probably to her medbay. Logan waited in silence as Maeve stared at the scarred and stained fibersteel floor.

Thousands of knights hadn't been able to stop the Devourers in Arcadia. Duaal cast them from Prianus, but hadn't been able to kill them. Logan had managed to kill a few Devourers, but it had cost him his ship. What could Maeve possibly do against the monsters? She had banished them from the White Kingdom a hundred years before. That had been different, though Maeve wasn't quite sure how or why...

Footsteps interrupted Maeve's worries and Panna came down the stairs.

"Can I have a minute?" she asked.

"Do you need something from the bay, too?" Maeve asked.

"What? Um, no. I... I wanted to talk to you about Mir," Panna said. "About the Arcadians there."

Again? Maeve shoved her hands into her pockets and realized that she was clenching her teeth.

"I am sorry for their plight," Maeve told Panna. "And I have tried to pay the price for my part in it. But that only caused more harm. Not only to myself, but to everyone on this ship. There is nothing more I can do to make amends for the White Kingdom's fall."

"That's... not what I mean," Panna answered, shaking her head. She drew a deep breath. "The Arcadians need a queen. They need leadership, Your Highness. They need *you*."

"No," Maeve said louder than she intended to. "I am no queen! That is Xartasia's right, not mine."

"And look at what she's doing with it!" Panna argued. "Xartasia worked with the Nihilists, who killed hundreds of people or more. She taught Gavriel Euvo magic that he used to terrorize Duaal and torture you! She helped Gavriel summon the Devourers, then betrayed him and took them for herself!"

"I am not arguing in favor of my cousin's crimes," Maeve said, shaking her head. "I know that we must stop her."

"The Arcadians want a queen. Right now, they have only one choice for that. You would be a much better queen than Xartasia!"

Panna's green eyes were bright with fear and passion. She must have been nerving herself up for hours for this confrontation. "You *should* be queen!"

"The crown is Xartasia's by Cavain's divine right," Maeve said. "I am as much a criminal to our people as she is... even if my crimes against the White Kingdom were unintentional. I have no place on the throne!"

"But–!" Panna began.

"No," Maeve said as firmly as she could.

Panna bit her trembling lower lip, then turned on her heels and retreated back upstairs. When she was gone, Logan replaced his assembled laser in its hip holster. The metal hissed quietly against aged and scarred leather. Logan's expression was neutral, but even with Panna gone, the conversation had made Maeve uncomfortable and she found herself wishing Logan hadn't heard it.

"You do not wish me to be a queen, do you?" Maeve asked, only half joking. She wanted – needed – him to agree.

Logan secured his Talon in the holster with a worn strap and turned back to Maeve.

"No," he said. "Your royalty doesn't particularly matter to me. It seems to bother you, though. Especially Panna's attention."

Maeve nodded, but didn't know what else to say to that. Logan was right. He usually was about her. Maeve spun her spear between her hands. The glass flashed brightly under the sunlights that illuminated Gripper's hanging garden. When she stopped, Logan ran one of his metal fingers up the blade's shining edge and the spear shivered slightly in Maeve's hands. Logan withdrew his cybernetic hand to inspect a new hairline score in the metal.

"Still sharp," he said, nodding. "Does Arcadian glass ever lose its edge?"

"Not really," Maeve answered. "It takes many, many years for a glass blade to dull. Unless it is broken, of course."

Logan nodded and Maeve frowned at him.

"Are you telling me I am still a useful blade?" she asked suspiciously. "That time and deeds have not diminished Cavain's blood within me?"

The Prian hunter's handsome face was hard, but Maeve swore that there was a faint twinkle in his ice-blue eyes. "I was only asking about the spear. Would it matter if I were making a point? You've made your feelings on the throne quite clear. In any case, our focus needs to be finding Xartasia. And surviving that encounter."

It always came back to that. Maeve drew a deep breath against the panic tightening her throat. The sour taste was stale, old.

"We must find her on Sunjarrah," she agreed.

"I know," Logan said. They all knew.

A bout of sparring with the much larger Prian eased some of Maeve's tension, but not by much. Logan was a skilled fighter and even mock battle against her hunter stirred bittersweet memories of his year as her adversary. After several rounds, the ship's intercom finally clicked on.

"We're about to drop out of FTL and should be arriving in high orbit of Sunjarrah in about two hours," Duaal announced. "Logan, can you come up here and lend a hand? I need to run a scan when we come out, but I can't juggle that and fly the Blue Phoenix at the same time."

Logan pulled his shirt back on over sweaty skin and hurried out of the cargo bay while Maeve combed fingers through her black hair. She retrieved her spear and made her way back toward her room while the Blue Phoenix vibrated all around her as it slowed.

But Maeve stopped outside the medical bay. Xia steadied herself on the counter as the ship shivered again.

"Almost there," she said.

Maeve walked carefully to the single small window, unable to use her wings for balance in the tight confines, and looked outside. The stars were haloed in shattered rainbows and then even those vanished suddenly as the Blue Phoenix slowed to sub-light speeds.

They were on the edge of the Sunjarrah system, a pair of large white-gold stars smeared dark across their equators by the inner asteroid belt.

"What is that?" Maeve asked, pointing.

Xia came over to look over her shoulder. "Where?"

"There," Maeve said. "Just above the asteroid belt, on the edge of the suns' glow."

Xia squinted her compound eyes. "I... don't see anything."

Maeve looked again, but could find no sign of the pale flashes of light she had seen before. She shook her head, dismissing the issue and then waved a short goodbye to Xia. Impatient and unsure what else to do, Maeve replaced her spear in her room and then went up to the cockpit. Duaal sat in Tiberius' worn and hawk-shredded old seat, flying the Blue Phoenix toward the paired suns. Logan was in the copilot's chair, fingers moving quickly over the sensor controls. Both men glanced back over their shoulders at Maeve and then returned to work.

"Anything out there?" Duaal asked.

Logan raised a wheat-colored eyebrow. "Plenty. There are thousands of ships in the system."

"One of those *must* be here for Xartasia," Maeve said. "To pick up the Arcadians."

"We won't be able to tell which one with any of these readings. These are mostly atmospheric sensors and densitometers," Logan said. "We need to land and get more information from the Arcadians. If Xartasia is here to pick them up, they should be able to tell us when and where."

The flight to Sunjarrah was as quiet as a prowling cat. When they finally arrived, the Blue Phoenix circled to the daylight side of the planet, a mottled brown and blue sphere with irregular patches of polar ice that gleamed pink in the sunlight. Knotted traceries of green and purple auroras glowed like a crown above the ice.

"Land in New Hennor," Panna said. She was crowded into the corridor outside the cockpit with Maeve and Gripper. "That's where most of the Arcadians on Sunjarrah live."

Panna's knowledge of the fairies was impressive. She might not have grown up in the White Kingdom, but she had made a dedicated study of their ways. Maeve was impressed, but more grateful for the direction. Duaal keyed into Sunjarrah orbital control from a panel in the center of the cockpit.

"Control, this is the Blue Phoenix. We need to put down in New Hennor as soon as possible," he said. "We have urgent business."

"Please hold," a computerized voice answered. "Please hold for an authorized flight control representative."

Duaal banged his fist into the com panel, but his frustration was no rival for the dents left by Tiberius. Gripper winced.

"Oh, come on!" Duaal growled. "Exactly what part of *urgent* is confusing, you stupid computer?"

"Please hold for an authorized flight control representative," the com system answered cheerfully.

Duaal was threatening to pull out the control system's wires one at a time – and Maeve was inclined to join him – when the mechanical voice suddenly cut out and a woman with the same automatic cheer as the computer informed them that they could now land in New Hennor. She sent coordinates to the Blue Phoenix navigational computer and bade them a good afternoon.

Duaal made a rude gesture at the com.

"Xartasia could have already landed and left again in the time that took us," he said. "Damned bureaucracy."

"Then get us down there and stop wasting time," Logan told the young captain.

Duaal stuck out his tongue, but angled the Blue Phoenix down toward Sunjarrah's surface. The view outside turned white-hot as the ship descended through the atmosphere, then dim and gray in the upper cloud layer. Finally, they punched through the gloom and into the warm orange sunlight of the Sunjarran afternoon.

Logan brought up the coordinates relayed by orbital control. Duaal nodded and turned the ship south.

The light of the twin suns cast the domes and arched windows of New Hennor in molten colors. The Blue Phoenix raced high over the bronzed cityscape and landed in a public field tiled in spiraling patterns like licking metal flames. As Maeve stepped off the ship, she rubbed her eyes until they adjusted to the bright sunlight.

Panna said that New Hennor wasn't a large city and taxis were expensive, so Maeve flew. Panna, Logan and Duaal walked briskly below, casting long shadows in the afternoon sun. Gripper and Xia had remained behind – there was work to do back on the Blue Phoenix. And Gripper was scared, Maeve knew. The Arboran was little more than a boy and they were going in search of dangerous enemies. So was Duaal, but without Tiberius, there was no one left who could tell the young mage what to do. He hurried along with Logan and Panna to keep up with the flying fairy princess.

New Hennor looked a lot like the cities on Mir. Other than the scorching suns – the back of Maeve's neck felt brittle and baked – it was almost as though they had not left Mir at all. The glaring afternoon light cast fragmented binary rainbows through the glass blade of her spear.

"Hey!"

Maeve looked down at the source of the loud shout. A Mirran cop leaned out the window of his green- and yellow-banded car. The null-field generator hummed, motionless against the curb.

The officer regarded Panna, Duaal and Logan through his tinted sunglasses. He waved Maeve down to the ground. She landed on the sidewalk, in a spot cleared by watchful pedestrians. Maeve had been in New Hennor for less than ten minutes and she was already in trouble.

"Where are you going with those weapons?" The cop nodded to Logan's Talon-9 and Maeve's spear. "You have permits for the firearm, I assume."

Logan hesitated. He didn't have a license to carry the weapon anymore and hadn't wanted to bring the laser, but Maeve was the one to point out that if they found Xartasia and her Devourers, they couldn't afford to be unarmed. The cop's mirrored gaze moved from the Talon-9 down to its owner's illonium hand. The Mirran's mouth worked under his green and brown mustache.

"Mister... Coldhand?" he asked hesitantly.

Logan's eyes flickered toward his own hand for a moment and then back to the police officer. "Yes."

"So what brings you to Sunjarrah?" the officer asked. His tone wasn't subservient – strictly speaking, his authority far outstripped a bounty hunter's on his own planet – but it was respectful. "Business or pleasure?"

Duaal and Panna exchanged a look, but they remained carefully silent.

"I'm looking for someone, actually," Logan answered. "An Arcadian woman."

"A fairy?" The Mirran cop looked at Maeve, who did her best to look like an appropriately stern bounty hunter's companion.

"The Arcadians tend to stick together," Logan said. "Usually in a single community. Anything like that in New Hennor?"

"Sure," the cop answered. He said it with a slightly buzzing burr. *Zure.* "Over by the old settlement. No one can grow anything there anymore, so it seemed like as good a place to put the immigrants as any. They have a sort of camp out there."

A camp. Fury kindled on Panna's face and Duaal had to grab the girl's shoulder.

"Great," Duaal said quickly. "Which way?"

The Mirran cop twisted in the driver's seat, looking at the street and getting his bearing. "Uh, a ways down Penton Road."

"What's the address?" Logan asked him. "We can just put it in my com."

"There's no system out that far," the cop answered. "Positioning doesn't bother keeping real close track of things out there. Just follow the road out until the pavement stops off."

With a final respectful nod to Logan, the police officer brought his window up again and pulled the striped squad car back out into the street. Every other vehicle slowed noticeably as law enforcement's attention turned back to them.

"The end of the road," Panna said. "That could be a long walk."

"Yeah," Duaal agreed. "Let's get back to the Blue Phoenix. If it's as empty out there as he says, there should be plenty of room to land."

They hurried back through New Hennor, attracting more stares and mutters. Duaal called ahead and Gripper had the airlock open for them. Maeve landed with a ringing thud on the fibersteel and ran inside. Duaal was already climbing the cargo bay stairs, taking them two at a time.

"Um, Glass? Where are we going?" Gripper asked, hanging from the edge of the catwalk by one huge hand.

"An Arcadian encampment outside New Hennor," Maeve said.

Xia pressed herself against the wall as Duaal ran by.

"And you think that they can tell us where to find Xartasia?" she asked.

"There are more Arcadians in New Hennor than anywhere else on Sunjarrah," Panna answered. "One of them must know something about Xartasia's pickup."

The Blue Phoenix rumbled and then jolted beneath them. Sun-washed cityscape raced beneath the ship and swiftly gave way to flat plains. Maeve steadied herself against the wall and stared out the airlock viewport. The ground was a patchwork of tough, pale grass and the lumpier green of scrubby bushes. An occasional solitary tree rose suddenly from the ground, casting a long, dark blue shadow and then was gone as the ship flew past. Logan and Panna looked over Maeve's shoulder.

"There," the Prian hunter said, pointing one of his metal fingers at a geometric smear of brown down below. Logan held down the green intercom button beside the raised cargo ramp. "Duaal, there are some buildings to our port side."

"I see them," the captain answered. "I'll take us in closer... if I can. The sky is full of fairies."

Maeve squinted into the twin suns' bright light. Duaal was right. She could just make out hundreds of pale-winged shapes wheeling and diving through the sky. Circling? Arcadians were not vultures who flew rings over the dead and dying.

So what were they doing?

"There's something down there," Panna said.

Logan jabbed the intercom button again. "Get us on the ground, Duaal."

In answer, the Blue Phoenix dropped precipitously, tumbling Maeve and Panna against the airlock. The window filled with green grass and brown stone as the ship turned sharply and swooped down toward the ground. It landed with a hard thump. Maeve recovered her balance and slapped the airlock button. The reinforced old doors creaked and groaned, then grated open.

Maeve was in the air within seconds, flying low and fast. Shouts and the clatter of footsteps followed her from the Blue Phoenix, but Maeve didn't slow. There was the old settler housing that the cop talked about. The buildings were long and low, with peeling siding and cracked solar panels lining the roof, cloudy and grayed by the years. An old quick-sink well sat crookedly in the middle of the old settlement, surrounded by plastic buckets and mycolar bottles that looked recently used.

But there was no one on the ground. All of the Arcadians arced and swooped through the white sky, casting flickering shadows on the ground below.

Maeve beat her wings and crested a three-story common hall, where Sunjarrah's early settlers would have gathered for meetings and emergencies. The overgrown cornfield was full of a hundred or more Arcadians, wheeling this way and that and crowding the skies with wings.

The dark, sleek shape of a ship crouched in the field's center, crushing dead brown stalks beneath it. An ember-red light glowed next to the closed airlock. Maeve landed hard, spear in hand. Logan and the rest of the Blue Phoenix crew sprinted around the corner of the common building and stopped beside her. Duaal and Logan took in the sight of the black ship and looked at Maeve.

"That's the Oslain'ii," Logan said.

"Xartasia's ship," Duaal finished. "She's already here."

[6]

OSLAIN'II

"That's Xartasia's ship?" Xia asked. "Did she beat us here?"

Maeve shook her head. She didn't know, but her heart slammed against her ribs and her pulse pounded a deafening drumbeat in her ears. Her chest felt too small for her lungs and Maeve found herself panting. For all the blood that she shared with Xartasia, it gave Maeve no better idea what her cousin might be doing. Was she inside that black ship?

"Gripper, call in the New Hennor police," Logan said. He stood beside Maeve, right hand on the laser at his hip. "Get them out here and we'll have the proof we need."

"Yeah, Coldhand," Gripper answered, his voice shaking. "I... I'm on it."

A scattering of feathers sifted down from the sky as the other Arcadians circled, staring and calling out in their own language. There was a click and the black ship's airlock light flashed twice, then turned green. Glossy doors slid slowly open and two shapes stood in the Oslain'ii's blue-lit hatchway: one slender and winged, the other huge and shrouded in black smoke. A Devourer.

The circling Arcadians moaned and then drew together, rising higher into the pale Sunjarrah sky. Duaal's green eyes took on the glassy, unfocused look that Maeve was beginning to associate with the young mage working on a spell. Logan tore his Talon-9 free and aimed it at the Devourer while Gripper stumbled hastily back, his com raised up to one ear. Panna and Xia stood together, the medic with unsteady fingers wrapped around her laser.

The Devourer's Arcadian companion stepped out into blinding sunlight. The fairy wasn't Xartasia, but a man in full and brilliantly sparkling glass armor. His lean body was wrapped with scarves beneath, as was Arcadian tradition, but they were sooty black slashed with scarlet like bloody wounds. His face was twisted and scarred across the brow and one cheek, turning his flesh into a knot of welts and lumps. The strange knight raised his spear skyward. Sunlight caught the glass and flashed brightly.

"Asi!" he called in Arcadian. *Wait.* *"Your queen summons you, sons and daughters of the White Kingdom. Titania Cavainna, heiress to the throne, lives and calls you to her court! All who were born of the White Kingdom shall have a home with her."*

Maeve crouched and prepared to spring into the air, to fall on the knight in black and his oddly unmoving Devourer. But Logan knelt and grabbed her shoulder.

"Wait," he said. "He's talking. Fast, but that's more than we've been able to get so far. What's he saying?"

Maeve's jaw clenched so hard that her teeth ached, but she had to admit that Logan was probably right. The knight in black was ignoring them entirely, focused instead on the flock of Arcadians overhead.

"He says that Titania is alive," Maeve repeated. "And that she summons them to her."

"The White Queen has tamed the Devourers," the knight shouted and Maeve recounted. *"They serve her now, my brothers and sisters. And in that service, our rightful and glorious queen summons you. She needs you! Together with our once-enemies, we shall restore the White Kingdom."*

"Wait, what does that mean?" Panna asked. "Is she going back to Arcadia?"

Maeve shook her head. She didn't know. Now the other knight raised his face, squinting upward to gauge the effect of his words. Suddenly, Maeve recognized him.

"Calathan!" she shouted. "Calathan la Nyra! How can you stand beside one of those who destroyed our kingdom?"

Calathan turned to look at Maeve. There was recognition in his eyes, but no affection for the fellow young squire who had helped him up from the grass after a tourney match, who had shared an entire bottle of wine when they both lost their winners' ribbons to the indomitable Sir Orthain Fyre and the royal consort, Sir Anthem Calloren. Rage twisted Calathan's already maimed face and he leveled his spear at Maeve. Even the ribbons hanging from the haft of his spear were as black as her own hair.

"Maeve," he snarled. "Twice now you have slaughtered my kin. You will answer for that!"

Twice... First Arcadia and then the Nihilists. That explained the black under Calathan's armor and how he knew about her role in the White Kingdom's fall. Behind Calathan, something pale flashed in the dark depths of the Devourer's face. Teeth? Was it smiling?

"The littlest Cavainna." The grating voice came not from the huge alien's mouth, but issued from the swarming black cloud of nanites. "I've heard your name. Commander Dhozo tells us we have *so* much to thank you for..."

Calathan leapt at Maeve, spear leveled at her unarmored midsection. Laserfire sliced past her and struck Calathan in the chest, but splintered into harmless red light against his glass breastplate.

Maeve jumped back to stand next to Logan, who was still aiming his Talon at the fairy. Calathan's spear came down, slashing a deep line of rage into the packed dirt.

"Have you got this, dove?" Logan asked, bringing his laser up to the Arcadian knight's face.

Panna screamed and Duaal shouted at her to get away from the Devourer. Maeve spun her spear down to a guard position.

"I do, enarri," Maeve said. "Go!"

Logan spared Calathan a single cold look before sprinting away toward Duaal. Xartasia's knight in black lunged, slashing his spear at Maeve's wings. She knocked the blade aside with her own and leapt into the air. The crumbling old settlement spun beneath her, flickering like disturbed water with the shadows of the frightened, swiftly scattering Arcadians.

The Devourer was a seething pillar of black blades, flashing red and blue-white with Logan's lasers and Duaal's lightning. Maeve still heard Panna shouting again.

"Wait...! Come back!" she cried. "That's your princess up there! She needs you!"

But no one seemed to be listening. Maeve had no time to spare for Panna or even her hunter fighting for his life below. Calathan vaulted into the air and arrowed past Maeve, forcing her to fold her wings and swoop beneath. He circled to make another pass and Maeve beat her wings hard, climbing. Calathan's armor protected him from both laser and blade, but its weight and restricting plates made him slower.

Maeve arced and dove again, throwing all of her weight behind her spear. Orthain always told his young squire that it was the height of dishonor to aim for an opponent's wings and force them to the ground. It was a cheap victory and hardly worthy of an Arcadian knight – but this was not the Morningfire Court and Maeve had given up her honor long ago. She could not afford chivalry when there were so many lives at stake.

Calathan had no honor left, either. He rolled and Maeve's spear glanced off his curved pauldron. He thrust back with his own spear, aiming for the delicate membrane of her left wing. Maeve spiraled away almost too slowly. The point of Calathan's spear raked her wings and several red-streaked feathers tore away. Pain burned a line along her injured wing.

The two fallen knights circled each other, trying to gain the higher position. Calathan's glass armor reflected the flashes of fire and lightning and churning darkness below and Maeve fought the urge to look down. She parried Calathan's spear again, but he used the momentum to spin the shaft and crack it against the crest of her flight-taut wing. Maeve ground her teeth and lost altitude as she wheeled to recover.

Calathan sang a resonating note of triumph. He shot at Maeve in a straight line, certain that his strike against her wing had slowed Maeve enough. But it was hardly the first time Maeve had fought with injured or even broken wings. Logan Coldhand knew nothing of Arcadian honor and had never hesitated to take advantage of the inviting targets. Maeve twisted and dove beneath Calathan's head-on aerial charge. She beat her wings hard at the bottom of her dive and soared up behind him. Calathan was slow to turn, to break the swift, straight line that had been his gamble. Maeve brought her spear down and drove the blade through his back, into the unarmored spot between his wings. The glass slid past his spine and into his heart. Calathan shuddered, raining blood to the ground below as he fell.

Maeve banked sharply. Beneath her, the Devourer raged like a terrible storm between Duaal and Logan. It lashed at both men with scythe-like blades of glittering black, but the nanite swarm was thin, as tenuous as shadow. Duaal threw up one arm and the curved blade shattered like cheap glass against an invisible barrier. The sharp shards didn't fall, though, but turned instead into shadow and flew back to the Devourer's amorphous armor.

Ignoring a deep, bloody gash through his calf, Logan circled the alien monster as the nanite swarm shifted, accommodating the returning machines. He found a thin spot and fired a long burst of laserfire that burned through the Devourer's thigh, driving him to one knee with a rasping bellow of pain.

Duaal raised both hands in front of him and then swept them down again. The nanite swarm sagged toward the ground around its master as though in a great wind, though Maeve felt nothing. Logan took aim as the Devourer's face was suddenly revealed. It was wide and gray-skinned, with a grimacing, sharkish mouth full of sharp teeth. Even as he staggered backward away from the alien, Gripper's shocked exclamation was clearly audible – the Devourer looked like some nightmare reflection of Maeve's Arboran friend.

Logan fired three carefully aimed shots through the back of the Devourer's exposed skull. The alien surged up to its feet, the holes through its head steaming slightly, and whirled in a wobbling circle to face Logan. Maeve dove, landing hard against the Devourer's broad shoulders and bearing him down to the ground. The creature fell and lay still. Maeve leapt free as the black nanites billowed like smoke all around her. The uncontrolled machines twisted this way and that and then fell on the dead Devourer. Blood welled up from the hairless gray skin and then vanished as the nanites consumed their own master. Maeve stared in revolted fascination as the huge body vanished.

"What the hells–?" Duaal asked, gasping. "Are they coming after us next?"

Even as he spoke, the black machine cloud was turning an ashy gray. Dying? Logan grabbed her wrist and pulled Maeve back.

"We don't want to be their next meal, dove," he said.

Xia and Panna crept closer – but not too close.

"What was that? Some sort of self-destruct?" Xia asked.

"Probably a system problem," Panna said. "Most cultures care at least a little about proper disposal of remains and wouldn't want their armor eating them after they die. We already know that the Devourer nanotech runs on chemical energy. So I'm guessing that without someone to operate them, the nanites turn on the nearest power source. Their dead owner... and then each other."

Gripper ran toward them, waving his arms and pointing.

"The ship!" he cried. "There's still someone in there!"

As if in answer, the Oslain'ii's open airlock slammed shut and the engines – sleek black bullet-shapes mounted under the back-swept wings – roared. Duaal shielded his face from the sudden tempest of hot wind and broken pieces of cornstalk.

"They're taking off!" he shouted over the noise. "Gripper, how far away are those police?"

"I don't know! I'm still on hold," the Arboran answered, brandishing his com.

"Get back onto the Blue Phoenix," Logan called out. "You, too, Gripper."

The hunter was already running. Xia and Duaal were close behind, Gripper bringing up the rear. Panna moved to follow, but then turned on her heels and bolted deeper into the wind-whipped field. Maeve shouted at her, but there was no time to go chasing after Panna. The Oslain'ii was already rising.

Reluctantly, Maeve leapt into the white Sunjarrah sky and dove after the others. By the time she landed and ran through the Blue Phoenix's airlock, Duaal was vanishing through the door that led to the front of the ship. Logan took the stairs two at a time, shouting for Gripper to follow. The bewildered Arboran loped after him, pulling himself up over the railing.

"But I need to be in the engine room–!" Gripper protested.

"We need you in the cockpit," Logan told him. "And bring your computer."

Xia jabbed the airlock controls as Maeve bolted past. The fairy clipped one of her wings on Gripper's planters, winced and landed on the fibersteel catwalk. She ran toward the cockpit, but her view was eclipsed by Gripper's wide silhouette. He ran a crooked line as he juggled his computer from hand to huge hand.

Maeve staggered into Gripper's back as the Blue Phoenix lifted off and then pivoted sharply. Even from the hallway, she could hear Duaal yelling at the Oslain'ii.

"Where the hells do you think you're going, you Narsus lump of slag? Get back here and let the cops get a good look at you! Tell me you've got a plan for this, Logan..."

"Just shut up and follow them," was the Prian's curt answer. "As close as you can."

Maeve and Gripper stumbled their way to the cockpit's door as the floor pitched beneath them. The big Arboran nearly crushed her as Duaal pulled the Blue Phoenix up, knifing through a thin layer of clouds and high into Sunjarrah's atmosphere. The planet spread out below, gently curved and smooth as far as Maeve could see. Above, the darkness of space was full of stars, celestial orbs of fire and the less impressive blinking green and yellow of planetary satellites. There were faster points of light sliding between them like shooting stars – other ships.

One of them slid past on the left, where Logan sat with his back absolutely straight and icy eyes narrowed. The ship was black and graceful, almost invisible against the darkness but for the stylish violet lights up and down its length. Duaal cried out and jerked on his controls, whipping the Phoenix around to face the Oslain'ii, but the black ship was already speeding past, silent in the cold emptiness of space.

"Damn, she's fast," Duaal grunted.

"That's a Narsus Predator," Logan said. "It can spin up the FTL drive in twenty seconds. If the Oslain'ii gets out of the system or above the stellar plane, it will be gone."

Duaal slammed down on the accelerator and gave chase. The Oslain'ii dove, back toward Sunjarrah's cloud layer, then up as the Blue Phoenix followed. Condensation streaked white along both ships' hulls and then boiled swiftly away as they raced through the atmosphere. Temperature gauges flashed orange and the canopy flickered with azure light as spots of phenno ignited in the rising heat. Duaal tightened his hands until his knuckles turned white and pulled the old freighter up after the Oslain'ii.

"Get us closer," Logan told him.

"I'm trying!" Duaal answered through clenched teeth. "But her engines are better than mine."

"Um, why are we trying to get closer?" Gripper asked.

Logan didn't answer. Maeve wondered what he had in mind, but now wasn't the time to question him. Logan worked fast, intense and hard, and asking him why or how was only a waste of precious time. Maeve was having trouble enough just remaining upright as the Blue Phoenix swerved in pursuit. Duaal pushed the accelerator down to full, but the Oslain'ii was vanishing into the distance.

Logan leaned forward, watching and frowning. "They're going around the autotraffic belt. We can catch up if we go through."

"Through?" Gripper squeaked. "Shimmer, you can't–!"

But Duaal was grinning, teeth bright in his dark face. He yanked the Blue Phoenix onto a new vector, smashing Maeve and Gripper into one another again in the narrow fibersteel corridor.

A stripe of strobing lights was coming closer outside, alarmingly close: the autotraffic belt, a band of latitude reserved for communications satellites and other computerized orbital objects. Maeve's stomach lurched, but before she could say anything, Duaal was diving between the lights. Metal and flickering points of color flashed past, one of them so close that Maeve swore she could reach out and touch it... The Blue Phoenix shuddered and there was a shrill metallic squeal. A cylinder of rotating segments careened away, tumbling awkwardly end over end until it collided with a delicate cloverleaf cluster of relay dishes.

Duaal grimaced, pulling back and easing up on the throttle. Sunjarrah's gravity pulled at the Blue Phoenix, slowing the ship and tugging the dented nose down planetward. Logan's metal fingers scraped loudly over the screens and readouts of the powerless co-pilot station.

"Give me control," he said.

Duaal spared a short, sharp look at Logan. Even in that fraction of a second, the Blue Phoenix drifted and Duaal had to wrestle it back on course. The Oslain'ii was barely visible through the lane of satellites, just a faintly shining spot of darkness. Duaal swore.

"You're losing them," Logan said. "Give me the controls!"

"Do you have any idea how long–?" Duaal asked.

Another impact rocked the Blue Phoenix. Duaal steadied his old ship with an effort and hissed out through his teeth. He flipped a striped toggle and the other half of the cockpit lit up like a sky full of stars.

Before the secondary controls had even finished powering up, Logan slammed down on the accelerator and the Blue Phoenix leapt forward into the close, crowded belt of satellites. Proximity sensors went from yellow to orange and then flashed red as the ship plunged into the autotraffic belt. Another coms relay flashed past, curving dishes and long, sweeping antennae dangerously close to fatal entanglement with the Blue Phoenix. Duaal held his breath while Gripper shrieked in terror.

"Watch out!" he screamed.

Maeve saw the cold fire burning in Logan's eyes, the fierce joy of a hunting hawk. He had lied to Maeve – her hunter *did* miss his Raptor.

Logan turned the Blue Phoenix up on edge, the curved horizon tilting dizzyingly. Maeve grabbed the doorframe and closed her eyes. The local gravity inside the ship was completely contrary to the view outside and it was making her stomach crawl up into her throat.

"There!" she heard Duaal shout. "There's the Oslain'ii!"

She forced her eyes open to look where Duaal was pointing. He was right. Through the mosaic of metal and lights, there was a barely visible curve of black and luminous violet. The Blue Phoenix slid from the dense field of satellites and dropped in behind the Oslain'ii.

The expensive Narsus ship rocked up to one side as the pilot inside saw them and started. But then the Oslain'ii pivoted to face the Blue Phoenix. A laser cannon blazed beneath the needle-like black nose and red light flared across the empty darkness, far too fast to react to. Logan jerked the Blue Phoenix into a tight spiral, but alarms blared deafeningly through the ship. A warning flashed on Duaal's controls and he glared at Logan.

"If you can avoid getting me and my ship blown to bung, I'd appreciate it," he said. "What in the three hundred hells do we do now, Logan? The Phoenix doesn't have any weapons!"

"That's the compression regulator!" Gripper shouted, pointing to a flashing light. "I've got to get down to the engine room."

"No," Logan said. The Oslain'ii fired again and the Blue Phoenix shuddered. "You stay right here. What's the range on a mainstream router?"

"What–?" Gripper began to ask, but Logan dropped them into a stomach-churning roll, streaking after the still-firing Oslain'ii. "Uh... about quarter mile! Less if there's radiation..."

"As soon as we're close enough, you need to get onto their wireless," Logan told him.

"What? Why?" Gripper asked.

The sleek black Narsus ship arced over a long, blocky hauler so huge that both the Blue Phoenix and the Oslain'ii could have fit comfortably inside and continued their chase. The Blue Phoenix rose up and over the hauler just as the Oslain'ii flipped around and changed direction, shooting back toward them. Logan flipped the old cargo ship end over end, just out of reach of the hot red spray of lasers.

"I can see–" Gripper said. He broke off, juggling his computer. "No, we're out of range again. You need to stay close."

Logan swung the Blue Phoenix from side to side as the Oslain'ii loosed bolts of laserfire at them. Sweat matted his blond hair flat against his face.

"This ship is too slow," he told no one in particular. "Move, damn you..."

Logan sounded so much like Tiberius in that moment, but there was no time to miss the old Prian. The two ships tumbled around each other, the Oslain'ii firing a near-constant barrage of molten red. Logan managed to keep out of the worst of it, but a dozen warnings blinked and blared in the cockpit.

"We can't keep this up much longer," Duaal said.

A huge passenger liner covered in a faceted grid of windows suddenly loomed up between the two ships. Faces stared out from behind glassteel, a hundred mouths wide with shock. The Oslain'ii swung around and fired through the sharp fin that attached one of the liner's maneuvering thrusters. The other engines flared and the whole ship began to spin right at the Blue Phoenix. Logan swore and pushed down on his control yoke.

Gripper worked thick fingers across the computer in his trembling hands.

"I... I'm in, Coldhand," he said. "What now?"

"Navigational system," Logan answered shortly. "Slave it to the Blue Phoenix's."

"Why? They don't need a tow!" Duaal shouted. "They're trying to kill us!"

"Just do it!"

Logan yanked the Blue Phoenix up again. Maeve threw a hand across her eyes. They were pointed right at Sunjarrah's binary suns. The glass in front of Logan and Duaal swiftly polarized, turning the great burning orbs into flat discs of gray. By the time Maeve could see again, the Oslain'ii was close. Too close to miss. A pair of missile ports slid open in the black ship's sleek underside.

"Gripper...?" Duaal asked. His green eyes were huge and wide. "Are you in?"

"Wait... wait..." Gripper said, biting his thick lower lip.

Logan's jaw was set. He stared at the Oslain'ii, facing down the other ship like an ancient gunslinger. There was movement barely visible in the missile bays, the deadly dark-within-dark pounce of a night-hunting cat. The Oslain'ii was firing.

"Got it!" Gripper shouted.

Logan was already pulling back on his controls, forcing the Blue Phoenix to rise sharply away from Sunjarrah and the Oslain'ii. The missiles closed quickly, leaving trails of frozen propellant. Logan rolled the Blue Phoenix again and sent the old ship the opposite direction, into a plummeting dive.

"Duaal, jump us into the corona of one of those stars," Logan said in a flat voice.

"Their FTL system is faster than ours," Duaal reminded him. His words came out in a breathless rush. "With their nav connected up to ours, the Oslain'ii will just follow us!"

"Into the sun," Maeve said, finally understanding Logan's plan.

Duaal punched up the coordinates. "Shit, there's a moon in our way... We hit that and we'll wish it had been the missiles."

"The other star then!" Logan said.

The Hyzaari mage swiped up another flight plan and sent it to the navigation system. Logan punched the FTL button, his metal hand slamming into the plastic cover and shattering it as he sent the command home to the Blue Phoenix's computers. The damaged ship screeched in protest, but the blue null-field indicator flashed and the faster-than-light engines roared.

Steel bulkheads trembled under Maeve's hands as she steadied herself. In a flash of multi-colored light, Sunjarrah, the missiles and the Oslain'ii vanished. Just for a moment, the soothing mosaic of superluminal flight washed over Maeve.

"Dropping!" Duaal shouted.

Light blazed through the cockpit, glorious golden celestial fire. Maeve scrubbed at her eyes, but could not wipe away the dark spots burning in her vision. The polarizing filter was no match for a star at this range. As if in answer to this blazing challenge, azure flames streaked across the Blue Phoenix's hull. Duaal's head dropped to his chest and he squinted at his instruments, tears streaming down his cheeks.

"The phenno's holding..." Duaal said, then jumped to his feet, smashing his head against the low ceiling. "Wait, the Oslain'ii!"

Maeve shielded her eyes and stared through the blue glow. Yes, one of the dark spots in her vision didn't move as she shook her head. It was Xartasia's ship, just off the Blue Phoenix's right side but very nearly swallowed by the star's brilliant corona. No, not nearly... Without phenno, the other ship was burning, searing red and then white as heat and radiation engulfed the Oslain'ii. The black ship lurched once as the pilot tried to fly away, but within seconds, the black ship listed to one side and sank deeper into the star's corona.

Gripper's hands shook and his computer clattered to the floor. "I... Coldhand... I just killed everyone on that ship, didn't I?"

"Yes," Logan said. He squinted after the vanishing Oslain'ii with hard eyes.

"They would have killed all of us," Duaal told Gripper.

But the big Arboran ran, bumping and stumbling, out of the cockpit. Maeve could hear his sobs long after Gripper was gone.

She took Logan's left hand. The illonium was cool to the touch, even as hot sweat ran down her skin. Maeve was shaking all over, but Logan's grip was steady. She kissed her hunter's temple once and then left to find Gripper.

[7]

LIGHTS

"What we know is fragile defense against what we don't."

Maeve sat silently next to Gripper while Duaal piloted the Blue Phoenix out of Sunjarrah's secondary star. She didn't know what to tell her friend. She had killed before and not always in self defense – as Gripper had today – but lives were gone, snuffed out like candle flames. The pain of that never dulled, Maeve knew. It honed itself against guilt and doubt to a razor edge.

They sat beside one another on Gripper's workbench. Maeve rested her head on his broad shoulder. She wrapped a wing around the Arboran as he cried, but could do little more. Even if she knew what to say, Gripper could not have heard it. The engines in the room's center thunked and ground unhealthily. The Oslain'ii had landed several shots before the Blue Phoenix could escape. The repairs would be expensive, but at least they were still flying. That was more than could be said for Xartasia's ship.

Had Maeve's cousin been onboard the Oslain'ii? Could Xartasia be dead?

Maeve doubted it. Why would Calathan make a speech on his queen's behalf if she was on the ship? Xartasia – the White Queen – was somewhere else, with the rest of the Devourers... And with the Arcadians she had gathered from Mir and who knew how many other planets.

The intercom light flashed on and Maeve heard Duaal's voice, but could not make out a word he said. She slid from the work-bench, went to the speaker and held down the button.

"Please say that again. Louder."

Maeve still had to lean in to hear over the noise of the laboring engine.

"We're heading back to New Hennor to get Panna," Duaal said, enunciating each word. "Should be there in about twenty minutes."

Maeve promised to be in the cargo bay by then to help retrieve the other Arcadian and returned to Gripper.

"Do you wish to stay here?" she asked.

"Yeah," Gripper said. He wiped his cheeks and nodded. "I... I should start on the repairs, I guess."

Maeve embraced Gripper and made her way to the cargo bay. Logan and Xia were already there. Maeve's stomach felt made of lead, heavy and toxic.

"How many do you think were on the Oslain'ii?" she asked.

"Probably just the pilot," Xia said. "Why?"

"You do not think that any Arcadians recruited from Mir were on the ship?"

"No," Logan answered. "The Oslain'ii wasn't big enough. It was expensive, but meant for personal use. There's only room for maybe ten or fifteen Arcadians, even if they crowded in. And that only works for a short flight. Calathan was only there to talk, I'd bet, to get them primed for the real pickup."

Maeve hoped Logan was right.

"That means another larger ship must be nearby," she said. "Not far from Sunjarrah."

The Blue Phoenix landed hard and sent a jolt up Maeve's spine. Black carbon scoring streaked the viewport, obscuring the view until Xia unsealed the airlock. Duaal had set down not far from where they had landed before. It was darker now, a deep blue-green twilight, but there were the dilapidated settlement houses, the collapsing common building and the withered cornfield.

But now there was something new. Several, Maeve saw when she stepped from the Blue Phoenix. Three banded police cars, with lights flashing on top, and a fourth vehicle that she didn't immediately recognize. It was only when Logan paused and frowned that Maeve looked again and read the letters stenciled on the larger, darker vehicle's side: CWAAF.

"They came," Xia sighed in relief.

"Gripper's call finally went through," Logan said, but he didn't sound pleased.

"Is this not precisely what we wanted?" Maeve asked him. "The authorities are here."

But Logan's gaze remained fixed ahead as he stalked toward the compound. Maeve and Xia hurried to keep up.

The police had rounded up what seemed to be every Arcadian living outside New Hennor. The winged fairies huddled together next to one of the broken-down gray houses, surrounded by armed and scowling officers. The Arcadians kept their heads down and murmured to one another. Maeve wasn't close enough to make out the words.

Panna stood to one side, flushed in the flashing police lights and arguing with a tall Ixthian woman in a neat green Alliance uniform and a starkly white braid falling down her back. When Panna saw Maeve, she broke off and called out.

"Can you *please* talk to the lieutenant here?" she shouted. "Tell her what happened!"

The CWAAF officer turned to Maeve, but looked right over the small fairy's head and nodded to Logan and Xia.

"Good evening," she said. "I'm Lieutenant Xal. We came out on a disturbance alert, but the call was dropped before we arrived."

"That was Gripper," Xia told the other Ixthian. "We had to leave before he could talk to you."

"We found an Arcadian body next to a scorch mark in that field there," Xal said. "Are you telling me you left a murder scene before the police arrived?"

"That knight was not the only one here!" Maeve said.

"There was a Devourer, too, and another ship," Panna told the lieutenant.

"A... Devourer?" Xal's antennae arched up from her snow-white hair. "You're shining, surely."

"No," Logan answered. "Panna's right. It was working with the dead knight you found. We fought and killed the Devourer, too."

"We found only one body – the Arcadian male whose murder you just confessed to."

"That's not a burn mark out there. That's where the nanites consumed the body," Logan said. His cybernetic hand ground at his side, clenched into a silver-gray fist.

The CWAAF lieutenant was not impressed.

"If we can verify that, you're going to owe something colorful," she said. "It's a damned good thing for you that it wasn't an Alliance citizen who attacked you."

Rage boiled inside Maeve, painful and hot and erupting before she could stop herself.

"That man was an Arcadian," she snarled. "That is what you are saying, yes? That it is a good thing he was *just a fairy*?"

Xia placed a restraining hand on Maeve's shoulder and looked at Lieutenant Xal.

"What about the Devourer?" Xia asked. "You have plenty of witnesses here of the attack on us and the alien."

"We've found no evidence of any monsters," Xal said dismissively. "There have been some stories of another assailant from the three Arcadians here who speak any Aver, but nothing conclusive. What happened to this other ship?"

Maeve opened her mouth to answer, but Logan was quicker.

"We chased it, but their ship was too fast," he said. "We lost it."

Xal sighed. "Did you catch its name or transponder code? I'd like to speak with the pilot."

"No," Logan said.

"So what's going to happen now?" Xia asked. "Are you going to report this to CWAAF?"

"Yes," Lieutenant Xal said. "Don't leave New Hennor. I'll have a lot more questions for you."

The Blue Phoenix was grounded on Sunjarrah for a week while the police questioned Logan, Xia, Gripper and Duaal about what had happened.

As a non-citizen, Maeve's testimony wasn't admissible in court and not deemed important in the investigation. Panna's presence and reactions raised questions and it wasn't long until a file sent from Tynerion revealed her Arcadian heritage.

The fine for falsifying her identity was five hundred cenmarks.

Fines for their illegal squatting in the old colony were less, but the Arcadians of New Hennor couldn't pay them anyway. So many fairies were incarcerated for their various petty crimes, dropped into a prison populace of violent criminals that they didn't know how to communicate with. The Arcadians would remain there for a month, but the numbers weren't in their favor.

Statistically, only fifty percent would survive their prison time. Those who made it out again had nowhere else to go. They would return to the same place they were fined for living.

It was not the police who told Maeve about this, but Panna. She ranted every afternoon, when she and the princess were alone on the Blue Phoenix, while the rest were gone answering a new round of the same questions. Maeve agreed with her rage, but what could they do? Only the Lyceum could change Alliance law.

The Lyceum was far away on Axis and there were no Arcadians on that council. The conversation always ended the same way, with Maeve sitting in unhappy silence while a red-faced Panna fought for her composure and fled the room before she lost it.

Panna wasn't the only one revealed as a fraud during the investigation. Logan's identity, too, was the subject of many questions, and for invoking the powers of his lapsed license, Logan Coldhand's fine was one thousand cenmarks.

As they suspected, the Oslain'ii hadn't registered a flight plan or landing coordinates. Several companies had noted damage to their satellites in the autotraffic belt. The damages were split between insurance companies and the captains of the two involved ships: Duaal Sinnay and the mysteriously absent pilot of the Oslain'ii. Even so, the reparations cost every chip of color that Maeve, Duaal and the rest could scrape together.

And then the investigation was over. Any interest in the dead Devourer never made it past a few disregarded initial testimonies. Lieutenant Xal and CWAAF only involved themselves in the affair because the Arcadians didn't fall under the jurisdiction of the Sunjarra police. Once the bird-backs were dealt with, Xal quickly and efficiently completed her datawork, then never appeared again.

Four days later, the whole thing was over. Broke and frustrated, everyone was free to return to the Blue Phoenix.

The crew's first dinner together in eight days was noodles and canned sauce from the back of the cupboard. Xia served the limp dinner to Duaal and Logan, then a larger bowl to Gripper. The Arboran sniffed at the sauce. His eyes were still rimmed in red. Xia offered some food to Panna, but the girl declined. Maeve accepted the bowl instead. They all ate in silence, heads down and shoulders slumped.

"Now what?" Duaal asked at last, finally breaking the monotonously mechanical sounds of chewing.

Eyes rose slowly to his – faceted red, forest green, glacial blue and stormy gray. Duaal seemed to realize too late that he asked his question aloud. He smoothed his dark hair and cleared his throat.

"Look, Maeve, I really want to help," Duaal said. "I do. But we've tried everything to get the Alliance involved. They don't believe us, even when we find a Devourer on one of our own planets. We know Xartasia is out there with them, but we don't know where and we don't know what the hells she's doing."

"I... I wish I could believe that all my cousin wants is to take our people home," Maeve answered. "But if that was true, what need does she have for the Devourers?"

"I don't know. We could fly after her to the end of the universe, Maeve," Duaal told her unhappily, "and never find her or figure it out. We're out of money and ideas."

Logan pushed his bowl back and tapped illonium fingers on the stained tabletop.

"We *do* know a few things," he corrected. "Xartasia is gathering Arcadians. Maeve's right. If all she wants is to take them home, she just needs ships. Not Devourers. Xartasia's got some sort of plan that involves the Arcadians she's summoning."

"But we don't know what that is," Duaal said again. "Or how to find out."

Logan held Duaal's gaze for a long moment, but it was the Prian who finally looked away. Gripper sniffled and Maeve wished she could tell him that all of his pain had been *for* something, to save the entire galaxy. But... it would be a lie. Maeve pushed her pasta around the bowl and couldn't convince herself to eat another bite.

"No. We're not out of the fight yet."

It was Panna who had spoken. The wingless young Arcadian jumped to her feet and slammed her hands down on the tabletop, making the dishes jump.

"Coldhand's right," she said. "We *know* that Xartasia is after the Arcadians. That may be the only thing we know, but we can still do something about it."

"What?" Gripper asked. His voice was raw and hoarse. "What are we supposed to do, Sprite?"

"We have to get to them first! We win the Arcadians to our side before Xartasia can," Panna said. She turned to Maeve. "You are a knight and a princess of the White Kingdom. You should be our queen, not her! Call to our people, Highness, and they will flock to your side."

"I am no queen," Maeve objected. "We have discussed this–"

"But you *could* be a queen," Duaal said. "Panna's right, Maeve. It's the only thing we can do against Xartasia. If we can make you into a queen, we might still be able to stop her. We don't know what she needs the Arcadians for, but we might be able to stop her from getting them."

"No." Maeve's fingernails were biting into her palms. "I cannot lead my people. I am unfit to be queen!"

"Then make yourself fit," Duaal said. When Maeve looked up, there was a hardness in his eyes that she had never seen before. "If you really want to stop Xartasia and the Devourers, this is it. This is the only plan we have, Maeve."

Her mouth was dry and felt like there was something thorny lodged inside. She turned to Logan.

"Tell them... tell me that this plan is insanity," she begged. "That it will not work. We cannot do this!"

"I don't know if it'll work," Logan said. His eyes were cold and unforgiving. "But Duaal's right. We have nothing else."

If she weren't already sitting, Maeve would have fallen. She felt stabbed in the heart, betrayed... but it wasn't Logan's fault. It was the only idea they had. Did she expect Logan to side with her just because they were lovers...? No, her hunter was too smart and too practical. There was no other way. Maeve slumped in her seat.

"Very well," she said almost inaudibly. "I will do it. I will... I will be queen."

Panna slapped her hand on the tabletop again. Her expression was grim, but there was a tiny smile curling her lips. Xia shook her head, disbelieving but not disapproving. Even Gripper smirked just a little, as though he had always expected this. Duaal leaned back and arched one dark brow.

"Great," he said. "Now how do we turn Maeve into a queen of Arcadia?"

"We can start now," Panna answered. "Here in New Hennor."

[8]
A'SHAE

"Don't play if you're not willing to lose."

- DUAAL SINNAY (233 PA)

"Go get dressed," Duaal said.

"I *am* dressed," Maeve answered.

"You can't seriously be thinking of wearing that!"

"What is wrong with it?"

Maeve was in the middle of reaching for the airlock handle, but stopped. She had showered, combed out her hair and dressed in a fresh pair of black spacer's pants with a plain blue shirt. Duaal had changed clothes, too, donning a pair of his favorite leather leggings and a red velvet vest with gold edging. He inspected his folded cuffs and then his polished boots.

"If you're going to be a queen," he said, "then you better look the part. Right now you just look like the galaxy's prettiest maintenance worker. Appearances matter. Come on, Maeve... I'll help you get dressed."

Duaal took Maeve's arm and hauled her up the stairs.

"Do I have any say in this matter?" she asked.

"None," Duaal answered cheerfully. "You may have royal blood, Maeve, but you've got a soldier's sense of style."

"I was a knight. I can dress myself!"

Panna trotted up behind them. "Well, it can't hurt to let him try. If you're going to be queen, then you need to get used to letting other people help you."

Maeve scowled at the other Arcadian as Duaal shoved her into her room and to the closet. After forcing her to try on everything inside, Duaal finally settled on a long skirt of golden cloth. One of the seams was frayed, but the intricately cross-tied crimson shirt he selected covered the poor repair. He found a pair of high-heeled sandals buried at the back of her closet.

"To make you just a bit taller," he told Maeve. "You're not exactly a towering woman."

Panna chose a scarf woven with threads of gold and used it to tie back Maeve's thick black hair.

"It looks like a crown," she said. "This will have to do until we can get the real thing."

"A crown...?" Maeve asked. "But this is all just a ruse... I do not need a crown!"

Duaal had already grabbed her wrist, though, and was towing Maeve across the bunkroom. He pushed her down into the chair.

"Now time for some makeup," Duaal said.

"I have none," Maeve answered truthfully. She had never seen much need for it and tended to sweat it right off.

"I've got a little," Panna offered.

Duaal waved a dark hand dismissively.

"Go get the blue case from my room," he said. "Not the gray one – the blue."

Panna returned a moment later with a large blue box. The Blue Phoenix's captain flipped it open and applied powder and blush, eyeliner and shadow. Duaal held Maeve's chin firmly as he applied a glossy red paint to her lips.

"You need to stop chewing these," he told her. "Your nails, too."

"I do *not* chew my nails!"

Duaal raised an eyebrow. "Then you must be using a hack saw to trim them. Stop it, princess."

"We should start calling her *a'shae* or *Queen Maeve*," Panna said.

"Why not *Queen Cavainna*?" Duaal asked. "I wish we had some jewelry for you, Queen Cavainna."

"Every single king or queen for ten thousand years has been a Cavainna," Panna reminded him. She perched on the edge of the desk, pinning up Maeve's black hair. "Including Xartasia."

Maeve felt like a pet being groomed for show. "Maybe it would lend an air of legitimacy to this… endeavor. I would not be opposed to simply using the Cavainna name–"

"No!" Duaal and Panna answered together.

Maeve snarled and stood, shook out her wings and then seized her spear from where it leaned in the doorway.

"Enough!" she said. "I do not need to paint my face in order to lead my people."

"Then you still have a lot to learn about leading," Duaal said.

But he and Panna followed their irritated creation as she stalked through the Blue Phoenix. Maeve staggered when one of her heels caught between the deckplates, then hissed an oath and wrenched her foot free. In the cargo bay, she swung her legs over the catwalk railing and jumped, gliding down to the ground. There was no way she was going to navigate the stairs in these ridiculous shoes. Why did she still have them at all?

The answer to that stood on the lowered cargo ramp, waiting with mismatched hands thrust into the pockets of a long gray coat. Logan's pale eyes went wide when he saw Maeve. He strode up into the bay, wrapped one arm around Maeve's waist and kissed her. Her hunter still tasted like his unsweetened black coffee.

"Hey, don't mess up her lipstick!" Duaal shouted as he bounded down the stairs.

Panna laughed. "Come on, it's time to go. I promised Ferris we'd be there in thirty minutes."

Logan eventually released Maeve. Duaal checked her makeup, sighed but let the princess go. Panna and Logan fell into step beside her as Duaal waved from the cargo bay and closed the Blue Phoenix behind them. Maeve wobbled a little and looked at Panna.

"Ferris?" she asked.

The blonde girl nodded. "Duke Ferris Verridian. That's who Sir Calathan came to speak to, but he never got the chance. He was a noble back in the White Kingdom and is the oldest Arcadian in the New Hennor camp. Duke Ferris' daughter just went to prison. Xal picked her up and he couldn't pay the fine. So..."

Panna shrugged, but her tightly clenched jaw undermined the casual gesture. Maeve didn't know what to say, so she just nodded. Panna was right, but what could be done about it? Maeve struggled during Xal's investigation to keep herself out of prison, too.

These were hardly the thoughts of a proper queen... But Maeve wasn't a queen. Not really.

It was a short walk to the Arcadian settlement. Or a short flight, in Maeve's case. The hard ground was pitted and the cracked foundations of long-collapsed or unfinished buildings lurked in the saw-toothed yellow weeds.

The Arcadians must have seen them approaching. The fairies – far fewer than those who had circled the Oslain'ii, perhaps twenty in total now – stood silent and still on the common hall's warped porch. Feathered wings rustled as Maeve landed.

Panna and Logan took up flanking positions on either side and Maeve wondered what they were doing. Protecting her? Supporting her? Advising her, maybe? Whatever it was, Maeve was simply glad not to have to do this alone.

As they walked into the old common hall's shadow, one of the Arcadians stepped slowly down from the porch. He was far older than Maeve, with deep worry lines creasing his brow and cheeks.

His clothes were many times mended but the fabrics were fluid and flowing – a knotted skirt of green material and a long, stained silver tunic.

That had to be Ferris. The duke's back was straight and the long braid that fell between his wings was still the same golden blond as Panna's, but shot through with coarse gray. He fixed brown eyes on first Logan, then Panna, and the lines around his mouth deepened as he frowned.

Finally, Ferris turned to Maeve. She felt like a child again, sent to see a stern and disapproving uncle. Ferris took in her clothes and black hair, then nodded once. The duke spread his wings out to either side and turned them down in the Arcadian version of a bow.

"A'cer," Ferris said. It was a general honorific, used for princesses and queens alike. Anyone with a drop of royal blood in her veins. "It is a pleasure to receive one of Cavain's daughters."

One of. Maeve glanced at Panna, who shrugged in reply. Maeve swallowed a sigh and inclined her head.

"Duke Ferris," she greeted him. "It is an honor."

"Sua an eru, a'cer?" Ferris asked. *Why are you here, Highness?*

"I..." Maeve chewed her lip. Where to begin? She couldn't seem to sort out her own tumbling thoughts. "I am... Xartasia, Princess Titania. I am not her, I mean, but my cousin has made an alliance... and is summoning our people. But her plan – which we know so little about – is too dangerous to... So I..."

Maeve trailed off, her throat as dry as the red Stray desert. Duke Ferris pursed his lips, unimpressed. Maeve's hands curled into angry, impotent fists and she squeezed her eyes shut until she heard blood rushing in her ears. She was still holding her spear, Maeve realized. She was a knight, not a queen.

"You saw that Devourer," Maeve said, eyes still shut. "Fighting here, with a knight in glass that invoked Titania's name. She killed many to summon our most terrible enemies here! I love my cousin, my own blood, but her pain..."

Maeve was losing it again, the tenuous thread of thought that only barely connected their fragmented information and plan together.

She opened her eyes. The Arcadians on the sagging porch had drawn together, wings rustling and voices murmuring. They were listening. So was Ferris. The duke's sharp chin had lifted and his eyes narrowed. Maeve's knees felt like water and her feet were going numb in their ridiculous high heels. She took a deep breath that tasted like burnt cornhusk.

"...But our pain," Maeve said, "the pain we all share, has twisted Xartasia's heart and soul until she no longer knows her friends from her enemies, her kin from her oppressors."

"Xartasia has offered us protection and relief," Ferris answered in Aver. "The White Queen promises a return to our home. Can she return us to our kingdom, a'cer?"

"I do not know," Maeve admitted. "But... but even if she can, at what price? The White Kingdom is more than planets–"

"*Ja'hirra morrae!*" one of the watching Arcadians cried out shrilly. *It is just a memory!*

"*Ja'hir morrae. Ja'hir la tasia!*" Maeve sang in reply, shocked at the heat in her own words. *It is a memory. It is the dream!* "The dream of light and beauty that we all remember every day. But what has been can never be again. What Xartasia builds now, she does upon blood and betrayal. That is not Arcadia!"

Panna elbowed Maeve lightly in the ribs.

"They don't care," she hissed quietly. "These people get arrested just because they have nowhere to live. The Alliance hasn't exactly taken good care of us. They need something else, some hope for a better future. So far, Xartasia's the only one offering that. Have you noticed how few there are here? It's not just the ones in prison... more of the fairies have left. They've gone to join Xartasia!"

Maeve swallowed. Her tongue felt swollen and heavy. She was no good at this! She was never supposed to ascend to the throne, not even by accident. It was Xartasia who had grown up on Illisem, surrounded by court politics. The throne was hers by right and by experience.

But there was no one else. Maeve looked out at the porch again and counted twenty-one other Arcadians, including Duke Ferris. It wasn't much of a kingdom, but there were twenty-one of her people here that she might be able to help. If only she knew what to say.

"You understand all this better than I do. Why do you not speak to them?" Maeve asked Panna.

"I don't have the black hair," she said. "Just talk!"

The fairies were all losing interest. The knowledge that some of their royal family had survived the White Kingdom's fall was pale comfort next to the realities of life in the Alliance. Black hair and a few drops of royal blood were not going to win Maeve's case for her.

"Xartasia will prey upon your need to summon you to her side. Our life here is hard, but we need not be prey," Maeve said. She felt Logan's eyes on her. "Together as one people, we can make a life not only of strength and safety, but of honor and dignity."

It was this last word that made Duke Ferris look up again. Was he thinking of his daughter? After a hundred years as refugees, of being neglected and despised by the people of the core, of having no rights and no protection under CWA law, the chance to live with pride was a nearly impossible dream.

"Xartasia would never ignore you," Maeve said. She took a step toward Ferris, her hand extended. "But she wants to use you... I do not know for what, but we cannot let Xartasia manipulate and trick us into joining her army of monsters. We are true children of the White Kingdom. Our fate is our own."

Duke Ferris lowered his graying wings until the tips touched the ground and took Maeve's hand in his. His skin was as brittle and dry as the dead grass under her feet. He kissed her hand in such an ancient gesture of respect and subservience that Maeve shuddered. Never in her entire life had she ever hoped to be queen, not even of this tiny fraction of her people. Something about it was deeply un-settling, but as she herself and the others kept pointing out, there was nothing else to do.

"Our fate is our own," Maeve repeated. "But we need not face it alone. We are one people and it is time we were united once more."

Ferris turned toward the other Arcadians and raised his wings high over his head.

"*Vaeli a'shae!*" he sang in a clear, loud voice.

One by one and then all together, the fairies took up the song. "*Vaeli a'shae! Eru ilvae Arcadi'na. Vaeli a'shae!*"

Logan shot a look at Panna. "What's that they're singing? Do we need to get Maeve out of here?"

Panna beamed. "No. They're agreeing with her. *Honor the Night! Vaeli a'shae!*"

Maeve floated, wings and arms spread, on the bittersweet tide of her people's voices. The suns were hot and sweat stung skin cut and abraded in her battle against Calathan. She was tired and hungry and there was makeup itching in her eyes, but Maeve couldn't bring herself to care. There was so much better and worse to come.

"*Vaeli a'shae,*" Logan agreed in awkward Arcadian.

Xia went to work examining all of the fairies, cleaning poorly cared for wounds and inoculating them against common diseases.

"Not very much point in bringing them all together only to start spreading rughalla," she told Maeve. The Ixthian's tone was matter-of-fact, but she couldn't conceal the pale green of concern in her compound eyes.

The Blue Phoenix's kitchen wasn't well stocked, but it was far better than the few scavenged supplies that were all the Arcadians could offer. Gripper picked everything edible from his garden and carried it to the kitchen, where even Duaal donned an apron and cooked whatever Gripper could bring him. There wasn't much to make out of the scattered assortment of their remaining cans and vegetables, but by that evening, there were three large pots of soup bubbling away on the stove and filling the Blue Phoenix with their warm, savory smell.

Maeve reported to the kitchen with her sleeves rolled up to the elbow to begin work on the pile of knives and cutting boards that filled the sink, but Panna was already there and stubbornly refused to let Maeve do her usual chore.

"You're a queen now," Panna said. She pointed toward the door with wet fingers. "Queens don't do dishes."

Maeve shrugged and then left the mess. At least there was one advantage to her new job. Maybe Duaal would stop making fun of her nails if they spent less time scrubbing pots.

Duke Ferris and the other Arcadians arrived just as the sun was setting. They crept together into the Blue Phoenix's cargo hold in a nervously huddled mass. Gripper and Panna had arranged empty cargo containers into a long row of impromptu tables. Duaal firmly seated Maeve at the head, with Ferris to one side and Panna on the other. Ferris offered so many toasts and praises to the royal line of Cavain that her own name quickly became nonsense in Maeve's ears.

That night was full of soup and introductions as every single remaining Arcadian of New Hennor presented themselves to their new queen. Maeve sat uncomfortably on her empty water canister and did her best to listen to twenty painful stories of hard life in the core, of friends and family lost to the Devourers, to disease and the hatred of the Alliance species. Was there any way to turn these lost, broken people into an Arcadian kingdom?

There were other introductions to make, too. The fairies had already met Xia, but many of them stared at Gripper. His size and stature were far too reminiscent of the Devourers. Nervous and still anguished by the death of the Oslain'ii's pilot, Gripper collected the dishes – feeding so many mouths had used every single bowl and bowl-like object on the ship – and he retreated to the kitchen.

"What about the captain?" Ferris asked. He glanced down along the table to where Duaal sat, telling stories. "He is not like most humans."

"He has been trained in our arts," Maeve answered. "It was not a pleasant verse of his life, but Duaal has become a powerful spell-singer. His skill surpasses even that of the Ivory Spire adepts."

Ferris' eyebrows shot up. He didn't seem to think that likely. "He must have learned at the wingtips of one of our own. Maybe you were his mentor, my queen?"

"No, it was not me," Maeve said sharply, then tried again, softening her tone. "I did not teach Duaal our songs. His teacher was another human, Gavriel. He led the Cult of Nihil."

Duke Ferris' expression was blank of recognition. Maeve tried again.

"The group to which Xartasia once belonged," she told him. She rubbed her hand against the back of her neck. The memories were as heavy as lead weights there. "After Gavriel died – when Xartasia killed him – my cousin sent the coreworlders who remained to be torn apart by Devourers."

Duke Ferris gave Maeve a long, serious look. "Does the boy pose a danger to you or the kingdom, a'shae?"

Maeve shocked herself by laughing.

"No," she answered. "Duaal is no enemy. He and I are – though it is strange to say – good friends. Duaal has devoted himself to this endeavor and he has been an invaluable ally."

Across the makeshift table, Panna grinned. "On Prianus, I really thought you two hated each other."

"We did," Maeve admitted, shaking her head. "It took Tiberius' loss to mend our relationship."

Panna fell silent, perhaps thinking of the Blue Phoenix's original captain... or maybe another man lost on Prianus. Maeve had long suspected Panna's feelings for her teacher, Professor Xen, had been more than a student's respect. Not unlike her own affection for Orthain, Maeve realized. Xen had protected Panna's genetic secret in defiance of his own Ixthian culture. It was easy to understand her infatuation.

Infatuation? Maeve wondered at her own thought. Was that fair to Panna? Duke Ferris cleared his throat.

"What of the other human?" he asked. "The man who was with you this afternoon?"

Maeve blinked and looked around the crowded cargo bay for Logan, but he was nowhere to be seen. Where had he gone?

The flat horizon was crimson, as though Sunjarrah itself burned a smokeless scarlet. Brilliant silver stars had already kindled high overhead, especially dense along the glowing line of the galactic plane. The river of stars flowed over the Blue Phoenix, bright and inviting.

"Waited until, by wind's tempest
I came to the old one's claim
'For a summer, I have searched...'"

The note went sour and Logan stopped singing. He frowned down at the guitar.

He sat on top of the Blue Phoenix, between two broken sensor spars. They had snapped off during the flight through Sunjarrah's autotraffic belt and there was no money left to repair them. The guitar across his lap had been battered and worn even before Logan bought it from one of the Poes Nor students on Tynerion, but now the neck was criss-crossed with deep scars. The wood was splintered in several places and held together with black engine tape.

Logan plucked one of the strings and carefully slid his metallic left hand up the neck to tighten it for the seventh time in the last hour. He twisted too hard and the string snapped.

Second one in an hour.

Logan set the instrument aside and took a mylon tangle of spare strings from his pocket. He had bought every one of them that he could find at Poes Nor, but his supply was dwindling swiftly.

Logan unwound the broken string and replaced it, then tried to thread the other end through the tiny hole in the tuning knob, but the guitar slid in his grip and Logan's fingers tightened reflexively. The wood crunched in his cybernetic grip and one of the fret bars twanged as it snapped free. Logan reached into his pocket again.

He had to glue the fret back down before replacing the string. Logan was tempted to glue the tuning peg into place, too, but knew that guitars didn't work that way. He examined the battle-scarred instrument as he waited for the glue to dry.

In spite of the damage done by his cybernetics, this guitar was still an improvement over his first one. He had been seven years old, running from another gang of bullies. Young Logan Centra had flung himself into a trash bin to hide. The reek of rot and the sharp pain of something jutting into his back were far better than the beating that awaited him if the older boys found him. Only when their rough voices and words had long since retreated did Logan finally dare to haul himself out of the bin and finally saw what had been spearing his spine – the broken neck of a guitar.

Little Logan had taken the instrument home and painstakingly repaired it. The guitar never really sounded quite right, but he had loved it all the same. There was no money for lessons, so Logan watched every video he could find on the mainstream. The work was even more meticulous and difficult than the repairs, but Logan learned to play.

A cop's income was better than a schoolboy's – although not by much. Logan's second guitar had not been new, either. It came to him third-hand, already dented in places and on its fourth set of strings. But it was a good instrument and Jess had painted a falcon over the largest stain in the varnish. It wasn't perfect either, but it was beautiful.

Now Logan tilted the guitar up to catch the fading sunlight, inspecting the replaced fret bar. It was hard to see much. A scattering of yellow and green indicators glowed on the Blue Phoenix's sensors and antennae, but they didn't help very much. Some glue had bubbled up around the thin line of metal and Logan picked away as much of it as he could with the tip of his knife, then began to play again.

"Two hundred eighty-eight days of light,
Will be desired by a night…"

Panna said that the Lay of Cavain was a piece of history, a story of how Cavain had conquered the pyrads and founded an empire that lasted over ten thousand years. A long and very, very proud history to which Maeve was now the heir.

She never wanted it. Logan knew that much. Maeve didn't really like being a princess, much less a queen. But Panna was right – there was no other way and no one else who could do it. After one hundred centuries, the Arcadians were used to the rulership of Cavain's raven-haired descendants. Of course, that meant many of them would go to Xartasia, too.

When the sun finished setting, the night grew quickly cold and Logan's fingers went numb. He flexed the stiff knuckles and kept playing. His voice echoed quietly through the dark and dilapidated settlement below.

Panna also said that the Lay of Cavain was about more than just history. The fairies of Arcadia believed that their rulers were literally descended from the gods. According to the song, Cavain was the son of the sun goddess, Aes, and an unknown fairy man. As a result, their divine blood entitled House Cavainna – the *Nights, a'shae* – to the respect and codified admiration of their people.

Now Maeve was a queen. Perhaps she didn't think of herself as one just yet, but Logan knew she would be a great queen. She was an amazing woman, strong and clever, though she would be the last to say so. There was nothing Maeve Cavainna would not give for her people. Panna and Duke Ferris knew it. Maeve's speech today had been awkward and unrehearsed. Beautiful and striking as she was – the desire to seize and kiss Maeve was never far away – it wasn't words that convinced Ferris. Not words alone, at least.

Maeve was down there, in the Blue Phoenix's cargo bay with her new subjects. It was a sad and shabby sort of court, true, but Maeve would make the best of it. She was more resilient than even Panna realized. Maeve would build up a new kingdom from nothing and Logan would protect her as she did it. He was no longer a bounty hunter, but he still had his Talon-9 and he knew how to fight. Logan Coldhand didn't know much else – the guitar twanged tunelessly in his hands again – but it all belonged to Maeve.

The Blue Phoenix's aft hatch clanked and popped open. Logan looked back to the small airlock. A black-haired head emerged from the ship, then white-feathered wings and a pale, lithe body. Maeve kicked the hatch closed behind her and came to sit beside Logan.

"There you are," she said. "We missed you at dinner."

"I wasn't hungry," Logan said, but then his jaw clenched. He didn't like to lie to Maeve. "That's not true. I don't want to embarrass you, dove."

"You? Embarrass me?" Maeve asked. She stroked one wingtip along Logan's spine and smiled. "You stood beside me today as I fell through that terrible speech. *You* cannot shame me, my enarri."

"A dinner party is a long way from being a silent bodyguard," Logan said. "You're a queen now, Maeve. I'm a... not even a bounty hunter anymore. And that cost us a lot of colour we couldn't afford this week."

"You are *my* hunter," Maeve told him. Her cheeks were flushed in the starlight. "My enarri. I always want you by my side."

Logan kissed Maeve, cradling his guitar in one arm. She cupped his face in her small hands and then ran delicate fingertips down his chest and arms to the guitar.

"I do not care much for dinner parties, either," Maeve admitted with a sly grin. "And am in no hurry to return to it. Will you sing for me, my love?"

Logan kissed her again and began to play.

[9]

WHERE

"Retreat isn't the same thing as running away. They're spelled completely differently."

— DUAAL SINNAY (234 PA)

There was a loud thump from the next room, the sound of a body hitting the floor. Jessica Centra ran out of the kitchen and skidded to a stop, hands splayed protectively over her belly. Logan was sprawled on the apartment floor, eyes closed and laying absolutely still. Jess put her hands on her hips and scowled.

"Vorus Reginald Centra, did you shoot your father again?" she asked.

The little boy standing on the cushions of their threadbare couch hung his head, but his unruly blond hair didn't hide his grin. Jess sighed and threw her hands into the air.

"Well, go kiss him back to life," she told her son.

Vorus jumped down from the couch and scampered across the living room to kiss his father's cheek. Logan sat up suddenly and wrapped his arms around the boy, who screeched and wriggled.

"Dad, no!"

"That's Captain Dad to you, rookie," Logan growled.

"Logan, you know I don't like you playing shooting games with him," Jess said. It wasn't the first time.

"What? But we were playing Cops and Also Cops. We were training," Logan answered. Vorus giggled until his father finally released him. "Go set the table for dinner. Commissioner Mom wants to talk to me."

Vorus pouted a little, but then scampered off to do as he was told. Jess winced and pressed her hands against her back. Logan jumped to his feet and helped his wife to sit. It was a sweet gesture, but she wasn't letting him off the hook that easily.

"Vorus is too young for those kinds of games," Jess said. "They're just too violent."

"He already knows," Logan countered. Logan's left hand went automatically to the worn old badge on his chest. He was still in uniform, of course. "Vorus knows I'm a cop. He's already asked what happened to the man he's named after."

"And you told him?" Jess asked, aghast.

"What did you want me to do, Jess? Lie? To our son?" Logan took her hands. His fingers were warm, rough and strong. "Jess, this is Prianus. There's no point in pretending it's safe."

"But it is safe in here," Jess said. "In our home. Besides, you know cops don't shoot other cops. Let's keep it to shooting bad guys, hawk. Imaginary ones."

"That's fair," Logan agreed. He smiled and kissed his wife. "What's for dinner? It smells great."

The Blue Phoenix made daily flights out to other Sunjarran cities, searching for more Arcadians. Maeve gave several speeches, better rehearsed this time, but still admittedly unpolished. The crowds were small, though. Sunjarrah was not one of the original worlds to which the Arcadians fled when the Devourers ravaged the White Kingdom. Fairies had come to Sunjarrah over the century since then, but never in great numbers. And most of those had already promised themselves to Xartasia's mysterious cause. After a week of searching and speeches, Maeve's new kingdom was far from impressive. With only thirty-seven members, it was more like a gang than a kingdom.

"This just isn't working," Duaal said. "Not the way we want it to. That we need it to."

Maeve looked at the young mage's reflection in the mirror. He stood behind her, helping Panna to style her hair. Panna held the comb while Duaal arranged sculpted black curls around Maeve's shoulders.

"Xartasia is spreading her message aggressively. We need to do the same," Panna said.

"If we weren't so damned broke, we could. Maybe hit the mainstream–" Duaal broke off with a sigh. "But we are broke."

"Perhaps we could take a job," Maeve suggested. "This is still a cargo ship, after all."

"I don't know that it is," Duaal answered. He stopped fussing over Maeve's hair long enough to pat the fibersteel bulkhead affectionately. "We're cramming thirty Arcadians into the hold every night to eat and to listen to you. There isn't room for cargo."

"And I don't know if we can take a week off to haul any," Panna agreed. "We *have* a job. We just need to figure out how to do it."

"We won't have much time to do it," said a new voice.

All three of them looked up. Maeve was already beaming, but Logan's expression was serious. Even more serious than usual. The Prian didn't come into the room, but remained in the hall, holding the door open.

"What is wrong?" Maeve asked.

"Xia just commed," Logan said. "We have to get back to New Hennor."

"We'll be there tonight." Duaal inspected Maeve's wings for any ruffled feathers. "After the speech."

"You need to get us in the air now," Logan told the captain. "The police are at the settlement right now. They're accusing Ferris and the other Arcadians of trying to start up a sovereign government on Sunjarran soil."

"What?" Panna asked. "How did they even know about that?"

"Ferris told them," Logan said. "According to Xia, he was quite indignant when the police arrived. He seems to think that Maeve should have authority over them."

"Shit." Duaal ran out of Maeve's room, past Logan and up to the front of the Blue Phoenix.

"We're not even Alliance citizens and yet they expect us to respect their government," Panna said. "Typical CWA politics."

Maeve, Panna and Logan hurried to the cargo bay. Gripper was already there, hanging from a support strut and planting the last of his seed reserves. He squeaked as the Blue Phoenix took off.

"What's going on?" he asked. "I thought we were staying put for a few hours."

"The police are trying to arrest my people," Maeve said. She paced back and forth across the cargo bay as Sunjarrah raced by in a green and orange blur below.

"I really hope you have another speech up your sleeve," Duaal said, his voice popping over the intercom. "There are nine cop cars down there and we can't get into a firefight with them."

Gripper swung down and landed with a clang beside Maeve. "What are you going to do, Glass?"

Maeve wasn't sure, but the Blue Phoenix landed and she hit the airlock controls. Gripper shied back, but Panna and Logan charged out alongside Maeve into the bright white sunlight. A pair of officers – a Mirran in dark glasses and a white-eyed Hadrian – turned toward the Blue Phoenix. Their guns were still holstered, but the cops rested hands on their weapons.

"You can't land here," shouted the Hadrian officer. She held an arm across her face. The Blue Phoenix's engines were still rumbling and rippled the yellow grass in hot waves. "We're in the middle of a police action."

"How many officers do you have here?" Logan asked.

"That's none of your business, sir," said the Mirran.

"How many?"

"Fifteen," the Hadrian cop answered. "Now we really need to ask you to leave."

"We're members of this Arcadian group," Panna said. "Queen Maeve needs to speak with your supervisor."

"Queen?" the Mirran asked.

The two cops looked at each other, and then the Mirran nodded slowly. "Come with me, miss. Hands off your weapons."

It took Maeve a moment to understand what the police officer meant. She didn't have her spear, but Logan had not forgotten his laser. He remained very close to Maeve as the cops led her through the ring of cars. The lights on top flashed. Maeve was escorted to one of the flat foundation slabs where Ferris stood silently, chin lifted proudly despite the dirty smears on his lined cheeks. When he saw Maeve, the duke spread his wings.

"Here is our queen," Ferris told another brown-striped Mirran cop rather smugly. "She will have a solution to all of this."

Maeve wanted to shake Ferris. They had already lost every last cenmark paying out fines. What did the duke think Maeve could do...? Still, she had to try to keep her people out of prison. Maeve took a deep breath and gave the officer – whose brass badge read *Lieutenant Sanhir* – her best smile.

"What seems to be the problem, captain?" Maeve asked, feeling foolish.

"This settlement was condemned three years ago," Lieutenant Sanhir said. He was a middle-aged man with dark eyes and was as thick around the middle as the gazelle-like Mirrans ever seemed to get. "It's illegal to live here. Your people have already been warned about it."

"Warned?" Panna repeated under her breath. "You call prison sentences *warnings*?"

Ferris narrowed his amber eyes at the girl and subtly shook his head. Panna's expression remained furious, but she fell silent once more. Maeve's urge to shake Ferris returned. Did he really think that Maeve was doing any better?

"They... we have nowhere else to go," Maeve answered. "Fining and imprisoning them does not change that truth."

"And it doesn't stop it from being illegal, either," Sanhir said. He looked over his sunglasses at Maeve. "Mister Vallerian here–"

"Verridian," Ferris corrected hotly. "Duke Ferris Verridian."

"Whatever." Sanhir kept his gaze leveled at Maeve. "He says that you've declared yourself queen of this little crowd. If that's true, it's in violation of about a dozen Sunjarran laws."

"Um–" Maeve didn't know what to say. She combed her fingers through her neatly arranged black curls. She could imagine Duaal wincing as he watched her from the Blue Phoenix. "What defines *squatting* under your laws?"

Sanhir arched one brow. His dark green hair was receding, but the Mirran's eyebrows remained thick and bushy. "Sleeping and storage of personal belongings in a non-residential zoned area for more than fifty-four hours."

Maeve seized on her tenuous idea.

"Then we can leave," she told him. "No one will remain here to violate your laws."

Sanhir crossed his arms over his chest and his sidearm shone brightly in the luminous sunlight. It looked well polished and cared for, but not unused and Maeve wondered if he was a good shot with it. Sanhir's nostrils flared as the cop took a long breath. He frowned down at Maeve.

"Technically, these fairies have already broken the law," he said. Maeve's wings curled angrily, but Sanhir wasn't done. The police lieutenant looked at Ferris before continuing. "But it's a civil issue, not a violent crime, and corrections *are* allowed in civil cases. It's going to take forever to collect you lot and more taxpayer cenmarks than any of you deserve."

Maeve swallowed the insult and kept smiling. "Then you will let us leave?"

"If you and your people are out of New Hennor by tonight, I can report the case corrected."

"Tonight?" Maeve repeated. "That is very little time."

"That's the best I can do," Sanhir said. He looked over her head at the Blue Phoenix. "And if you're really calling yourself queen of this little flock, I suggest you leave Sunjarrah entirely."

"I... Yes," Maeve said.

Tonight? How could she move thirty-seven people by morning?

"We'll be back at seven tomorrow," Lieutenant Sanhir told her. "Anyone still here by then will be leaving with us."

Maeve nodded dumbly. Sanhir said something into a silver com hooked around his ear. The police withdrew to their cars, turned on humming orange null-inertia fields and drove away toward New Hennor. Duaal jogged across the sunburnt grass to Maeve, looking back over his shoulder at the retreating police.

"What happened?" he asked.

"We need to get everyone onto the ship and then off Sunjarrah," Logan said. "And it needs to be done by seven tomorrow morning."

"Off Sunjarrah?" Duaal asked. He rubbed his cheek. "Can't we just take them back to Nanpoor? That's where you were supposed to talk tonight."

"No," Logan answered. "We can make one pickup tonight, but then we need to get off the planet."

"You really think the cops will chase us off Sunjarrah?" Panna asked.

"We will not be welcome anywhere on this world," Maeve said. She shook herself and looked at Duaal. "Logan is right. We will take with us those we can from Nanpoor, and then we must go."

"More than thirty Arcadians on the Blue Phoenix? It's going to be a tight fit, Maeve," the Hyzaari said, frowning. "And that's not including anyone you pick up tonight."

Ferris drew himself up and gave Maeve an unhappy look.

"Do you truly intend us to leave Sunjarrah, a'shae?" he asked.

"I am afraid that we must," Maeve told him. "We cannot remain here. I am sorry. I know that your daughter is still in prison here."

The old fairy noble closed his eyes and rubbed them. "Il'mani was attacked in prison last night. No one will say who did it. They broke both of her wings."

"That's why the police came out," Panna said. "Isn't it? To tell you what happened? But you don't have a proper address in New Hennor, so they came back to the last location of record."

"Are you saying that this is my fault, little wingless one?" Ferris asked in a raw, angry voice. For the first time, Maeve noticed how red the other Arcadian's eyes were, as though he had run out of tears and would soon begin weeping blood. "You blame me?"

"No," Maeve answered. She stepped between Panna and Ferris. "It does not matter why it has happened. We must take action, not lay blame."

"What action?" Duaal asked. "Maeve, we'll have a ship full of fairies. What are we going to do with them? There isn't space and there sure aren't enough filters or food to handle them for long."

"We are meant for the sky, not the empty darkness of space," Ferris said. His expression remained unhappy, but the duke would clearly rather be working on the problem at hand than worrying over his own.

"We have to take them somewhere else," Logan said.

"Where?" Duaal put his hands in his pocket and kicked a clump of brown grass. It clung stubbornly to the ground, not quite dead and ready to be uprooted. "We're not exactly in the middle of New Hennor out here and the police are still routing them. Where can we go that isn't going to invite more police visits?"

"Prianus," Logan said. "There are Arcadians there and the Prian police have their priorities straight. They won't bother rousting squatters when there's plenty of real crime to deal with. And the Prians don't have the same distaste for Arcadians that the rest of the Alliance does."

Ferris and Panna flinched at Logan's bluntness, but Maeve knew he was right. Most coreworld species wanted the Arcadians off their planets and would do much the same as the Sunjarrans did now. But Prianus was a long, long way from the deep core. It was dangerous, too – cold and full of predators.

"No. Though I would never begrudge you the chance to return to your homeworld, enarri–" Maeve said. Logan opened his mouth to protest, but she held up one hand. "–I have another thought. It is a little closer and a little less dangerous than Prianus. Stray."

"Stray?" Panna said, loudly and suddenly. "Maeve, you can't be serious!"

"This is your *queen* you address!" Ferris hissed.

Panna's face went quite red.

"Sorry, Highness," she muttered. "But Stray? That's where the old Church of Nihil was! Stray is dangerous."

"More dangerous than Prianus?" Maeve asked.

Panna chewed her lip and sighed. "I... I guess not. And there is a lot more ship traffic going to and from Stray than Prianus. If we intend to steal more Arcadians from Xartasia and bring them to us, then we'll need that advantage."

"We have some allies on Stray," Maeve told her. "And the police, we know all too well, will not raise their hand against us unless well paid to do so."

"Stray, then," Duaal said. "I'll get the Blue Phoenix prepped. It's going to be a crowded trip. We'd better make it as short as possible."

The Hyzaari mage turned on his heels and headed back toward the Blue Phoenix, already calling Gripper on his com. Panna moved to follow, then stopped and looked back.

"Maeve... Majesty... What about Xartasia?" she asked. The question was barely audible. "She's doing the same thing as we are. Do you think she's had the same problem?"

"I doubt it," Maeve said. "The police have tracked and reported us, and would do the same for her, but we have heard nothing. I do not think Xartasia is on any Alliance planet."

"Then where do you think she is?"

"Khylor hasn't returned yet. Neither have those little wing-rats that went with him."

It was Orix, the youngest of the Glorious. He stood with four of the other huge aliens, starlight playing over his nanite-slicked gray skin and long, sharp teeth. Smoky tendrils of his swarm snaked out and back, gathering information that it sent back to the Devourer's implanted computer and transmitting data to the rest of his alien squadron.

"Sir Calathan is a knight of the White Kingdom," Xartasia said. She didn't turn to look at the Devourer. "You will speak of him with due respect."

"He is a slave, aerad," Orix snarled. "A meal–"

Dhozo cut him off. "Enough."

Orix's grinding, grating voice said something else, something he didn't bother to send to his nanites for translation. Dhozo held up a fist the size of Xartasia's head and made a curt motion with it. Orix reluctantly quieted, though the young Devourer glared balefully at his commander.

Xartasia smoothed the skirts of her gleaming pearl-white gown. An Arcadian woman, Ailo, stood up on her tiptoes to place the delicate glass crown on her queen's brow. It caught the glow of lights in the high ceiling and threw back brilliant rainbows. Dhozo regarded Xartasia's clothes.

"Again?" he asked.

"Yes," she said. "As often as it takes to soothe my people's spirits. They do not like being in space, so far from any open sky. You are the commander of your team, Dhozo. You should know the value of trust. I would not violate my people's faith. You will aid me in that."

Ailo arranged Xartasia's flowing white skirts behind her. They flowed like cream along the floor. Orix took a long step toward her, looming over the Arcadian queen and Ailo leapt back with a frightened moan, hiding behind her wings. Unflinching, Xartasia looked up into the Devourer's wide onyx face. Orix's nanite armor writhed across his skin like a living thing.

"I do not fear you," Xartasia reminded him. "You and yours have already taken from me what I loved most. Now you will help me to get him... get it all back."

"Why are we helping this little wing-rat slave?" Orix rumbled like an encroaching storm. "We were supposed to take the Projector, open it and bring the rest through!"

"You know why," Dhozo said. The sound was like water being poured over coals, hot enough to burn and blister. "There is more than meat for us here. We cannot reopen the Projectors ourselves, not without the old science."

"The *magic* she says she can teach us?" Orix hissed. He waved a huge, razor-clawed hand at Xartasia. "She hasn't given us anything, commander!"

"Your people picked this galaxy clean and when there was no more to eat, you left to find a new one," Xartasia said. She stared down both of the monstrous aliens, unafraid of their teeth or claws, of the nanites clinging to their skin that could become a deadly cloud of blades in a heartbeat. "Now *that* galaxy is no more than bones and your people are starving to death. The whole of the universe will be your hunting ground when you control the Waygates once more. But I will not give that to you until my people are home and whole again. When that is done..."

"Anzo b'ho khavvna ghotek! Anzo khamen!" Orix snarled at Dhozo. "You believe her?"

"We must eat," said the Devourer commander. His voice – his *real* voice, not the metallic approximation of his nanite swarm – was as hard and cold as ice. "The Glorious must eat. Your pride can take the cut, Orix. So shut it."

The door slid open, metal ringing on metal. A pair of glass-armored Arcadian men burst into the room, spears held with points low and wings spread wide to leap. One of them turned to Xartasia while the other kept his weapon leveled at the Devourers.

"We heard shouting, Highness," he said. "Are you alright?"

"Of course," Xartasia told him. "Go wait outside."

Reluctantly, the two knights bowed and withdrew. Voices came from the corridor outside, echoing back and forth so that Xartasia couldn't pick out their exact numbers. But those numbers were growing... The chanting and singing faded again as the door closed.

Xartasia beckoned to Ailo. The woman crept closer, trembling as she emerged from the shadows. Clean, processed air whispered through the vents and ruffled her pale golden hair. She came slowly to her queen. The glass crown was cool and smooth against Xartasia's skin.

"You need not fear them," she said, pointing with one wingtip to Dhozo and Orix. "They are our allies, our brothers and sisters."

"We won't be helpful to anyone if we don't get to work," Dhozo rasped. "When do we begin? We need data, little queen, before we even know if what you want can be done."

"Not yet. You know that, Dhozo," Xartasia said. "You are an engineer. You made the calculations. We need more of my people before we make any attempt. Many more."

She smiled beautifully at Ailo and strode out through the door. Arcadians and Devourers alike fell into step behind her. They made their way down the black metal corridor, toward the sound of voices raised in song, in praise to the White Queen.

Xartasia paused before the final door, listening, and let the song wash over her like a tide over sand. It pushed and pulled, guiding her... The sound was almost enough to drown out the century-long silence of everything she loved – her kingdom, her family, her beloved Anthem...

Even through the sealed bulkheads and airlocks, Xartasia could hear her people sing. They called out for her, for change. For the restoration of the White Kingdom and all they had lost.

[10]

IN THE BLACK

"Horrible mistakes are simply life lessons that *really* wanted to get
your attention."

- DUAAL SINNAY (234 PA)

Duaal need not have worried about collecting too many Arcadians in
Nanpoor. There were no fairies in the city, only a mob of angry Ixthians
and humans. They shouted at Maeve and threatened to call the police if
she didn't leave at once. Unwilling to face Sunjarran law enforcement
again, Maeve retreated to the Blue Phoenix. Panna, Duaal and Logan
were less eager to leave and followed her into the ship only at a distance.
Duaal was still yelling at the crowd as the airlock sealed behind him.

Disappointed and dispirited, they finally returned back to New
Hennor, where Duke Ferris waited with the other Arcadians at the
edge of the sun-scorched cornfield. The fairies all carried their few
meager possessions clutched in stick-thin arms: moth-eaten blankets and near-empty sacks of food, a spare change of clothes and an
occasional rainbow-hued shard of glass or cloth brought from their
homeworld.

Maeve greeted them at the cargo ramp. It would be a cramped and uncomfortable journey, but when they arrived on Stray, they could begin building a true home. A new kingdom. Maeve repeated her promise as reassuringly as she could manage.

Xia and Gripper escorted each Arcadian to where they would be staying for the next few weeks. Every room of the Blue Phoenix was full, everything that could be made into a bed or table pressed into service. The survival raft had even been patched and covered with a reflective blanket. Panna gave up her room in favor of Duke Ferris. The nobleman thanked her in a perfunctory sort of way that suggested he expected no less. Logan volunteered his own bunk to an old Arcadian woman from the city of Hallipon named A'lanu. Duke Ferris watched Duaal carefully guide A'lanu through the crowded hold and up the stairs.

"That is very kind of you," the duke said.

Logan shrugged. "I never use it anyway."

"No, I expect not," Ferris said. "A man as skilled and dangerous as Logan Coldhand is surely busy at all hours. It is said by some that you do not sleep."

"You've heard of me?"

The Arcadian nobleman gave a noncommittal hum and swept off to look after a pair of younger fairies who were having trouble finding space to lay out their small basket of belongings.

Maeve waited nearby. When Ferris was gone, she stepped close to Logan and kissed his illonium fingertips. Many of the Arcadians stared at them and Maeve tried not to blush.

"It is getting late," she told Logan, "and we need to leave Sunjarrah. Duaal wants you to copilot the takeoff. We are carrying many more passengers and weight than usual."

"If he needs the help, sure."

Logan hurried up the stairs out of the cargo bay and Maeve smiled after him. Whatever else her hunter said, she knew better –

Logan was Prian. He loved to fly, even if only as occasional copilot on an old cargo ship.

A shadow fell over Maeve and she stepped back, trying to get out of the way of whoever was pushing their way through.

"A queen should not have to carry messages for a mere ship's captain," Duke Ferris said. He hadn't gone far, it seemed.

"Duaal tried to call to Logan over the intercom," Maeve told the other fairy, "but it was too loud in here."

"But your ship has others to..." Ferris struggled to find the word in Aver. "*Dryan'ii a nyan'ii.* Your duties are greater than those of a simple courier."

"My duties are whatever need to be done," Maeve said. "Whatever is required, I will do."

Ferris bowed his head. "Of course, a'shae."

He dipped his wings to Maeve and the two of them went back to the cargo ramp to bring in the last of the Arcadians. The sun was rising bright blue-violet over the condemned Sunjarrah settlement. It was time to leave.

● ● ●

Every last spare cenmark collected from the Arcadians and the Blue Phoenix crew had been spent on food and fuel, but by the end of the second week, everyone on board had to skip meals. The fairies were accustomed to going hungry, but they had hoped for more from their new queen.

Tempers frayed and in the close confines of the little freighter, there was no place to get away from each other. There were arguments over food and space, and even a few blows traded. Ferris did an impressive job of smoothing things over, but occasionally had to bring Arcadians to Maeve for a royal decision.

The new queen was not above hiding from Duke Ferris when he came seeking her wisdom. He was older and wiser than Maeve, she reasoned. Ferris was a nobleman, probably raised in the heart of the court. Leadership was considerably harder than doing dishes, or than giving speeches. Let those who were suited to it settle the disputes.

Maeve spotted Duke Ferris at the door to her room. His arms were crossed over his chest and he was accompanied by five Arcadians who stood packed together in the narrow hall. Maeve turned and strode quickly back the way she had come. A'lanu saw her in the corridor, though, and lowered her wingtip to the floor, wincing as her arthritic joints struggled with the deferent gesture.

Maeve moved swiftly past, feeling uncomfortable. She stopped briefly in the mess, but it was crowded with other fairies searching for food or sitting listlessly at the table. Instead, Maeve went to the medbay. The Arcadians were mistrustful of coreworld science and while they didn't refuse Xia and her medicine, neither were they very comfortable around the Ixthian.

But to Maeve's shock, there was a pair of other Arcadians in the small medical bay. Both were young, less than a century old. Like Panna, they had been born since the fall of the White Kingdom. These two didn't even remember their home. One of them – a young man about Panna's age with his blond hair in a pair of long braids – perched on the edge of Xia's exam table, holding his right arm gingerly. The Ixthian medic sat on a metal stool, cleaning a painful-looking red burn that extended from the boy's wrist almost to the singed elbow of his shirt.

"You shouldn't be practicing fire spells on the ship," Xia said.

"It's just magic," the other Arcadian answered sullenly. "I need to practice."

She looked a little bit older than the boy with the burnt elbow and wore her hair the same way. At least, she used to – now one of the braids was gone, burned away with no more than a few blackened strands left in its place. Soot smudged her face as if the girl had fallen into ink.

Maeve paused in the doorway, struggling to remember the two younger fairies' names. Malla and... Hanno? No, Hannu. They were brother and sister, but their parents were not among those Arcadians on the Blue Phoenix.

"Fire is fire," Xia told the pair. "It consumes oxygen and we don't have that much to spare. If you must practice, please no fire or lightning."

Malla started to roll her eyes, but caught sight of Maeve halfway through and jerked upright.

"Your Highness," she gasped.

Hannu sat up straighter on the exam table and tried to pull his hand from Xia's grasp, but the Ixthian was much larger and had six silver fingers wrapped around the boy's wrist. He had to settle for inclining his head, cheeks flaming. Xia looked up, too, and smiled at Maeve.

"I thought I was done with this sort of thing," she said. "Duaal doesn't butcher his spells anymore."

"No," Maeve agreed. "He has become a great mage."

"That's the human man who captains this ship, isn't it?" Hannu asked. "The Hyzaari?"

Maeve nodded. "He used to burn himself, as well. And much of the ship. There is a spot on the ceiling of the hold that still bears the scars of his younger days. That was before Gripper put his planters in."

"Did you teach him, Highness?" Malla asked. She tugged self-consciously on the remains of her burnt braid.

"No," Maeve said. "I know only a few charms. I was a knight, not a spell-singer."

"But I thought that..." Hannu trailed off, blushing even brighter.

"What?" Maeve asked.

Malla exchanged a look with her brother that suggested there was a good smack in store for him as soon as there was no royalty watching.

"We heard that the queen–" Malla began then corrected herself. "That is, Xartasia... Sir Calathan said that she is a great mage. We assumed you were, too."

"You spoke to Calathan?"

"No," Hannu said. "Not ourselves, at least. But we heard him in Rassinmar, before he came to New Hennor."

"It's a good thing you were more eloquent, Maeve," Xia said. She finished cleaning his burnt arm and wrapped it in soft white gauze.

Malla and Hannu looked at each other again. This time, it was the fairy girl who colored. Maeve cocked her head.

"What is it?" she asked the younger Arcadians.

"Nothing," Malla mumbled.

"Tell me, please."

"Well... We're very glad to be here, Your Highness," Malla said in a rush, the words running together like spilled paint. "But we... we would have gone to Xartasia if we had been allowed. Most of the others in Rassinmar went to Xartasia, but Sir Calathan wouldn't take us."

"Why not?" Maeve asked.

"He said that we were too young," Hannu answered. "Anyone born in the core isn't welcome in the White Queen's court."

Maeve scowled. Was her cousin truly so cold? Would Xartasia really turn away the youngest of their people just because they had never known the green grass and endless blue skies of Arcadia? Maeve supposed she should be grateful, whatever Xartasia's reasons might be. Hannu and Malla were here on the Blue Phoenix because of them.

"Listen to Xia," Maeve said. "I am glad you are practicing the charm songs. There are so few spell-singers left among our people. But do avoid fire and lightning while we are in flight."

"Yes, Your Highness," Malla and Hannu answered.

Xia checked over her work and then released Hannu. He and his sister lowered their wings toward Maeve and edged around the medbay to the door. The siblings vanished quickly down the fiber-steel corridor, whispering behind their wings.

"Do you think they will listen?" Maeve asked.

"Did Duaal?" Xia asked as she cleaned up the supplies she used on Hannu's burn. She replaced the remaining gauze and sighed. The cupboards were looking more than a little bare.

"Not to me, perhaps, but Duaal listens to you," Maeve said.

The Ixthian laughed. "Really? I hadn't noticed."

Maeve closed the medbay door. She didn't want Ferris walking past and noticing his wayward queen.

"Since Prianus," she said. "You and Duaal grew very close while we were there."

"Yes." Xia locked the supply cabinets. "I suppose we did."

"What happened after?" Maeve asked. "You are no longer..."

She wasn't exactly sure how to say it, but Xia seemed to understand. The Ixthian peeled her gloves off, went to the sink and began scrubbing her hands. She had no fingernails, Maeve noticed for the first time – all twelve digits came to smooth, soft tips. They looked fragile, but Maeve doubted that they actually were. The Ixthians were too large to sustain a proper exoskeleton, but their insectoid heritage had made their skin nearly as resilient as one. In a test of strength, Maeve's short, unpainted fingernails would lose out against Xia's smooth silver skin.

"No, Duaal and I aren't seeing each other any longer," she said. The doctor looked down at the soap on her hands rather than face Maeve's curious gray eyes. "He just outgrew me, I suppose. Duaal needed someone to take care of him, but that's a boy's need. He's a man now."

Maeve was sorry she asked.

"That must be painful," she said.

"It's not so bad, really," Xia answered with a shrug. She dried her hands and smoothed back her white hair. "Duaal has his work and I have mine. We all do what we have to, Maeve."

"Did you love him?"

Now Xia actually turned to Maeve and smiled.

"Not like you love that hard-hearted bounty hunter of yours," she said. "I've been meaning to ask you about that."

"You are changing the subject," Maeve objected.

"Only because I'm legitimately curious," Xia said. "And a little concerned. You really should bring him in for some tests. Logan's human – they're a resilient species. And he's Prian, too. He could be carrying a dozen diseases that he doesn't even know about. Arcadian immune systems just aren't up to that sort of challenge."

"Oh." Maeve hadn't thought of that. "That seems wise."

Xia sat on the corner of the exam table and propped her elbows up on her long, thin legs. "And that's only one factor of biology."

Maeve wanted to hide behind her wings, but that wasn't very queenly. She put her hands on her hips.

"Ixthian males are smaller than their females," Maeve pointed out, remembering her embarrassing conversation with Panna. "But Duaal is nearly as tall as you are!"

Xia's teeth flashed in a smirk. "True, but not what I was saying. Humans and Arcadians share a lot of genetics, but not enough. You and Logan can't have children. Not naturally and maybe not ever."

"I know."

"Doesn't that bother you?" Xia asked when Maeve said nothing else. "You can never have a family with him."

"I have not given it much thought," Maeve admitted. "It seems so unlikely we will live long enough for such concerns. With everything else going on, it hardly seems important."

"With so few Arcadians left," Xia countered, "maybe you should be considering your population a little more seriously."

Maeve lied that she would and then fled the medical bay.

"Can you hand me the um... the... um..."

"What do you need?" Logan asked.

"The U-wrench," Gripper squeaked.

Logan found it on the bottom tier of the toolbox and handed it up to the Arboran. Gripper's arm vanished up to the shoulder into the vent.

"Even the heavy filters just can't handle this much feather fluff," he muttered. "I need to install a five gauge."

Gripper grunted and pulled the filter out, maneuvering it carefully free of the duct. The mesh was entirely covered in fine white down like snow. Logan passed up a new one and Gripper's tongue poked out from between his teeth as he examined the new filter. He sighed.

"This kind is for the rear vents. I'll need to cut it down to size," Gripper said. He climbed down and began making measurements. He hesitated and looked at Logan. "I... You can go, if you want. I know the captain asked you to help out, but–"

"It's fine," Logan answered. He held the filter frame steady as Gripper marked out the cuts with a stick of blue wax. "Maeve's busy and there isn't much piloting to be done while traveling SL. Duaal can manage that on his own."

"Oh." Gripper chewed his lip as he worked. "We only have a few more of these. Getting to Stray before we all choke on feathers is going to be close."

Logan nodded, but Gripper wasn't looking. Instead, the young alien sat cross-legged down on the metal floor, hunched over his work and muttering numbers to himself. Gripper's large, powerful muscles bunched beneath his oil-stained shirt, knotted and tense-looking. Logan was silent for a moment before he spoke.

"You're still upset about the Oslain'ii," he said.

Gripper flinched and didn't even try to protest.

"Yeah, I am," he said. "I know I shouldn't be. They were trying to shoot us and all, but I never wanted to..."

Gripper sighed and took a laser cutter from the dented green toolbox. He flicked it on with a massive thumb and began cutting, wielding the tool with a delicacy that surprised Logan. The fine red beam sliced easily through the filter's metal frame.

"You didn't know," Logan said. "You were just doing what I told you to."

"I know." Gripper turned off the laser and picked a file from his case. "The raw edges will tear up the duct lining if I don't smooth them down some. I told myself that it was your fault. For a while."

"I was sixteen the first time I killed someone," Logan said.

He leaned against the wall beneath the open vent and crossed his arms under the small of his back, making his cybernetic arm scrape along the bulkhead.

"Young, but not as young as some on Prianus," Logan said. "Jess was flying with a gang in those days. The Harrowhawks. Getting her out came down to a duel with her leader. I was too young and too broke to have a bird of my own, but Vorus loaned me his."

"Vorus?" Gripper asked. The file in his hand wasn't moving.

"My teacher. He ran the palaestrum where I spent most of my time. Vorus taught me to fight and how to fly a bird. A blue-banded falcon named Bella. On my command, she tore out the Harrowhawk boy's throat. His hawk gave me this."

Logan tugged the collar of his shirt down and showed Gripper a set of three faded lines that ran over his right collarbone. They were pale now, but had been livid red for more than a year after the duel.

"And then she went with you?" Gripper asked. "The girl?"

"Jess. Yes, she did. A few years later, we were engaged."

"To a girl from a gang?"

Logan pulled his shirt back into place. "Everyone on Prianus flies with a gang at some point in their life. Even the cops. You don't survive long alone."

"So... are you saying I'm like the hawk?" Gripper dropped the file back into his toolbox. "That I just followed your orders? But I'm not dumb, Coldhand. I should have figured it out, what we were doing. I just didn't."

"You're not an animal," Logan said. His voice was harder than he meant it to be. "We love our birds, but they're just animals. They just follow commands and kill when told."

"I don't get it."

"You're right, Gripper. You could have figured out that we were towing the Oslain'ii into the star," Logan said. He lifted the cutdown filter and held it out. "But would it have changed what you did? Would you still have done it?"

Gripper didn't take the filter.

"I had to!" he said. "That pilot was trying to kill us!"

"So?" Logan asked. "One of us was going to die. But you got to decide which one. Choosing yourself is a legitimate option, Gripper. You could have died instead of becoming a killer. Plenty make that choice, even on Prianus. Not everyone has it in them to fight. But you did."

"I... I had to," Gripper answered quietly. "We have to stop the Devourers, Coldhand. We're trying to save the whole galaxy here."

"And by taking out the Oslain'ii, you saved Maeve, for which I'll always be grateful. We can't remake our choices. We live with the consequences of our actions and they make us who we are. We can only hope that we help more than we hurt."

Gripper finally accepted the filter and climbed up to wedge it into place.

"Yeah. I guess so," he said. The Arboran's voice echoed in the duct. "Hey... Thanks, Logan."

It was strange to hear his given name from the Arboran. It made Gripper seem older, somehow, but Logan doubted that it was just the sound of his name. Death changed a person, one way or the other. He and Gripper finished their work in silence.

"Queen Maeve, Dellan requests an audience."

The Blue Phoenix wasn't large enough to avoid Ferris forever. Maeve sat at the dinner table with her chin in her hands. Lunch sat half-eaten in her bowl, a rehydrated salad made from Gripper's emergency stores. Maeve's stomach growled.

"Yes, I would be happy to see him," she lied.

Duke Ferris bowed and went to get Dellan while Maeve finished her salad in a few large, hasty bites. But before she could take her empty bowl to the sink, an Arcadian woman swept it away. Another swiftly polished the table clean with a dish towel. Clean as the old table got, at least. Maeve thought it might have been Malla, but the girl was gone again in a moment.

Panna stepped through the door that led up to the cockpit. She looked around the mess and then squeezed through to take a seat next to Maeve.

"It sure is crowded in here," she said. "What's going on?"

"Audiences," Maeve grumped. "I am not even permitted to do my own dishes. And Dellan wishes to speak with me, apparently."

"Well, I've told you that a queen can't do dishes," Panna said. "You don't think King Illain did the laundry, do you? That was probably some nyad's job."

Maeve had no answer to that. Duke Ferris returned a moment later, leading Dellan, a middle-aged man who walked with his head down. He held one of his wings out at a stiff angle from his body and did his best to lower them before the dinner table where his queen sat. Maeve felt ridiculous.

"A'shae," Duke Ferris said. His expression was pinched with disapproval. "Dellan has asked to speak with you alone."

"Of course," Maeve answered. She couldn't imagine why Ferris objected and didn't feel like asking. She looked around at the other fairies filling the room. "Will you please give us just a moment?"

Panna stood, too, and filed out with Ferris and the rest. When they were gone, Dellan rose slowly.

"*Vaelin, a cerri,*" he said. *Thank you, my queen.*

"*Ai'li eru Aver?*" Maeve asked. *Do you speak Aver?*

Dellan shook his head. "*No, Highness. I never learned.*"

It wasn't uncommon. How many fights between Arcadians and the coreworlders had started because they couldn't communicate? If Maeve was really a queen, could she change that? Institute some sort of... educational program? All the Alliance worlds had contributed to Aver and then learned the common language. Maybe the fairies could, too.

But was Maeve truly a queen at all? Her sudden monarchy was not out of any ability or sense of obligation, but because Panna and Duaal were sure that it was the only way to thwart Xartasia. Playing queen didn't actually mean that Maeve could change anything.

Maeve realized she hadn't been listening to a word Dellan said. She sighed and apologized.

"*Please say that again.*"

"*It is Gael,*" Dellan said. The man was upset – his hands clasped before him so hard that the knuckles had turned pale – but it didn't seem to be directed at Maeve. "*He has never... He is my friend, but Gael lost his whole family at the fall. He takes* Deep–" The name was spoken in heavily accented Aver. "*–to forget. He falls asleep for days at a time. Please, my queen... Can you help him?*"

"Me?" Maeve asked. She sat up and banged her elbow painfully into the table's edge. "*How can I help him?*"

"*Speak to Gael, Your Highness. I beg you. He is here on your ship so he must believe in you, in the new kingdom that you promise. If you ask him to stop, maybe he finally will.*"

"*I... can try,*" Maeve said uncertainly. "*Where is he now?*"

"*There is one of the closets, full of cleaning things. It is small and dark and no one seems to go there much. Gael sleeps there when he has taken too much.*"

Maeve nodded and stood. Dellan bowed and then followed her from the mess. The corridor outside was still crowded by those banished from the room. Ferris and Panna began to walk with her, but Maeve waved them off. The old duke gave her another disapproving look, but Panna just shrugged and returned to the mess.

Maeve and Dellan made their way through the Blue Phoenix to a small door just down the hall from the medbay. The tiny closet was all that remained of the larger storage room that had been converted for Xia's use. Maeve knocked on the gray metal door, but there was no answer.

The medical bay door slid open and Xia's head poked out, silver antennae arched. "Anything wrong?"

"Maybe. Did you see anyone go in here?" Maeve asked.

Xia shook her head. "The closet? No. But I've been redprinting all of the new blood samples. I only heard you knocking because I was already on my way out."

Maeve held her breath and opened the closet door. There were shelves of bleach and hylox, all marked with peeling and yellowed labels. The lower shelves held boxes of sponges and a splitting mycolar bag full of old rags. At the bottom of the closet was the curled-up shape of an Arcadian, his limbs drawn close and wings wrapped tightly around his skinny body.

Dellan let out a low, unhappy moan.

Xia emerged from her medbay and gasped when she saw Gael. "We need to get him out of there. What happened?"

"He has been taking Deep," Maeve said.

With Xia's help, she managed to pull the unconscious man from the closet and carry him to the medbay. His limbs were tightly contorted, knotted up like rope. Xia peeled back Gael's eyelids and shined a penlight across his dilated pupil.

Maeve looked up at Xia. "Can you wake him?"

"You say he's been taking Deep, right?" Xia asked. She went to the computer attached to the wall and slid her fingers across the keyboard. "Deoxyhexabromine, street name *Deep* or *Deepblack*. Yes, I can wake him up."

Xia unlocked one of the medbay cabinets and withdrew an air needle. Muttering to herself, the Ixthian selected a vial of something as yellow as butter. She added a few drops of a thicker blue substance and then shook the vial. The whole thing turned a bright orange as the chemicals reacted inside. Xia slid it into her air injector and pressed the device against the inside of Gael's elbow.

Within seconds, his arms and legs began to uncurl. Dellan held Gael's bony hand and he whispered something into his friend's ear. Gael's eyes finally fluttered open. One of them was dim and cloudy, but the other fixed on Maeve. He struggled to rise, but Xia pushed him gently down again.

"Relax," she said. Gael looked up at the Ixthian with fear and no comprehension.

"*Anlae,*" Maeve repeated in Arcadian. Gael didn't seem to speak Aver, either. "*Dellan asked us for help. He is worried about you.*"

Gael's eye flicked toward Dellan. There was a mixture of anger and gratitude there. Dellan ducked his head and would only look at Maeve.

"*Dellan worries too much,*" Gael said. His voice was roughened by too much sleep. "*I am fine, Your Majesty.*"

"*You are using Deep to forget.*" Maeve took Gael's hand and tried to summon some sort of queenly bearing. This was just like giving one of her speeches. "*We have all lost so much. The Arcadians can only fly forward from that together. That cannot be done from the darkness of a closet or the deeper dark of a drugged haze. Dellan is here. I am here. Fly with us, not away.*"

"*You are my queen,*" Gael said.

There was respect in his voice, but disbelief, too. He didn't think Maeve understood any of it.

"*I have taken more White and drunk more narcohol than the most dedicated human inebriate,*" she told the other Arcadian. "*There is so much pain that I want to forget, Gael. That I would gladly cut out of my own life and flesh if I had a blade sharp enough. I know the skies you fly now.*"

Gael swallowed hard. He squeezed his eyes shut and nodded slowly.

"*Yes, my queen,*" he said.

"*Do you have more of it?*" Dellan asked. "*Of the Deep?*"

The other Arcadian man's jaw clenched, but he nodded again. "*It is in the closet where I slept, wrapped up in the rags. What will you do with it?*"

"*We will destroy it,*" Maeve said. "*No one here needs it anymore.*"

Gael drew a shuddering breath and visibly steeled himself.

"Yes," he agreed. "*Destroy it before I beg for more.*"

[11]

RED STAR, RED SAND

"Moments are but grains of sand. Life is the beach and truth is the blue ocean dancing across them."

- TITANIA CAVAINNA (234 PA)

A'lanu didn't survive to see Stray. She was an old woman, too sick to fly anymore. She fell down the stairs into the hold, shattering her left hip, shoulder and both wings. Xia did all she could for A'lanu, but the old fairy woman's immune system was too ravaged by age and exposure to alien diseases to recover.

It was dangerously unsanitary to leave A'lanu's body on the Blue Phoenix, so Xia and Panna wrapped her in a white sheet and some colorful scarves donated by the other Arcadians. She should have been buried with a circlet of birch on her head, but there was no wood on the Blue Phoenix. Panna did her best with a dried somato vine around A'lanu's white-shrouded temples.

At Ferris' insistence, Maeve spoke at the funeral, bidding A'lanu farewell and safe flight into Aes' golden embrace. Maeve had to stop every couple of words to wipe her eyes. It was a short and awkward speech, but no one complained.

When Maeve finished, Gripper placed A'lanu's body in the air-lock and with a bit of instruction, Duke Ferris released the outer door. Evacuating air ruffled the shroud, and then Duaal cut the gravity and A'lanu floated gently away. Within seconds, she was just another white spot against the stars. A moment later, she was gone.

Three days after A'lanu's funeral, The Blue Phoenix entered the Bannon system. Everyone on the ship was hungry, but according to Xia, more or less in good health considering the long and cramped flight.

Duaal called down from the cockpit to Maeve on the internal system. "We should be on Stray in a couple of hours. Where do you want me to land?"

"Gharib," Maeve answered.

Panna and Duke Ferris were nearby – they always were these days. Panna looked up from a datadex in her hands.

"Gharib?" she asked. "Where Gavriel's cathedral used to be?"

"Yes," Maeve said. "But it is also a city that we know, police we can rely on to be unhelpful and where we can find Xyn. We are out of phenno now, after all."

"Gharib it is, Queen Maeve," Duaal said only a little bit mock-ingly. "I'll have you on the ground by noon, local time."

Their young Hyzaari captain was true to his word. The Blue Phoenix shook as it landed and dim, ruddy red sunlight streamed in through the viewports. The Arcadians crowded into the cargo bay, muttering and murmuring. Maeve stood at the top of the stairs with Logan and Duaal. Gripper looked up at her from the airlock. When Maeve nodded, he lowered the cargo ramp. A storm of white wings burst from the Blue Phoenix, thirty fairies kept too long away from the sky and eager to fly again. They filled the dingy orange sky like a flock of birds, wheeling and circling over the ship.

Duaal looked at Maeve. "Now what?"

"Why are you asking me?"

"You are the queen," Logan said.

In case she had forgotten... Maeve resisted the childish urge to stick out her tongue. "I am not sure. What do we need first?"

"We're on the western edge of Gharib, in the landing crescent," Duaal said. "Not far from where we were last time, actually. We don't have the color for landing fees, though. It'll go unnoticed for a while, but someone will come demanding their money eventually."

Maeve climbed over the catwalk railing and glided down to the blanket-strewn floor of the cargo hold. Everything stank of sweat. Logan and Duaal came down the stairs to meet her. Panna and Xia were with Gripper next to the airlock.

Duke Ferris stood out on the lowered ramp, stretching his wings out, but he hadn't joined the other fairies in the sky. He squinted out over the sandy red landing field. Maeve could just make out the humped bulk of another hauler, one much larger than the Phoenix. But it was late winter on Stray – the windy season – and any more detail was obscured by dust.

Ferris came back inside, shaking a fine coat of rust-colored sand from his wings.

"Is the whole world like this?" he asked. "Covered in sand?"

"Mostly," Gripper said. "There's some ice at the poles and some farmable land around the equator, but the rest of Stray is all sandy desert."

The duke looked speculative, but then he turned to Maeve and dipped his wings. He was not a young man and Maeve wondered if all the bowing hurt. Would he stop if his queen asked him to? Or was tradition even more important than royalty?

"There are other Arcadians here, a'shae," Ferris said. "Panna has told me as much. You will want to speak to them, of course."

"Yes, of course," Maeve agreed sullenly. The urge to spare Duke Ferris bow-related wing pain passed.

"We will find them, Your Highness," Ferris promised.

"Um... where should we bring them?" Panna asked. She looked between Maeve and Ferris. "It can't be here. We're already out of space on the Blue Phoenix. Part of the reason we came to Stray was to make a home."

Logan had his arm around Maeve – the right one – and pulled her close to him. He was warm and smelled faintly of metal. Logan looked down at Maeve, caught her staring and smiled faintly. He already knew what she had in mind. They had discussed it several nights before, with her head resting in the hollow of his shoulder and sweat-damp hair plastered against his bare chest.

"The site of the old Nihilist cathedral," Logan said.

Ferris did not look at the Prian. But everyone else did, mostly in confusion.

"What? No," Panna objected. "We can't go there!"

"We can," Maeve said. "I think it will help. It will be... cleansing. The police collected and removed all of the evidence."

She avoided the word *bodies*. It didn't help her case at all.

"Gavriel built a large cathedral there," Xia said in what Maeve hoped was agreement. "And had gatherings there every week or so, but nobody stopped him. Either no one owns that land or else the owner doesn't care."

"Sprite, you did a lot of research into the Gharib thing," Gripper said. "Do you know? Did anyone get mad after we crashed into the church?"

"No, not that I know of," Panna answered with a shrug. Without the extra bones of her wings, it looked almost like a human gesture. "But as far as I know, someone owns everything on Stray. It's got to at least belong to Channik Grale's family. That's the Lyran man who bought the whole planet."

"It's not exactly a prime location," Duaal said. "It's off the roads and outside town. I could see forgetting about it."

"I... guess it's a good enough place to start," Panna conceded.

Ferris frowned at the girl. "Ours is not to question the queen."

"Please do question your queen," Maeve said sourly. "She is very new to this and needs a great deal of help."

"It seems a wise place to begin, a'shae," Ferris said. "We will tell our people to seek you there."

With that, he stepped out into the dim red daylight, spread his wings and soared into the sky. He circled once, singing instructions and then wheeled off in the direction of Gharib. About half of the other Arcadians followed him. The rest remained, including Malla and Hannu, who landed lightly on one of the Blue Phoenix's wings. Maeve had not been able to hear Ferris' orders, but suspected that the sibling's lingering was not of their own choice.

Duaal buttoned up his silver-trimmed coat. It was beginning to look a little threadbare, but Maeve thought better of saying anything. Duaal checked his com and slid it back into his pocket.

"I'm going over to Unbreakers to see Xyn," he told Maeve. "We need phenno and any current news about what's been going on in Gharib. We're flat broke, so I'm going to have to carry that phenno back. I could use a hand. Gripper?"

"Sure, captain."

"Anyone else?" Duaal asked.

"I'll walk into town with you, but I will be helping to bring in the Arcadians," Panna said.

"Gharib isn't the nicest city in the Alliance," Xia told her. "I'll go with you."

"Can I go, too?" Maeve asked. She had no desire to stand uselessly around the Blue Phoenix being a figurehead for the next few hours. "To Unbreakers, I mean. I would like to give my regards to Kessa and her family, if they are still here."

"I knew you had another reason for choosing Gharib," Logan said. He gave Maeve a hard, icy look. "You should have told me."

"I–" she began, but then Logan stopped her with a kiss and an awkward, unpracticed smile.

"It's sweet," Panna said.

"I'll go along with Maeve. And I'm sure our escort will follow, too." Logan jerked an illonium thumb back over his shoulder to the wing of the Blue Phoenix, where Malla and Hannu stood.

"I do not need a bodyguard," Maeve said. She ruffled her wings in irritation.

"It couldn't hurt to have some eyes in the sky," Logan told her.

Maeve hated when her hunter agreed with Duke Ferris, but at least the Arcadians following her wouldn't be treading on her wing-tips. Duaal waited for everyone to make their way down the cargo ramp, then raised and sealed it behind them.

"Let's get this done," he said. The mage coughed and spat some red mud onto the sandy ground. "You sure know how to pick them, Maeve. Do you really want to found a new kingdom here?"

"No," she answered. "But I fear we have no other choice."

— • • • —

"Is that a command, Your Highness?"

"Yes," Maeve said. "It is."

Hannu and Malla exchanged a look, but then they shrugged. The pair took up positions to either side of the doors and Maeve turned back to Unbreakers. Duaal, Gripper and Logan waited at the door for her. Light from the multicolored holographic sign played over their skin. The shop's windows were cloudy with old static sheets that were no longer doing their job very well. Dust gathered in the curling edges.

Duaal pushed the door open and they went inside. Unbreakers was, if possible, even more cluttered than it had been on their last visit. The already small store was full of precariously stacked boxes and crates full of parts and pieces of every known starship, from expensive Starwind and Narsus models to cheaper Gallex knock-offs and generic manufacturers.

A hundred 'floor' models sagged on orange null-fields overhead. Maeve didn't need to duck beneath them, but all of her male companions walked stooped over like old men. Duaal slouched to the corner of the shop, where there was a long counter covered in loose nuts and bolts and dust. A black-haired young Dailon in long beige sleeves was trying in vain to sweep up the sand without sending the bits of metal flying and looked up at the sound of customers. A grin spread across their blue face.

"Maeve!"

"Kessa…?"

Maeve braced herself as the Dailon girl vaulted over the counter and threw her arms around Maeve.

No longer pregnant, Kessa had taken on the lean, androgynous look of most of her species – flat-chested and narrow-hipped. Only her large, long-lashed black eyes belied her gender. To Maeve, at least. Dailons didn't seem to have the slightest trouble identifying their own.

Kessa released Maeve quickly and backed away, blushing a deep sapphire color.

"Sorry," she said.

"No apologies necessary," Maeve answered with a smile. "It is good to see you, my friend."

Kessa returned her smile and gave the Arcadian another hug. She embraced Duaal and Gripper, too, but then looked uncertainly at Logan.

"Are… are you in trouble again, Maeve?" Kessa asked.

"Yes, but not from Logan this time," Duaal said. "You remember Xartasia, I'm sure."

"Oh yes." Kessa frowned. "So she lived? What about Gavriel?"

"Oh, he survived the cathedral's collapse, too," Duaal said. "But Xartasia stabbed him on Prianus. That took care of the old bastard."

Duaal's voice was full of cold venom and Kessa's black eyebrows rose. She looked them over again.

"Where are Xia and Captain Myles?" Kessa asked.

"Silver is out there in Gharib, looking for the Arcadians who live here," Gripper said. His eyes welled up with tears and the Arboran tugged on his shortened left ear. "But Claws... he..."

"Tiberius is dead," Logan said. "Gavriel killed him."

Maeve looked up at Logan. His expression wasn't as hard as it usually was when facing death and she remembered him at the service on Prianus. Logan had respected Tiberius Myles, maybe even liked the surly old captain. Maeve took Logan's metal hand in hers. A silent moment passed before he felt it and gently squeezed her fingers.

"Oh, no... I'm so sorry," Kessa said, wiping her eyes. "Captain Myles was a good man."

"Yes, he was," Duaal agreed. He wiped his eyes with his sleeve, too, and then grinned roguishly at the Dailon. "But that's not why we're here. Is Xyn in?"

"Sure," Kessa said. "He's in the lab. Go on back."

Duaal gestured to Gripper, who squeezed through Unbreakers to a small, box-obscured door marked *Storage*.

"Where is Vyron?" Maeve asked. "And Baliend? Are they well?"

"They're at home. Actually, Vyron is usually here, but it's his day off. And Baliend is growing like a little weed. He's ready to start walking any day now." Kessa glowed with maternal pride. "Are you going to be on Stray for a while?"

"Yes," Maeve said. "We do not yet know exactly how long, but it will be some time."

"You have to come over for dinner!" Kessa told her, clapping her dusty blue hands. "You will, won't you? Come have dinner with us?"

Maeve nodded and hoped that Kessa didn't notice her mouth watering.

● ● ●

"Damned stubborn old fool," Xyn grumbled. He waddled to the mixer, set the timer and flipped the switch. "He was doing something stupid, wasn't he?"

"Tiberius was buying us time," Duaal told the fat little Ixthian man with pride. "Tiberius sacrificed himself to save all of Prianus. Maybe the whole dumb galaxy."

"That sounds like him."

Xyn didn't look at Duaal, or even at the confounding alien Gripper. Instead, he paced up and down the rows of steel tables covered in beakers and test tubes and bottled chemicals. He opened a stout white refrigerator, closed it again and moved on. Eventually, Xyn returned with a green glass bottle. Using a pair of tongs, the Ixthian pried the cork free and held the wine aloft.

"You wouldn't appreciate this, Tiberius, you sour old bastard," Xyn said. "But rest well or fly fast or whatever you Prians do."

He took a long drink and wiped his mouth, then held the bottle out. Gripper accepted it and took a sip. He made a face.

"This used to be grapes?" he asked. "Gross."

But Gripper drank again, longer and deeper before passing the bottle to Duaal. "Do you have glasses?"

"Don't push your luck," Xyn grunted.

"We miss you, Tiberius," Duaal said quietly. He drank.

Panna coughed. She wished she had taken Xia's advice and brought a scarf. There was sand and dust everywhere. It was gritty on her tongue and she had to stop every few minutes to scrub it out of her eyes. How did anyone manage to breathe on Stray?

"Arcadians actually live here?" Panna asked.

Xia nodded. She had wrapped a pair of scarves around her head and face, leaving only her colorful compound eyes squinting out across Gharib.

"I've met a few," she said. "We got some information from them when we brought Kessa here a year ago."

The two women made their way down the cracked and sandy sidewalk. Cars and other pedestrians passed them by, all hurrying to get back indoors. Panna shielded her eyes and looked up into the late red and violet afternoon. A pair of Arcadians flew by overhead, but she couldn't tell whether they were some of Queen Maeve's.

Panna watched the winged shapes vanish into the low, brackish clouds. It was a bitter irony that it was the removal of her own wings and ear tips that had made Panna suddenly curious about her own culture. As a child, it was the only world she knew. But once she left it, when she could look in instead of out, only then did Panna begin to wonder what she had given up.

She didn't regret the decision, but neither could she ignore the irony of it.

"How did you get caught up in all that?" Panna asked, turning her attention back to Xia. "The whole thing with Kessa, I mean."

The tall Ixthian stepped around a human sitting in the lee of a stairwell, his head down and a hood pulled down over his face.

"I thought you read all about it," Xia said. "You certainly seem well-educated on the issue."

Panna nodded. "I read all of the news, sure. Everything I could find. I had no idea until then that anyone from the House of Cavain had survived and I was fascinated by the sociological implications. But none of you did interviews."

"No one asked. It wasn't exactly huge news."

"So what happened, then?" Panna asked. "How did you end up bringing Kessa here?"

"Maeve and Logan found her," Xia said. "Kessa ran into them on one of the lower levels of Axis. She was running from her gang, the Sisterhood."

"Maeve and Logan...?" Panna asked. She squinted through the billowing dust at Xia. "Really? When I met them, they didn't seem to care about much. Alright, that's not true... Logan cared about finding Maeve. But not much else."

"We were all surprised, too," Xia said with a shrug. "But those two are the only reason we got involved in this whole thing. Even if I don't entirely understand why."

Panna turned up her collar against the wind. "Me too, I guess. Without them, I wouldn't be here."

"I thought that would have been Xen."

Panna's eyes stung with tears and they walked in silence for a while. A man tried to sell them bread wrapped in sheets of mycolar and Panna wished she could afford some, but the fines back on Sunjarrah had bankrupted them all. She waved him off regretfully.

"Professor Xen was why I went to Prianus," Panna said at last. Her throat was dry and her voice seemed to stick. "I didn't know there was a Waygate until we arrived. He was a good teacher and a good man... I guess you know that. You knew him better than I did, Xia. But if you really want to trace it back, it was my parents."

"We can all trace our lives back to our parents," Xia pointed out. She pulled down the scarf across her face so Panna could see that she was smiling.

"Trust an Ixthian to think I meant biology," Panna said. She smiled, too, but not for very long. "They were so unhappy, Xia. All the Arcadians on Cyrus were. It wasn't a bad planet and the human colonists there didn't treat us particularly poorly. They worked any Arcadian laborers hard, but Cyrus is a farming world. *Everyone* worked hard.

"But that didn't stop every fairy there from being miserable, lost. When I was a girl, I couldn't understand why. Hells, I'm not sure I do now. Maybe I can't. I'm not sure anyone born since the fall can truly understand that loss."

The two women waited for a traffic light to change, then hurried across the street to a long series of empty lots, all overgrown with wiry weeds and white-green lichen. Panna followed Xia and hoped the Ixthian had some idea where she was going. They scrambled over the remains of a crumbling ashblock wall. A pack of scruffy Lyrans snarled until Xia and Panna hurried on.

"So did you ever figure it out?" Xia asked.

"Anthropology isn't an exact science," Panna answered. "No, not really. But it's why I think we need Queen Maeve. Or why we would need Xartasia, if she weren't deranged. Only a Cavainna can unite us, can give us back the sense of pride and unity we once had."

"This isn't just about stopping Xartasia for you, is it?"

Panna blushed and ducked her head. "Don't misunderstand... I don't want her to succeed in whatever she's up to. But even without wings, I'm an Arcadian first."

They came around a chipped and graffitied corner to a leaning light post with a flickering yellow tube. An Arcadian man wearing little more than a stained and transparent skirt slumped under it. Not provocatively, Panna thought, just tired.

Xia cocked her head. "I don't think I met that man last time, but I'm guessing he's in the same line of work. Let's go talk to him about your ideals of cultural unity."

She probably meant it as a sort of joke, but Panna's enthusiasm was sincere as she hurried to speak to the other fairy. He looked up nervously, darting furtive looks up and down the sandy street. Panna raised her hand and called out a greeting.

"*Sua cerri shae!*" Panna said.

The expression on the fairy man's face when he heard his own language was of such painful relief that it broke Panna's heart. But he raised a dirty hand in reply.

"*Sua aes'ii.*"

[12]

WHAT FALLING IS FOR

"Our duties to our families are a model for our place in the rest of the world."

- CENDRA HALLOS, SUNJARRAN CONSUL (48 PA)

Xia was on the Blue Phoenix when Maeve returned, but Panna wasn't with her. The Arcadian girl was still in Gharib, talking to the other fairies they had found.

"Panna said she would call later," Xia told Maeve.

"Her loss," Duaal said with a shrug. "Kessa's invited us to dinner."

"How is Baliend?" Xia asked.

"We'll find out tonight. Gripper, put that over here."

Duaal pointed to a relatively uncluttered corner of the cargo bay and Gripper set down the heavy canister of phennomethylln with a grunt. It was about the size of a small barrel, with handles welded to each side and a red nozzle on the top.

Maeve looked outside. It was swiftly growing dark and the night was cooling. The Arcadians were returning to the Blue Phoenix, one by one and then in small groups. They lowered their wings and bowed their heads to Maeve as they came inside before going to their scattered blankets.

"It hardly seems fair that we go to dinner while they have only a spoonful of beans and nutrient injections," Maeve said.

"No, it doesn't," Duaal agreed. "But hey, going hungry ourselves won't help. And you said you want to coo over the baby. What else can we do? We have no money."

Logan stood at the top of the lowered cargo ramp, arms crossed and watching the sky as the stars began to flicker against the violet evening sky. He turned back to the Blue Phoenix.

"What about that?" he asked.

Maeve looked back to where Logan was pointing – the canister of phenno. Xia and Gripper looked, too.

"What about it?" Duaal asked, frowning. "Xyn always gives us a fresh batch when we come to Stray. What about it?"

"That's a very expensive gift," Logan said. "You could get at least a thousand cenmarks for that much phennomethylln."

"Not enough money to found a kingdom, but it is enough to eat for a while," Maeve agreed.

"You want me to sell our phenno?" Duaal asked. "What about the Blue Phoenix?"

"You're not planning on diving into another star anytime soon, are you?" Logan asked him.

"Well, no..."

"We have to sell it," Maeve said. She sighed and then gave Duaal a smile. "I am sorry for your loss, captain, but I thank you for saving my people."

Duaal scowled at her for a long moment and looked as though he might start shouting at Maeve... But at last, the young mage laughed.

"You really are turning into a little queen," he said. "Fine, I'll sell the phenno. I assume that sooner is better than later?"

"They are hungry," Maeve answered. She gestured around the hold. "Our dinner can wait."

Gripper nodded and then checked his pockets until he found his com.

"I'll call Blue and let her know we're running late," Gripper said. He began delicately pressing the tiny buttons. Tiny compared to his huge claws, at least. "I think that will be alright. She wasn't sure she could get dinner ready in time, anyway."

"Where the hells do we sell phenno, anyway?" Duaal asked. "I have no idea where to start."

"I do," Logan said.

"You do?" Duaal asked. "But you are... were a bounty hunter. Phenno is highly illegal. Weren't you sort of on the other side of the black market?"

Logan nodded. "I was, yes. But I've hunted smugglers by letting them think that I had phenno or other illegal items to sell. And I've actually used it a couple of times, so I'm familiar with both buying and selling."

"Xyn sells it, too," Xia pointed out.

"So let's make sure we're not going to be competing with him," Duaal said. "This stuff was a present and I don't want to get on his bad side."

Logan spent the next few hours on the mainstream. Eventually, he gave Duaal a list of names and com frequencies. Duaal scanned the datadex and whistled.

"Head out to dinner," he told the rest of his crew. "I'm probably going to be on this until late."

"You've grown into a captain far better than I have any kind of queen," Maeve said.

Duaal flushed. It hadn't been so long since he and the princess were petty enemies that compliments came easily to either of them. But Maeve had to admit to herself that she would have been lost without Duaal.

"Maybe," Duaal said. "Just save me some food, alright?"

Maeve, Logan, Gripper and Xia covered themselves with hoods and scarves and set out toward Gharib. They passed several more Arcadians, the fairies on their way back to the Blue Phoenix. Those that saw Maeve sang out a respectful greeting to their queen, but didn't ask her business.

At the edge of the dusty landing crescent, they made their way through a neat line of huge Starwind haulers and into the city. Taxis lined the crescent's edge with drivers leaning out of their doors and hawking their rides to the passing travelers, but Maeve and her friends didn't have the money to rent one. So they walked through the shadow-steeped sandstone of Gharib to the address that Kessa had given them.

Two hours after they planned to arrive, they finally stood on the low concrete porch of a small brown house. Gripper knocked on the door. In a shocking display of impish humor, Kessa had not told her mate about the visit. When Vyron spotted Logan outside, the Dailon man shouted in terror and tried to slam the door shut. But Gripper's hand was in the way and the door only bounced off his thick knuckles. The Arboran leapt back, groaning and cradling his injured hand. Vyron had fallen to the floor and stared up at the rest of them.

"Maeve?" he asked, black eyes wide. "Xia? What are you doing here? Why is Coldhand with you?"

Logan stepped into the door and extended his hand to Vyron.

"That's a long story," Logan told him. "But I'm not here for you or your family."

Vyron didn't look at all certain about this confounding change to the order of the universe. He stood on his own and invited them inside. Vyron had cut off his glossy black ponytail – probably un-comfortable in the Stray heat, Maeve guessed – and wore his hair cut close to his head. But when Gripper asked Vyron about it, the Dailon grimaced and touched his temple.

"Baliend is a bit of a hair puller," he said. "You'll want to watch out, Maeve."

Vyron's house was small and inexpensive, but brightly lit and cheerful. Kessa was waiting for them in the kitchen, giggling as she cut up a loaf of bread. Vyron scowled at his wife.

"Very funny, dear," he said. "At least I know why we needed so many eggs."

Kessa hugged Xia and thanked the Ixthian for coming.

"Where's Duaal?" she asked.

"Just finishing up some business," Xia told her. "We're selling off the phenno."

"Selling phennomethylln?" Vyron asked. He took over slicing the bread so Kessa could pour glasses of pink-tinged lemonade for everyone. "Xyn won't like that."

"We've already called him about it," Gripper said. "Mixer knows it's just a one-time thing."

"We need the money," Maeve told them with a dismissive flip of her wings. She had been quite patient, Maeve thought, and now she wanted to see the baby. "Where is Baliend?"

"Oh, he's asleep in his room," Kessa said.

The disappointment must have shown on Maeve's face. Vyron shared a look with Kessa and then turned to the Arcadian.

"It's about time for him to eat again. Do you want to get him?" he asked. "He'll probably need a diaper change, though."

"It would be my honor," Maeve said sincerely.

Xia and Kessa giggled, but Maeve didn't think there was anything disapproving in their laughter. Vyron pointed down a narrow hallway to a closed door painted in blue and yellow stars.

"May I help?"

The question came from Logan. Xia's eyes turned a surprised orange and Gripper's mouth hung open in surprise. Vyron looked nervous, but Kessa smiled at the Prian.

"Sure," she said. "Baliend's kind of a handful when he wakes up. I'm sure Maeve could use the help."

Logan nodded. He and Maeve made their way down the hall to the star-studded door and stepped quietly inside. The bedroom on the other side was barely lit by a small nightlight shaped like a seashell that was out of place on dry, sandy Stray. Baliend lay asleep in a tiny bed, tightly swaddled in a blanket to keep him from falling out. His fine hair had darkened from its snowy white to a dark jet color, just like his parents.

"He has grown so much," Maeve whispered. She crouched and stroked the baby's soft, fine hair. "I wonder if he is talking yet."

Quiet and gentle though she tried to be, Baliend's large obsidian eyes popped open. He yawned impressively, displaying lavender gums with a couple of small white teeth winking in the nightlight. Baliend burbled at Maeve so adorably that it took her several moments to realize she was holding her breath against the smell. The infant Dailon squirmed in his blanket.

Maeve had no idea what to do. She squinted around the nursery for something that looked like diapers. Were those them, the rolled-up bundles of... paper?

But Logan had already unwound Baliend from his blankets and carried him to a changing table. The boy's tiny blue face screwed up in indignant infant fury and he began to cry. Logan placed an illonium fingertip very carefully between Baliend's lips. The baby bit once on the cold metal and continued to cry.

"Do you–?"

Maeve began to ask if Logan wanted her to try, but her hunter's expression was intent and Maeve's heart skipped. She knew that look. Logan was planning, weighing the tactics of his next move.

"Tumble down baby," he sang.

The words came haltingly, but his voice was strong and smooth. There was something bright and sweet there, too. Logan sang like no Arcadian man. His voice was thicker and deeper and had some tone, somehow, of the stone and ice of his homeworld.

> "Tumble down baby
> From the cold clouds
> Finding your wings
> Is what falling is for..."

By the middle of the second verse, Baliend had stopped crying. He regarded Logan with large, serious black eyes but made no more fuss over his diaper change. Logan cleaned his hands with a clear gel that smelled sharply of chemicals and picked up the now-clean Baliend.

"Where did you learn so much about children? I thought that you had no siblings," Maeve said as she took Baliend. She cradled the baby against her chest. He was heavier than she expected. "Your song sounded almost Arcadian."

"It's a Prian lullaby," Logan answered. He smoothed Baliend's hair, which had been ruffled during the change. "My mother used to sing it. My parents had two daughters before me. I'm just the only one who lived past my first year. Infant mortality is high on Prianus. But there were plenty of children in our building and I needed to make some colour."

"So you... cared for them?" Maeve asked. The idea was insanity. Logan Coldhand had been a baby-sitter.

"No. I rented them out as cheap labor," Logan answered.

Maeve looked up from Baliend's round blue face just in time to catch the last of her hunter's quick smile. She laughed and stood up on her toes to kiss him. The baby was warm and slightly squirming between them.

Kessa and Vyron were just outside the door when they emerged, hovering protectively. Maeve handed Baliend back to his mother and assured her that he had behaved perfectly. They returned to the kitchen and Logan helped Kessa wrestle Baliend into a high chair at the dinner table.

Duaal arrived just in time to eat, stamping the dust out of his boots and grinning happily at Vyron and Kessa. The Blue Phoenix's young captain swept into the dining room and sat with a flourish.

"Smells delicious," he said, winking at Vyron. "I can't wait to eat. Maeve, Ferris called in after you left. He's planning your first speech here in three days. There's something else he wants to talk to you about, but he wouldn't tell me what it was."

"Speech?" Vyron asked.

"Gripper and Xia told us a lbit of what's been going on while you were taking care of Baliend," Kessa said. The baby cooed at the sound of his own name and threw his milk cup on the floor. Kessa jumped to her feet with a sigh and gave chase as it rolled away.

"They said you're making yourself queen of the fairies?" Vyron asked skeptically, as though he didn't quite trust his understanding of the situation.

Duaal nodded. "To compete with Xartasia and keep the Arcadians out of her Devourers' claws."

"Devourers?" Kessa asked. She returned the bottle to Baliend, who took one drink and dropped it again. "What?"

Xia sighed. "Of course you didn't hear about that. It happened on Prianus."

Vyron and Kessa were full of questions. Maeve and the rest took turns answering while the rest filled their plates with roasted ham and minnas and leafy green jouk. They told Vyron and Kessa about the events of Prianus, the Waygate and Gavriel's death, arguing with the Alliance on Tynerion and again on Mir, then the final decision to take on the problem of Xartasia themselves.

"So now you've got a ship full of fairies?" Kessa asked. "Did you have any trouble getting out to Stray with that many people and no weapons?"

"No," Gripper said. "Is that strange?"

Vyron shrugged.

"I don't know," he said. "The galaxy is a big place."

"But there have been attacks in extra-system space," Kessa told them. "Pirates, they're saying on the mainstream."

"Pirates," Xia hissed with shocking anger. "My shiny silver ass."

Gripper choked on a sip of purple juice at that and blushed furiously. Maeve was more than a little surprised to hear such language from the gentle and cultured doctor, too. She blinked at Xia and was not the only one. The Ixthian put a hand over her mouth.

"Sorry," she said. "Not in front of the baby."

"That's alright," Kessa assured her. "It's not like he can understand yet."

Baliend wasn't paying attention to the adults at all. Instead, he intently smeared mashed minnas on his face, making starchy white paint on his round blue cheeks. He stuck out his tongue at Duaal, who did the same.

"It's the Devourers out there," Xia said. "I'd bet my license on it."

"And I would bet mine – if I still had it – that Arcadians are vanishing nearby with each attack," Logan added. "But that won't make it onto the mainstream."

Vyron rubbed his jaw and looked at the Prian. The news that Logan Coldhand was no longer a bounty hunter had rocked him and the Dailon father was clearly still struggling to keep up.

"What are you going to do now?" Vyron asked.

"Now we need to build a fairy kingdom," Duaal answered. "How many Arcadians are there on Stray?"

"Nine thousand?" Vyron said. "Maybe ten?"

"That's enough to get started." Logan turned in his chair to look at Maeve sitting beside him. "There's another Arcadian that I think we should bring here. His name is Ballad."

"The one you met on Prianus? We just got to Stray!" Duaal said. "We can't just pack everyone up again and head to the other side of the Alliance. It's a five-week flight from here!"

"No," agreed Logan. "We need to stay on Stray. I'll send word to Prianus. And money to make the flight, if we can get it. Ballad will want to bring his gang and his family with him."

"We can loan it to you," Kessa offered quickly.

"Kes, are you sure?" Vyron asked.

"We wouldn't be here without him and Maeve and Tiberius," Kessa answered. She enfolded one of Vyron's hands in hers. "Come on. It's just money. We can always make more."

"You're right, Kes," Vyron agreed. He kissed his wife and then stood up to get Baliend some more milk.

Gripper cleared his throat and then tentatively held up one big hand. "Um, Talon–"

"Is that what you're calling me now?" Logan asked.

"I'm trying it out."

"That's the model of my gun."

"Yeah," Gripper admitted. "That's where I got it."

"You can't call me that. Coldhand is an assumed name. Just keep using that."

"Nah," said the Arboran. "It isn't really *you* anymore."

"It isn't?" Logan arched an eyebrow at Gripper.

"I'll figure something out. How are we going to get a message to your friend? I don't think I saw a single mainstream terminal in that whole part of Pylos."

"Not many Arcadians even know how to use your computers," Maeve said.

Logan frowned thoughtfully and then nodded. "I know who can get the message to Ballad. If he's willing to let me give it to him."

Ballad Avadain felt eyes on him.

The dark Prian night was deep and cold, and the midnight chill sliced through even the thick leather of his jacket like a nanoknife.

Ballad shivered and surveyed the narrow, crooked streets of Pylos. There were Arcadians and humans below, all bundled up in coats and scarves against the cold. The season was well into summer now, but there was still sleet mixed in with the rain that spattered across Ballad's shoulders and soaked into his feathers.

But the shiver that ran down his spine had nothing to do with the weather. Someone was watching him.

Ballad spread his wings, leapt from the crumbling cornice and soared into the darkness. Lamps jutted up from the cracked sidewalk, but only one in ten glowed through the clinging gray fog. He landed on the concrete and searched the street. The crowds were thinning for the night as everyone went home. Ballad stuffed his hands into the pockets of his jacket and found the fibersteel straps hidden there. He slid his hands through the flexible metal and felt a bit better with them on, but still uneasy.

A shape in dark clothes stepped out of the shadows and stalked purposefully toward Ballad. It was a human man, broad across the shoulders but not much taller than the young Arcadian.

Ballad leapt in with a pair of punches, trying to drive the interloper back. The human shuffled aside with deceptive speed, stepping into the flickering light of a streetlamp. He was Prian, but older than most Ballad had ever seen, with a heavily lined face and no hair left. He stepped inside another punch and jabbed two gnarled fingers into Ballad's bicep. The Arcadian pulled back, wincing. He kicked at the Prian's knee. Fighting such an old man made Ballad more than a little uncomfortable, but the human had swiftly proven himself an able warrior.

The Prian melted back and then back again, forcing Ballad to reach for him. When he did, the human grabbed one wrist, twisted and yanked Ballad down to his knees on the cracked and jagged sidewalk.

"Ballad Avadain?" the man asked, not even out of breath.

"What are you doing in my piece of Pylos?" Ballad asked. He writhed, but couldn't break the old Prian's grip.

"My name is Arctan. I'm carrying a message for you."

Vorus released Ballad's wrist and the young Arcadian jumped back, rubbing his wounded hand.

"Arctan Vorus? You were Jocasta's teacher. It's an honor to meet you." Ballad extended his hand hesitantly. "Wish I could say this is the first time this happened. Who's your message from?"

Vorus shook the fairy's offered hand firmly. His palm was rough and dry. "Another old student of mine. He says you've already met."

Ballad grinned. "Yes, we have. What does Logan Coldhand got to tell me?"

"He says that your queen needs you, Ballad. She summons you to Stray."

[13]
GLASS

"It was in a place of desolation and dust that we found ourselves."

- FERRIS VERRIDIAN (234 PA)

Duaal's haste in selling the phennomethylln had cost him some of the profits, but the money was enough to feed the growing number of Arcadians for a while. There was even some color left over to buy tents and pavilions to set up on the site of the old Nihilist cathedral.

But before sending anyone there, Panna and Logan wanted to check the site.

This time, Panna borrowed a scarf to wear over her face. It was more of a veil, really, but if it would keep Stray's endless red dust out of her mouth, Panna would have worn a bag over her head. She wiped the steam from the mirror and checked her reflection. She looked so... human.

Even after years without them, Panna was always surprised and a little sad not to see her wings rising up from between her shoulders. She had lived more of her life without wings than with them... Did that make her less Arcadian? Duke Ferris certainly seemed to think so.

There was so little of the old Arcadian nobility left. That hadn't always been the case, of course. Those of noble blood had been evacuated from the failing White Kingdom first, leaving behind the common fairies and most of the knights to cover their hasty exits. But the same virtue that had given them the first chance to flee Arcadia had made them poorly suited to their new lives as Alliance refugees. Without their riches and high glass towers, servants and knights, the fairy nobles fell quickly into the depths of depression. Those not killed by coreworld diseases took their own lives.

Logan was waiting for Panna at the cargo bay airlock. The Prian had not changed his wardrobe for Stray, but she didn't think that he cared very much about the local weather. Duke Ferris was there, too, standing on the other side of the airlock with his arms tucked into long, pale sleeves.

Panna inclined her head to the duke.

"Your Grace," she said. "What can we do for you?"

"He wants to come with us," Logan answered.

"You... do?" Panna looked at Ferris. The old Arcadian man had his gray-streaked golden braids and pointed ears covered in a deep lavender hood. "We're only inspecting the old cathedral site, Your Grace. Just to make sure it's stable and clean enough for our use."

"Vyron's trying to find out who owns it," Logan said. "No luck yet. There's a record of the sale, but the name on it is a fake."

"Gavriel didn't own it?" Panna asked.

Logan shook his head. "He had no money. Gavriel didn't own anything."

"That does not sound unlike us," Duke Ferris answered. "Let us begin."

Duaal had landed the Blue Phoenix near the collapsed cathedral and Logan opened the airlock, then led the Arcadians outside. It was early in the day and the dim, oversized sun squatted on the horizon. The wind hadn't picked up yet. Panna pulled off her scarf with a sigh and stalked out of the ship after Logan.

In the year since the Nihilist church's collapse, the desert had almost entirely reclaimed the land. If Panna had not seen images of Gavriel's black cathedral, she would have had no idea that anything ever stood in the sifting orange sands. All that remained were red dunes and a few dark patches of tough black weeds.

"What happened to the Nihilists' cathedral?" Panna asked. "Did the Gharib police tear it down?"

Logan crouched on one of the small dunes and dug through the dust. He pulled a piece of twisted metal free and inspected it.

"No," he said. "It's just been buried by the desert."

Duke Ferris flew to the top of a larger dune and landed to pick up a handful of fine sand. It sifted from between his fingers and fell in red and orange-brown streams to the ground.

"An entire cathedral lies buried beneath us?" the old nobleman asked, frowning.

Logan shrugged. "Not intact. Tiberius knocked it down with the Blue Phoenix. Without maintenance, the tunnels beneath probably filled with sand, too. But we won't know for sure until we can get a survey densitometer out here."

"It's going to take a lot of upkeep to build anything here," Panna said. She sat down on a russet rock and sighed, feeling suddenly drained. "The desert is just going to bury us alive. Maybe this isn't such a good idea."

Ferris glided down to Panna and, to her surprise, smiled.

"The queen does not think so," he told her. "She agrees that this remains an excellent location for our new home."

"Has Maeve *seen* it?" Panna asked a little more sharply than she intended.

Duke Ferris noticed and his more familiar frown returned. "You should not question Queen Maeve."

Panna wanted to point out that she had actually known Maeve far longer than the duke had, that she was one of those who had urged the queen to take the throne, but Ferris wasn't done.

"We discussed it this morning," the duke said. He brushed some sand from his sleeve. "The sands here are not a curse, but a blessing. It is not the same as that of our lost home, but I believe that we can make glass from it."

"Glass?" Panna repeated. "You mean Arcadian glass?"

"He certainly doesn't mean the kind we put in windows," Logan answered. He was rubbing some dull red-orange sand between the fingers of his right hand. "This isn't going to be the same as the kind of glass in Maeve's spear."

"Do we have anyone who knows how to make it?" Panna asked.

She had studied everything she could find about the hard and strong Arcadian glass, including the molecular structure and chemical composition, but that didn't mean she could create it.

"I spent some time glass-singing as a younger man," Ferris said. "Only small things, sculptures and such. But both Hyra and Lorren know the songs."

"They do?" Panna asked, shaking her head. "Then why didn't I see a single piece of glass on Sunjarrah? If all they need is sand..."

The older Arcadian gave her a pitying look. If she didn't understand already, Ferris didn't seem to think she could learn.

Panna sighed and hoped that he didn't hear her. The duke was just as bad as Xartasia, in his way. Neither of them thought much of the young fairies. Xartasia left them behind and Panna wondered if Ferris would do the same – if only Maeve would let him.

Panna stifled another sigh. It was an unkind and unfair thought. Ferris' idea about the glass was a good one. Even with all the coreworlders' extensive and impressive science, they couldn't reproduce Arcadian glass. It was unique to the White Kingdom. Panna knelt and ran her fingers through the red sand.

"Coldhand, how long are the profits from the phenno going to feed us?" she asked.

The tall Prian considered for a moment before answering. "At our current head count, with cheap food and no fuel for the Blue

Phoenix, about five weeks. But if our numbers rise, that estimate is going to fall drastically."

"Queen Maeve will win the hearts of all the Arcadians here on Stray," Ferris assured him confidently.

"And they'll need somewhere to live," Panna said. "So we had better get started. Where can we get a densitometer?"

"Sure, we've got a densitometer," Vyron told Duaal. "It's on a survey truck. The old owner couldn't pay his repair bill and left the whole thing. I can pull it out tonight, if you want."

"Don't bother," Duaal told the Dailon man cheerfully. "Does the truck run?"

"Not very well."

"As long as we can get it over to the old cathedral site, it will do the job."

Vyron nodded and took a few notes on a datadex. "Are you sure you don't want a proper survey team?"

Duaal shook his head. "No. There isn't enough money or time for that. Maeve's making her first speech tomorrow night."

Unbreakers was actually quite busy, with a dozen customers all squeezing through the narrow aisles and filling shopping baskets with bits of electronics and machinery, or waiting surreptitiously to buy a canister of Xyn's black-market phennomethylln. Vyron leaned over the counter and asked if they needed anything, but those who acknowledged him at all did so only with grunts or waves of their hands.

"Kessa's been asking about the speech," Vyron said, returning his attention to Duaal. "Do you think we could come to listen?"

Duaal hesitated. Maeve liked the little Dailon family and talked about them all the time, but she seemed nervous about the speech.

The new fairy queen had locked herself in the Blue Phoenix mess with Panna and Duke Ferris to review every word.

Duaal grinned.

"Sure," he told Vyron. "I think Maeve would *love* for you and Kessa to be there."

Maeve wondered if she was going to pass out. Her head swam and spots of color burst like miniature fireworks behind her closed eyelids. Logan held her upright like a fainting bounty mark.

"How many?" Panna asked, stunned.

"Three hundred or so," Ferris repeated.

"So many?" Maeve whispered. She wasn't sure if anyone heard her, or if she had spoken aloud at all.

"Sir Calathan addressed at least that number on Sunjarrah," the duke continued. "And Xartasia's numbers far surpass our own. By the time this is done, we must be able to sway thousands."

"Thousands?" Maeve asked. Her mouth was as dry as the desert outside. "I cannot do this! I am not a politician. I... I am not even a knight anymore!"

"No," Ferris told her. "You are the queen of Arcadia. Your people need you."

How often had she heard those exact words from Panna? More times than Maeve could easily count. But did her black hair really mean anything? If Cavain's blood ran through her veins, why didn't she feel more like a queen? Shouldn't she feel some sort of glorious righteousness? But Maeve only felt sick.

She ran to the sink and retched, but all that came up was a thin trickle of acidic saliva. The would-be queen spat and leaned against the counter until she could stand on her own again. Maeve felt Logan, Ferris and Panna watching her. She splashed water on her face.

Maeve's reflection was warped and indistinct in the metal of the sink's bottom. All Maeve could see was a pale oval with dark smears in place of her eyes. It was the face of a ghost, of one long dead and set to wander the worlds without a home.

Was that how Arcadians looked to the Alliance, forlorn shrouds empty of life?

Perhaps. But that is how we see ourselves, Maeve thought. *That is how Xartasia sees us. However terrible her plan is, at least she gives our people a purpose.*

It didn't matter how sick it made her, how watery her knees felt or how much her wings shook. Maeve didn't feel glorious, but she had to pretend.

It was a lie, but maybe it was better than Xartasia's lie.

Maeve scowled at her distorted reflection. At least Xartasia had Calathan's help, and probably many others. Briefly, Maeve considered asking Panna or Ferris to make the speech for her, but decided that it was hardly fair. It wasn't the other fairies' fault that Maeve was nervous.

She turned away from the sink and smiled a little.

"Three hundred," she said as clearly as she could manage. "It is a good start. We will hope for more next time."

It had been Panna's idea to join the rest of the crowd for Maeve's speech, but now she was beginning to wonder if it was a good idea.

The other Arcadians were staring at her. Some seemed to think she was human, but it was those who recognized her as one of their own that made Panna bite her lip and bury her hands deep in her pockets.

The three hundred or so pale-haired and white-winged fairies gathered in the sandy bowl between two dunes. A camp of dusty tents rose up on one side like the solidified peaks of choppy water.

They were all empty, though. At Duke Ferris' request, the Sunjarrah Arcadians were mixed into the crowd, not unlike Panna.

Logan and Vyron had raised a small stage on top of the smaller dune. It was little more than a sheet of metal bolted to four concrete blocks. Hyra and Lorren were still trying to figure out how to sing the strange Stray sand. The only glass they had managed so far was cloudy and brittle, prone to shattering under the slightest pressure.

On the other side of the audience basin, Panna saw a tall Dailon holding their black-eyed baby up for a better view. Panna hurried through the maze of feathered wings and extended her hand.

"You must be Kessa," she said. "I'm Panna Sul."

The Dailon balanced Baliend against her hip and shook Panna's smaller hand.

"Maeve told us a lot about you," Kessa said. "She says you know more about fairies than she does."

"Queen Maeve said that?" Panna knew she shouldn't grin at the praise, but she couldn't help herself.

Kessa laughed.

"Queen Maeve," she repeated. "It's strange to hear you call her that. She yelled at me once just for thanking her. Maeve was a very unhappy woman."

Panna had a hard time imagining it. Not Maeve being unhappy, but being impolite. She knew it had happened... Duaal had plenty of stories about the queen's misdeeds and Panna knew that Logan Coldhand had tried to capture Maeve for a bounty not so long ago.

But now Maeve Cavainna was her queen. Panna could admit to herself that she might not have been as naturally commanding as Xartasia seemed to be, but the younger Cavainna really was trying.

"There she is," Kessa said suddenly, pointing.

Panna looked up to see Maeve landing on the makeshift stage. Duaal and Ferris – who had landed beside the queen and furled his wings against his back – must have selected her clothes. Maeve Cavainna wore flowing red and gold that streamed out behind her in the dry wind like a flaming banner. Her long black hair danced as though alive.

Logan climbed up the dune to stand beside the queen. Panna smiled to herself. He was never very far from Maeve and it drove Ferris to distraction. Logan Coldhand wasn't Arcadian, as the duke so often pointed out. He had no business in their politics.

It struck Panna as more than a bit unfair. Duaal Sinnay was not Arcadian, either, but Ferris didn't seem to object to his help.

Kessa cheered Maeve's appearance wildly and Panna joined in. Other voices rose through the crowd, but not as many as Panna had hoped. Probably only the Sunjarrah fairies, who were already at least somewhat loyal to their new queen. The far more numerous and suspicious Stray Arcadians remained silent.

They had been here before, Panna realized. Here, on this spot in the unwelcoming Gharib desert, listening to Gavriel and his talk of comforting death.

Maeve seemed to be saying something, but Panna couldn't hear her. Ferris spoke into the young queen's ear and she nodded, then stepped up to the edge of the stage and raised her white wings. A figure dressed in purple that Panna thought might be Duaal raised one palm toward the crowd.

"I thank you for coming today," Maeve said.

Her voice shook, but now Panna could hear her clearly.

"After a hundred years of exile in the core, it is no easy thing to reach for hope. What I tell you now is difficult, but hope and pain are two wings of the same set.

"You have heard, I am sure, of two queens who would lead you. Xartasia, who was Princess Titania and daughter of King Illain before the fall. And me. I am Maeve Cavainna, daughter of Princess Beltain. I have no claim to the throne of the White Kingdom and to your fealty, but I fear that I must ask it.

"It is Xartasia who should be before you now, who should lead the Arcadians. My cousin says that she can restore Arcadia. She claims that the White Kingdom will be as it once was. But she has cheated and killed in her purpose, and summoned the Devourers themselves! She has taken up the mantle of the Nameless, the dark goddess that brought pain and death to our people.

"I am not my cousin," Maeve said. "I was never prepared to take the throne. I was trained as a knight. I was taught to protect, not to lead. But I see our people suffering, without Xartasia and with her, though they may not know what they have given up to her. I never wished to rule. I stand here before you not out of ambition, but because I cannot kneel before her."

Maeve gestured broadly to the dunes and then up into the thin blue-green sky of Stray. Panna looked at Kessa and then at the Arcadians all around them. They were watching, staring intensely at the little queen in red and gold. Was it working? There was hard work ahead and the Arcadians were an exhausted and broken people. Could she convince them?

"We are all sons and daughters of Aes and Erris, sun and song," Maeve said. "Our gods made us to sing and dance and create anew when they could not. What has been can never be again. But we can create something new. Here, on Stray.

"We have lived as refugees long enough. We have waited for the Alliance to recognize us, to admit to our loss, but they have problems of their own. So be it! We are Arcadian! We are stronger than they know! We will sing glass towers from the sands of Stray. With you, I will build a new kingdom in this very place. A new home, here and now."

Maeve held out her hands toward the audience.

"We cannot bring back the past," she said. "But neither will I allow our people to go on suffering. The time has come to rise, to fly again. The time has come to build a new kingdom and to build our future."

The fairies didn't applaud. They sang. Just a few dozen voices at first, and some of the Arcadians spread their wings to fly back into

Gharib, but more of the fairies remained. They lifted their faces and wings. A handful of voices became a hundred and then two hundred until the air thrummed with the single word.

"A'shae."

The night.

Your Majesty.

Panna sang, too.

[14]

A CROWN OF BLADES

"What is beauty in the dark?"

- ANNETH ZHYRESS (218 PA)

The great black fleet glided silently through space, eclipsing stars but casting no shadows in the endless darkness. Devourer nanites covered the fleet's hulls, collecting data and transmitting it to the ships' computers and their alien operators. But the seething black was as hungry as its creators, slowly devouring the ships they had themselves restructured and built.

The Starwind convoy never saw them coming. Seventeen networked ships dropped out of superluminal flight on the edge of the Giadeen system, seven hundred thousand miles from the outermost asteroid projections. Faintly luminous orange bubbles faded from around the cylindrical haulers as null-fields powered down and the Starwind computers gathered new route information.

Dhozo looked at Xartasia and she nodded.

"Now," he ordered. "Tear them apart."

The Devourer's swirling black cloud of armor transmitted his command across the fleet in nanoseconds. Five thousand Arcadian voices rose in broadcast songs of praise as a wing of sharp-looking black fighters soared through the middle of the convoy. Red lasers and long black hooks tore open four of the Starwind haulers before any of the ships could react.

The lead cargo ship turned ponderously against the backdrop of starlight, bringing the tiny, bulbous control deck around to face the threat. It fired a few laser pulses, but the Devourer fighters were too fast. They spiraled tightly around the remaining haulers, each cutting their violent way into one of Starwind's ships.

A pair of blade-winged fighters engaged the better-armed lead vessel. Angry scarlet laserfire seared along one of the black fighter's armored underside. The other Devourer slammed into the hauler's flank, making the whole huge ship shudder and buckle. The sharp, backswept wings curled like clawed fingers into the fibersteel hull. Air hemorrhaged from deep tears in the hauler's side and froze into white plumes in the absolute cold of empty space.

"Return all mineral salvage to the Sozsarus for reconstruction," Dhozo commanded. "Consume the crew and then report back to the VSS Illisem."

Xartasia wasn't sure if the Devourer pilot's com channels were closed or if the fairies' song simply drowned out the screams.

"*All* of the metal?" Orix objected from nearby. "Commander, we need it to replenish our swarms!"

"My people require starships more than you need your robots," Xartasia told the young Devourer coldly. "Every scrap will go to new vessels."

The seething black cloud that surrounded Orix swirled like a brewing storm. But it had lost some of its iridescent glitter, Xartasia noticed. Were the nanites actually ailing somehow, breaking down? They were machines and machines required power, fuel. Food, like their masters.

A steely dark shape jutted suddenly from Commander Dhozo's armor, a shield between Xartasia and Orix.

"There will be plenty to eat on Anzhotek," Dhozo reminded his subordinate. "We're going there soon. Until then, let your appetite keep you sharp, not angry."

Xartasia shrugged to herself and turned to the knights flanking the door. A dozen fairies in shining glass armor stood at attention, wings and spears held upright.

"Commander, you said someone wanted to talk to me?" Xartasia prompted.

A knight wearing red and violet scarves wound under his glass armor nodded.

"Yes, my queen," he answered. "Sharlon Artain. He is new. Sir Varris and Tarno brought him from Arrideen. He has been asking to see you ever since he arrived, a'shae."

"Bring him."

The knight bowed and left, then returned a few minutes later with another Arcadian man limping behind. Xartasia stood at the head of the gleaming silver table and its polished surface cast her reflection all down its length, ending in the diamond points of her glass crown like a circle of daggers leveled at Sharlon.

"What is it?" Xartasia asked.

Sharlon stared at Dhozo and the other Devourers. The huge aliens stood behind Xartasia, but their black armor was never still, swirling and transmitting and gathering data and translating.

And eating. The energy demands of their bodies and implanted nanite systems meant that the Devourers, the Glorious, were always eating. Mostly metal, though not always... The dark carbon fiber floor beneath Orix was turning a brittle-looking gray. Sharlon tore his gaze from the monsters and back to his queen.

"I... thank you for seeing me, Your Majesty," he stammered. His voice was smoke-roughened, but still less abrasive than the Devourers' buzzing rasp.

Xartasia raised a slim, perfectly manicured hand in acknowledgment of her subject's thanks.

"What is it?" she asked again.

"Before I left Arrideen, they... they said that there was another queen. Is it true?"

Xartasia fixed violet eyes on the cowering fairy. "I have had no word of this. Tell me more."

Sharlon swallowed hard. "Her name is Maeve Cavainna, they say. She is on Stray. There have been no emissaries, my queen, as you send. But word has spread. They say she is even raising towers of glass in the Stray desert."

Xartasia's eyes flickered over the glass armor of the knights at the door. Every atom of carbon for those suits had been collected from ships and shipments, sifted and selected with meticulous care. It was the finest glass the galaxy had ever seen. Xartasia remembered the dull red sands of Stray.

"If this is true," she said. "If my cousin sings glass from Stray's dry sand, what she builds will be as brittle as any coreworlder glass. And the throne she claims for herself is just as fragile."

"They call her the Gray Queen, a'shae," Sharlon told Xartasia. "And... and they say that she is accompanied by a great beast, like... like one of your Devourers. But not the same... brown and green where the Devourers are all darkness."

"Ah, yes," Xartasia said. "The Arboran. He is a coward. There is nothing we need fear from him."

"Arboran," Orix sneered.

Sharlon jumped and very nearly fell. One of the knights stood forward and steadied the terrified Arcadian. Dhozo growled something at the younger Devourer in their own language.

Xartasia held her hand out, palm up. "Thank you for this information, Sharlon. It will be dealt with."

"Yes, my queen." Sharlon bowed deeply, still trembling. "Thank you for seeing me."

He turned back toward the door to leave and Dhozo stepped close beside Xartasia.

"This isn't news that should spread through the fleet," he said. "It could split loyalties. You need to control the information."

"Sharlon has probably already spoken of it," Xartasia answered with a shrug.

Sharlon heard her and turned back.

"Only to a few friends, Your Majesty," he assured her. "I thought I should tell you..."

"Which friends?" Xartasia asked.

"Errulin Aesus, Lannui and Shae de Wen," Sharlon answered. "And... and Ollen Certanan, I think."

Xartasia sighed and looked up at Dhozo. "Very well. If it must be. You may have Sharlon and his friends. Deal with them swiftly and privately."

"What?" Sharlon asked. He jumped back, but two of the glass-armored knights grabbed his arms and dragged the fairy forward. "But I–!"

Xartasia glided to the panicked Arcadian and touched her cool red lips to his cheek. "Go in peace and dignity, Sharlon Artain. I shall remember your name, my brother. This pain will not last and matters not. The White Kingdom will return and you with it."

"I do not understand–" Sharlon began, but Orix was already on him. Claws and hooks and teeth flashed in the dark and blood pooled on the deckplates.

Xartasia stepped back from the spreading red, but even this was swiftly devoured by the boiling nanite swarm. Orix slowly turned his dark, nearly invisible eyes on Xartasia. His wide, fanged maw gaped open.

"Enough, lieutenant," Dhozo snapped. "Zhyress, V'lox, go with the aerad knights and collect Sharlon's friends. Savor the meal."

Two of the tall, shadowy Devourers saluted and left with four of the glass-armored fairies. Dhozo returned his attention to Xartasia.

"How does this information change our schedule?" he asked the white-clothed Arcadian queen.

"It does not."

"You're just going to ignore this other queen?" Dhozo asked. It was difficult to tell whether his tone was of incredulity or grudging admiration.

But Xartasia didn't care what Dhozo thought. "No. I do not think that Maeve understands at all what I do, else she would not raise arms against me. But I cannot risk the trouble she may bring."

"What will you do, then?"

Xartasia pointed to the armored knight in red and purple again. He approached and dipped his wings. "Yes, my queen?"

"Bring Syle to me," she told him. "I find myself in need of his skills."

The knight saluted and then left. Dhozo's swarm of dark nanites parted just long enough for Xartasia to glimpse his fang-filled grin. She didn't think that was coincidental.

"You're sending an assassin after your own cousin?" he asked. There was no mistaking the approval in his voice this time.

"Syle is not an assassin," Xartasia said. "His skills are far more... creative than that. There will be death, I am certain, but I would not send an assassin after my own blood. I am not like you, Dhozo."

Titania alighted delicately on the soft green grass. The dryad gardeners did their jobs well and in utter silence... She didn't even see any of the green-skinned fairies in the royal garden.

The knight landed beside her, the wind of his passage shaking free a handful of pale pink petals from the nearby rose tree. They tangled in the princess' black hair and hung there like beads. The handsome knight fell into step beside her. Together, they walked through the royal gardens.

"Your father summoned me last night," he said.

"I thought that he might." Titania smiled triumphantly. "And what did the king want with you, Sir Anthem?"

"You already know."

"But I want to hear you say it."

She stopped beside a curling green and blue topiary that looked like cresting waves and took Anthem's hands. He smiled indulgently.

"He has asked me to remain at court," Anthem told Titania. "If I am to be consort to his eldest daughter, to the future queen of Arcadia, King Illain believes that I must learn more of politics."

Titania balanced herself with outstretched wings and leaned close to the knight. "Little does he know that you have already been learning."

"You are a good teacher, my enarri," Anthem told her between kisses. "It has been most pleasant to be your student."

"Still, I hope you intend to do as the king asks."

"Of course. I will learn all I can," Anthem said. He cupped her cheek in one hand and brushed back her black hair. "You will rule the White Kingdom one day, Titania. You will be a great queen. I wish only to be a good prince to you."

Titania pulled Anthem close and wrapped her arms around him. The royal palace rose up above them, over the gardens, towers casting glowing shadows across the lawns and blooming vines. That castle of gleaming glass, the crown of the worlds, would one day be hers. It was a frightening prospect, but not today. Titania could do anything at all, so long as her enarri was by her side.

[15]

SHADES OF SUNSET

"A queen's love must not be for a consort, but for her people."

- FERRIS VERRIDIAN (234 PA)

"We're out of money," Panna said.

"Again?" Duaal looked up from a datadex he was sketching on. "But we sold that new batch of phenno just three days ago."

"There are nearly six thousand Arcadians out there now," Panna pointed out. "And more arriving every week."

"We've got seven glass-smiths working on housing and towers," Duaal said. "If Stray's got one abundant free thing, it's sand. We're moving fairies out of those tents at a good rate."

"But they can't eat sand," Xia told him. "There is the cost of their medical care, too. Kessa's helping out – unpaid, by the way – but that doesn't reduce the cost of the medications I need."

"And there's the passage we're paying for off-world Arcadians to come here," Panna added. "There aren't that many yet, but hopefully that cost will only go up."

Duaal groaned and threw his datadex down on the table and Panna picked it up curiously. It was another crown design. This one was less elaborate than the others, little more than a circlet of glass with a single raised point. Panna liked it. She held the datadex out to Xia. The Ixthian nodded.

"I think Maeve will love it," Xia said.

"She had better," Duaal grumbled. "It's the seventh one I've designed. I liked number three better."

"It looked like a glass hedgehog," Xia said.

"It looked *grand*," Duaal corrected primly. "Maeve could use a little grand."

"I think this one is just perfect," Panna said. She pointed to the row of windows along the Blue Phoenix's mess. "Besides, the grand crown is out there."

A dozen slender spires rose from the desert, shining under the pale sky. Another five spiraled up half-finished, slender lattices like translucent vines spun up into soaring towers. As hard as Hyra and Lorren worked, they couldn't entirely clarify the rust-colored Stray sand and the glass towers were shot all through with streaks of red, orange and yellow that turned them into elongated, frozen flames. The citizens of the little desert city had begun calling it Kaellisem – *Firehome*.

Arcadians flew between the glass towers, indistinct silhouettes from this distance. Kaellisem wasn't much like true Arcadia, Panna suspected, but she had never seen the five worlds of the old White Kingdom. For a girl from the farms of Cyrus, Kaellisem was something out of myth.

"I suppose it *is* rather lovely," Duaal said grudgingly. "Speaking of lovely, where is our little queen?"

"She's greeting the new arrivals," Panna said. She didn't take her eyes from the view outside. "Coldhand and Gripper went with her. The ship from Prianus is finally here."

"It's been more than a month since Logan sent that message. No wonder we're spending so much on shipping," Duaal said. He stood and took his datadex back from Xia. "Well, I guess I'd better get this down to Hyra. We'll need something to put on Maeve's head at the coronation tomorrow night."

No one offered to help Ballad with his bags. That was fine with him – the young Arcadian didn't own much and didn't particularly want someone else handling it. But they could have helped Vellania. The old woman struggled with a sack that had gotten wedged between two seats. Kashan pushed and glared his way past a pair of chattering humans to help her pull it free.

Ballad landed at the bottom of the narrow exit stairs. Stray was nothing like Prianus. The sun was large, dim and red, arcing ponderously across a pale sky. There was a low, dusty city to one side and sandy rust-red dunes on the other. The air was dry and dirty. Ballad broke into a fit of coughing. When he recovered, scrubbing his eyes and straightening with a rustle of feathers, Ballad saw a pair of familiar shapes making their way across the blastphalt. It was Logan Coldhand and the strange alien who had accompanied him back in Pylos, Gripper. Ballad squinted against the red sun. Was the bounty hunter... smiling?

"Hey!" Gripper shouted, waving Ballad over. He enveloped one of the Arcadian's hands in his own and shook it enthusiastically. "We've been waiting for you!"

Ballad had questions, but there was no chance to ask them before Logan pulled him into a tight embrace. Ballad gaped as the Prian released him. Was this really the same haunted, harried man he had met in Pylos? There were the scarred illonium hand and the dark blond hair, the ice-blue eyes and even the Talon laser on his hip. But this Logan looked years younger, full of life and purpose – and sincere pleasure to see Ballad again.

"Vorus found you, then," Logan said as he released the fairy boy. "How was he?"

"Good," Ballad answered. "The palaestrum is doing well, he said to tell you."

"He didn't come with you, did he?" Logan asked, then shook his head and sighed. "No, he wouldn't have. Vorus would never leave Prianus. Where are Kashan and An'assi?"

"Kashan's still on the ship, helping the others. We brought more. Vellania and her family and some others. We couldn't leave them. An'assi died about a week before I got your message," Ballad said. The loss still hurt deeply. "He caught something. It went right to his lungs and killed him in two weeks."

Logan bowed his head for a moment and then turned, gesturing for Ballad to follow. "Gripper, help Kashan and the rest. I'm taking him to Maeve."

"Sure, Hunter," Gripper said. He ignored the strange looks that he was getting and made his way into the passenger liner.

"Maeve?" Ballad asked. He had to jog to keep up with the much taller Prian. "That's the dove you were looking for back in Pylos, isn't it? Sounds like you found her."

"Yes, I did."

The fierce note of joy and pride in Logan's voice made Ballad wonder. This was all too strange... Vorus appearing in Pylos with money and an invitation to Stray, saying that there was an Arcadian queen in Gharib. Logan led Ballad around a small, unstaffed control center and he stopped short.

A woman stood in the dusty gray shadows, an Arcadian in elaborately knotted red and gold scarves, with silver eyes and hair as black as the void between stars. Ballad whistled.

"That's Maeve?" he asked. "The new queen?"

He suddenly understood the change in Logan, at least in part. Ballad had lived his whole life on Prianus, among the desperate and dying remains of the White Kingdom, worlds he had never known. Maeve seemed a piece of that history, a fragment honed to a spear point and hung with banner-ribbons like the knights of old. He wondered if he should bow.

Maeve – Queen Maeve – bit her lip like a nervous schoolgirl.

"Logan tells me it is to you I owe my rescue in Pylos," she said.

"Well, he's the one who found you, Majesty," Ballad answered, then gave Logan a sidelong look. "Right?"

"Not without a lot of help," he said. "But you were the one who sent me to the Kayton base camp."

Ballad smirked. So he really *had* helped.

"They say there was a Waygate there and the cops had a claws-out war with the Devourers over it. Is that true?" Ballad asked.

Maeve and Logan exchanged a look and the raven-haired Arcadian queen nodded slowly.

"Yes," she admitted. "And we failed to entirely banish them. The Devourers are still out there, under the command of my cousin."

"We have a lot to talk about," Logan said. "And some important things to show you. Once we collect Vellania and the rest, we'll get back to Kaellisem."

"Kaellisem?" Ballad asked. It sounded Arcadian, but there were no Arcadian cities in CWA space. Were there?

Duke Ferris was waiting for her at the gates. At least, that was what the residents of Kaellisem called them: The Gates of the Sun. There were no real gates, just two red-streaked pillars of glass that rose up from the desert floor and came to sharp points high in the sky. They were actually just experiments, tests of the Stray glass' integrity. But the two pointed pillars had become symbols of Kaellisem, of the new Arcadia. Maeve hoped they wouldn't fall over during the next sandstorm.

Ferris stood in the flame-colored shadows with hands tucked into the sleeves of his flowing blue robe and his braids whipping in the dry wind. They were woven with silver ribbons almost indistinguishable from the streaks of gray through his blond hair. Maeve stopped between the glass pillars.

"Is this important?" she asked. She nodded back toward Ballad and the rest of the new Arcadians who had landed behind her. "We have tired newcomers."

Ferris took in Ballad's appearance – his worn denims torn out at one knee, short Prian-styled hair and the leather jacket cut up the back to fit over his wings – and frowned. Ballad frowned right back.

"It concerns your coronation tomorrow," Ferris said, shifting his gaze back to Maeve.

"It's fine, Glass," Gripper told her. "Hunter and I can help them settle. They're going to the new tower, right?"

Maeve nodded and Logan shifted one of Vellania's bags across his shoulder, then bent to kiss Maeve before heading away to escort the Arcadians down the road toward one of the delicate glass spires. Ballad waved to Maeve, spread his wings and followed the rest of the fairies.

Ferris' lips remained in a tight, unhappy line. "That is the one Coldhand wanted so much money to bring here? Where is he from? He has the manners of a dryad."

"Prianus," Maeve answered. "Logan was hunting the Nihilists in Pylos when Ballad accosted him. He was trained by someone Logan greatly respected. Ballad is very brave and very capable."

"Capable of what?" Ferris asked sourly, but then shook his head. "Forgive me, a'shae. All are welcome in Kaellisem, naturally."

Maeve was grateful that the duke didn't want to argue about Ballad.

"You wished to speak with me about the coronation?" she asked.

"About after you are crowned, in truth," Ferris said. "Please, my queen, will you fly with me?"

Maeve vaulted into the air beside Ferris. The wind was hot but strong, lifting them high into the pale sky over Kaellisem. The small

– but gleaming – glass city spread out below them, red and gold and fiery orange and deep, secretive russet. Winged Arcadians stood or sat on translucent balconies. Some walked down the single central road. There were a few stalls set up, staffed by humans and Lyra in hopes of wheedling a few cenmarks from the new settlers. Maeve caught a glimpse of Logan and the others just before they vanished into one of the half-finished towers.

"Kaellisem is amazing," Ferris said softly, just loud enough to carry over the wind to Maeve's pointed ears. "You have done more for our people in six weeks than anyone has in decades, my queen. You have given us a home and hope we thought long dead."

Maeve chewed her lip. Ferris gave her too much credit for Kaellisem. It was the glass-singers, under Hyra's direction and leadership, who were building the new city, not Maeve. But it was good to see glass towers rising up toward the sun again, even an alien sun. Kaellisem *was* beautiful.

Duke Ferris landed on top of a slender rose-colored bridge that connected a pair of Kaellisem's tallest towers. Another Arcadian man waited in the center of the translucent span. He was older than Maeve, but much younger than Duke Ferris. He wore his hair in a smooth fall of blond braids woven with midnight blue ribbons. His clothes, too, were simple: pants and a sleeveless shirt of a smooth silver fabric. He turned to face them as Maeve and Ferris landed.

Maeve gasped. She *knew* him.

"Anthem? What are you doing here?" Maeve narrowed her eyes and took several steps back. "Ferris, this man is Anthem Calloren. He was Titania's consort before the fall!"

"He knows who I am," Anthem said. He held up his hands. He wasn't carrying a spear, or any kind of blade that Maeve could see. "Whatever else you decide... I want only to speak with you."

"Why? Has Xartasia sent you to kill me?" Maeve asked.

Her heart raced. She had to fly. She needed her spear. She had to get to Logan. Maeve was no match for Anthem Calloren alone, but with her hunter, she might be able to fight him... Ferris placed a gently restraining hand on Maeve's tensed arm. Was the old duke a traitor? After all this, was he going to deliver Maeve to her cousin? Or perhaps just her head...?

"Listen to him," Ferris said urgently.

Anthem took a half-step closer, his hands held open as though approaching a dangerous animal. Maeve glared at the pale-haired knight.

"Speak quickly," she hissed. "What could my cousin's lover want of me?"

"To join you," Anthem answered. "I saw the royal palace fall on Illisem. For a hundred years, I believed Titania dead. Now you tell us that she lives... but I cannot rejoice."

"Sir Anthem was here in Gharib," Duke Ferris told Maeve. "He sought me out and begged an audience with you."

Anthem looked at her with eyes of the same dark sapphire color as the ribbons in his hair. "I would join you, Queen Maeve. If it is true that the woman I loved has become a monster, then you are all I have left of her."

Maeve stared. Could it be true? Anthem Calloren was one of the greatest knights of the White Kingdom, rivaling even Orthain Fyre. Kaellisem had no knights, but with Anthem's help, maybe Maeve could change that...

"Thank you, Sir Anthem," she said, voice wavering. "I..."

Before she could share her idea, Ferris' fingers tightened on her shoulder. Maeve tore her eyes from Anthem to look at the duke.

"My queen..." Ferris said. "There is more here before you than a knight. I see what the human hunter, Coldhand, means to you. But he is not of noble blood. He is not even Arcadian."

The glass city spun around Maeve.

"What?" she asked. "What does that matter?"

"You have given our people a queen, but now they need a king," Ferris told her. "An Arcadian king, a'shae."

Maeve tore herself from Ferris' grasp and staggered away. There was empty air under her heels and Maeve had to beat her wings once, swiftly, to propel her back onto the bridge.

"Logan is my enarri," she shouted. "I love him! He walked alone through the storm to find me. We have shared bed and battle and bloodshed!"

"I do not doubt his worth as a man," Ferris said, though the sour note of distaste in his voice made it quite clear that he did. "But your people thought the House of Cavain dead for a hundred years. They see your black hair now and hope that the White Kingdom may be theirs again. The pride and the history, my queen... But there can be no royal line without heirs, a'shae. Even if the people could ever respect a human consort, Logan Coldhand cannot father Arcadian children."

"And so you would... would have me give him up?" Maeve said. Blood roared in her ears like a stormy ocean. She pointed a shaking finger at Anthem. "My enarri? For *this* man?"

"Sir Calloren was a worthy consort to King Illain's eldest daughter, heir to the throne," Ferris reminded her. "He is an unparalleled knight of a well-known noble house. He is a good match for you, Highness. Your people would cheer to see Sir Anthem beside their new crowned queen tomorrow."

Maeve couldn't speak. She spun to stare at Anthem. Surely he would have nothing to do with this... madness. But he looked up at Maeve with blue-black eyes.

"I would be honored to serve however I may," Anthem said. "I offer myself freely as knight or consort, my queen."

No. Maeve could never do it. She *loved* Logan. No one could make her give him up...

But Ferris' idea did make a wretched sort of sense. Maeve and Xartasia were the last of their line and without an Arcadian mate, there would never be another black-haired fairy ever again. Cavain's house would fail. After ten thousand years, it would die.

Maeve reeled, threw out her wings and dove off the bridge. Hot tears seared her eyes and she very nearly smashed into a golden-streaked tower before she finally found Logan standing out in the street, talking to Ballad's friend, Kashan. Maeve fell to the ground and threw herself into her hunter's arms.

"Maeve...?" Logan asked, surprised. His ice-blue eyes went hard and dangerous. "What's wrong, dove?"

[16]

BROKEN ARMOR

"Love is a blade. Any weapon can be taken away and used to cut the one who treasured it most."

– ANTHEM CALLOREN (294 PA)

Maeve walked beside Logan all the way up the spiraling glass stairs of her tower. It was one of few spires in Kaellisem that had a staircase, crafted by Hyra at Maeve's insistence. When they reached the top, Logan sat in one of the open windows and pulled Maeve into his mismatched arms. She closed her eyes, resting her head in the hollow of his shoulder, and wrapped her long white wings around them both. Logan stroked the soft skin between Maeve's wings.

"Ferris isn't wrong," he told her. "You and I can never have children, dove. You know that."

"I do not care!" Maeve said. At least, that's what Logan thought she said. It was hard to make out the words with her face buried against the side of his neck. "I love you. You are my enarri."

"And I–" The words caught in Logan's throat as though they had thorns. He laid his cheek against the top of Maeve's head. Her black hair was smooth and soft. "Dove, don't be so quick to discount this."

Maeve slid out of Logan's arms and jumped to her feet. "Do not dare to tell me that you would give me up to Anthem Calloren!"

Logan remained sitting on the windowsill. His cybernetic hand slipped on the smooth glass and scraped loudly. The tower room was full of a diffused orange glow as the sun shined through the delicate walls and the warm wind smelled of dust. Maeve began to pace, stalking back and forth like a caged animal. Her eyes were rimmed in red.

"If I am truly queen," she said, "then I may make any law I wish, take any lover that I desire! And I desire you, Logan. I will have you or no one!"

Logan couldn't keep from smiling at his furious angel. Maeve had such fire. Even when he felt coldest, numbed and chilled by his mechanical heart, a single kiss or moment in her arms made him feel so alive.

Logan stood and stepped into the path of Maeve's angry pacing. She bumped into him and hissed with rage.

"Do not dare–" Maeve started, but Logan caught her wrist in the unbreakable grasp of his illonium fingers.

"You know it's not that simple," Logan said. "Maeve, you know what I'm like. You're here to inspire, to take your people away from whatever Xartasia's got planned for them, for the whole galaxy. I'm no good at that. Do you think this Anthem hawk might be?"

Maeve swiped tears out of her gray eyes and one splashed onto Logan's hand. It sparkled in the filtered sunlight, but he couldn't feel the wet heat.

"Sir Anthem is an accomplished knight," Maeve admitted as reluctantly as if Logan had tortured the answer out of her. "Ferris did not exaggerate that. He was well known in the White Kingdom."

"And was Xartasia's consort, right?" Logan said. "If they see him by your side instead of hers, that's going to look bad for her."

Maeve tried to yank her hand from Logan's metal one. "Yes, I suppose. You have a better head for politics than you claim. And in the name of these higher ideals, you would let me go? After you fought so hard to find me again?"

Logan's hand clenched around the Arcadian's delicate wrist. She squirmed, but her expression remained defiant.

"I would do anything for you, Maeve," he told her in a low voice. "Anything. Including letting you go, if I have to. What we're doing here is important, dove. I know what it means to you."

"Not more than you do!" Maeve shouted. She put her free hand over Logan's cybernetic one and kissed the flat gray illonium.

"Yes, more than me," Logan said. He pulled Maeve close again and closed his eyes. They burned with tears. "Maeve, I told you that you would be a great queen. Your people need you."

Maeve cried and beat her fists against Logan's chest until she finally collapsed sobbing to the ground. He sank to the ground and held her until the storm of tears subsided. Maeve's wings draped across the glass floor behind her like a bridal train. She lifted her face and kissed Logan.

"You are right," she said. "Tomorrow, I will go to Ferris. I will tell him that... that I accept Anthem as my consort. But not now."

Logan kissed Maeve again and together they stumbled into the bedroom, tearing off each other's clothes with a terrible, desperate need. Maeve twined her arms around her hunter's neck and would not let go. She whispered and sang out her passion in lyrical Arcadian, in words Logan did not understand. Maybe it was better that he couldn't.

He traced his fingertips over the pale, slender curves of Maeve's body, memorizing every bit of her. The scent of her hair and sun-warmed feathers, the taste of tears and sweat on her silky skin, the sound of Maeve's cries and his name on her lips...

Logan held her long after their bodies could no longer endure their need. Starlight shone weakly through the glass tower and outlined them both in faded silver. Maeve's eyes fluttered, fighting sleep. Logan kissed her forehead.

"Sleep, dove," he told her. "Tomorrow is an important day."

"Do not leave," Maeve whispered, splaying her fingers over his heart, over the knotted white scar there. "Stay with me."

Logan put his hand on top of hers.

"I won't go. Not until morning," he promised.

Maeve nodded and fell at last into a deep, still sleep. Logan lay awake until dawn, watching her.

Maeve woke up alone in the pale pink light of dawn. Logan was gone. His clothes, his gun and even the warm spot beside her in the bed had all vanished. Maeve drew a deep, shuddering breath. The time for tears was over.

The Gray Queen rose and prepared. She wrapped herself in a long, soft robe and stood before a polished silver mirror. The night before had left her long black hair a tousled mess. Maeve reached for her brush and pulled it mechanically through her hair.

Duaal arrived a few minutes later, leading a pair of young Arcadian girls – Dain and Verra – that each struggled with an armload of glass plates.

"Good morning," Duaal said with a smile. "It's as hot as five or six hells out there today. Are you ready to try on your armor?"

Maeve didn't look up, but stared fixedly at her reflection.

"Armor?" she asked.

Duaal pulled a chair beside Maeve and sat. He frowned into the mirror at her.

"We talked about this yesterday," he said. "You wanted to wear armor tonight. You're still a knight, you said, and were one long before you were queen. Ferris had a fit. A civil one, of course, but I swear his ears were about to pop off. Don't you remember that?"

Maeve did – now that Duaal mentioned it – but the scene wasn't so funny anymore.

She stood, dropping her robe without pretense. If her heart and body were only mere tools of statecraft, then what point was there in modesty? Logan's Talon-9 did not blush when drawn.

Duaal arched one dark brow as the Arcadian girls whispered. He crossed his arms over his chest and frowned. He looked so much like Tiberius when he did that, Maeve thought. She smiled sadly at the mirror.

"What's wrong, Maeve?" Duaal asked. "I would have thought you would be excited to suit up. You haven't worn Arcadian armor in... how many years? You should be excited about this! Hyra was up all night getting it finished in time. Why are you just standing here like a stuffed bird?"

"Nothing," Maeve answered. She made herself smile at the Blue Phoenix's young captain. "You are right. Let us inspect Hyra's work."

Duaal gave her a suspicious look as she went to the table where Dain and Verra had set down her armor. There was a twisted rope of scarlet scarves. Maeve uncoiled them and began wrapping herself in the colorful fabric.

"Where is Duke Ferris?" she asked as Duaal stepped up behind her and helped Maeve wrap the red silk.

"He's downstairs," he answered.

"Is there anyone with him?"

"Other than Panna? Yeah, actually," Duaal said. "Another Arcadian man. Older than you, I'd guess. Braided hair, great legs. Is that Logan's friend Ballad?"

Maeve shook her head. "No. I suspect that is Sir Anthem. Good, I am glad he is here."

"*Sir...?* Another knight?" Duaal asked. He untangled two more of the blood-colored scarves. "Why isn't he up here instead of me? He must know how your armor works."

"He is probably being respectful of my privacy," Maeve said. "He does not yet know if it is acceptable to see me like this before we are wed."

Maeve gestured to the mirror, to her still half-nude image there, but Duaal wasn't listening. He jumped, dropping the scarves. The red silk drifted lazily to the floor.

"What?" Duaal asked. "*Wed?* You mean married? What in the three hundred hells are you talking about?"

"I will announce Anthem Calloren as my consort at my coronation tonight." Maeve closed her eyes and fought for breath again. It was as though a Devourer had closed its great black claw around her ribs. "I will tell Duke Ferris when we are done here."

"Consort?" Duaal shouted. "But... what about Logan? You love him! He loves you!"

"Love does not build kingdoms," Maeve said. She wound a red scarf around her neck and then pulled her hair free of the cloth. "And it does not win wars. Do not forget that we are here to contest Xartasia and that we must beat her at her own game."

Duaal gaped. His mouth worked but nothing came out. Maeve finished knotting the scarlet silks under her wings and turned back.

"I can put on this armor myself," she said, "but it will take three times longer."

The young mage shook his head and picked up her delicate-looking glass breastplate.

"You can't be serious about this," Duaal said as he helped tie the armor in place. "You and Logan have something amazing together. Maybe not something entirely sane, but–"

"I am queen," Maeve interrupted. "I must love my people more than any one man."

"Who the hells told you that? Ferris?"

"No," Maeve said. "It was Logan."

Gripper hung from the edge of the balcony, watching Xia talk to a group of fairies.

She gestured to the small white plastic box in her other hand. The top and sides were printed with the circled blue cross emblem of the Alliance medical corps. Xyn had placed the order, but Maeve hadn't been able to pay him back. They all owed the little Ixthian scientist a great deal of money, Gripper knew, but only Panna and Xia kept track of exactly how much. He had asked, but Xia only smiled a pretty silver smile and told him not to worry about it even as her compound eyes turned a concerned red.

Xia was good at taking care of everyone, Gripper reflected. She was kind and generous and sweet right down to the root. Gripper wondered what he should do. Nothing – not the flowers or other gifts on Prianus – had done anything to earn Xia's affection. Well, her *special* affection. Xia liked everyone. That was one of so many great things about her.

Gripper swung back and forth from the balcony's edge. There was no railing around it. There were no rails or banisters anywhere in Kaellisem, actually. A species with wings didn't need them very much, Gripper supposed.

Footsteps rang on the pink glass and the Arboran pulled himself easily up onto the balcony. A human stood in the arched doorway, hands buried in his pockets and shoulders slumped. It wasn't until Gripper saw that the left one was made of dark gray illonium that he recognized Logan. The posture was all wrong.

"Hunter? What's wrong?" Gripper asked. "Where's Glass?"

Logan stared out at the colorful crystal spires of Kaellisem, flickering like kindling fire in the dawn sunlight. And then he slammed his cybernetic fist into the tower's wall. The glass cracked with a sharp retort and pale lines raced out in a jagged spiderweb around Logan's metal hand. A few peach-colored shards fell to the balcony floor, each no larger than a single seed. Gripper jumped, but didn't retreat.

"I left her."

"What?" Gripper asked. He must have misheard. "Left? But you adore her."

"More than anything. But Queen Maeve's people need an Arcadian king," Logan said. He raked his hand up the back of his neck, through his hair and over his face. "I was learning more Arcadian. So I could sing the oathsongs to her."

"Oathsongs?" Gripper asked, gasping. If he understood right – and Gripper had spent a great deal of time with Maeve – Arcadian oathsongs were shared only between family or those who wanted to *become* family. "You were going to...?"

Logan nodded and punched the tower's glass wall again, but the blow was softer, almost gentle. In the street below, Xia had finished her instructions and handed the medical case to one of the fairies. She shaded her eyes against the red rising sun and stared up at the balcony.

"What are you going to do?" Gripper asked.

"I will serve my queen," Logan answered in a dead voice. "However I can."

"Your queen?" Gripper repeated. "But you're not Arcadian."

"She's still my queen."

[17]

THE GRAY QUEEN

"Honor the people you rule and they will honor you."

- ILLAIN CAVAINNA (28 PA)

Maeve alighted softly on the wide, gently curved sill of the bedroom. But for the faint violet filtering through the tower's glass walls, the room was dark. Maeve could just make out the pale shape of Orthain in the circular bed. His long, lovely wings draped across the silk sheets.

Maeve gestured to a nyad who stood silently in one corner. Her dark blue skin and hair blended perfectly into shadows, making her and her kind ideal nighttime servants. She bobbed a quick bow and helped her mistress out of her glass armor. When Maeve wore only a maroon scarf around her hips, she waved the nyad off and crept through the darkness to her bed. She slid under the silky sheets and wrapped her wings around Orthain's warmth.

The knight stirred and rolled onto his side to look at Maeve. His eyes caught the moonlight, turning into pools of shimmering silver.

"It is late. Where were you?" Orthain asked. But his voice didn't have that rough-soft burr of sleep. "No, do not answer. I know. You were out with Caith again."

"We were working," Maeve answered. "You know that I have duties, enarri."

"I am a knight, too," Orthain said. "I was your father's squire before you were even born and I taught you the arts by which you now live. Yet I have been here in our bed for hours. Waiting for you."

Maeve sat up, suddenly hot and prickly all over with anger.

"What exactly are you saying?" she asked. "What are you accusing me of?"

Orthain sat up in the shimmering sheets, too. They pooled like water around him. "You are gone all day and all night, Maeve. You are always with Caith."

"He is my brother!" Maeve said. "The day he was born, you told me to go to him. How dare you tell me to turn my back on him now?"

"When I told you to go…" her husband repeated in a ragged voice. "When you left, I wanted you to come back to me. But you never did, Maeve. And you never will."

He stood up out of their bed, shuddering and rustling in anger. Maeve rose, too, and clenched her fists at her sides. She didn't embrace her enarri or kiss him.

"The bond between Caith and I is of blood, Sir Orthain," Maeve said. "What you and I have traded are just songs."

Orthain turned away from his wife. The light reflected from the pale nighttime orbs of Wynerian and Orindell streaked his body in ribbons of milky radiance. His long hair was bronze in the wan light and hung in smooth waves between his outstretched wings. Orthain was so lovely, but Maeve still shook all over with rage. How dare he question her right to see her own brother?

"Your heart already belongs entirely to Caith," Orthain told Maeve. "There is no room left there for me. Or here. So goodnight and goodbye, Maeve… my enarri."

Without looking back, Orthain strode to the open window and leapt out. His wings swept down once and then he rose on the midnight wind, vanishing into the dark sky before Maeve could answer.

"I would change nothing!" she shouted after him. "All I have done, I have done for love!"

Maeve stood like a statue in her new suit of gleaming glass armor as Duaal and Anthem checked the fit. The golden-haired fairy knight tugged gently on her greaves and the back of her breastplate.

"It sits too high against the wings," Anthem said.

"Yeah, I bet it does," Duaal muttered.

Maeve had no idea what that was supposed to mean and suspected Duaal didn't either. But Anthem either didn't hear him or pretended not to.

Ferris returned with Panna and the wingless fairy girl carried a small, plain mycoboard box, but grinned from ear to rounded ear.

"It looks *just* like Duaal's design," she said triumphantly. "You're going to love your new crown, Your Majesty."

Maeve glanced over her shoulder at Panna. The armor pinched beneath her left wing and Maeve winced. Anthem was right about the fit. Panna put the box down on a table and stepped out onto the balcony.

"Please lift your arm, my queen," Anthem instructed.

Maeve did as he asked while Duke Ferris finished a quiet conversation with her young handmaidens and then strode outside.

"Sir Anthem," he said.

The knight knelt down on the colorful balcony at Maeve's feet, inspecting her knee-high glass boots. It was often a sticking point in armor. Arcadian knights fought most of their battles in the air, making it easy to overlook the state of their footwear. But all battles came to ground at some point, even if only in defeat.

"The right boot is too tight," Anthem told Duaal. The Hyzaari captain rolled his eyes but dutifully wrote down what he had said. Anthem looked up at Duke Ferris. "Yes, Your Grace?"

"Sir Anthem, you will be taking over responsibilities for Queen Maeve's protection," Ferris said.

"Taking over? Who was responsible before?"

"Logan Coldhand," Maeve said. She narrowed her eyes at Ferris. "Is it not enough that I have accepted Sir Anthem as a consort? Do you no longer trust Logan to protect me?"

"Coldhand was not here with you this morning," Ferris pointed out. "When Verra and Dain arrived with Captain Sinnay, you were unprotected, my queen."

"Unprotected...?" Maeve asked bitterly. "From what? If Xartasia knows at all what we do here, she has ignored us."

"Thank God," Duaal said. "We're in no shape to take on anyone. Especially the Devourers."

Maeve sighed. Duaal was right. They *were* poorly prepared for a fight and wasn't that their ultimate purpose here on Stray? But protecting Maeve was hardly the solution.

She looked down at Anthem, who held one of her hands in his. Carefully, he inspected each joint of her gauntlet for strength and flexibility.

"Stand, Sir Anthem," Maeve said. "I have a more important task for you than serving in my guard."

Anthem straightened and gave his queen a curious look. "Anything you wish, a'shae. I am yours to command."

"We need knights," Maeve told him. "The Devourers killed most of them during the fall. Yet you lived, Sir Anthem."

He didn't look certain if this was praise or an insult. Good.

Maeve knew she wasn't being charitable, but she found it hard to care. Anthem had flown to her banner instead of Xartasia's and Maeve *knew* that had been an amazing stroke of political luck – Logan was right about that, and so was Ferris – but she just couldn't forgive Anthem for any of it just yet.

"You were Princess Titania's consort and most favored knight for a long time," Maeve said. "None living know more of our training, of our arms and armor. And so you will train a new generation of knights, Sir Anthem."

He listened intently and then swept a wing across his chest. "As you say, my queen. It would be my honor."

"Have Hyra fit you for armor of your own." Maeve clenched her left fist and had to admire the sparkle of the golden-swirled glass. The fit was not perfect, but it was close. "And then you will begin. Your first student will be Ballad Avadain, a boy from Prianus."

"The one in leather?" Duke Ferris asked her. "Your Highness, are you sure he is... suitable to be one of your knights?"

"They will not be *my* knights," Maeve said. "They are knights of Kaellisem. Even this small kingdom comes from many worlds."

"They're all Arcadian," Duaal said.

"Well... I'm from Cyrus," Panna pointed out. She smirked up at Duaal and Duke Ferris. "Ballad is Prian. Kinrae and Selphia were both born on Axis."

"And if we are as successful in building Kaellisem as we plan to be, there will be Arcadians flocking here from all across the core," Maeve agreed. "Ballad is a good man and already an accomplished fighter. A boxer, I believe."

"Boxer? *En summari?*" Ferris asked incredulously.

He used the old Arcadian word for *brawler*, usually reserved for dryads or nyads who fought one another – and the term was *not* a flattering one. Arcadians didn't fight with their empty hands. Ten thousand years of knightly training and tradition focused on the spear. Duke Ferris' scowl would have wilted grass, if there were any on Stray.

"Malla and Hannu will begin training as well, I assume," Ferris said, struggling to regain control of the situation. "They are loyal and dedicated."

Maeve nodded her agreement. The siblings would make good knights. But even better, it would give them something more important to do than follow her around.

"But there is still the matter of your guard," Duke Ferris said, as though he had heard Maeve's thoughts. "You must be protected at all times, my queen."

"I can and will serve," Anthem answered too quickly for Maeve's taste.

"You will be training knights," she reminded him coldly. "You will be busy."

"Sir Anthem is to be your consort," Ferris said. "He will be with you much of the time, a'shae. And it shall come naturally, I know, to protect the beloved and royal person."

Maeve sighed and closed her eyes as she nodded.

"Fine," she said without enthusiasm.

"What about the rest of the time?" Panna asked. "Sir Anthem will be working with the new knights a lot of the time."

"I'll do it," Logan said from the doorway. "I can still protect her."

Maeve's heart leapt at the sight of her hunter, but then fell just as swiftly at the Prian's icy, frozen expression. Duke Ferris scowled at Coldhand.

"You?" he said. "Where were you this morning? As soon as you were banished from Queen Maeve's bed, you vanished off into the rising sun!"

Panna and Duaal gasped, and Logan fixed his glacial gaze on the old Arcadian duke. Gripper crept out onto the balcony behind Logan, chewing worriedly on a thick claw.

"I was never far away," Logan told Ferris. "I would – and have – protected Maeve with my life."

Anthem gave Logan a long, appraising look. Dark blue eyes met pale and Logan's illonium-plated hand curled slowly into a tight fist. Anthem's wings stretched out, long pinions fanning like a hundred slender fingers. The two men stood still for a moment, silently appraising one another.

"You managed the queen's guard before?" Anthem asked at last.

"I did," Logan said.

"What management needed to be done," Duaal said. "We didn't have a lot of personnel and we still don't."

"All the more reason not to waste it," Anthem said. He turned to address Maeve and Duke Ferris. "I will take over leadership of Her Majesty's guard."

"They *will* be knights," Ferris agreed forcefully. "Those trained and selected by you."

Anthem nodded. "But Logan Coldhand has served our queen loyally and until we have knights enough, we will need his help to maintain a constant guard."

Duke Ferris pursed his lips, but then he inclined his long-haired head in acquiescence. "Of course, Sir Anthem. I am certain that all propriety will be observed."

Here, Ferris arched a blond brow at Maeve, who felt an acidic stab in her gut. What did that mean?

"Well, this has been awkward," Duaal said cheerfully. "Anthem, are you done staring at Maeve?"

"I have finished my inspection of her armor," Anthem said after a moment's thought. His Aver was far more heavily accented than Maeve's.

"We can take it back to Hyra to get the changes made," Duaal offered. "I'm sure he'll finish them by tonight."

"I will go with you," Anthem said. The Blue Phoenix's captain scowled. "I need armor, too. And I must speak with the glass-singer about his work. We will need many spears, but there is little wood for hafts on Stray. Can it be imported?"

Maeve shook her head. "We have little money, I am afraid. What we bring from off world are Arcadians, not wood."

"Yes, my queen," Anthem said. "Then we will need some other material."

"Fiber-carbon tubings might work," Logan suggested. "It's light, strong and fairly flexible."

Anthem cocked his head at the Prian hunter.

"Flexible?" he asked. "You have seen our spears in battle, then? Most assume that they are like stone. Unbending."

"Maeve and I fought many times," Logan said flatly. Anthem frowned.

"But that was a long time ago," Gripper added. "Right, Hunter?"

Logan shrugged.

"Take care of the glass," he told Anthem. "I'll watch Maeve."

The Arcadian knight nodded slowly and then turned to Maeve. "I can meet with Ballad, Malla and Hannu. Perhaps they will know of others who may make suitable knights to serve Kaellisem. I will return when I am able."

They all went back inside the tower. Dain and Duaal began unstrapping Maeve's crystal armor and piling it up on the floor.

"This stuff is a lot heavier than it looks," Duaal said when they were done. He gestured to Maeve's other handmaiden, Verra. "How about lending me a wing again?"

The young fairy nodded and moved to scoop up Maeve's glass pauldrons, but Duke Ferris shook his head. "Verra and Dain should remain with the queen. After all, they are her handmaidens. What if she needs her hair brushed while you are away?"

"I can do it myself," Maeve said.

Duke Ferris waved a hand dismissively. "There are any number of other needs to consider. Take Panna with you instead, Captain Sinnay."

Dain looked uncertain, but handed her armful of glass plates to Panna. Gripper hurried to help.

"I've got much bigger hands, Sprite," he told Panna.

Gripper followed Panna and Duaal down the stairs as Anthem bowed his wings once more to Maeve.

"I will return soon, my queen and lady," he said.

Anthem took Maeve's hand and kissed it lightly, then went to the balcony and leapt into the air. He beat his long wings once and was gone. Duke Ferris turned to Maeve with a stiff-looking smile.

"Let us begin, then," he said, gesturing through a doorway to the room that served as Maeve's office.

"Begin what, exactly?" she asked.

Maeve hadn't spent much time in the office and did not particularly want to. She slid her arms through the gauzy sleeves of a rose-colored dress that Dain held out and took a silver scarf from Verra that she wound several times around her waist.

"I have some ideas," Duke Ferris said. "We must begin building funds, Your Highness."

"I want to fight Xartasia, not buy her gifts," Maeve snapped. "We have enough money."

"With respect," Ferris said, "we do not. I have spoken to Panna and Captain Sinnay about it. Kaellisem survives on loans and gifts from your friend, Xyn. But that will not hold out much longer and we owe him a great deal of money. Majesty, We *must* begin generating revenue."

Maeve stalked into her office. Ferris, Logan and the two Arcadian girls followed her like a line of ducklings.

"Your Grace, is it not enough that I have agreed to take Anthem as my consort? That I will let you put a crown on my head tonight?" Maeve asked.

She paced furiously back and forth across the smooth, shining floor until one of her bare feet slid on the glass. Why couldn't they afford carpet...?

"How many more of these ridiculous displays must I make to be a queen?" Maeve asked.

"That *is* being queen," Ferris told her. "You are our future, Your Majesty. You show us what to be."

These last words were slightly strained. Maeve stopped pacing and looked at the fairy duke. "So stop acting like a petulant child? Is that what you are telling me?"

Ferris spread his hand and politely chose not to answer.

But Logan did.

"Yes," he said. "It is. You will be whatever your people need you to be, Maeve. You know that."

She looked into the Prian's sky-colored eyes, then turned back to Ferris.

"Money, then," Maeve said. "If Kaellisem requires me to become an accountant, then an accountant I will become."

"Not an accountant, my queen, but we must begin considering ways to make money. I have already outlined a course of action. We can discuss it now, while you have some breakfast."

Maeve went to her desk. "I am not hungry. Tell me your plan, Duke Ferris."

Duaal and Gripper left hastily after delivering the queen's armor back to Hyra's workshop. The two young men walked close, whispering urgently to one another and darting angry glances back at Sir Anthem. Panna couldn't hear what they were talking about, but she could guess.

Hyra, the one-winged glass-smith, was happy enough to make the changes that Anthem requested, but was less pleased about the knight's request for a dozen more suits of armor and three times that many spears.

"I can make the spears easy, yes," the white-haired old Arcadian said, scratching the back of his calloused hand. "Those are simple. But armor is a more complicated business. I need Lorren for fine pieces and she is working on the towers."

"You need more smiths?" Anthem asked Hyra. "I thought you had several apprentices?"

"Yes," he answered. "But they do not know much yet."

They stood beneath a patched plastic awning that was coated in a thick layer of brown-red dust. The wind was quiet, but that never stopped the sand from getting everywhere. Hyra pointed with his remaining wing to a pair of young fairies standing across a table from one another. They held their hands flat on the tabletop, on either side of a tall heap of sifted and washed red Stray sand. The Arcadians sang together in low, sibilantly smooth voices. Their eyes were squeezed shut in concentration. Visualizing the results, Panna knew. Magic didn't work unless the caster knew *exactly* what they wanted to happen.

The pile of sand began to move, spreading out across the table like a blanket tugged at the corners. It flowed like water and turned that same non-color as it stretched and shaped... almost. Veins of scarlet and orange swirled through the sheet of finished glass. Heat shimmered over its smooth surface, but not nearly as much as there would have been in a coreworlder forge.

Panna had seen the process before – she insisted upon watching the very first pieces of Arcadian glass that Hyra forged on Stray. But it still astonished her every time. She grinned at Hyra, but the smith was watching Sir Anthem.

"Fallo and Dellanon are two of my best students," Hyra told the knight. "The glass there is the clearest that we can make. The others are out with Lorren, singing up the new towers from the sand plots. It is not as pure as what we make in sheets here, but it is faster and good enough for walls. We sing them a little thicker than we would like to keep them strong."

"But this is the quality of glass we need for armor," Sir Anthem said. It wasn't a question. "Make the spears first. Knights must know how to fight. We will armor them as we may."

"The queen wants you in armor, though," Panna reminded him. "It'll be nice to see a real knight in real glass armor."

Hyra looked Anthem up and down. "I can have a suit ready in a week. Three days if I pull Lorren off the towers."

Anthem considered a moment and then nodded.

"Do that," he said. "I will find you some additional singers. We will need a lot of glass."

"As you say, sir," Hyra agreed. The one-winged smith whistled sharply to his apprentices. "Come over here. We have work to do on Her Majesty's armor. Did she like the crown?"

"I don't know. Maeve hasn't seen it yet," Panna admitted, but gave Hyra a reassuring smile when the smith's wing sagged. "Everyone will see it tonight."

Hyra straightened a bit at that. Panna said goodbye, then she and Anthem left.

The sandy streets of Kaellisem were far from crowded, but she was still proud. It wasn't the largest gathering of Arcadians in the galaxy – not yet – but it was close. And by far the most beautiful. Stray's ruddy sun cast only hazy shadows and pale glows through the glass city. Kaellisem was nothing like the imperial White City, less than a hundredth Arcadia's size and grandeur. But Panna had never been to Cavain's home.

Kaellisem was the most amazing thing she had ever seen. Panna loved it even as she choked on a mouthful of dust and spat into the unpaved street. The desert drained away the moisture in seconds.

It was not until he repeated himself loudly that Panna realized Sir Anthem was speaking to her.

"What?" she asked. "Sorry, I was thinking. What did you say?"

Anthem rearranged a gray scarf across his face. He must have spent a lot of time on Stray, Panna thought. The native ones were used to the unpredictable wind and dust storms, always prepared and covered.

"I asked you where to find Ballad Avadain," Anthem repeated.

"Oh." Panna thought for a moment. "Well, I'm not sure. I haven't actually met him. But he's Prian and Duke Ferris said that he wears leather. I'm sure we can find him without too much trouble."

It didn't take long to locate Ballad. Only a few other fairies knew the newcomer's name, but several remembered him by description and pointed Panna to one of the new towers. It was banded like a Mirran in dark yellows and oranges.

Panna groaned. Like most of the Kaellisem towers, it had no stairs. There was a door at ground level, but it led only into a single room where a small group of older fairies clustered around an even older Arcadian woman.

"Is Ballad Avadain here?" Panna asked. The old woman stared blankly, so she tried again. *"En alla Ballad Avadain?"*

"I'm right here," said a voice to one side.

A young winged man stood in the doorway. Just as Ferris had complained, he wore his hair cut Prian short. A blue scarf hung around his neck in acquiescence to the necessities of Stray, but the rest of his clothes were Prian, too. Denims with ragged and often-patched knees, sturdy boots and a black leather jacket with long gashes up the back where his wings jutted through. Panna wondered if she imagined the Prian squareness to his features. It was not as if humans and Arcadians could interbreed.

"Who are you?" Ballad asked. "You want something?"

He stalked into the room, followed by another similarly dressed young fairy. The pair eyed Panna and Anthem suspiciously. Panna crossed her arms over her narrow chest.

"Stop that," she said. "We're not your enemies. No one in Kaellisem is."

Ballad stopped his circling and narrowed suspicious olive-green eyes at Panna.

"You're Arcadian," he said, frowning. "What the hells happened to your wings?"

"I had them removed," Panna answered. Her face was flaming, she knew. She felt the heat in her cheeks like a sunburn.

"Why?" Ballad asked.

"That's none of your business. And not really relevant right now. I'm not the one who wanted to see you," Panna said. She gestured toward Anthem. "This is Sir Anthem Calloren, the queen's consort and first of her knights."

Panna stood back. Let Anthem deal with the prickly Prian Arcadian boy. Ballad scowled at the knight.

"Consort?" he asked. "Queen Maeve's got a hawk. He's a friend of mine. Maybe you've met him... Tall, human, got a hand made of illonium. Good fighter."

"As am I." Anthem strode across the room to peer closely at the much younger fairy. "And I am Queen Maeve's consort now. Do you challenge my right to court her?"

Ballad's jaw clenched. "Ain't my place. Logan should have the pleasure of ripping you apart."

"Logan Coldhand has agreed to the situation."

"Like hells. He would *never*–"

"He has agreed," Anthem said with blade-edged finality. "This is the queen's decree. And it is also her wish that you become first of my students and newest knight of the White Kingdom."

Ballad's mouth worked a moment before the sound came out.

"You want *me* to be a knight? A proper glass knight?" he asked.

"Queen Maeve Beltain Cavainna summons you to honor and glory," Anthem said in a ringing, formal tone. "Will you answer her call, Ballad Avadain? Will you take up your spear for your queen and your people?"

"Yes!" Ballad answered fiercely. "Yes, I'll fight!"

The other Arcadians sang out short, bright cries of pride and pleasure. Anthem held out his hand to Ballad, who hesitated and then clasped the other man's wrist.

"I still don't like you," Ballad told him.

"But we both serve the queen," Anthem said.

"No," Panna corrected. "We all serve Arcadia."

Anthem and Ballad shared a look, then nodded in agreement.

[18]

DUE

"Taxes are an investment in the future."

- CWA PUBLIC CAMPAIGN SLOGAN (210 PA)

"Anthem Calloren?" Xia asked. "Are you sure that's his name? Long hair, dark eyes? Awkward Aver?"

"That's him," Duaal said.

"I know the man. At least, I've spoken with him," Xia said.

She leaned forward, propping her elbows on the dining room table as her eyes turned a pale blue-green. Her lunch still sat on the top, untouched.

"What?" Kessa asked. She repositioned Baliend on her knee and the baby giggled. "When?"

"Remember when we first brought you to Stray? We were trying to find out if the Sisterhood had any groups here," Xia said. "I spoke with an Arcadian prostitute. That was Anthem."

"Are you sure it's the same man? He says he's a knight," Gripper said. The big Arboran perched precariously on a chair far too small for him and the plastic creaked in protest at his every movement. "Is he lying?"

"No, I don't think so," Xia answered. "Anthem mentioned having once been a knight. *In service to the Night*, I think he said."

"You remember that, Silver?" Gripper asked, impressed.

Xia smiled modestly. "It was only a year ago. As I understand it, *a'shae* – what Ferris always calls Maeve – means *the night*. Anthem must have worked for the royal family."

"He used to be Xartasia's man back when she went by *Titania*," Duaal said. "She and Anthem apparently traded several oathsongs. The two were effectively engaged."

"Wait, Anthem was engaged to Xartasia?" Kessa asked. In her lap, Baliend whined. "Does Maeve know that?"

"Glass knows," Gripper said. "So does Hunter. He's the one who convinced her to take Anthem. Hunter told her that it's a good political move. Anthem chose Glass over Xartasia and everyone in Kaellisem will know it."

"Logan *wants* Maeve to do this?" Kessa asked. "But... why?"

"I don't know, Blue. He told me what he said to Glass last night, but he didn't tell me why he said it." Gripper clasped his long arms around his knees. "Sometimes I don't think Hunter feels like he's good enough for Glass. Especially since this queen thing."

"That's silly," Kessa said. "They're perfect for each other."

Xia picked up her fork and rolled it between her smooth silver fingers.

"Perhaps. But there *are* issues," she said. "Their different lifespans, for example. Arcadians live for nine centuries or more. Maeve is only two hundred. If he can learn to take care of himself, Coldhand might survive another hundred years. And they can't breed. Humans and Arcadians don't have similar enough redprints."

"Slow down there," Duaal protested. "You *know* there is more to it than just how perfect your children will be."

Xia looked across the table and her antennae curled. "Look, I'm not saying I agree with their decision, but the Arcadian government has been a hereditary monarchy for ten thousand years. That black hair means a lot to them. If Maeve doesn't take an Arcadian mate, that part of their history will be lost forever."

"That doesn't mean that she should have to drop Logan," Duaal argued.

Gripper nodded emphatically. "Politics don't mean anything up against love."

But to his shock, Kessa actually frowned. She ran blunt fingers through Baliend's fine black hair and the baby boy sucked seriously on his chubby blue toes.

"If love really won all battles," Kessa said, "then I wouldn't have had to run away from Axis."

"But you're here, Blue," Gripper protested. "With your husband and baby and a nice little house. Your love *did* win!"

"Only after I gave up everything," Kessa said. "Even then, it took a lot of luck to get here. And Maeve is trying to save a lot more than one family."

Vyron pulled the thick scarf back up around his mouth. As the sun set and the temperature dropped, the wind was whipping up and filling the deepening twilight with red dust. He bent nearly double to hear Xyn.

"What?" he asked his employer. "What did you say?"

"That I'm starving," Xyn grumped. "Where's the food?"

"We paid for all this," Vyron reminded the Ixthian. "Duke Ferris wanted a feast, but we couldn't afford it."

Xyn groaned. "Damn it. How can these people basically live in diamond towers and still be so poor?"

The two men were walking – slowly to match Xyn's short stride – down the central road of Kaellisem. Towers rose up around them, slender and pointed as a line of spears. Arcadians flew overhead like huge birds, singing as they soared through the darkening sky.

Coreworlders walked and drove along the road below them. Not as numerous as the fairies, but more than Vyron had expected. They moved in close, curious groups through the flame-colored shadows of Kaellisem.

"Who the hells are all these people?" Xyn asked. He frowned at a nearby family of Lyrans. "This is an Arcadian coronation."

Vyron laughed. "Did you forget your wings at home? You're not Arcadian, either. You don't even like them."

"Well, I *am* footing the bill for this whole thing," Xyn said. "And I'm curious."

"So are they." Vyron nodded to the Lyrans, who had stopped to admire an arch of ruby-colored glass.

A horn blared behind them and Vyron pulled Xyn off to the side of the road. A black police car floated by on its cloudy orange null-field and bright lights flashed on top.

"What do they want out here?" Xyn asked. "We never see cops in Gharib."

Vyron wasn't sure. He broke into a jog and then a run, following the police car through Kaellisem's narrow streets and leaving Xyn to curse in the road behind him.

Kaellisem was a small town and Vyron was barely winded when he caught up with the police. They had stopped at Kaellisem's edge, where the Arcadian towers gave way to desert once more. The patchwork stage where Maeve had given her first speech had been replaced by a polished plateau of multi-colored glass. The sun was a tiny sliver of red on the horizon and Stray's single moon shone the color of pewter between the sparse lavender clouds. For now, the glass stage was empty.

Two thousand Arcadians and coreworlders drew back from the police car. Vyron could just make out several more parked around the edge of the crowd. People muttered unhappily.

Two humans stepped out of the car Vyron had followed – a man and a woman, both with white-filmed Hadrian eyes. Their hands remained close to the lasers on their belts. Vyron smoothed his hair and put on his best salesman's smile.

"Good evening, officers," he said, waving to the cops. "What can we do for you?"

"We heard you folks are planning to crown up a fairy queen," said the female police officer. A black plastic badge on her shoulder read *Janse.*

"That's right," Vyron answered slowly. "Is there a problem? It's going to be a peaceful affair."

"Stray already has a government," Janse said. "You can't create a sovereign nation on our planet. You establish a formalized government and that's exactly what you'll have."

A shadow fell across Vyron and an Arcadian man landed beside him. Vyron had heard of Duke Ferris and seen him a few times, but never met the old fairy noble. Ferris' hair was only half braided and the sash that held his silver robes closed was hastily tied.

"What is the meaning of this?" he demanded of the two Gharib cops. "This is an Arcadian matter! You have no right to be here."

Vyron groaned inwardly. Duke Ferris was *not* helping the situation. The Dailon brightened his smile.

"It's alright," Vyron said. "These officers are just here to discuss some legal issues."

"You have no right or ability to found a sovereign nation on this planet," Janse told Ferris. "That is rebellion under CWA law."

"We're not trying to," Vyron answered quickly. "Arcadians aren't Alliance citizens, right?"

"Right," Janse agreed.

"Well, then they can't really rebel, can they? They're just setting up a sort of enclave," Vyron said.

The two cops looked at each other, unconvinced. Vyron ran his tongue over his teeth, thinking fast. A year ago, Kessa had to all but bribe the Gharib police into helping Maeve and the rest of the Blue Phoenix crew. They were not out here on the fringes of their city to enforce Alliance law. That was CWAAF's job, as they had told Kessa a year ago. These cops wanted something else.

"The Arcadians are just building up a small population center," Vyron told them. "Like any of the apartment blocks all over Gharib. Maeve Cavainna is simply a community leader."

Still nothing from the humans. Vyron sighed.

"They'll need to pay all municipal taxes, naturally."

There. Slow smiles spread across both of the cops' faces. Vyron licked suddenly dry lips and looked back along the road. Xyn came puffing and panting up the street, scowling at Vyron. The nervous Dailon turned back to the cops.

"Taxes...?" Duke Ferris bristled and shook his finger at the cops. "Taxes paid to a government that ignores the plight of our people?"

"We *want* them to keep ignoring you," Vyron hissed under his breath. "Be quiet!"

"We need to collect the first quarter's worth of taxes," Janse said. "As a gesture of good will."

"Of course," Vyron agreed. "Duke Ferris, can you go collect the color from Queen Maeve?"

"How much money will they require?" Ferris asked quietly. "We do not have very much."

"It doesn't matter," Vyron answered. He just wanted Ferris gone before the fairy duke's pride made things worse. "Uh, a hundred cenmarks should cover it."

Ferris looked worried, but flew away toward the colorful glass dais. The male police officer went to his sleek black squad car and called to the other cops. Janse folded impressively muscled arms over her chest and regarded Vyron, who cleared his throat uncomfortably and waved urgently to Xyn. The scientist waddled over and squinted at Vyron. The Dailon wondered why he did that. Xyn was Ixthian. Surely his parents had bred him with better eyes than that.

"So what is this?" Xyn puffed. "You're not in cuffs yet."

"I need your blackchip," Vyron told him.

"What?" Xyn scowled and pressed his six-fingered hands protectively to his pockets.

"They–" Vyron gestured toward the two police officers, then out to the other squad cars. "–came to warn us that Kaellisem is behind on their taxes. If we can give them the money now, Janse and her fellows will deliver it and make sure we don't accrue any penalties."

"Oh?" Xyn asked. He curled his stubby silver antennae at Vyron. "That's awful fine of them. How much does the crown owe?"

"One thousand cenmarks," Janse supplied.

"A *thousand*?" Xyn said.

His round face pinched and the Ixthian's compound eyes went a dark red, but Xyn took a black plastic credit chip from his wallet and handed it to Janse. The Gharib cop took a slender reader from her pocket and swiped the black square of plastic through it. Xyn thumbprinted the transaction and snatched it back. Janse eyed the reader until the blinking green light turned blue. Then she smiled at Vyron and Xyn.

"You're paid up for the next month," she told them.

"One *month...?*" Xyn asked. The Ixthian's cheeks were turning a subtle scarlet under his thick skin. "But you said–"

"Thanks," Vyron interrupted. "We'll see you next month."

The two cops got back into their car. The null-field hummed as the sleek black vehicle rose a foot into the air, pivoted smoothly and drove away. Xyn was turning purple.

"One thousand cenmarks?" he said again, flapping his arms in agitation. "You didn't even try to negotiate with them, Vyron! What the hells kind of salesman are you? You're fired!"

"You pay half that every month just to keep Unbreakers' doors open," Vyron pointed out. "And you used to pay even more before you hired me."

"Exactly! So why didn't you try to talk those sharks down?"

"We don't need to give them any excuses to drive Maeve and her Arcadians out. Let's keep the cops happy and far away, alright?"

Xyn struggled for an answer. The sun was gone now and the sky grew swiftly dark but for the sparse light of scattered stars. Ferris landed softly and looked around for the cops.

"Where have they gone?" he asked.

"Already paid off and on their way back into Gharib," Vyron told the duke. "But bad news. It's going to cost you a thousand cen each month to keep Kaellisem in operation."

"One thousand?" The fairy sounded just like Xyn. But his sharp-angled face didn't fold up in anger like the Ixthian's had. Ferris only nodded. "Very well. We will need to speed production."

"Production?" Vyron asked. "Of what?"

"Glass," Ferris answered. "We have nothing else to export from Kaellisem and the coreworlds have nothing quite like it."

"That's pretty much manufacturing diamond. Not many people on Stray can afford that," Xyn pointed out. "Other than those cops."

"Most of your clients are the owners of starships, are they not?" Ferris asked. "Surely they can pay for our work."

"You might be surprised," Xyn said. He had to speak up over the rising murmur of the waiting crowd. "Myles never seemed to have enough color to make half a rainbow."

"Not just diamonds," Vyron told Xyn. "Think of all the glassteel and fused ceramics in a ship. The Arcadians can make stuff much stronger just by singing to the sand."

"What about your supply chain?" Xyn asked with a flip of his hands. "I suppose you want me to set that up. Make introductions, pay for permits."

The look that Ferris gave Xyn was shrewd.

"Right now, the Arcadian crown will never be able to repay the money owed on behalf of our people," Ferris said. "You would be enabling us to repay your kindness."

"But Xyn's right that building out a new enterprise is a lengthy process," Vyron interjected. He fought to keep the smirk off his face. "It's going to take a major investment of time and personnel hours."

"We would be pleased to take on most of that burden," Ferris offered with a politician's smile. "It is our own industry we seek to build, after all."

"But you're going to be working hard just to produce the glass," Vyron pointed out. "You can barely keep up with the needs of your own city. Besides, *we're* the ones that the local ship captains know and sort of trust. You'd lose more in buying their business than any percentage we ask for."

"And what portion *are* you asking for, Master Fethru?"

"Twenty," Vyron said.

Duke Ferris covered his surprise quite well, the Dailon thought, except that he was blinking too much.

"A fifth of our income?" Ferris said. "We have a city's population to feed and house on these proceeds. The crown could only give up five percent and still be able to care for her people."

Vyron cocked his head. "We can expand your distribution much further than you ever could alone. Better a loss of fifteen percent of more money than keeping all of none."

Ferris' pointed ears turned red, but his tone remained civil, even urbane. The man was born and bred nobility, Vyron thought.

"In the greater interest of providing for all Kaellisem, the crown could probably give up a tenth of the money earned," Ferris said reluctantly. "I will have to speak with the queen about the matter."

"Ten percent," Vyron agreed. "That doesn't include the cost of shipment, but we can negotiate a good rate for you. I'm sure Maeve will approve. We'll talk to her about it tomorrow. She has enough to worry about tonight."

"Yes, she does," Ferris agreed. A little sullenly. "I should return to her side. She will be pleased to know that the Gharib police are dealt with, if not the cost at which it was done."

"Please extend our apologies to Queen Maeve," Vyron said with a smooth smile. "And tell her that we'll work together to more than make up for the loss."

Ferris nodded once and leapt into the air. Vyron let himself grin and turned back to Xyn. The Ixthian scientist stared at Vyron with wide, bright blue eyes. His antennae twitched so hard and fast that they were nearly vibrating.

"Ten percent of an entire town's profits from a brand new and exclusive product," Vyron said. "You'll be wanting to hire me back on, I assume. And I'm going to need a raise."

———— • • • ————

Maeve stood in the door of the little room under the glass mesa. There were no windows, just the translucent patches and colorful streaks that ran through the cloudy material.

The only fresh air came in through the door. So that was where Maeve stood, panting and wondering why her lungs couldn't seem to do their ridiculously singular job. She felt faint.

"Just breathe, my queen," Anthem said again.

Maeve whirled toward the knight. "I am breathing! What else do you think I am doing? Gods, if only I could…"

"You are shouting," Anthem pointed out, unfazed.

Maeve stalked across the sandy floor.

"Where is Logan?" she asked, still shouting.

"Outside," her new consort reminded her. "He took Malla and Hannu. Since Duke Ferris told us of the Gharib police, Coldhand is watching the perimeter against further intrusion."

"He should be here," Maeve fumed. She couldn't pace far in the small room, even less when crowded with people.

"Coldhand is doing his duty," Anthem said. "And we are already late to begin yours."

"I cannot do this!" Maeve cried. "I… I was wrong. I am no queen! I cannot wear the crown."

"But you have to, Maeve," Panna told her. "Remember Xartasia. Remember the Devourers. Remember your people. We need you."

Duaal lounged in a corner of the tiny glass chamber. His velvet coattails brushed the sand, leaving a red blush of dust on the deep blue fabric.

"It's just a little glass hat, Maeve," he said. "You've already done the hardest parts. And Panna is right – this isn't for you. This is for them."

Duaal gestured to the wall behind him. Maeve could just make out the indistinct blur of the crowd outside, gathered on the dune's slope. Maeve gulped.

"I need Logan," she said. "I cannot do this alone."

Duaal nodded and reached into his beaded sapphire coat for a com, but Duke Ferris stood in the door and gestured to Maeve.

"It is time to go," he said.

"Call Logan," Maeve told Duaal.

"No, a'shae," Ferris said. "You must be up on that stage with Sir Anthem and he alone."

"You will be there!" Maeve hissed at the old nobleman.

"Someone must crown you, my lady," Anthem said. "It is time to go."

He held his hand out to Maeve. His long blond hair had been washed and intricately braided down his back. The knight was dressed in a plain white robe of the sort that squires wore on the night of their vigil. His feet and hands were bare. Maeve lifted her hand to his. Her glass gauntlet shook so hard that the fine crystal plates rang off one another.

Maeve felt like an imposter, a liar. She had no right to wear the armor of a knight, much less the crown of the White Kingdom.

It wasn't the true crown of her home, she reasoned. King Illain's birchwood crown had perished with him when the Devourers took the White City. There were no trees at all on Stray, so Duaal's circlet wasn't even a good approximation. It was not at all the same thing...

It didn't work. Maeve couldn't make herself believe her own lie, even for a moment.

But the others were right. No one needed her to believe. They needed her to *do*.

She took Anthem's hand, gripping hard. If she hurt the knight, he gave no sign. With her new consort in tow, Maeve stormed out and onto the glass stage to the choral cheers of her people. Duke Ferris followed, the glass crown of Kaellisem cradled delicately in his hands.

There was more than a bit of awkwardness after the coronation. Maeve and Anthem were left alone at the top of her tower, and Duke Ferris made it quite clear that Maeve's rooms were Anthem's. He was her consort and was to share her tower, her responsibilities, her life and her bed.

Maeve stared at her reflection in the mirror, at the glass crown nestled in her black hair. It really was beautiful, she had to admit. She would tell Duaal so in the morning. The circlet was simple, elegant and regal. Delicate red and gold scrollwork wound through the glass like Stray's blazing wind given form.

The queen removed her crown and set it down on its cushion. There were no clouds in the sky and the starlight sparkled off the glass. She turned away to find Anthem waiting for her in front of the window. His white wings were luminous in the darkness.

"Are you planning to stay?" Maeve asked.

"I am your consort, a'shae," Sir Anthem answered. "I will protect you until the dawn... when that duty belongs to Logan Coldhand again."

Maeve sat and began unpinning her dark hair. Dain and Verra had offered to help, but with Anthem there, Ferris had let Maeve send the girls away. It had been a long night and despite his general fascination with preserving every tradition of the White Kingdom,

Ferris seemed more interested in giving his queen some quality time with her new consort.

Maeve's black hair fell around the glass shoulders of her armor and she dug her fingers under one shining pauldron, then pried at the knotted cords that held it in place. Maybe she shouldn't have refused Dain and Verra's assistance.

"Do you need help?" Anthem asked.

"No," Maeve said. "I will manage."

She pinched and picked until the cord finally released and the curved glass plate clattered to the floor. Maeve winced at the noise and looked at Anthem. The knight stood still against the backdrop of Stray's dark sky and bright white stars, watching her. A shiver ran up Maeve's spine and she turned away, yanking on another strap of her armor.

"Let me help you, my queen," Anthem said. "You will never get to sleep if you spend all night undressing."

"Sleep?" Maeve asked, not looking at him. "Do you intend to let me sleep, Sir Anthem? Or do you intend to keep me awake into the morning?"

"I will do whatever you wish me to, a'shae."

Maeve yanked off one of her gauntlets and let it clatter to the tower floor. "Whatever I wish? And if I told you to leave?"

"I am to protect you," Anthem answered. "I will leave the room, if you wish, but I cannot go far."

"Then what is the point?" Maeve hissed. She glared venom at the other knight. "You loved my cousin. How can you give yourself to me?"

Anthem's eyes shone and he bowed his head. "There are more important things than love. Titania has turned to destruction. *Allu ma'saena...* It wounds me that in one day, I learned that my beloved lives and that she has become my enemy. But my pain and my love do not stop the worlds' turning."

Maeve shook her head and gave her armor another yank.

"Help me with this," she told Anthem. He nodded and began carefully untying the chords. Maeve was still furious. "Do you love her still, even after what she has done?"

Anthem hesitated as he worked at Maeve's intricately wrought breastplate.

"I do not know. I love my Titania. But this White Queen, Xartasia... She is someone else, I fear. I do not know my enarri anymore," Anthem said. He moved to stand in front of Maeve, brows furrowed as he detangled Maeve's long black hair from a joint between two plates of glass. "But in time, I think we may be able to love each other, a'shae. You remind me much of Titania in her youth. There are differences, but..."

Maeve's stomach churned and she wondered if she would be sick. Her skin was hot all over and the horrid sensation seemed to be pushing through like needles.

"You think that you could love me?" Maeve asked. "There are so many things you do not know about me. I fight Xartasia, but you should know that my sins are no less than hers."

Anthem frowned and finished unfastening Maeve's breastplate. He carefully put it aside on the stand that Verra had brought but she had entirely ignored.

"I do not understand, my queen," he said.

"It was me. I opened the Tamlin Waygate," Maeve told him. The painful swirl in her stomach became a boiling storm. "My brother wanted to see his lover and so I opened the gate in his stead. When I failed, it triggered some internal mechanism that called back to its creators, the Devourers. By unhappy chance, they actually heard that call and came."

"*Asi allu?*" Anthem asked. *That was you?*

"Yes," Maeve said. "And I have spent every day since trying to atone for what I did. Out of shame, I tried to die... That is how I met Logan. I placed a bounty on my own head. Xartasia called Tamlin a mere accident, the fall of our kingdom, but..."

She trailed off, unsure how to put the complex emotions into words. Xartasia's forgiveness was true but tainted by her own crimes and bloody ambitions. The fault was not Maeve's, but belonged to the black-storm Devourers who tore Caith from the air and eaten him while he screamed in the bloodstained grass.

Still, the pain had never left Maeve. It was a deep scar, at least as terrible as the one through Logan's heart.

Anthem removed Maeve's remaining gauntlet and slid it onto the stand.

"I was a prostitute," he said. "Has your Ixthian friend, Xia, told you that yet?"

"No," Maeve admitted.

She hadn't seen the doctor much in the last few days. There was so much to do.

"I am a knight," Anthem said. "I could have found other work. I could have at least died honorably after the White Kingdom's fall. But I was lost, Maeve. Titania was gone. My home was gone. I had nothing."

Maeve suddenly remembered seeing him dressed in blue and silver rags, the colors of House Calloren. She recalled the woman who took Anthem away after Xia spoke to him. She remembered the rage, the disgust... and then that she had done nothing. Maeve and Xia had just walked away.

"We have all done terrible things," Anthem said. "Panna Sul cut off her own wings so she could have a life among the humans. Duke Ferris told me that he left his only living child back on Sunjarrah so that he could serve Kaellisem. She is in a prison hospital and he doubts that she will survive to see him again. We have all done what we must."

Maeve's teeth ground and her jaw ached. What Anthem told her was true. Every Arcadian had their own tale of pain and shame. It hurt, but it was a terrible sort of relief, as well. Maeve wasn't alone.

She wasn't the only one who had failed. And Logan – her scarred and tormented hunter – wasn't the only one who could understand.

"I wanted to tell them," Maeve said, stabbing one wing toward the window and the spires of Kaellisem. "I have no desire to keep these secrets!"

"But to fight Xartasia, we must be unified," Anthem said. "If you drive them away now, no one will stand between your cousin and trillions of Alliance lives. I think you are right not to tell them this secret."

"Then tell me," Maeve said. "Do you still think that you could love me?"

"Yes," Anthem said. "Will you ever love me, a'shae?"

Maeve turned away from the knight. "I can manage the rest of my armor, Sir Anthem. There is another room across the hall. Make yourself comfortable there."

Anthem stepped back and lowered his wings.

"Yes, my queen," he said. "Sleep well."

[19]
NEVER TELL

"There are truths and lies. In between, there are secrets."

- LOGAN CENTRA (234 PA)

Ferris had planned to sell finished art and arms, pieces of Arcadian culture, but Vyron argued that the real money was in fabrication. Fairy glass was much easier and cheaper to produce than the plastics used in ship and starscraper windows. It would be useful as an electronics insulator, too, Vyron pointed out. The glass didn't require the same curing time that ceramics did or the energy costs of high-fire processes.

Maeve agreed with Vyron. There was training time to consider, too. Hyra and Lorren were already working long days to train the hundreds who had volunteered to learn their craft. To create the sort of fine work that Ferris wanted to export would require years of training and practice, but it took only a few weeks to learn the basic songs, those used to sing the sand into simple, flat sheets of glass.

The structure was very simple, Panna said. Even the newest and least skilled Arcadians had little trouble holding the basic honeycomb molecular structure in their mind. Kaellisem's first exported glass was too cloudy and impure for use in windows or anything else that someone had to see through, but served as a cheap and effective insulator.

There was an incident aboard the Nova Jumper, when a sample sheet contained too much iron and exploded as a nearby magnetic clamp activated. But no one was in the engine room at the time and Vyron quickly smoothed over the incident by promising replacements and a percentage share from any Arcadian wares shipped out aboard the Nova Jumper. Maeve apologized in person to the ship's Lyran captain and mechanic. The two wolfin women agreed that it was just the growing pains of a new industry and that they were still simply glad to be involved at this early stage. Both grinned with sharp teeth at the little Arcadian queen and then hurried back onto their cargo ship.

Vyron crossed his arms as the Nova Jumper vanished up into Stray's pale sky.

"Those two-faced bitch harpies," he said cheerfully. "They absolutely loathe fairies. We tried to hire the Nova a month ago and they wouldn't even entertain the idea. Now that there's a profit..."

Vyron trailed off, shaking his head. Maeve shaded her eyes and surveyed the rest of Gharib's dusty landing crescent.

"Do you think they faked the explosion?" she asked.

"Maybe," Logan answered. He stood on Maeve's other side. "But unlikely. Ferris says that there actually have been some production issues. They're running out of usable sand near Kaellisem. The further they have to go for sand, the fewer hours are being put in on sifting and singing it."

Maeve nodded without looking at the Prian hunter. "Even the best sand we can find in Gharib is not pure enough. We need pure carbon and silicon, not the iron and copper that color the sand here. Is there a better source on Stray?"

"Um," Panna said, thumbing through one of the datadexes she always seemed to be carrying these days. "Actually, the polar sand is lighter than at the equator, where we are now. Want me to put together an estimate on shipping some down to Kaellisem?"

"Yes," Maeve answered. Panna smiled and took a note.

"I can help with that," Vyron offered.

"Thanks," Panna said. "Do you think any of your contacts might be willing to make some runs for us? Moving that much sand in a ship would be a lot easier than by truck."

"Use the Blue Phoenix," Logan told her. "Don't pay some other local captain for such a short flight. They'll cheat you. There are too many Arcadians looking for work, more than Hyra can train. They can help load the Blue Phoenix."

"Good idea," Panna said. She took another note. "There's a city nearby called Bherrosi. We'll need to pay someone there to let us collect the sand. But they've got a bad reputation for treatment of Arcadians up there. Some of our first people came from Bherrosi."

"Talk to them," Maeve told Panna. "Collect the names of anyone that we may need to pay off and I will speak with Anthem. We will send the best of his new knights to Bherrosi with the Blue Phoenix to protect our workers."

"We still need to tell Captain Sinnay that we want to fill his ship with sand," Panna pointed out with a smile. "Duaal's not going to like that."

"He will understand," Maeve said. "He helped us so much. This is a small thing when held against what Duaal has already done... and what lies ahead."

Panna nodded. "I think he likes getting to work with a queen. It makes him feel important."

"Because he is," Maeve said. She searched her scarlet sash for her com, found it and switched it on. "Duaal? Can you hear me?"

"I hear you," came Duaal's voice from the device, echoing a bit. "What can I do for you, little fairy queen?"

Maeve related Logan and Panna's plan. As she had anticipated, the Blue Phoenix's captain was quick to agree.

"I'll let Gripper know to fuel us up. We've been grounded for weeks now," Duaal said. "It'll be good to fly. Can't let my extensive skills atrophy. Are you and Logan going to be coming along?"

"No. Only some of Anthem's knights to keep the others safe in Bherrosi."

There was a pause on the other end of the line. "Anthem's only been working on those new knights for a few weeks, Maeve. Maybe you better send Anthem himself. To make sure the job gets done right. We want this to go well."

Maeve considered that. She glanced at Panna, who shrugged at her.

"The knight stuff is Sir Anthem's area or expertise," Panna said. "Not mine. I have no idea how the training is going."

"That is a good idea," Maeve told Duaal through her com. "I will ask him."

"Great," Duaal answered. "Well, I better talk to Gripper. Have a nice time queening."

Maeve thanked her friend and then turned off the com. Panna and Vyron were already talking about distribution of the new glass. Logan watched Maeve, expressionless. She walked back to the car and the other three fell into step beside her.

When had Logan last played his battered guitar? The last time that Maeve could remember was that night on Sunjarrah, sitting on top of the Blue Phoenix, under the stars. Had he touched the instrument at all since then? Frowning, Maeve watched her hunter. He was scanning the landing fields, searching for any potential dangers to the Gray Queen. Maeve doubted his guitar had been touched in weeks and she longed to hear him play.

The thought made her heart ache. But what good would it do? Logan Coldhand was neither her lover nor one of her people. She had no right to ask him to live his life any particular way.

Logan held the car door for Maeve and then closed it behind her. Through the window, Maeve saw the Talon-9 on Logan's hip, the metal and ceramic scarred by age and use but freshly polished. The weapon certainly had not been neglected.

Maeve leaned forward in the front seat, trying in vain to make room for her swiftly cramping wings. No one in the core made cars for Arcadians. It would have been much more comfortable to fly, but Logan had no wings. What good was a guardian if she left him behind? Ferris had pointed out several times that Anthem and the Arcadian knights he was training could easily fly with their queen. Maeve had to admit that he was right about that.

She sighed and crossed her arms on the sun-heated dashboard as her companions and guard climbed into the car. Logan grabbed the hot steering wheel with his unfeeling illonium hand and started the engine.

"Hm, would you mind dropping me off at home?" Vyron asked. "Baliend's teething again – he's on his third set already – and Kes needs a hand."

"Sure," Logan said.

Vyron and Panna sat quietly in the back seats behind Maeve, each with a datadex in hand. Occasionally, they conferred on some financial point, but kept their voices lowered. Logan drove in utter silence, eyes riveted to Gharib's cracked and dusty roads. He delivered Vyron to his home, where Kessa waited at one of the windows. She held Baliend against her shoulder and waved. Maeve raised her hand and waved back.

"Would you like to come in for dinner?" Vyron asked, pausing in the middle of climbing out. He stuck his head back into the car. "If you don't mind listening to Baliend screech a little bit, we'd love to have you over."

Maeve looked over to Panna and Logan.

"Do I have plans this evening?" she asked.

"I'm afraid so," Panna answered. "Duke Ferris has asked to talk to you about the Bherrosi trip. Sir Anthem has three new potentials that you need to approve."

"Can I not do that with a call?" Maeve asked. "Do I truly need to return to Kaellisem?"

Panna cocked her head and frowned. "Sir Anthem's knights are the only sort of security or police force in Kaellisem. Do you really want to approve new knights without even meeting them?"

"No," Maeve sighed. "I suppose not."

Vyron made a sympathetic click with his tongue and looked at Logan. "What about you? I'm sure Panna could drive Maeve back into the glass city."

"No." Logan wasn't looking at Vyron as he gave his flat answer. "I'm working."

"...Alright, then," Vyron said. He glanced at Panna, who shook her head.

"No thanks," she said far more graciously than the Prian hunter had. "I'm working, too."

Vyron said goodbye and then went back to his family. Logan put the car into gear and pulled back out into the street. Maeve swallowed. Everyone remained uncomfortably silent as Gharib streaked past outside the windows.

The bloated sun was sinking swiftly, appearing to flatten like a rotting piece of fruit against the horizon. Maeve knew that Logan could have accepted Vyron's invitation. The training of Kaellisem's knight force was a largely outdoor business and took place during the daylight hours. Once night fell, Anthem was free to take up his more personal responsibilities with his queen.

In theory, Logan had plenty of time to spend visiting Vyron's family. Did he have some other plans? A date, perhaps? Something bitter churned in Maeve's stomach. She had no right to be possessive. But knowing that did nothing to banish the sick sensation.

The blocky concrete and sandstone of Gharib ended suddenly, giving way to rolling red desert. Then those sands turned into the sunset-colored spires of Kaellisem. The glass sparkled and seemed to dance in the fading sunlight like flames. Maeve forgot about her cramped wings and even about Logan's evening plans as they drove between the delicate crystal towers. Faces appeared in windows and doors, all framed by yellow hair and white wings. Not many vehicles came through Kaellisem. There were the trucks that picked up shipments of glass and the occasional curious visitor, but the hum of an engine usually meant royal business.

Panna touched the controls for her window and the tinted glass slid down. Hot, dry air blew into the car, full of fine dust and music. The Arcadians were all singing a high, clear song as the car glided past. Maeve couldn't make out the words – not over the rush of wind and the sound of the engine – but goosebumps rose between her wings.

Panna was staring out, biting her lip and managing to smile at the same time. She hummed along with Kaellisem as the small city welcomed their queen home. The song rang from the glass towers, making the desert air vibrate with a palpable energy. *Praise, thanks, purpose...* The rising harmonies spiraled around one another like a flock of birds soaring in perfect, natural formation.

"I... I have not heard this song before," Maeve said in a choked voice.

"It's been spreading around town for the last few days," Panna told her. "I don't know who first wrote it, but it's very popular."

Maeve slid her window down, too, and listened. Logan slowed the car until it was barely moving and nearly silent.

"*Lua en shae sammai,*" Kaellisem sang. "*Ae na pa'eru illanae mae. Lua ossinae shae ra.*"

Maeve blinked. "*Mae* and *ra?*"

Panna shrugged. "The rhyme's a bit awkward and I'm not sure about the *from bones* part, but it's beautiful."

"Yes," Maeve agreed. She leaned against the window frame and let her black hair fan out in the cooling air. In spite of the Arcadian words, the melody reminded her much more of Logan singing to Baliend. "It is beautiful."

Logan stopped the car in front of Maeve's gold glass tower and held the door for her again. The hunter remained silent as Panna bade them a smiling farewell and hurried off into the evening.

"I'll call Duke Ferris and Sir Anthem to let them know you're back," Panna said over her shoulder.

Maeve nodded and thanked the girl.

Logan climbed out of the car and followed Maeve up into the tower. She stopped in the kitchen – a small room with a few basic appliances with which Dain always managed to work miracles, but Maeve was far less skilled – and found some mycolar envelopes of condensed poultry. She tossed one to Logan. He caught it deftly in his right hand.

They went out to one of the many balconies that extended from the tower's curving walls. The underside was fluted like a seashell and rippled with captured twilight. Maeve tore the top off the packaged chicken with her teeth, then squeezed the pale yellow protein and vitamins into her mouth. The wonders of coreworld food... She didn't even have to chew.

The cooling air against the daylight-heated sands of the desert made the wind gust unpredictably. It tugged Maeve's filmy crimson dress around her ankles and rustled her feathers. The wind caught her emptied dinner envelope and tugged it away and the shiny mycolar flashed once, then vanished into the evening.

"I think I was supposed to heat that," Maeve said.

She ran her tongue over her teeth. The slightly grainy protein stuck stubbornly to them. Logan held the other poultry pack unopened in his hand.

"Still hungry?" he asked.

"A little," Maeve admitted.

Logan went inside the tower and heated the ground chicken in the microwave. He poured it into a bowl with some pepper and then returned with a spoon before handing it to Maeve. She took a tentative bite. The sludge still didn't taste good, but it was better than the cold gluey paste had been.

"Thank you," Maeve said as she finished. "I did not realize that I was so hungry."

Logan took the dishes away, then returned with a glass of water and Maeve drank thirstily. There must have been a lot of salt in the food. Something about sodium being a necessary component in a healthy nervous system... Another bit of interesting but ultimately unhelpful information from Xia.

Maeve rubbed her eyes. The makeup that Verra had painted on that morning smudged and Maeve frowned at the streaks of gold and bronze on her fingers.

Logan watched her closely. What must Maeve look like to those ice-blue eyes? A traitor...? One with wind-tangled hair and ruined makeup, no less. But Logan's expression was as unreadable as it ever had been during the year he hunted her.

Maeve squeezed her eyes shut against a sudden flurry of hot, sandy wind that blew already disarrayed hair into her face. She felt smooth coolness on her raw red cheek, brushing cold and careful across her skin. Maeve opened her eyes to find Logan pushing back her tangled black hair with his cybernetic left hand. The metal felt good in the Stray heat. Maeve leaned her face into his touch and put her hands over Logan's. The illonium was hard, unyielding beneath her fingertips.

"A'shae–" gasped a voice from the door behind them.

Maeve jumped guiltily and turned. Duke Ferris stared at them, scowling. Logan's hand dropped to his side once more.

Ferris schooled his expression into something less disapproving and cleared his throat. "Where are your handmaidens, my queen? It is not seemly that you should be unattended."

"I was not unattended," Maeve said, hating the tight, defensive note in her voice. "Logan was–"

The duke shot Logan such a look of venom that Maeve couldn't bring herself to finish the sentence.

"I suspect my handmaidens are upstairs somewhere, tending to something," she said instead. "We... I did not announce my arrival."

"I will have to speak to them about being more attentive," Ferris said – apparently to himself and inviting no answer from his audience. "Your consort, Sir Anthem, awaits you with his knights in the south field."

"Yes," Maeve answered quickly. "I will go at once."

"I shall fly with you, my queen," Ferris said. he managed to look imperiously up at the much larger and taller Logan Coldhand. "You are no longer needed tonight."

The Prian nodded once and turned to leave. He had not said a word since Ferris' abrupt arrival. Maeve reached toward Logan, but caught the duke watching and stopped herself.

Instead, Maeve flew further up the tower at Ferris' suggestion, and asked her handmaidens to fix her hair and makeup. The two girls efficiently did as she asked, faltering only when the duke chastened them for leaving the queen alone. Verra nodded as she wove ribbons into Maeve's hair while the younger Dain barely held back tears and withdrew downstairs to take care of the dishes.

"Please tell Dain not to worry," Maeve told Verra as the young woman finished painting her lips. "No harm was done."

"But see that it never happens again," Ferris said. Verra inclined her head and withdrew. The duke smiled tightly at Maeve's reflection and nodded. "We are late already. We should fly swiftly."

Maeve went to the wide window, spread her wings and leapt out into the sky.

It was a short flight to the south field, a half-acre expanse of sand and stone pounded more or less flat. There were several large glass rings rising above the desert floor on stout poles. White-winged men and women flew a tightly curving race that wound through them.

In the fading light, one of the flying fairies nearly collided with the translucent crystal. He folded his wings at the last moment and plummeted, landing with a loud thump on the ground. The trainee knight glared up at the ring, then caught sight of Maeve and Duke Ferris. He raised his closed fist and she recognized Ballad's close-cropped hair. She waved.

In the center of the training field, Sir Anthem stood with wings raised over his head like blades and holding a long, slender spear that streamed with brightly colored ribbons. His glass armor glittered with the sheen of an exotic gemstone.

Anthem raised his spear and called the other Arcadians to him. Ballad and the others – twenty-four in total – landed and arranged themselves into a pair of neat lines. Unlike their commander, these younger knights did not yet wear their glass armor and their spear blades were wrapped protectively in scarves.

They knelt as Maeve and Duke Ferris landed, lowering their heads. Anthem strode down the line and kissed the queen's hand.

"A'shae," he said. "Welcome. We are honored by your presence."

"You asked me to come," Maeve pointed out.

Somehow, despite a day of training, Anthem's hair remained in a neat but simple braid that fell in a golden line down between his long wings. Maeve was suddenly very embarrassed by the intricate, colorful coils of her own hair. What sort of knight wore her hair like that?

But Maeve hadn't put on her armor since the coronation or even held her spear in days.

"And... I am late," she added.

"I did ask," Anthem agreed. He smiled at Maeve and spread his arms. "But you are my lady and queen of the White Kingdom. The tides would wait for you."

"There are no oceans on Stray," Maeve said.

The nearest of the knights laughed. He was older than Maeve and a bit taller, with eyes almost the same tawny yellow as his hair.

He flushed and swept his wing across his chest in a salute again to cover his embarrassment.

"I am sorry, Your Majesty," he mumbled.

"It would have been funnier if it weren't true," Ballad said from further down the line. The Prian fairy boy had put aside his sliced leather jacket, but still dressed in the worn blue-gray denims he favored rather than the lighter, flowing fabrics of traditional Arcadian dress. "This sandball's as dry as a taxman's eyes at collection time."

The golden-eyed knight and several others tried to stifle their laughter. Anthem shook his wings, silencing them.

"Respect your queen," he said. "Without her, none of you would be here. It was her decree to train new knights."

"It is alright," Maeve assured them. "We need more laughter in Kaellisem. It has been a long and hard century."

Anthem's expression softened and he lowered his white wings. "As you say, a'shae. Please, let me introduce our newest."

He gestured to a pair of nearby young women, closer to Ballad's age than Maeve's. Both were slender and small, still showing the ravages of long years of malnutrition. Their pale skin was slicked with sweat and trembling from the day's training, but they stood up proudly straight when Anthem introduced them.

"Cyrene and Eranna," Anthem said. "Both from Farnum, here on Stray."

The two girls saluted Maeve, who returned the gesture. Strictly speaking, that wasn't traditional or proper – and Maeve could feel Ferris' eyes on her – but she had endured the knighthood training. She knew what Eranna and Cyrene had volunteered for.

Sir Anthem turned toward the older prospective knight, the one with the wolf-yellow eyes who had laughed at Maeve's comment. The knight fell at once to one knee.

"This is Syle," Anthem introduced him. "He just arrived from Axis last week."

"Thank you for your service, Syle," Maeve said, wishing that the other Arcadian would stop kneeling.

Syle rose slowly to his feet and fixed intent gold eyes on Maeve.

"It is my greatest honor to serve the queen," he said. "I will do anything she requires of me."

[20]
ENASSUI

"It's not about beauty. What's important is the inspiration behind the beauty."

- BALLAD AVADAIN (232 PA)

Ballad stood in front of the scuffed little porthole window long after Kaellisem had vanished from sight. The glass city was beautiful, a shining jewel out of legend for a boy born on hard gray Prianus, but that wasn't what arrested Ballad's attention. It was the crowd that had turned out to bid farewell to the knights and workers on their way to Bherrosi. It was hardly all of Kaellisem, but the two hundred or so Arcadians who came to sing their farewells was a vision that would not leave Ballad.

He had fought with his parents – and those just like them – for years, trying in vain to convince them to make something, *anything* of their new home on Prianus. But the Arcadians were resigned to their fate, to the disease and death that ran rampant across the planet. Ballad's own family never thought much of his desire to fight. Even when his younger sister, Aria, was raped and beaten to death by a gang of Prian boys, they would not raise a wing and sang sadly when Ballad did.

But Kaellisem wasn't like that. Almost half of the Arcadians there were younger than the queen. Ballad knew that Xartasia was rejecting those fairies born after the fall of their homeworlds. Malla and Hannu talked about it often, always quick to assure their fellow squires how glad they were that Xartasia sent them away. Not that anyone ever accused the siblings of lacking loyalty, as far as Ballad knew. Hannu and Malla had been the first of Maeve's guardians.

Her first Arcadian ones, at least. Logan Coldhand was truly the first, though. Back on Prianus, before anyone ever heard the name Kaellisem, Logan had been by the queen's side.

Ballad couldn't help but feel a little perhaps undue pride in his human friend. Logan had been so broken when Ballad met him in Pylos. But now he burned with purpose... If not with joy these days. Ballad glanced out of the corner of his eye at his commander.

Anthem had landed on the cargo hold's worn catwalk and was organizing the Arcadian volunteers as they stored the canisters, boxes and crates they had collected to hold and then transport the sand they would take from Bherrosi.

The senior knight was admittedly handsome and glorious in his shining glass armor and twined blue and silver scarves. The wingless girl, Panna, stood next to him, reading something out from a datadex. Her hair was pulled back in a tail, not even trying to hide the surgically altered curves of her ears. Unconsciously, Ballad's wings pulled close against his back. He couldn't imagine giving up his wings. But despite the twinge of revulsion, Ballad had to admit to some admiration for the wingless fairy girl. Surrounded by her own natural-born people, it must have been hard not to question her decision, but she never seemed to. Panna Sul was always busy, always smiling as she worked.

"What is so fascinating?" someone asked from next to Ballad. The voice had what he always thought of as the old world accent, even though Ballad knew perfectly well that *he* was the one with a strange Prian accent. "You are staring."

"Sorry," Ballad said. He turned to find one of the other knight trainees standing at the airlock, holding an armload of collapsible shovels. It was the one with the strange eyes that reminded Ballad of a Lyran. "Syle, right? Let me help you with those."

"Thank you." Syle allowed Ballad to take half of the awkward load and secure it into one corner of the Blue Phoenix's hold. "But you still have not answered my question."

Ballad gestured with the tip of one wing at where Anthem and Panna worked.

Syle smiled. "She is pretty, even mutilated as she is. Or perhaps you mean our lord commander, Sir Anthem. He, too, is lovely. You would not be the first to think him so."

"You mean Queen Maeve?" Ballad asked.

He caught himself scowling and tried to stop. Syle's smile was just as wolfish as his eyes. The older squire rolled up the sleeves of his shirt and finished hooking an orange cargo net around the pile of shovels.

"There were others before our queen," Syle said, lowering his voice. "I did not even realize that Sir Anthem survived the fall of Arcadia, and now I learn that he has spent the last hundred years selling himself to coreworlders."

"Selling...?" Ballad asked. "You mean that he was a whore? Sir Anthem?"

Syle nodded and Ballad looked up again. Sir Anthem Calloren was a prostitute? It was hard to imagine, but he knew that plenty of Arcadians had turned to the sex trade on Prianus and all across the Alliance. It was honest work, if dangerous, and Ballad couldn't hate Anthem for that. But Syle's yellow eyes were narrowed.

"It is strange, is it not?" he said, echoing Ballad's thoughts. "Sir Anthem is the paramount knight and consort to the queen herself, yet..."

Ballad could think of all too many ways to finish Syle's sentence. Anthem had given up, sold himself and refused to fight until Maeve Cavainna commanded him to.

Ballad turned away with a frown. Anthem was training them to be knights, the first knights since the White Kingdom's fall. Whatever else Ballad felt about the man, Sir Anthem deserved his respect for that.

But what about the queen? Was Anthem worthy of her?

Ballad's thoughts weren't comfortable – they tumbled heavily down into his chest and would not sit still. He looked for Syle, but the other squire had vanished into the crowd of busy Arcadians. Sir Anthem and Panna were gone, too, working elsewhere on the Blue Phoenix. Ballad stood under the swinging cargo net full of tools as the ship flew north over the desert.

"We'll have to make more than one trip," Panna told Anthem.

"If you say. I am here simply to keep you and your workers safe. Economics and industry are beyond me, I fear."

"You're the prince consort, Sir Anthem," Panna said. She pushed her datadex across the table to him. "You represent Queen Maeve when she isn't here."

"You can simply call the queen for any decisions that need to be made," Anthem pointed out.

Panna raised an eyebrow. "Yes, that's true. But something could go wrong. Gripper insisted on staying back in Kaellisem, for some reason. So if the com system breaks, we're on our own."

Anthem looked a little alarmed at this idea.

"That would be a problem," he said.

"And there's more than that," Panna told the knight. "You know what Maeve means to the people of Kaellisem. But without her on the Blue Phoenix, that's what you mean to them."

Panna waited for Anthem to sigh, to argue or to tell her that it wasn't really *that* important, but the royal consort just picked up the datadex and began to read. His brow furrowed as he struggled to read the Aver, but Sir Anthem otherwise worked quietly. Panna blinked a few times and stood, not sure what else to do. She was so used to arguing with Maeve that this felt like cheating somehow.

Panna cooked up a bowl of noodles, offered some to Sir Anthem – who declined politely – and then went up to the cockpit to see if Duaal was hungry. The Hyzaari captain sat in Tiberius' scarred old seat, eyes fixed on the clouds streaming by the Blue Phoenix. He actually jumped when Panna interrupted him.

"Bloody hells, woman," he gasped. "Don't do that!"

"Sorry," Panna apologized. "I just wanted to know if you wanted some lunch."

"Sure." Duaal glanced back over his shoulder, down the narrow corridor past Panna. "Where's Anthem?"

"In the mess. Do you need to talk to him?"

"God, no," Duaal said. "Just making sure he's not trying to call up Maeve."

"Why not?" Panna asked. "He *is* her consort. Anthem will probably need to talk to her at some point during this trip."

"Good luck with that," Duaal said with a laugh.

Panna blinked. "What?"

"The external coms don't work."

"Why not? Gripper said everything was ready!"

"It was," Duaal confided with a wink. "Gripper broke it before we left. And he can't repair it while he's back in Kaellisem, can he?"

"No," Panna agreed through gritted teeth. "He can't. Why under the bone heel of the Nameless would you do that?"

"Sir Anthem is going to leave Maeve and Logan alone for a few days," Duaal said, sounding quite smug and satisfied with himself. "And I'm sure that we'll run into a few other snags and delays along the way."

"Like contacting Bherrosi air control without external coms?" Duaal frowned. "Yeah, like that."

Maeve watched the Blue Phoenix vanish into the wispy pink clouds with an unexpected weight in the pit of her stomach. She had been first mate and then a passenger on the old ship for almost five years. Not very long in the lifespan of an Arcadian, really, but so much had changed in those years.

When Tiberius first found Maeve on Stray, she had been struggling clumsily to slit her own wrists with her spear. And now she was queen of a city of her own people. Maeve had not touched any chems or even a narcohol bottle in over a year. The bounty hunter she had hired to kill her was her ally now, her friend and...

Logan stood between Maeve and the small crowd that had gathered to sing their farewell to the Blue Phoenix. Several of Anthem's students had gone with the knight, leaving fourteen behind in Kaellisem. But it was the Prian with his mismatched arms crossed over his chest that held the little mob back from their queen. His pale eyes were cold and unyielding.

Maeve retreated from the relentless heat of the crimson sun and into the slightly cooler shadows of Kaellisem. She dismissed her remaining knights – led by Malla until Sir Anthem returned – at the door to her tower. Logan climbed the stairs beside her without a word. Sweat dripped down the back of his neck, soaking and darkening his hair. It stuck like damp feathers to his skin.

At the top of the tower, Dain was filling crystal bowls with some sort of scented oil while Verra struggled with a portable air conditioner. Both girls stopped their work and inclined their heads as Maeve entered the room.

"What can we do for you, Your Highness?" Verra asked.

"Nothing," Maeve answered quickly. "I am fine."

Despite her assurances, the Arcadian girls insisted on following Maeve as she went to the bathroom to rinse the sweat from her face. Dain offered to comb her hair and Verra suggested that it was time to polish the queen's nails again, but Maeve declined.

"Duke Ferris would like to see you at ten," Dain told her.

Suddenly, pointlessly preening her hair and nails didn't seem like such a bad idea. Maeve sighed. "Did he say why?"

"His Grace mentioned an enassui," Verra answered.

An enassui? Maeve had to admit that she was curious. That didn't sound much like the tedious sort of thing Duke Ferris usually wanted to discuss. She checked the clock next to the window. Nine forty-seven. Ferris would arrive soon.

Maeve's com chimed and Logan held it out. There had been nowhere to carry it in her dress.

Maeve pressed the worn button on the side. "Yes?"

"Hey, Glass. It's Gripper."

Maeve smiled at the little collection of metal and circuits. Yes, she had gathered that much. "What is it?"

"Um... Is Duke Ferris there?" Gripper asked, his voice flattened and tinny through the com.

"Not yet, though the girls say he wants to talk to me."

"Well, I... need you to come look at something," Gripper said. "You and Hunter. Both of you."

Maeve looked at Logan, who watched her without expression. Dain and Verra hovered in the doorway, supervising the queen and her guardian.

"What is it?" Maeve asked. "What requires our attention?"

"Just a... thing," Gripper said. He sounded nervous. "Out at the new tower."

Maeve didn't understand what Gripper needed, but didn't want to dismiss her friend's concerns. "I am sending Logan to you. I will join you as soon as I am finished with Duke Ferris. He wishes to talk about an enassui."

"Enassui?" Gripper asked. "What's that?"

"It is..." Maeve hesitated. Trying to explain Arcadian ways to non-fairies was like... like trying to tell them what it felt like to fly. They could *almost* understand. "It is rather like an opera. A story told in song before an audience. I have not heard one since the White Kingdom's fall."

"So this is important?" Gripper asked, crestfallen.

"Yes," Maeve said.

"Oh."

Feeling obscurely guilty, Maeve turned off the com and gestured to Logan. "You heard that?"

"I'll go take care of it," said the Prian hunter.

Maeve watched Logan leave, staring at the door long after Dain and Verra had scurried out of his path and the tall human vanished down the staircase. Dain asked if she wanted... something. Maeve ignored her.

Duke Ferris arrived a few minutes later, smiling broadly. Was it the enassui? Or was the old duke simply that pleased to find Logan absent? Maeve chastised herself for the thought. Duke Ferris' first and only loyalty was their people.

"Good morning, Your Grace," Maeve said, hoping that she didn't sound as sullen as she felt. "The girls tell me that you want to talk about an enassui."

Ferris turned his approving smile on the two handmaidens.

"Indeed so, a'shae," he said. "There is a troupe here in Kaellisem composing a new one."

A *new* enassui? Maeve blinked.

"I thought you simply meant a performance," she said. "There has not been one in a long time."

"No," Ferris agreed. "But the enassuanii have a new idea. A story of you, my queen."

"Me...?" Maeve asked. "That will not make for a very interesting performance."

"Do not underestimate your importance, a'shae," Ferris told her. "You are not only Kaellisem's leader, but her heart. And all songs, as they say, are sung first in the heart. The enassuanii wish to speak with you, Queen Maeve, and better learn about you for their songs. May I bring them to you?"

"Yes," Maeve said, torn between reluctance and excitement. "I would be happy to see them."

For all its glittering sunset-colored glory, Kaellisem was still a small city and it took Logan less than ten minutes to drive across it.

Hyra or one of his singers could have paved the road in glass, but Xia had recommended against it. Arcadian glass was strong, but vehicles were very heavy and the sand beneath was far from stable. Shattered glass in the road was a recipe for trouble.

Logan found Gripper exactly where the young Arboran said he would be, standing in the meager but colorful shade of a half-built tower. The slender spire leaned at a dangerous angle. The endlessly shifting sands of Stray were not just trouble for the streets.

Gripper watched the road and waved rather limply to Logan as the Prian parked. The Arboran's thick brown hide was wet with sweat and the big alien looked miserable.

"What's wrong?" Logan asked when he had climbed out of the car and approached the new tower. None of the Arcadian workers were anywhere to be seen.

"Hey, Hunter," Gripper said. His wide shoulders slumped and he sat heavily on the ground. "Glass isn't coming out. She called just before you arrived. She's going to be busy for the rest of the day."

Logan nodded, unsurprised, and peered at Gripper.

"What's wrong?" he asked again.

The mechanic wound his thick fingers together and sighed. "I asked all the glass-smiths to go away so it would be... you know...

private out here. And with the knights gone, I thought that you and Glass could um… be alone."

Stray's hot red sun beat down mercilessly on the back of Logan's neck. It was nothing like the small and distant star of his home-world. This glowering red sun filled the sky and made the glass towers shimmer like impossibly tall flames. Logan sat down beside Gripper.

"This was a trick?" he asked. "Just to get Maeve and me together for a while?"

"Yeah," Gripper admitted. "It was Shimmer's idea."

Logan combed his illonium fingers through his hair. He needed a shower. "That's why Anthem is on his way to Bherrosi, isn't it?"

"Sort of. There really are problems for Arcadians in the north, but I doubt anyone will notice the Blue Phoenix up there. Bherrosi is three times bigger than Gharib."

It was silly, Logan knew. Gripper and Duaal were teenagers and their ploy was ridiculously juvenile. But Logan still couldn't help wishing that it had worked. He closed his eyes and let his head thud back against the glass wall of the unfinished fairy tower.

"Do you miss her?" Gripper asked. "I mean, I know you just saw her, but…"

"Yes," Logan said.

They sat together in the heat. Eventually, Gripper speared one finger into the sand beneath them and spoke.

"What do you know about this enassui thing?" he asked.

"Like Maeve said, it's similar to an opera," Logan told him. "It's a traditional Arcadian format. They closely follow the five oathsongs, actually."

Gripper cocked his wide head at Logan. "And you were studying them. That song that's so popular in the city… You wrote that, didn't you? For Glass?"

Logan nodded. "I mangled some of the words."

"Does she know?"

"That the words were wrong? Yes."

"That's not what I meant."

"No," Logan answered. "Maeve doesn't know that I wrote it."

"You should tell her, Hunter."

"Why?"

Gripper didn't seem to have an answer for that. He scooped up a handful of sand. It sifted out from between his fingers.

"I haven't seen you with your guitar for a while," he said. "Actually, I meant to tell you to bring it out here with Glass... but I uh... sort of panicked and forgot."

It was Logan's turn not to answer. It had been weeks since the last time he played. Only twice since Maeve had left him... No, that wasn't fair. He was the one who told Maeve to do it. He had pushed Maeve toward Anthem's open arms.

Logan stood.

"I'm going back," he said.

"Why?" Gripper asked. "Glass will be working."

"So will I."

Sighing, Gripper followed Logan back toward Kaellisem.

"The fleet has reached twelve thousand."

Xartasia looked up at Dhozo. The smooth black floor reflected her white silhouette, but the Glorious commander cast no reflection. The slick layer of nanites against his skin absorbed most light to supplement its power supply. Only one in a hundred photons escaped the nanomachines' metallic surface. They were not actually black, but reflected so little light of any color that they might as well have been.

"Is that number sufficient?" Xartasia asked.

Dhozo shrugged his huge shoulders. The observation deck was plenty large enough to keep more distance, but he stood close to the little aerad queen, looming over her. Xartasia did not flinch or back away from Dhozo.

"I don't know," he rasped. "Until we actually go to Anzhotek, we won't know how many of your aerads you will need. It could be ten or ten million."

"There are not that many Arcadians in the galaxy."

"Then I suggest we get the information, little queen."

Xartasia turned away from Dhozo. Not out of any fear or even distaste, he suspected, but simply to enjoy the view. The black fleet had caught another small freighter. The crew had provided an all too small meal and Dhozo's stomach ached again already.

Now the ship was being rapidly torn apart for metal and minerals. The fibersteel that seemed so popular in the old worlds was flexible but easy to tear. Zhyress and her team would restructure it into strong and thick armor, slick and black and invisible to all but the most sophisticated of sensors, the kind of instrumentation that this galaxy had not seen for millions of years.

"We will set course for Anzhotek, Commander Dhozo," Xartasia said as the ship outside broke into ragged, disintegrating pieces. Even those dwindled swiftly away to skeletal struts and supports, barely visible in the darkness. "I visited that world once, years ago, in search of secrets. I did not ever think to return."

Xartasia turned toward one of the silent knights that followed her everywhere. Unlike Dhozo and his soldiers, their armor was brightly polished glass. Too shiny, too visible. When the time came to fight, how long would these aerad knights last? They were slaves; bred to serve, not to fight.

But Dhozo was older and smarter than Orix. Underestimating Xartasia and her kind – as his young subordinate often did – would not put meat on the table.

Dhozo remembered the first time the old Projector had flared and opened in the forgotten bowels of the VSS Forge. Then the feasting that followed... He was just a junior engineer in those days, without enough rank to earn fresh meat. But Dhozo remembered the smell of blood, coppery and salty. It had been months since the Forge's last kill and there had been near madness across the ship. The Glorious tore at each other in their desperation to get through the Projector, to hunt and to kill and to taste meat again.

Even after it was over and the Projector was closed again – shut down by an aerad operator on the other side – Dhozo never forgot that feeling of fresh, unprocessed wind on his face as he brought down aerads, dryads and nyads by the dozens. Nothing else ever tasted as good as that feast in the old galaxy.

Even after the closure triggered the emergency safety protocols to yank the Glorious back home, Dhozo became obsessed with opening the Projector again. He had studied the ancient technology every waking moment, poring over files so old that the computer no longer even indexed them. And when the gate opened again, he was the first one through.

But for all Dhozo had learned, it was not enough. He needed the information on Anzhotek.

Xartasia spoke quietly with some of her knights. They nodded and flew away to carry out her orders. There were fifty ships in the fleet and it would take organization to get them all to Anzhotek.

Fifty starships full of aerads... These fairies were thinner than the ones Dhozo had hunted a century ago, and many of them had diseases, but the commander's mouth watered as Xartasia turned to face him again.

"You are staring," she said in her musical voice.

"You are tempting, little queen," Dhozo told her.

"Focus, commander. I would make a small meal. But the use of the Waygates will feed you for millennia to come."

[21]

WHITE AS SNOW

"It is darkness that sends us in search of light."

- ANYA BOWDEN, QUARRAN EDUCATION MINISTER (193 PA)

"What's Varrth charging us to haul this stuff?" Ballad asked.

Panna squinted at him through her sunglasses. Stray's sun was dim as ever, but the bright white sand of Bherrosi managed to make it blinding. Panna hoped that boded well for its future as Arcadian glass.

"Three hundred cenmarks a ton," she answered. "Less than half the next best offer Vyron managed to find."

Ballad stood nearby, squinting out across the gleaming desert.

"How the hells did we get a discount?" the young knight asked suspiciously.

"Varrth wants to turn all this into farmland," Panna said. "He's already got a contract to irrigate it with polar runoff. He just needs to change the nitrogen content of the ground to support plant life. He's tried twice, but this sand just absorbs the infusions and doesn't do any good. So we're actually doing Varrth a favor in hauling the stuff away."

"And he's still charging us?"

"Yes, he is. Do you have any idea how much seven hundred tons of fertilizer costs?" Panna asked, raising an eyebrow at the short-haired fairy boy. "Varrth threw away a lot more into this land than he'll make off us. If he's lucky and gets a good rate, we'll be buying him one-quarter of his next nitrogen infusion."

"Still seems like we're being cheated."

Ballad turned his slit-eyed gaze to the Arcadians working the snow-colored dune, laboring under Duaal and Sir Anthem's direction to large plastic canisters and then drag them onto the null-inertia loader. The white sand hill hid the Blue Phoenix from view. Panna wondered if she would be able to see it when they had sifted and removed enough of the dune to fill the old hauler's hold.

"Is the nitrogen going to be a problem?" Ballad asked suddenly. "When Hyra and his birds make all this into glass?"

"What? Of course not," Panna answered. "Have you *ever* taken a science class?"

"No," Ballad said. "There aren't lots of schools on Prianus and I sure as hells wouldn't cut off my wings just to go to one."

Panna scowled at Ballad. "It shows."

"Wait, are you calling me stupid?"

"Nitrogen is a gas, Sir Ballad," Panna pointed out. "And unlike the heavy metals in Gharib sand, the nitrogen will vaporize as soon as the glass-singers begin working the molecules."

"How the hells was I supposed to know that?" Ballad asked.

"That's what school is for!"

Ballad fumed, gripping his spear so tight that his knuckles went the same white as the dunes.

"I'm going up," he said. "I may be dumb, but I can carry sand."

"But you're supposed to be watching for trouble from the city!" Panna protested.

She pointed to the barely-visible silhouette of Bherrosi in the distance. Ballad flicked his wings.

"We've been here all day," he said. "No one in Bherrosi has even noticed. I'm just standing here and getting a sunburn, not doing anything useful."

"If Sir Anthem needed you up there, he would call," Panna told him. "You stay right here."

"Yes, ma'am," Ballad said sourly. "Because I need another old-fashioned fairy ordering me around."

Panna was so pleased that Ballad was listening to something she said that it took a moment to register what *he* said.

"Old fashioned?" she asked. "Me? I had my wings removed and went to a coreworld college. I'm the most progressive Arcadian that you'll ever meet!"

Bored or maybe just showing off, Ballad spun his glass-bladed spear in a flashing circle. A pair of blue ribbons streamed from the haft, probably awarded for success in some sort of training exercise.

"Really?" Ballad asked, arching an eyebrow. "Queen Maeve left my friend for Sir Anthem. Let me guess where you stand on that."

"Hey, I like Logan, too," Panna protested. "But it's important for the queen to have an Arcadian consort!"

"Why?" Ballad asked.

He twirled his spear again and thumped the butt down into the sand. Panna shook her head in disbelief.

"Because Maeve's our queen," she said. "Because she's the living embodiment of ten thousand years of history and culture. *Arcadian* history and culture."

"So?" Ballad asked plainly. "Anthem gave up fighting to become a prostitute! He's a coward!"

"What?" Panna asked, blinking her streaming eyes. "Who told you that? And anyway, it doesn't matter anymore! Sir Anthem is an anointed knight and one of precious few noble-born Arcadians left in the universe. Queen Maeve needs him!"

"By that logic, she should marry Duke Ferris! And the one who *should* get to keep the dove is the hawk who fights for her!"

"That's sexist," Panna said. "Queen Maeve can fight for herself. And even if it *were* true, by that logic, Logan still lost Maeve. He left her, and was right to do so. We all make sacrifices for our people, Ballad. Maybe you'll understand that someday."

The young fairy man shot Panna a furious glare and took to the air. His takeoff kicked up a cloud of pale dust that made her cough.

"Well, I'm going to get some actual work done," Ballad shouted down to Panna. "But you can watch Bherrosi, if you want to waste your time."

When Panna finally figured out an answer, Ballad was already gone.

"What are those?" Logan asked.

Maeve looked up from her datadex full of numbers. Logan stood at the open window, ostensibly to watch the street far below, but his pale blue eyes were fixed instead on the fairy queen at her desk. The Prian looked like some kind of monstrous giant in the delicate glass room, with his decidedly un-Arcadian features, blocky metal hand and height generally towering over everyone and everything else.

"Reports from Bherrosi," Maeve said. "Panna tells me that they have collected and loaded over seventy tons of sand. They should be done and ready to return to Kaellisem in just two more days."

"A day early?"

Maeve's smile faltered. That meant Anthem would be back, too. Duke Ferris had kept her busy for the last week, working on the new enassui and Panna's reports had been sitting on her desk for the better part of a day. The time had gone by quickly, but it was lonely. Logan was there beside her every day, but it was nothing like it had been before and Maeve ached to kiss him. Or just to hold his hand...

"Do you need anything, a'shae?" Verra asked from her seat in the corner.

Maeve shook her head, then returned her attention to Panna's report. She still felt Logan's eyes on her, but she didn't let herself look up again.

"We should be done by nine or ten tomorrow morning," Panna told Anthem.

"Good," said the royal consort. "Everyone is tired and ready to return to Kaellisem. We have all breathed much dust here. Do you think it will do any harm?"

"Probably some," Panna admitted. "I'll ask Xia about it when we get back."

She was a little self-conscious sitting in Sir Anthem's presence, but she was exhausted. Panna propped her chin on her hand and stifled a yawn. The sky outside the Blue Phoenix was dark and the ship was full of the muffled sounds of singing: the evening prayer-song before sleep. The Arcadians always sang and Panna quickly found herself humming along. Anthem watched her.

"I do not know how anyone ever mistook you for human, child," Anthem said, even managing to not to sound condescending when he said *child*. "You are a true daughter of Arcadia."

"Really?" Panna asked. "Would you mind telling Ballad that?"

"Is there trouble with him?" Anthem asked with a frown.

Panna bit her lip and wished she weren't so tired. Weighing and tallying barrels of sand wasn't that hard, but it was so *hot*.

"It's nothing," she said. "Nothing important."

But that didn't seem to satisfy the knight commander.

"Ballad is an interesting disciplinary challenge," Anthem said. "He is fierce and dedicated to the kingdom, but has little respect for the traditions of our people."

"I can't argue with that," Panna said.

"You can," Anthem told her. "But you would be wrong."

Panna blinked a few times and burst out into nervous laughter. The prince consort was teasing her. Smiling at her... Panna's cheeks went quite hot. Anthem was a handsome man. She knew that he had been a prostitute even before Ballad had said anything. Xia had discreetly put the knight through a series of medical tests to ensure that he could transmit nothing dangerous to Maeve. But Panna had a hard time imagining Sir Anthem on a street corner.

A sudden shout interrupted her thoughts and Panna jumped to her feet, banging her knees on the underside of the table. By the time she managed to stand and run toward the sound, Anthem was already through the door and sprinting down the cargo bay catwalk. At night, the bulky airlock doors were kept open to cool the overheated hold and its crowded contents of Arcadians and barrels of sand.

Someone stood in the airlock. Panna thought for a moment that it was Duaal. The shape was human, as tall as the Hyzaari captain but with a wider build.

The man stepped into the hold. It was a human with sunburnt red skin and a slit-eyed black hood pulled down over his face. He held a piece of pitted steel pipe in his hands. It was only about the length of his forearm and was hardly the most dangerous weapon Panna had ever seen, but that piece of dented metal somehow filled her with an instant sense of dread. A pair of tall Dailons came in behind the human, then several others whose racial marks Panna couldn't make out from this distance. The Arcadian diggers shied away from the intruders, whispering and humming with the same fear that knotted Panna's stomach.

"What the hells are you doing on my ship?"

The loud question came from Captain Sinnay as he pushed his way through the ranks of nervous Arcadians. The furious scowl on his face would have made Tiberius proud.

The hooded human looked Duaal up and down, taking in the captain's lavender silk pants and black brocade vest, then swung the pipe in a short arc. The metal impacted with a loud thump against Duaal's temple and he collapsed to the floor, blood oozing from the side of his head. The intruder lifted his hood enough to spit on the crumpled Duaal.

"Roodin' fairy lover," he said and then pointed with the pipe in his hand at the Arcadians. Duaal's blood shone on the steel. "You come all the way back to Bherrosi to steal from me? You aren't going to get another chance, you little rats!"

Steal? Steal what? Panna did not have much time to wonder. Sir Anthem was already unfolding his long wings and diving from the catwalk. When had he grabbed his spear? More of Anthem's trainee knights pushed their way toward the armed coreworlders, who spread out in response, readying themselves for a fight... Panna saw more clubs emerge from desert robes and the greasy shine of several nanoblades, then a storm of wings obscured everything.

The Arcadians were breaking ranks, flying up and further into the ship. They scrambled over the stairs, through the catwalk where Panna stood and past her. Feathers drifted through the air like oversized snowflakes as Panna fought to keep her feet beneath her. She clung to the railing and gasped. Below, the fairies and coreworlders came together.

"Kill no one!" Anthem commanded, even as his own glass spear darted out.

Anthem lunged to one side, then beat his wings and was somehow behind a snarling Lyran that was reaching for him with claws extended. Panna gasped when he thrust his spear, but Anthem had twirled it around so that it connected butt-first with the back of the Lyran's head.

An Arcadian in black leapt on one of the humans. It was Ballad, the sliced leather jacket he wore even in Stray's heat making him stand out against the more colorful squires. Panna bit her lip. Only

Anthem had glass armor... Ballad's spear thrust out more awkwardly than Anthem's, but it drove his opponent back and the kick that he delivered connected with an audible thud.

There were cries of pain whose source Panna couldn't distinguish, and a few feathers floated on eddying currents as the cooling night air swirled through the hold. Some were spotted red with blood. She looked around the bay for something to do, for *some* way to help.

One of the invading humans loomed up over Duaal. The young Hyzaari captain groaned and struggled to push himself upright. He didn't seem to notice the shadow falling over him. Panna swore. There was nothing like a weapon up on the catwalk. All of the tools were stowed down in the hold, in the middle of the fighting, to say nothing of any real weapons. The only thing nearby was a plastic barrel someone must have set up here to get out of the way.

Panna grabbed the bottom and thanked Aes that it was empty – she never would have been able to lift it full. Panna heaved and the barrel balanced on the rail for a moment, then overbalanced and tumbled down into the hold. It didn't actually hit the man below, but it clipped his head and shoulder and knocked him sprawling to the ground.

By the time he managed to regain his feet, so had Duaal. The mage blinked blood from his eyes, and then they narrowed and fixed on the other man. Duaal raised his hand, songless and silent, and sent the Bherrosi man flying backward across the hold with a spell. He hit two more of their attackers and they tumbled together into a heap on the floor. One of Anthem's squires – bleeding from her own stomach wound – retreated back toward Duaal and began helping the captain up the stairs.

Panna searched for Anthem and Ballad again. There were fewer people fighting now. Anthem held his spear to the throat of a man on his knees. The wolf-eyed new squire, Syle, drove his spear deep into the back of the Lyran that Panna had seen earlier, who howled in pain as blood gushed from his muzzle. Anthem turned on Syle, rage blazing in his dark eyes, but the younger knight was already leaping and diving away, as graceful as a hunting bird, at another coreworlder.

Ballad's spear had fallen to the ground, but one of the Dailons lay curled in a fetal ball at his feet, gasping and groaning while the Prian fairy traded jabbing punches with the other one. When the remaining Dailon swung a blue fist nearly as big as Ballad's head, Panna tried to cry out a warning, but all that came out was a strangled choking sound.

Ballad slid under the blow and answered with a flurry of his own, but the impacts didn't seem to faze the bigger man at all. The black-clad young knight curled his fingers into a sort of claw and grabbed the Dailon, who shrieked far louder than Panna had managed and sank to his knees on the floor. He grabbed weakly for Ballad's hand until Anthem stalked close behind him and slid his spear under the Dailon's jaw.

"Leave!" Anthem commanded.

The kneeling Dailon nodded gingerly and Ballad released him. A midnight bruise was already spreading under the skin as they yanked the other Dailon to his feet and the two stumbled out the airlock, back into the cooling Bherrosi night. One by one, the others staggered or crawled from the Blue Phoenix.

Panna sprinted down the stairs as quickly as her trembling legs would carry her. Two of Anthem's knights were on the ground and did not rise. Cyrene lay still in a pool of blood, a nanoblade buried to the hilt in her throat. The other young knight was dead, too, the left side of his skull crushed like an eggshell. Panna sobbed and closed the knight's dull eyes. She crawled across the hold to do the same for the Lyran that Syle had killed.

Ballad grabbed the last man by his collar. It was the one in the black hood and now the cloth was torn and tacky with blood, but the human wasn't wounded. That blood wasn't his. Ballad swept the man's feet out from under him and sent him crashing to the floor of the Blue Phoenix.

"We didn't do anything to you!" Ballad shouted. "What the hells was this?"

"You stole my money, you roodin' bird-back," the man snarled back, angry but lacking the molten venom it once held.

"You're lying! We never went anywhere near Bherrosi. And now Cyrene and Sellesian are dead!"

Ballad yanked the man's hood off, making him suddenly squint in the bright cargo bay lights. Panna blinked. Their attacker had a round, friendly-looking face, with sparse brown hair and very pink cheeks. Ballad's hands trembled and Anthem put his hand on the young fairy's shoulder.

"And his Lyran friend is dead," said the prince consort. "Release him, Ballad. There is no justice to be had tonight. Your brother and sister fought for their people, as they swore to do. They are with the All-Singer now."

"Can't we call the Stray police? We can't just let this crime go unanswered!"

"The police on Stray are not like those of Prianus," Anthem reminded Ballad. "They will not care that our own are dead, but may punish us badly for the Lyran."

With a choked sob, Ballad threw the hood down to the floor and shoved its owner toward the airlock. "Get the hells out of here!"

The human jumped to his feet and ran. Only Anthem, Syle and Ballad remained in the hold with Panna. Anthem whirled on Syle.

"You killed one of them," he sang angrily. "I ordered you to kill no one!"

"*En xarri ma'anni,*" Syle answered. *They were killing us.*

"*Ae vae'ii si ven!*" Anthem hissed. *You will obey my orders!*

"You must deserve obedience," Syle told Anthem coolly. "Ballad is right. Cyrene and Sellesian are dead."

Panna gasped. "You can't blame Sir Anthem for that!"

Syle fixed his golden eyes on Panna and bowed his head.

"No," he said. "Please, Sir Anthem, forgive me. I was angry."

Syle hadn't *sounded* angry, Panna thought, but Anthem shook his head.

"Forgiven," he told Syle. "But a knight must obey orders, even if he does not agree with them. There is a time to ask questions and to argue, but in the midst of battle is not that time."

"No, it is not," Syle agreed. The yellow-eyed knight turned away and went to the bodies of his fallen comrades.

"We can't stay here," Panna said. "I doubt that man will call the police, but just in case I'm wrong, we should be gone."

"We have not yet collected the sands that we promised Queen Maeve," Anthem said.

"I think that our queen would rather keep her people alive than make more glass," Panna told him. "Besides, if this goes at all well, we can use some of the profits to send someone else up here to collect sand. Someone that the locals won't accuse of theft."

"Perhaps that man's accusation was not a lie," Syle interrupted. Anthem shot him an angry look, but Syle held up a handful of red cenmark chips. "Cyrene had them."

Panna wondered where she could have kept them. Cyrene didn't have a suit of glass armor yet and her pale body was dressed in only a few scarves, much better suited to the warm, overcrowded cargo hold than Ballad's leather. But Anthem took the plastic squares and clenched his fist around them. He thought a moment and then stalked to the airlock. He threw the plastic cenmark chips into the sand outside and slammed the doors shut.

"We are done here," Anthem announced. "Panna, please check on Captain Sinnay. If he is well enough, ask him to return us to Kaellisem at once. Ballad, get our people back into the hold and secured for the flight."

"What of me, sir?" Syle asked.

"Clean the blood from the floor, remove the bodies and reflect on the life you have taken," Anthem told him.

"Yes, sir."

Panna climbed up the stairs into the Blue Phoenix, but paused to look down at Syle as the fairy squire searched the cargo hold for a mop. Was he smiling?

[22]

BLACK AS NIGHT

"Love doesn't overlook flaws. It helps you correct them."

- XIA (233 PA)

"You flew with a head injury?"

Duaal winced at the sound of Xia's scolding.

"Just a little," he protested. "Bherrosi isn't that far away. And the ship's com was uh... slightly broken."

"I should have been there with you," Xia said. She examined the medbay computer screen. "We could have waited until I finished with the inoculation cycle. Luckily, you don't seem to have done any serious damage. You have a very hard skull, Duaal."

"Don't I know it?" he answered with a groan. "This whole thing really backfired on me. We were supposed to keep Anthem out of Maeve's hair for a week, but now we're back early and with two of her knights dead."

"I *told* you to leave that alone," Xia said.

Duaal ignored her.

"Did Logan manage to get that crown off Maeve while we were gone?" he asked.

"No, I don't think so. Gripper says when Maeve isn't running Kaellisem, Ferris is having her work on some sort of... show."

"Damn it." Duaal examined the Ixthian's work in a small mirror. The cut along his scalp was gone and the bruise already fading to a yellowish brown. "We'll just have to try harder. Nice work, Xia. I'll be back to my handsome self in no time."

Xia sighed and turned away, gleaming metal instruments in her silver hands. They clattered into the sink, bouncing off one another and nearly out of the shallow basin. Duaal slid off the cold exam table and put his hand on Xia's shoulder.

"What's wrong?" he asked.

"I should have been there with you," Xia said again. "Maybe I could have–"

"You can't be everywhere," Duaal told her. "You can't, Xia. You stayed because the Arcadians here need you. They've never had a doctor. And we needed you to stay close to Maeve. She's the key to everything we're trying to do here. If she dies, Xartasia wins."

"Maeve is fine," Xia said. She stared down into the sink with red eyes. She took a deep breath. "At least, her body is. There's nothing I can do for all of the other stuff she's going through. But people are dead because I–"

"You couldn't have known what was going to happen in Bherrosi," Duaal told Xia gently. "And you can't go back and change it. Don't break your heart over what could have been."

Xia sighed again, but the sound was more resigned this time. Her compound eyes shifted rapidly through a rainbow of colors.

"You've grown up so much," Xia told him. "You're a good man, Captain Sinnay."

Duaal turned away to cover his blush and laughed.

"Don't tell anyone," he said. "You'll ruin my reputation."

——————— • • •

Xia sat at the kitchen table, reading the news and ignoring the clinking and crashing from the kitchen as her daughter dropped another cup. Xas' new skin had not entirely hardened yet and the soft spots were slippery. She would have to learn how to deal with it. After all, the girl had four more molts before reaching her adult size.

The front door slid open and then shut with a pair of hydraulic hisses. Xia looked up from the computer screen.

"Good evening, love," she said. "How were classes today?"

"Successful," Xen told her as he came around the corner. He hung his coat on the rack and carried a large datadex to the dinner table. "How are the larvae?"

"Successful," Xia answered with a smile. "For the most part. Xas is trying to do the dishes."

"Can't you get Xol or Xid to help?" her husband asked.

Xia shrugged. "Xas needs to figure out for herself when she needs help and ask for it. Pride isn't a very useful trait."

Xen nodded in agreement. "I suppose not. You're as wise a mother as you ever were a doctor."

"I was an excellent doctor," Xia pointed out.

"And now you're an excellent mother."

"I could have been both."

Xen picked up his datadex and turned it on with a flick of his finger. "Unless you want to trust the upbringing of our children to someone else, one of us needs to be available to them. I would be happy to take up your position, if you like."

"No," Xia answered. "My superior size, patience and medical knowledge make me the better choice."

"Until adolescence. When schooling becomes a major factor, and my experience at Poes Nor changes things, we'll renegotiate."

"Agreed," Xia said.

There was another crash from the direction of the kitchen and then the sharp scent of anger. Xas knew better than to swear in her mother's house, but the young Ixthian couldn't help the rush of chemical language.

Not yet, at least. Another thing she would have to learn. It was not only Ixthians who could understand those smells, but the Lyra and Dailons. If Xas really wanted to become a politician — that was the girl's ambition this week — she would have to school not only her verbal habits, but her silent ones as well.

"A new student has just transferred into my two-ten class," Xen said suddenly.

"Now?" Xia asked. "It's halfway through the semester."

Xen shrugged, not looking up from his datadex. He was a proficient multitasker, a trait he had made sure to pass along to their offspring.

"I warned her and even gave her the opportunity to take the test next week," Zen said. "But she finished today and scored in the top percentile."

"Did she transfer from a similar course at another college?"

"No," Xen told Xia. His long antennae waved rhythmically as he read. "She came straight from Cyrus."

"The farming colony?" Xia asked. "The human one?"

"Yes. I was surprised, as well. Humans usually can't keep up with my advanced courses, but this one seems to be an exception."

"You'll have to see if she will agree to a redprint," Xia said. "I would be curious to take a look."

"So would I," Xen agreed.

"What's this brilliant girl's name?"

"Elsa De Marn."

— • • • —

Maeve shook her head and recentered the slippery glass crown atop her black hair.

"Please, do not let the numbers concern you," she said. "You and Sir Anthem brought back plenty of Bherrosi sands... and at far too high a price."

"Yes," Panna agreed in a soft voice. The wingless girl's eyes were rimmed in red.

"The fault for that lies with me, my queen," Anthem said. The knight was on one knee, his wings pressed to the sandy ground in a gesture of utter subservience. "I am sorry."

"It is *not* your fault," Maeve told her consort. "Now get up! I have read a dozen accounts of what happened in Bherrosi, Anthem, and only your own report blames you. Ballad, in fact, takes responsibility for the whole thing, as well."

"Ballad was only assigned daytime duties for guarding against–" Anthem began, but Maeve raised her hand and the knight fell instantly silent. There were *some* benefits to being queen.

"Enough," she told him and then turned to Panna. "I have not gotten to your report yet. Please, tell me whether any of my knights are to blame for this tragedy."

"No, they're not," Panna said. "None of the living ones, at least. The man who led the attack said that someone had stolen from him and Syle found some money on Cyrene. That seems to be what started all of this."

Maeve nodded. Anthem had gathered all twenty-two of his remaining knights in the flat red northern field, along with the white-wrapped bundles of their dead. Ferris had already flown away to take care of the funerary details, for which Maeve was grateful. She raised her wings.

"Sir Anthem," she said. "Stand forward."

Anthem stood and stepped forward. His dark eyes were not red like Panna's, but remained downcast. He held his spear point-down, the ribbons trailing in the dust. He truly was ashamed. After all Maeve had admitted to him, after she had shouted at him and sent him away to Bherrosi, Anthem Calloren was actually sorry that he had disappointed her. Maeve reached out and touched her fingertip to the knight's cheek. He raised his eyes to Maeve's.

"No knight can win all battles," she told him. "No matter how bravely fought – especially those begun from within. Fight for me and for Kaellisem as you have, Sir Anthem, and I will be forever proud. You are master of my knights and my heart, now and ever."

Maeve was rather proud of the little speech. She hadn't even asked for Panna's help with it. But Maeve could not help a glance behind her, to where Logan Coldhand stood his daytime vigil over Kaellisem's queen. His expression was stony. If Maeve's politic endearment bothered the Prian hunter, she couldn't tell.

Maeve returned her attention to the assembled knights. "Ballad, come here."

The young Prian fairy approached slowly. He was still wearing his black leather, but Maeve was sure that some of the deep slashes in the battered jacket were new. Ballad went down on one knee, as Anthem had.

"I'm so sorry, my queen–" he said.

"Enough," Maeve told him. She was tired of apologies. They did not bring back the dead. "You have done no wrong, Ballad Avadain. By all counts, you fought hard and honorably for the safety of our people and your fellow knights."

"Cyrene and Sellesian died," Ballad said.

"We cannot save everyone. Not yet. Are you arguing that with your queen?"

"No," Ballad said and then blushed, correcting himself. "I mean, not anymore. I'm done now."

"Good," Maeve said. "Now, if you insist upon some punishment, I will grant it. Sir Anthem, give me your spear."

Anthem dusted his weapon clean and held it out haft first to Maeve. She took the spear with a sudden rush of excitement. Gods, how long had it been since Maeve held her own? Since she wore armor? Not since her coronation... Maeve spun the spear, bringing the gleaming blade around to point at the kneeling Ballad.

"By the grace granted to me by Erris All-Singer and the first of our order, Anslin Sky-Knight," Maeve declared, touching the spear's glass blade to the crest of Ballad's right wing, "you are now a royal knight. Rise, Sir Ballad."

Ballad jumped up and spread his wings, sweeping the right one across to his shoulder. His eyes were bright.

"I will not fail you, my queen!" Ballad said.

Maeve still held the spear leveled at him. "You are the first Arcadian to be knighted since the fall of our kingdom. In Kaellisem, at least. I cannot say who my cousin may have raised up. But a great burden falls to you, Sir Ballad. Thousands of years of glory and responsibility lives again with you. Be strong. Be great."

"Yes, a'shae!"

Despite the gravity of the moment, Maeve smiled helplessly at Ballad's enthusiasm. Reluctantly, she returned the spear to Anthem.

"Have Hyra make Ballad's armor," she instructed. "And for your other students, too."

"It will set back our other glass orders, Majesty," Anthem said.

Maeve stopped smiling. "I know. But see it done. I will not send my knights into more danger without armor. Perhaps if Sellesian and Cyrene had theirs, they may have lived."

"Yes, my queen," Anthem said.

"You knighted Ballad?" Ferris gasped. "The Prian boy with no hair and the skin jacket?"

"It was more armor than anyone but Sir Anthem wore in Bherrosi," Maeve told the duke. "It may well have saved his life. And yes, I did. He is well suited to knighthood. Ballad is loyal and an able combatant."

"Your Majesty, he fights with his *hands!*" Ferris protested.

"And did our spears save us from the Devourers, Your Grace?"

Maeve stalked across the glass balcony to Duke Ferris, his withered hand against the tower wall as though the shock of it all might send him toppling into the street below. The hot wind tugged at her long black hair.

"Our enemies are no longer a few feral beasts or angry dryads," Maeve said. "Nor even the coreworlders who so despise us! Do not forget what I first told you on Sunjarrah, Ferris. What I do now, I do to fight Xartasia, the Devourers and *our own people* who have joined them. If we are to win that battle, we cannot fight with spears alone. These are weapons that have already failed against the Devourers. We need knights like Sir Ballad."

Duke Ferris stood up straight. "If we give up all of our ways, my queen, we have given up ourselves! What then remains to fight for?"

"We are not fighting for ourselves," Maeve told him. "The White Kingdom is already lost, and has been for a century. We fight for everyone else, for the scattered survivors. We fight for the Alliance, so that they will not face the terrible losses that we have."

"Yes, my queen," The old fairy duke answered stiffly. "If you will excuse me, the enassuanii have final preparations to discuss. It has clearly been a long and trying day for you. I should see to them on my own."

It was barely noon, but Maeve sighed and nodded. "Thank you, Your Grace. Please tell the enassuanii that I am sorry to miss them and that I eagerly await their performance tomorrow night."

Ferris spread his wings, inclined his head and leapt up into the sky. He wheeled once around the red and gold royal tower and then soared away across Kaellisem. Maeve watched him go and took a deep breath. The hot, dry air smelled acridly of dust. It always did... Maeve almost didn't notice anymore. Almost.

Maeve went back inside, where Logan Coldhand and her hand-maidens awaited her in the shifting ruby light. Verra hurried to offer lunch, but Maeve wasn't hungry and waved the girl off. Dain stood quietly in the corner, dusting the queen's armor. Logan raised one dark blond eyebrow.

"Ferris wasn't happy about Ballad," he said.

"You heard that?" Maeve asked. She combed fingers through her hair, ruining another one of Verra's delicate braids. "The venerable duke shall just have to deal with my decision. I doubt that my appointment of Sir Ballad will tear Kaellisem apart."

"Probably not," Logan agreed. "The Arcadians have never had a civil war."

Maeve smirked at him. "You have become very knowledgeable in our history, my hunter."

"Panna's been able to answer most of my questions."

"She knows far more about my kingdom than I do. I have never been suited to my own blood! But the color of my hair condemns me to the throne..." Maeve pulled off her crown and then stared at the delicate circlet of glass. "No, Arcadians have not fought each other in ten thousand years. But my own ancestor wiped out the pyrads for less purpose than we have now. We can fight, Logan. We *will* fight."

"If Kaellisem has half your ferocity, dove, it will be a short fight," Logan said.

Maeve thought that she saw a tiny smile on the Prian's face. But when she looked up, it was gone. On the other side of the room, Dain was singing to herself as she worked. Verra returned with the lunch Maeve had not asked for and began asking the queen what she wanted to wear to the enassui the next night.

[23]

RED AS FLAME

"Some things are just too important to talk about. For those, you
need songs."

- LOGAN CENTRA (234 PA)

The site of the enassui as much a practical decision as a creative
one. There was only one stage in Kaellisem and it happened to be
where the royal subject of the performance had been crowned. In
between their other work, the harried glass-smiths raised ranks of
semi-circle tiered audience stands and a few small private viewing
towers. The best of these seats was reserved for Maeve Cavainna
herself. It was the royal tower in miniature, a spiraling needle of red
and golden glass like a great flower that rose up over Kaellisem's
theater.

Syle Lamanna stalked between the low tiers of seats, pretending
to inspect the glass-singers' work along with his fellow squires. He
raised yellow eyes to the sky where Sir Ballad flew in circles over
the theater, speaking into a coreworlder's com. In his ugly black
leathers, the boy looked like a raven. The oldest knight and royal
consort, Sir Anthem, stood at the top of the queen's box and peered

down at the rows of glass seats below. Neither Ballad nor Anthem watched Syle. Even after Bherrosi, the other knights suspected nothing.

Syle stared down the sloped tiers to the stage. Red and dun-colored sand was still heaped around the little glass plateau, despite the best efforts to sweep it away. Stray was a world of dry sand. Not even the desperate beauty of Kaellisem could change that. But tonight, this theater would house the first enassui sung in a century. After a hundred years of silence, the fairies would offer their song to the gods once more.

It was almost a pity that it would all end in blood and fire.

Maeve batted Duaal's hands away and scowled at Verra until the girl backed off.

"I look fine," she told them. "All eyes will be on the stage, not on me. I could show up in a sack and no one would notice."

"Not *everyone* will be watching the show," Duaal said with an irritatingly mysterious smirk.

"And anyways, this whole opera thing is about you," Gripper pointed out. Even the big Arboran was dressed up in a fresh, clean pair of pants and a huge shirt that nonetheless fit him like a second skin. Gripper gave Duaal a stern look. "But don't worry. Everything will go just fine."

Maeve paused, not really sure what Gripper's reassurances were supposed to mean, but Verra saw her opportunity and lunged at the queen, hurriedly applying a silvery eye shadow that made Maeve's nose itch. She sneezed and Verra laughed at her. It was a soft, bell-like little sound.

"Sir Anthem will be unable to look away," she told Maeve. "You are beautiful, my queen."

She didn't really want to think about that. Instead, she looked at Panna. "Where is Duke Ferris?"

"Already at the theater," said the young anthropologist. "There are some coreworlders that came in from Gharib to watch the en-assui tonight. Duke Ferris has gone to make introductions."

Maeve nodded at her reflection. This time, Dain had firmly fixed the queen's crown with an armory of pins and some sort of hair product that made Maeve think of the resin Xia used to preserve specimens. Verra painted a pink gloss onto Maeve's lips, telling her not to bite them and she had to admit that the effect of her handmaidens' work was impressive. Her silver gown was delicately embroidered like the foam of a sea never seen on Stray.

The queen in the mirror was a statue of ice and moonlight. She was royal, regal and commanding. She looked nothing like Maeve.

"Fifteen minutes," Logan said from the doorway.

Maeve rose, her silver dress whispering softly around her.

"And where is Sir Anthem?" she asked. "He was supposed to be here by now."

"Don't worry about him," Gripper answered. "He's uh... already at the theater with the duke."

"Anthem's right where he needs to be," Duaal agreed. "Let's get going. You don't want to miss this."

Anthem Calloren looked around the Blue Phoenix hold. But for a few tangled orange cargo nets and a pair of large magclamps, it was empty. The barrels of white Bherrosi sand had already been removed and carted to Hyra's smithy.

Where was Captain Sinnay? Anthem called out, but the only reply was an empty echo. Why had Duaal called Anthem here...? Behind him, the airlock light flashed from green to red.

"O2 leak," warned a flat, recorded voice. "Now sealing all bulkheads."

The airlock slid shut and locked with a loud thunk. Anthem ran to the controls and then stopped. He had no idea what to do.

How could there be an air leak on the Blue Phoenix? The ship was on the ground and – until a moment ago – the doors had been open. Something had to be wrong with the ship's computer, but Anthem had no more idea how to fix it than how to kindle a star.

The knight remembered his com. It was a new addition to his equipment, but the coreworlder device had already proved useful on several occasions. Anthem was grateful that Gripper had given it to him. He scrolled through the pre-programmed contacts until he found Duaal's name and then selected it. The com beeped as it signaled out. Just once and then there was the unmistakable click of someone answering.

"Um... hi," said a nervous voice that was definitely not that of the young Captain Sinnay. "Hello there. I guess the airlocks closed up on you."

"Gripper?" Anthem asked, confused. Had he called the wrong man? No matter – Gripper could surely help. "Yes, your computer seems to believe that there is some sort of leak."

"Yeah," Gripper said, his voice staticky and sheepish. "I kind of programmed it to. And your com. It's not going to call anyone but me for the next few hours, Spear."

"You have locked me away on your ship."

"Sorry about that."

Anthem sighed and switched off the com. Gripper – and Duaal, he suspected – would release him when the enassui was over. Probably. The knight folded his legs under him and sat in front of the airlock to wait.

———— • • • ————

Maeve left Gripper and the rest of her friends on a lower floor of the theater tower. There were seats set aside for each of them, but the top level was reserved for the queen and her consort alone.

Panna and Ferris were both there, grinning with excitement and eager for the show to begin. Duaal argued heatedly with Verra to convince her that Maeve would not need her handmaidens during the enassui. The queen would have her consort soon, after all, and who better to take care of her needs? It was the wink that Duaal gave Verra and the suggestion that it might be better to leave Maeve alone with Anthem that finally seemed to convince her.

Maeve wondered how unqueenly it would be to punch Duaal.

Only Logan, as her guard, was allowed to accompany Maeve all the way up to the top of the tower. She had to admit that it had been almost worth the bother. Her box was a small, intimate balcony decorated with vines of tiny white flowers that filled the warm evening air with their sweet, delicate scent. Where had anyone found such things on Stray? Nestled among the blossoms was a deep, backless Arcadian-styled seat, just wide enough for two and cushioned in a dark wine-colored red.

The theater spread out below, glass tiers full of winged shapes surrounded by slender glass tower seats all lit by the pale silver of Stray's large, dim moon. The starkly simple stage rose up from the sand in the center and glowed in a brilliant spotlight. A circle of enassuanii knelt in the center of the smooth glass surface, creating a ring of overlapped white wings. They faced inward as they prayed in preparation for their performance.

Maeve knew the enassuanii had already been there for hours. Their song was more than a show; it was a holy obeisance, a sacred rite and duty before Erris All-Singer. He had created the Arcadians to sing what he could not, to create anew. There was no mistaking the Kaellisem theater for one of those lost with the fall of the White Kingdom, but the sight still brought tears to Maeve's eyes.

"Where's Anthem?" Logan asked suddenly.

Maeve turned back to look across the top of the tower. Logan was right... They were alone on the balcony. Maeve's knight consort was nowhere to be seen. She frowned.

"I do not know," she said. "He would not want to miss this."

On the stage, the circle of Arcadian singers moved, swaying like willows in the wind. As one, they turned outward, facing the audience with hands and wings raised. Maeve's heart sped. The enassui was beginning. She grabbed her flowing silver skirts and hurried to take her seat. Anthem could join Maeve later, but she had no intention of missing the show.

Logan stood behind Maeve. He wasn't watching the Arcadians on the stage below, but the queen. She was so beautiful. Perfect. It wasn't the gown or her sculpted black curls or the carefully painted makeup that made her silver eyes outshine the stars. Maeve leaned forward, grinning like a girl as the enassuanii beat their wings and rose into the violet evening sky. Logan would have given anything in the worlds to kiss those smiling lips.

Maeve grabbed his hand – his metal one – in hers and Logan's heart nearly stopped. She turned that delighted grin on him, gray eyes sparkling. She tugged and Logan let her pull him down into the seat beside her. Maeve didn't let go of his hand.

Below, the Arcadian enassuanii had risen into the air above the stage, circling one another on the evening breeze like great birds. What Logan had first taken for the soft sigh of the wind rose and swelled until he realized that it was the voices of the enassuanii.

The words were slow, long and sustained until each one became an alien, abstract sculpture of sound. The harmonies were subtle and close, layered and as intricate as circuitry. Logan couldn't understand most of the words – his Arcadian still wasn't very good and the complex music made the task no easier – but that detracted nothing at all from the beauty of the song. They were singing about Maeve. That was all he needed to know.

The enassuanii below had unwound long, flowing ribbons that trailed through the air as they flew. One by one, the singers added more flowing strands of color until the entire stage was alive with a shifting, slithering rainbow. The song rose as slowly as building storm clouds and the Arcadians above the glass stage began to swoop closer to one another, delicately brushing fingers and wings.

Maeve leaned against Logan, her wing brushing soft feathers along the back of his neck. His illonium fingers tightened on hers, making the queen hiss quietly in pain. But she was still smiling and her fingers curled warm and soft around Logan's. His heart raced. The enassui was rising into a crescendo, flowing Arcadian voices that filled the theater as the first act reached its climax. Logan recognized one of the words... Not Arcadian, but the sound of his own name.

"They are singing of you," Maeve whispered. "About my hunter chasing me."

"You told them about me. Why?" Logan asked. "The enassui is supposed to be about you."

"My story is hollow without you, Logan," Maeve answered so softly that he had to lean close to catch the words. "My hunter. My enarri."

"My enarri," Logan repeated. *My beloved.*

The singers had threaded their flowing ribbons into an intricate knot, weaving strands of color into a spiraling coil, but Maeve was no longer watching them. She stared at Logan with bright, wide silver eyes and clasped his cybernetic hand tightly, as though afraid to let go. Afraid she would drown if she did.

Logan raised his other hand and traced the sharp, fine line of Maeve's jaw. How could one woman be so strong – the queen of an entire race and the spear point for their war against Xartasia – and still be so vulnerable? How could Maeve Cavainna still need Logan?

He was just an uneducated Prian man, a disgraced police officer, an unlicensed bounty hunter and her ex-lover.

But she *did* need him. Maeve still needed him...

She was so close, those silver storm-cloud eyes filling Logan's vision. And her lips, as soft as silk and gently seeking his. Where was Anthem? He was supposed to be here, not Logan. Here with Maeve, surrounded by song and gleaming golden glass and the gentle fragrance of jasmine... His fingers curled against the back of Maeve's neck, pulling her up, pulling her close. Her lips found his and she kissed him. She tasted like the jasmine smelled, so sweet and heady that Logan was dizzy with the sensation.

Maeve... My dove, my enarri...

Logan's eyes closed and he pulled Maeve against him, hearing the queen's soft, surprised gasp and tasting it in their kiss. The enassui surrounded them in sound, intimate yet concealing. Thousands of Arcadians below watched the show, not their queen in the arms of the man she was not supposed to love. They couldn't hear her small cries as Logan's hands moved across her smooth skin. It was just like playing his guitar... He had not forgotten how. He couldn't forget. Not ever.

Thunder boomed out across the theater. No, not thunder, Logan realized nearly too late. An explosion. The enassuanii's song tore apart into screams and glass filled the air in a rain of blazing crystal daggers. One of them tumbled and sliced a hot, deep line of pain along Logan's spine.

Arcadians were everywhere, flinging themselves into the air in every direction, smashing into one another in storms of blood and feathers and seared clothes. Many of the fairies were on fire, hair and wings blazing. They screamed and fell to the shattered theater floor. The acrid stench of seared flesh made Logan's throat burn.

The stage was gone and smoke billowed from the crater where it had stood. Glass glowed white-hot and flowed in melted rivulets across the blackened sand. One of the enassuanii singers was on the ground, pinned there by an overturned piece of the stage and screaming as liquid glass ran over his sizzling skin. More Arcadians lay dead and dying, torn apart by the explosion or impaled by shattered glass. Their blood was invisible against the red Gharib sand. Beneath Logan's feet, the royal tower shuddered. Glass snapped and shattered with sharp, brittle retorts and the whole building swayed.

"Logan..."

The voice was quiet, strained. Logan spun to find Maeve on her knees, blood spattered across her diaphanous silver gown. One of her wings was stained red; the one that had been draped around Logan. The blade of shattered glass that had cut his back had sliced right through the delicate membrane of Maeve's wing. Her feathers were sticky and matted with blood. There was no way she could fly.

Logan swept Maeve into his arms. She weighed no more than a child, but the glass beneath his feet cracked, opaque lines racing out in all directions like fleeing snakes. An Arcadian man in seared and smoking rags tumbled from the churning sky and down to the tower top. He smashed into breaking glass, leaving smears of red across the shattered remains.

There were shouts from the stairwell. Gripper shoved his way through the narrow confines.

"Hunter!"

"I'm here," Logan called out.

He leapt over the widening crack across the glass. Logan wished that he could see the floor beneath his feet as he ran, but Maeve's wings obscured his view. The theater tower shivered again and swayed like a tree in the wind. Logan landed hard, sooner than he expected, and the impact shivered up his aching, injured spine. The crumbling floor was slick with blood. Logan fought for footing and then Gripper's huge hand closed on his shoulder.

"This tower's falling!" the Arboran shouted. "Shimmer's doing his best to keep it up, but he says the pattern's too complicated. We have to get out of here!"

Logan nodded. His throat felt raw. There must have been glass in the smoke, too. He followed Gripper down the stairs, slamming into the translucent walls every time the tower moved and struggling to keep Maeve sheltered. Cracks snaked like bolts of lightning through the collapsing walls. The tower was full of jagged shards and deafening shrills of tearing glass. Blades of broken crystal tore at Logan's clothes and the flesh beneath. Gripper's thick skin was covered in cuts, many of them shallow but all oozing dark blood.

They staggered out of the tower at last, into the hellishly flickering firelight and billowing black smoke. Panna, Duke Ferris and Xia ran to Logan as he set Maeve down. The queen's legs wobbled, but held. Xia gasped at the bloody rent in her wing and Panna went pale. Duaal stood a little distance away, fists clenched before him and his dark, ash-smeared jaw set as he stared at the tower.

"Everybody out?" he shouted in a strained voice.

"All clear!" Gripper called back.

Sweat shone on Duaal's brow as he uncurled his fingers and raised his hands. The theater tower went milky all along its length with cracks. Duaal lowered his hands, palms down, and the glass spire fell in on itself like a house of cards. A few motes of glittering diamond dust rolled out from the stump of the tower, but the Hyzaari mage contained the rest of the dangerous razor shrapnel.

Maeve was pushing Xia away and struggling toward the chaos.

"What happened?" she asked.

"We have no idea," Panna said. She coughed and held her hand to her side.

"Bomb," Logan answered shortly. He pointed across the ruins of the theater to what had once been the stage. "There."

Several winged shapes plummeted through the smoke, landed hard and ran toward Maeve. Logan moved to intercept them, but recognized Ballad and Syle leading the other young knights. The Prian fairy's face was smeared in ash and blood. The Arcadians stopped in front of Logan, eyes wide as they stared at their queen.

"Is she...?" Syle asked.

"I am fine," Maeve said. "How many are not?"

"Don't know yet. We came to find you and Sir Anthem," Ballad answered. "Where is he?"

"You do not know? Find him at once!" Maeve commanded.

Duaal and Gripper exchanged a guilty look.

"We know where Anthem is, Maeve," Duaal said. "He's back on the Blue Phoenix."

"I programmed the airlock to seal as soon as he went into the hold. We thought that you and Hunter..." Gripper trailed off, pale-faced and trembling.

"You imprisoned the royal consort?" Ferris cried. "How dare–!"

"Enough!" Maeve shouted. She whirled on Gripper, blood still streaming from her wounded wing. "Get him out of the Phoenix and back into Kaellisem. I need all of my knights!"

"Maeve, we just–" Duaal said.

She ignored him. She turned back to Ballad and Syle. "Begin a search of the theater. Help those who can be helped and count the dead. Take those who need medical attention to the Blue Phoenix. Gripper, get Xia back to the ship and her medbay. You will need to return there, too, after all."

"Yes, Glass," Gripper said. He followed Xia from the theater at a stoop-shouldered trot.

"Panna, go with Duaal," Maeve told the blonde girl. "Reinforce any compromised buildings and help the knights retrieve the dead and wounded."

"Yes, Your Majesty," Panna said. She grabbed Duaal's elbow and the two of them ran off into the shattered ruins of the theater.

"Ferris, find Hyra or Lorren," Maeve instructed the old noble-man. "This much broken glass is dangerous and only they know how to deal with it."

"My queen, you could have been killed! For all we know, that was the very purpose of this attack," Ferris said. "Syle!"

The yellow-eyed knight had not flown far. He wheeled and then landed again.

"Yes, Your Grace?" Syle asked.

"Remain with Queen Maeve," Ferris told the knight. "Do not let her out of your sight and protect her with your life!"

"Yes, Your Grace," Syle answered at once.

Satisfied for the moment, Duke Ferris took a step across the blasted glass and then took to the air in search of the smiths. He vanished quickly into the dark smoke. Logan looked at Maeve.

"What do you want me to do?" he asked.

Maeve's gray eyes were narrowed slits like steel blades.

"You are released from my guard," she said in a low, furious hiss. "You have a new duty, my hunter. Find the one who did this!"

Logan bowed. "Yes, Your Majesty."

Jessica Centra had not brought an umbrella. Stupid... It had been raining for two months. Why should it stop today? It was just another day on Prianus, no different from any other. The acidic rain fell in sharp diagonal lines, yanked north by the cold, razor winds. It probably didn't matter whether she had an umbrella, Jess decided.

Captain Lain stood under the leafless old alder tree. He did not have an umbrella, either. The rain splashed unnoticed from the shoulders of his dark blue uniform. The left one was a slightly different shade than the rest of the uniform. Patched, probably shredded by a hawk's talons... or by the bullet that had taken its previous owner's life. There was always a bird, always a bullet, and always rain on Prianus.

Captain Lain raised his right hand. He was young. Barely more than a boy, Jess thought. A large oil-fed torch burned on his right side, hissing and popping and twisting in the rain.

"Our lives are only the last things we give for our world," Lain said loudly, but still only barely audible over the drumming rain. "We each

knew that when we put on the uniform and we face our life's end without fear. But what about those left behind? We miss our brothers and sisters, husbands and wives, sons and daughters when they are gone."

When they were taken. Stolen away on a routine chem investigation, right after finally making detective.

Jess barely saw Captain Lain. She had eyes only for the line of white-wrapped bodies on their biers, shrouded and soaked by the rain. All seven bodies looked the same, faceless and anonymous. Shouldn't she be able to tell? Some instinct, some otherworldly sense that drew her? But there was nothing. There was only the rain and the fire.

Captain Lain was still talking, but Jess wasn't listening anymore. She just stared at the dead.

Which one? Which one was her husband? Had been her husband? Beside her, Vorus tugged on his mother's rain-soaked dress. Jess pushed him away. Where was Logan? Where was her hawk?

Captain Lain had finished his speech and took up the torch, walking slowly through the rain along the line of biers. Jess wanted to jump to her feet, to scream at the police captain to stop. Not yet, she had to find Logan! But she sat still as a statue while Vorus cried silently beside her. Rain ran down her face, burning and stinking of chemicals.

The first bier caught fire, red and gold flames spread along the cloth, turning it as black as the boiling clouds filling the sky. The wet wood threw sparks like miniature lightning bolts into the darkening night, cracked and popped like tiny booms of thunder. But the flames burned low and pale under the unceasing torrent. Captain Lain moved down the line, setting the second, third and more funeral pyres ablaze. Faceless white bodies became flickering golems of flame and then faceless black ash.

Where was Logan? Where was he?

Jess sat in the rain long after the fires had burned out.

[24]

BURN AWAY

"The moment you decided to fight, you lost the battle."

- SYLE LAMANNA (234 PA)

Glass did not burn well. The fires went out within minutes of the explosion, sinking the ruined theater into darkness. The lights had either been blown to fragments or crushed under falling debris. The knights searched by flashlight and wavering glow spells, one of the first charms that Anthem had taught those who could learn Arcadian magic. The prince consort joined the search as soon as Gripper released him from the Blue Phoenix, asking no questions of the Arboran or anyone else until much later.

Not until his job was done.

By midnight, Panna had collected and confirmed the knights' counts – sixty-eight dead, including all eight of the enassui singers and two royal knights. One hundred thirty-seven injured. By dawn, both numbers had climbed even higher. Duke Ferris estimated that more than three hundred Arcadians had fled Kaellisem.

"Where are they going?" Maeve asked.

Ferris shrugged. His wingtips dragged wearily on the floor.

"I do not know, a'shae," he told her. "I doubt that they do, either. They are frightened. Some may return, but..."

Maeve didn't ask the duke to finish. He did not need to. Those who left would not return. If they had the chance, they might even fly away to Xartasia. She could protect them. If they were frightened enough, it would not matter if she used Devourers to do it.

Maeve beat her wings in futile frustration, wincing at the bright slash of pain along the right one. Xia had cleaned and stitched the wound shut, but she still didn't have a nanite supply to hasten the healing. Even if she had access to some of the microscopic surgical machines, there were those who needed them more.

The bloated red sun was rising slowly outside. Maeve had reluctantly withdrawn to her tower back in Kaellisem. She didn't want to leave the theater, but she was only getting in the way of those with actual work to do amid the broken glass.

"Has Coldhand found anything yet?" Duke Ferris asked.

He asked the question grudgingly. Ferris liked the Prian hunter even less now, after Gripper and Duaal's trick, but even the hidebound old nobleman had to admit that Logan Coldhand was the only one in Kaellisem with any sort of police experience. Maeve wished she could smile, but she was too tired.

"Logan found the remains of a bomb placed beneath the stage. Any..." Maeve searched for the words that Logan had used. "...trace evidence was destroyed in the blast. He is speaking with the knights who were at the theater yesterday. Perhaps one of them witnessed something of use."

"I cannot imagine why anyone would disrupt the enassui, Your Majesty," Ferris said. He held out a glass and Verra hurried to refill it from a decanter of watered-down wine.

"Really?" Maeve asked darkly. "You cannot? I have no difficulty. We have plenty of enemies, from local malcontents to Xartasia herself. Surely she knows we are here and that I am raising a kingdom against her."

"If that is true, my queen, then this will not be the end."

"No," Maeve agreed. "There will be more. Arcadians will die. They will bleed and they will leave. If they go to Xartasia, all we have built here will be for nothing."

Dain came into the room and waited until Maeve gestured her closer. The girl bobbed her wings. "Queen Maeve, Sir Anthem is here to see you."

"Please bring him."

Maeve felt as if she were choking on the words. The last time she had spoken with Anthem was before the enassui. Before kissing Logan at the theater, before the bomb. When Dain returned with the knight, Maeve dismissed Ferris and her two handmaidens. With Anthem there and Logan Coldhand notably absent, Ferris seemed happy enough to leave the queen alone.

Anthem's glass armor was dull with dust and he wasn't carrying his spear. But even now, his pale blond hair remained smooth and shone like Aes' light. Sir Anthem inclined his head to Maeve.

"A'shae," he said in a voice roughened by smoke. "Are you well? Ballad told me that you were injured."

"Just my wing," Maeve answered. Her mouth was as dry as dust. "I am alright, Sir Anthem. Thank you."

He searched her face with midnight blue eyes.

"I came to receive your orders, a'shae. What would you have of your knights?" Anthem asked.

Sleep, Maeve thought at once. Anthem and the rest had worked throughout the night. They all needed rest. But she swallowed hard and took a deep breath.

"I... I must apologize for Gripper and Duaal," Maeve said. "I am sorry, Anthem. They were trying to–"

"I know what they did," Anthem interrupted. When he smiled, it was sad and gentle. "My queen... Maeve... I am not a fool. I know what you share with Logan Coldhand. I know that you love him with all your heart. Swearing yourself to me has not changed that."

Maeve had no idea what to say. Her head spun. She needed to sleep, too. "But our people—"

"Need an Arcadian king," Anthem said. "Yes, I know what Duke Ferris said to you. And I agree. Kaellisem needs us. But I understand perhaps better than you can know."

"Understand what?"

"I still love Titania. Even though I know that she is a traitor to her blood. I know that she is our enemy and that the day will come when we must deal with that. But I love her still, Maeve. I always will." Anthem took Maeve's hands delicately. They were dirty with ash and curled immediately into fists. Anthem ran his thumbs over the tightened fingers. "But you are a noble woman, Maeve. You are strong, fierce and beautiful. I see why Logan loves you, how you fill even his icy heart with fire. I said that I could love you and I asked you the same. You have never answered."

Maeve's stomach twisted into a hard, painful knot.

Could she...? Anthem was a good knight. He had been nothing but kind to Maeve, even as she spat insults at him. Anthem was noble and intelligent. He had already taken up some of the burden of rulership from Maeve, but never with the overbearing disapproval that she faced so often with Duke Ferris.

Anthem was beautiful, Maeve had to admit to herself. He even shared Logan's blond hair and blue eyes...

And Anthem was Arcadian. Humans made for difficult lovers, so much larger and stronger than a fairy partner. There were always their wings, too, which humans couldn't seem to figure out how to handle. Anthem understood Maeve's culture and her language. She would never need to translate for him. She would never need to explain the Arcadian gods to him, or why an enassui was different from a coreworld opera.

But Anthem would never love Maeve as Logan did. Her hunter. Logan had been there through her brightest and darkest moments, always holding her in that unwavering ice-blue gaze.

Sir Anthem still held her hands and drew Maeve to him. Something inside her wanted to struggle, to pull away from the knight, but something else craved Anthem's closeness. Her work kept her so busy. She barely saw Duaal, Xia and Gripper anymore. Logan was usually nearby, but Ferris and her handmaidens watched over them always, ever on guard against impropriety. They had shared only that first act of the enassui, interrupted by the explosion. And then Maeve herself had sent Logan away to find the bomber.

The queen was lonely. Anthem leaned in slowly. Maeve could have stopped the kiss, but she didn't. He held her there against his armored chest and did not comment on her tears. Maeve, in return, said nothing of his.

● ● ●

Xia worked through the night. Gripper wished that she wouldn't, but the Ixthian would not listen to anything he had to say. Every time he poked his large brown head into the medical bay, Xia ignored Gripper and kept working on the endless stream of wounded Arcadians. Eventually, he brought a bowl of soup and a large cup of coffee. He put them on the counter and left without trying to talk to Xia.

Duaal was waiting for him in the corridor outside. Other than Xia's busy medbay – which smelled now of blood and burnt feathers, finally overwhelming the pungent chemical scent of disinfectants – the Blue Phoenix was eerily quiet. Was it still night outside? Gripper had not looked out a window in a while and found that he didn't really care. He missed having Maeve and Logan on the ship. He missed grumpy old Tiberius and even the ill-tempered, sharp-taloned Orphia.

"Is she still mad at us?" Duaal asked Gripper.

"Who?"

"Xia."

"Yeah, I think so."

Duaal couldn't walk beside the huge Arboran in the ship corridors, but followed close behind Gripper as he made his way to the engine room. The old ship groaned metallically all around them. She didn't like sitting in the sand and gravity so long. The Blue Phoenix was meant to fly. Not unlike Maeve, Gripper thought unhappily. All he and Duaal had tried to give her was a little time to be herself. To be Maeve, Glass... not the queen of Kaellisem.

Gripper ducked through the human-sized door into his favorite room. The engine was quiet and still inside its cylindrical fibersteel case. Cables and pipes and colored wires snaked across the ceiling and floor, out into the rest of the Blue Phoenix. Duaal pushed himself up to sit on the edge of Gripper's oil-stained workbench and looked around the engine room.

"I don't think I've ever been back here," he said. "What's that?"

Duaal pointed to one of the walls of the engine room. It was a patchwork grid of lights and monitors. Most of the screens were dark, but a few displayed readouts, columns of numbers or blinking cursors.

"That's the computer core," Gripper told him. "It pretty much runs the whole ship."

"I thought that was my job."

Gripper did not have the heart to smile. He wasn't even sure that Duaal was joking.

"There are way too many things on a starship to keep track of," Gripper said. "When you bank the Blue Phoenix, there are seventeen systems that need to do stuff at the same time. Do you know how many filters and pumps work to keep us all from asphyxiating? The Blue Phoenix has over a thousand subsystems. There isn't a captain in the galaxy that doesn't rely on a computer. That's why it was so bad when Hunter had me get into the Oslain'ii's system."

Gripper fell silent and Duaal kicked his feet, polished boots flashing under the lights. His shirt was torn, missing most of the left sleeve and there were several blackened scorch marks on Duaal's cream-colored pants. But his boots were still somehow as shiny as beetle shells.

"Do you need something, captain?" Gripper asked at last.

Duaal looked up from his boots, which seemed to have captivated him as much as they had Gripper. "No. I just don't know what else to do. There's nowhere to fly. What do we do now?"

"I'm not sure," Gripper admitted.

"You can help me with this."

They turned to find Logan standing in the doorway. The Prian tossed a folded mycolar bag to Duaal, who caught it out of the air and held it up. There was maybe a spoonful of black ash inside.

"What's this?" the mage asked.

"A piece of explosive, I think," Logan answered. "But it's been completely fused by the heat. So I need you to tell me what it used to be."

"Xia has a bay full of equipment," Duaal pointed out.

"This isn't organic," Logan said. "It's chemical. Nothing Xia's got can reconstruct consumed fuel, which I think is what we've got here. But your magic deals with things like chemical reactions. Can you figure out what it was?"

Duaal turned the bag over in his hands and shook his head.

"I... don't think so," he said. "I have to be able to visualize or at least conceptualize what I'm trying to do. I have no idea how this used to be structured, so I can't revert it. Sorry."

He tossed the bag of ash back. Logan pocketed it and nodded. He turned to go, but Gripper spoke up.

"Hunter, can't the Gharib police help you with that?" he asked. "They must have labs to analyze this sort of thing."

"Yes," Logan lingered in the door. His pale eyes were hard. "But they won't talk to me. I'm not a licensed bounty hunter anymore."

"Why the hells not?" Duaal asked. He jumped down from Gripper's workbench. "This is just ridiculous. Let me give Kessa a call.

She got the Gharib police to come to the rescue once. Maybe she can make them do it again."

Duaal's determined march out of the engine room was somewhat undermined by having to squeeze sideways past Logan in the door, but made up for it by swearing blisteringly the whole way across the ship. Gripper waited until the captain's voice had faded.

"Hunter?" he asked at last.

Logan looked up. "Yes?"

Gripper hesitated. Was Logan angry? Gripper could never tell what his friend was thinking. Was Coldhand really his friend? The thought tripped Gripper up all over again and he almost couldn't speak. But he had to know.

"Is... is what happened tonight our fault?" Gripper asked. "Me and Shimmer? Because of what we did?"

For a terrible moment, Logan didn't answer. When he did, there was nothing gentle or even friendly in his voice.

"No," Logan said. "You and Duaal had nothing to do with that bomb. Anthem couldn't have stopped it from going off. He might have been able to organize the knights a little faster, but Ballad did a good job bringing them to Maeve for orders."

Gripper's eyes filled with tears.

"Are you sure, Hunter?" he asked. "We... I didn't kill all those fairies?"

"You shouldn't have locked Anthem in the Blue Phoenix. That was a dishonorable way to deal with him and it was dangerous... But no, the bombing wasn't your fault."

Before Logan could protest, Gripper bounded across the engine room. He banged his head on a pipe, but didn't care as he grabbed the hunter up into a long-armed hug and squeezed.

"Thank you," Gripper said, lifting Logan up into the air. "It was so awful, what I did to the Oslain'ii pilot, but he was trying to kill us. I couldn't stand that I might have killed a bunch of innocent fairies. Thank you!"

Logan remained still in Gripper's embrace, even though the relieved, over-exuberant hug probably hurt.

"But until we find the one who is responsible, Maeve and all the Arcadians in Kaellisem are still in danger," Logan said. "Duaal and Kessa won't get any assistance from the Gharib police. They only helped before because Kessa promised them Maeve's bounty. Unless we pay them, the local cops won't raise a finger. I'll be working alone on this."

Gripper put the Prian down. "No way. I'm going to help you."

— ● ● ● —

Panna felt guilty sleeping when she was sure that Maeve was not. But she knew she would be useless to the queen exhausted, so she grabbed a few hours of rest before reporting to the royal tower.

In the pale pink dawn, Kaellisem was eerily quiet. Panna walked through the dust along the wide central street. Not empty... There were Arcadians in the windows of every tower, all with wide, tired eyes and closed mouths.

No one was singing. There were other fairies in the street, too, lining up in front of the Blue Phoenix. Late last night, Xia had called Xyn in from Gharib to help with the wounded. Panna suspected that the grumpy little scientist had come quickly and probably worked through the night alongside Xia. The Ixthians were an amazing species. They could seem so cold and distant at times, but little would stop an Ixthian from coming to the aid of the sick and injured.

Panna felt another pang in her breast, but this one wasn't guilt. She missed Professor Xen. He had taken Panna under his wing and guided her education, even though she had lied to him about her genetic heritage. Xen had been brilliant, discerning and even handsome in a strange, alien sort of way.

Had she loved the Ixthian professor? Panna suspected so.

But now Xen was dead, killed and consumed by the Devourers. Though Panna had never set foot on Arcadian soil, the Devourers had still managed to take away what she loved best...

Panna walked past the Blue Phoenix. In the back, the cargo ramp was lowered into the dusty Kaellisem road. Kessa and Vyron both stood at the bottom, taking down names and entering information into datadexes. Panna waved to them and at Xyn, who was just inside the ship's hold, bandaging up a young Arcadian's wing. All three nodded to Panna, but didn't pause in their work.

The Stray morning was dry and dim. Panna's indistinct shadow stretched out behind her like a dark bridal train. There were two knights stationed at the base of Maeve's tower and she saw four more circling in the dawn-violet sky or landed on balconies. Panna made her way past the pair outside and climbed the narrow glass stairs. They were a little too shallow to mount easily but too deep to just skip every other one. Hyra had insisted upon singing up the royal spire himself and the glass-smith clearly had a purely academic understanding of a staircase's workings. It was depressing to think that Panna was the only Arcadian in Kaellisem who had to use them, but she reminded herself that Maeve often did, too.

Panna paused in front of a window a few stories up the tower. Outside, a flock of Arcadians flew over Kaellisem and toward the square silhouettes of Gharib. Leaving. Panna grabbed for her com and stared at it for several seconds before she realized that she had no idea who was leaving or how to contact them. Most fairies didn't even carry coms.

She sighed and replaced her com into the pocket of her pants. They were made of a smooth, slithery blue fabric, woven by one of the Arcadians of Kaellisem. Maybe one of those flying away right now... Panna rubbed the cloth between her fingers and wondered what would become of its maker.

The queen was in an airy, light-filled room that was part parlor, part audience chamber. Maeve sat in a backless chair and a long cream-colored gown pooled around her bare feet. There were dark circles under her eyes, but they were barely visible beneath the skillfully painted makeup. Sir Anthem stood behind her. Someone had cleaned his armor. The plates shined like a frozen ocean over the blue and silver scarves. One of Anthem's glass-gauntleted hands was wrapped around his spear, but the other rested on Maeve's bare shoulder.

Panna blinked. Had she *ever* seen Sir Anthem touching Maeve before? She didn't think so. Panna was suddenly quite certain that Anthem had never left the queen's company that night. Gods, did Logan know...?

"Good morning, Your Majesty," Panna stammered, covering her confusion with a deep bow. "You wanted to see me?"

"Yes," Maeve answered. "Thank you for coming so early."

There were footsteps behind her and Panna turned to find Sir Ballad in the doorway. His short blond hair stuck to his forehead in sweaty points. He spread his wings and inclined his head.

"Sorry I'm late, Majesty," he said through his Prian accent.

"It has been a long night for us all," Maeve told him. "But I fear that I only have more work for you two."

Panna glanced sidelong at the young knight. "Both of us?"

Queen Maeve nodded. She looked at Ballad.

"What I must ask of Panna is dangerous," she told the knight. "I need you to protect her and help her, Sir Ballad."

"Yes, Your Majesty."

Maeve returned her attention to Panna.

"You began this, Panna," she said. "You were the first to suggest that I should take up the crown."

Panna's mouth went suddenly as dry as the desert outside. Did Maeve blame her for what had happened at the theater? For the end of her relationship with Logan Coldhand? For all of it? Was this dangerous work some sort of punishment? Panna couldn't imagine Maeve doing anything like that, but the queen was a descendant of

Cavain, the man who had wiped out the pyrads to build Arcadia. What would Maeve sacrifice for Kaellisem? Panna suspected it was much more than one wingless little anthropologist.

"Too many died last night," Maeve went on. "And many more are leaving our city out of fear. You know what that may cost us against Xartasia."

"Yes... yes, a'shae," Panna said. "What do you want me to do?"

"The same thing that I have. We need to continue seeking out and speaking to the Arcadians scattered across the galaxy. I cannot leave Kaellisem right now, Duke Ferris tells me," Maeve said sourly. "I must remain on Stray, but you must find our people."

"Me?" Panna asked.

Maeve nodded and smiled at her. "Yes, you. You wrote most of my speeches, anyway. Now I ask you to go to more Alliance worlds to give them yourself."

"Me?" Panna repeated, stunned.

"We will send you with whatever money Kaellisem can spare," Maeve said. "Use it to send as many to Stray as you can convince. We can give them a home here and keep them from Xartasia's grasp. Sir Ballad will be your protector and assistant."

Panna was a little pleased to note that Ballad looked unhappy with this new assignment. Sir Anthem noticed, too, and gave the proud young Prian knight a stern look. Ballad's wings drooped.

Maeve either did not notice or else simply said nothing.

"First, you will go to Hadra," she continued. "The gravity there is much greater than what you are used to on Prianus or Stray, Sir Ballad. Have care. It is a hard world for Arcadians. Please, reach as many as you can and send them back to Kaellisem."

"But I don't even look Arcadian," Panna pointed out.

Maeve nodded. "And so you will encounter less resistance from the Alliance. Tell your story. Tell all of our stories. Tell our people what we have built here."

"I will, Queen Maeve," Panna promised.

"I wish that I could send you on the Blue Phoenix, but I fear that I need Duaal and his ship to remain. Xia's medbay there is all the help we have for most of those injured last night. Xyn has offered his help, for which we are unendingly grateful, but his facilities are of limited use. So Vyron has arranged passage to Hadra aboard another cargo ship. It will not be lavish, Panna, and I am sorry that I cannot offer you better."

"It's fine," Ballad said quickly. "We'll manage, Majesty."

Panna didn't really want to agree with the crude young knight, but had to nod. "The money will be much better spent getting Arcadians off Hadra."

Maeve smiled, but her expression was tired and tight. Was she angry? Sad? Both, Panna suspected. A queen's responsibilities were many and her worries many more.

"We'll depart at once," Panna said. She would get started at once and make Maeve proud.

"Your ship, the Vostra Sann, will not be leaving until tomorrow morning," Sir Anthem told her.

Panna blushed.

"Oh," she said sheepishly. "Right. We'll leave tomorrow, then."

[25]

ANZHOTEK

"The end of night is the beginning of day."

- TITANIA CAVAINNA (220 PA)

The sun had set hours ago and the thickly overlapping leaves were beginning to curl at the edges for their nocturnal retreat. Within an hour, the thick, verdant green shell that covered this part of Weh-Weh would become unclimbable, tightly furled spears of vegetation until the sun rose again. If Anandrou didn't get back to the branches of the village tree in the next hour, he would be stranded in the branches of the old sycona.

But that was an entire hour away. Anandrou picked another large purple flower and pulled off the petals one by one with his teeth. They were soft and sweet and far tastier than anything his mother made for dinner. She would probably scold her youngest child for spoiling his appetite, but it was more than a fair trade, Anandrou thought.

Something bright streaked across the darkening sky. A meteorite...? Anandrou's father always said they were celestial seeds falling through the sky to plant themselves in Weh-Weh's rich, dark soil. But others said they were pieces of the distant stars. No one knew for sure... When they burned all the way down into the forest, the meteorites seared blackened holes through the trees and down onto the surface. Once down below the canopy, they were gone forever.

Burning light blazed in the sky for a moment and then was gone. Had it landed? Anandrou wondered if he could find it. He was the best and fastest climber in his village. Anandrou swung up into a higher branch and stared after the fallen star. He could find it. He could see for himself.

But Anandrou picked a handful of sweet blossoms and began making his way home, chewing slowly on one of the purple sweets. What did it matter what the stars were made of? He would never reach them.

———— ● ● ●

Another great tree toppled, smoking from the laser burns that seared through its huge trunk. The sycona tree crashed through the branches of smaller trees, down to the distant ground and filled the air with long spears of shattered wood. Delicate purple flowers fell through the fire-hot air, curling and blackening all around Xartasia. The toppled tree left a deep, dark chasm in the thick green canopy.

Dhozo and his Devourers had surrounded the frightened aliens of Anzhotek. They were almost as tall as the Devourers, all with the same long arms and ears. But they lacked the slick, utterly hairless gray skin. Instead, they had rough brown hide and patches of dark green fur, usually around their forearms, but Xartasia saw some of the mossy-looking hair sprouting from shoulders and heads. For all their size and massive, impressively clawed hands, the Arborans cowered among their leaf huts. They screamed in a language that Xartasia did not know as Dhozo and Orix and the rest tore them apart. Blood ran bright red across green Anzhotek.

Fifty of Xartasia's knights surrounded their queen, spears held at the ready. Some of the aliens – Arborans, as she knew them, degenerate cousins and food to Dhozo – had already tried to run. They weren't warriors, but they were large and frightened... Their blood already dripped from some of the knights' glass spear blades.

The bodies through which it once flowed were gone, of course. Dhozo's Devourers preferred to kill their food themselves, but no meat could be ignored.

An Arboran child – young but still as tall as Xartasia herself – broke from her terrified parents as Orix descended on them in a storm of black barbs and blades. The Arboran girl was naked, skin bare to the warm yellow suns. She bolted across the thick layers of leaves that made up her village's foundation and under Orix's curling, cutting nanite storm. Her parents cried out. Were they calling her back or urging their child on, to run and climb away? Whatever their words, they didn't last long as Orix's gleaming black nanites stabbed a hundred tiny serrated blades into the two adult Arborans.

The girl wailed, tugging her long ears with her hands, and kept running. The rest of her treetop village was in flames and the Devourers had cut away the trees to close off their escape, so she fled the only way left to her – toward Xartasia. Her knights shared uneasy glances but lowered their spears in a defensive ring of blades. The young Arboran skidded and stumbled to a stop, her green eyes huge and terrified.

"Drive her back into the Devourers," Xartasia ordered. "Kill her yourselves if you must."

"But my queen, she is only a child," said one of the knights. Her spear wavered. "Surely she does not have to die..."

Several other fairies hummed their agreement. Dhozo stalked across the thick, overlapping leaves toward the circle of Arcadians. The green surface turned brown and then black around him. The Arboran girl whimpered and scrambled away from Dhozo.

Xartasia pushed through the line of her knights and seized the terrified alien girl by her knobby shoulder. She screeched, gaping at the approaching Devourer commander. But the Arboran's mass was much greater than Xartasia's and she was wriggling rapidly away. Xartasia drew the dagger from her white sash and slid it across the girl's throat. Her thick skin was no match for the glass' razor edge.

Xartasia stepped swiftly back as blood sprayed into the humid air. Dhozo's nanites swirled, catching the salty, iron-rich red from the air and the blackening leaves under his feet. She did not let herself turn away as Dhozo dissected and consumed the Arboran child.

"A'shae!" another knight said in a choked voice. "Why...?"

"For the White Kingdom and all of our people who died there," Xartasia answered the unfinished question. She had to raise her musical voice over the sickening sound of breaking bones. "The price is high, Sir Corrus. You knew that it would be. But remember what we buy with it."

Corrus nodded slowly and lifted up his spear. Violet and blue ribbons streamed out from the haft in the hot, damp wind. Bright orange embers swirled up from the burning village and singed tiny black spots into the green ground like diseased sores.

Xartasia watched Dhozo chew up the last of the Arboran child's entrails with sharp white teeth. She might have agreed to the price, but she did not have to like it and she did not have to remain silent. Dhozo licked his lips with a long, dark purple tongue and then his swarming nanite armor obscured his face in smoky darkness again.

"Surely your own people deserve a cleaner death, commander," Xartasia said.

"These are *not* my people," Dhozo snarled.

"They look like you."

"These degenerates are not Glorious," Dhozo said. "Some of the Anzhotekki researchers objected to the empire's expansion when we left this galaxy. We assumed that they would just die out. But they became... herbivores."

Dhozo said this last word with such a deep disgust that Xartasia glanced down around the Devourer's feet. His nanite swarm was burning, harvesting and consuming the thick layer of foliage, but Dhozo himself ate not a single bite.

"They became the Arborans," Xartasia said. She looked back up at the Devourer. "And we survived, as well. You created the fairies, servants that looked like creatures from your own stories. Why did you leave your slaves behind?"

Dhozo's nanites carried her words to be translated by the computer implanted in his brain.

"There was no room," he answered. "We required every ship to save ourselves from the famine. You and your worlds were luxury resources, anyway. Delicacies."

Xartasia nodded shortly. She didn't need the Devourers to flatter her, just to obey.

"If you have eaten your fill, commander," she said, "it is time to move on."

"The Glorious are never sated. But we need data." Dhozo raised his voice. "Form up!"

Fifteen of the hulking aliens returned at once to Commander Dhozo's side, but the last two – Orix and Tekker – didn't report until he repeated his order twice more.

They descended through the huge hole in the canopy left by the toppled sycona tree, down into the dark. The fairies soared easily on the warm, wet air, down below the fires burning above and the billowing black smoke, but the Devourers simply jumped. Hook-tipped black tendrils tore through bark and dug deep into the living wood beneath, breaking their owners' falls. They dropped the final distance and landed on glimmering red force fields that reminded Xartasia of the coreworlders' null-inertia technology.

The queen alighted gently on the spongy loam of the planet's surface. Some sunlight filtered down from the distant canopy, but not much. Xartasia's knights and the Devourers were little more than slightly darker shadows in the deeper green-tinged blackness. The great trees of Arborus creaked and groaned ominously all around, forbidding this invasion in an ancient and indecipherable tongue.

Xartasia sang a charm and a sourceless glow kindled around her. The other knights echoed their queen's spell as the Devourers squinted, muttering at the Arcadians. It was good to remind them that Xartasia still had knowledge the Devourers needed.

Arborus was just as dark and mysterious as it had been six years ago, when Xartasia had first found her way to the strange green planet in search of the secrets of the Waygates. The ground was as black as night, barren of any sort of undergrowth. There were the trees felled by the Devourers' lasers to cut off the Arboran's escape, too, columns of wood like starscrapers smashed across the forest floor, but even these had an eerie sort of agelessness about them.

Xartasia couldn't help remembering the cathedral in Gharib, the black columns cracked and broken by Maeve's ship when her captain came to save her. Gavriel very nearly died, his old bones crushed by the falling stone and sand. But Xartasia had saved him... only to kill him in the mountains above Pylos.

By then, Gavriel had served his purpose. Xartasia's purpose, in truth... She could teach magic to those not born to it, force the skills and power into an adult mind. With that, she could buy the Devourers. She had made servants of the greatest predators the galaxy had ever known.

But that night beneath the graveyard, Xartasia nearly lost everything. It had been a bloody reminder of just how fragile her plans truly were, and how tenuous the future was. How easily one woman could shatter everything...

Xartasia never returned to the place where the black cathedral had stood. It was just one of many pieces of land that she had purchased, tools in her long and intricate plan. Not bought in her own name, of course. Arcadians were not Alliance citizens and could not own land on CWA planets. The fallen black cathedral belonged to someone who did not really exist.

I do not exist, Xartasia reminded herself sternly. *I am the dream of death. Princess Titania died. Not all at once... But when I lost my home and my love, it began. The first frost of a hundred-year winter.*

But it will be spring again. All that has died will grow again.

Xartasia raised her right wing, a gesture for the rest to follow. The Arcadian knights took to the air alongside their queen and the Devourers fell into step below. Even in their own light, they slid like shadows through the darkness of Anzhotek's surface.

Other shadows moved between the huge trees, smaller than the Devourers but still large. They bounded between the trees on four legs covered in sleek green and brown fur. There was something lupine in the elongated muzzle and sharply pricked ears, like the Lyrans or wolves of Prianus. But the long, sinuously curling tail and slit-pupiled eyes were more feline. Whatever the creatures were, they were hungry and pounced, trying to swarm Orix and Zhyress at the column's rear.

The Devourers were hungrier.

Xartasia landed once, three hours into their journey, and peered up at the vast cathedral of trees. Dhozo loomed over her.

"Which way?" he asked.

"You ask me?" Xartasia settled her wings against her back. "It is your research center we are looking for, commander."

"It's four million years old now," Dhozo's nanite swarm buzzed. "It may as well be yours. You know more about the old science than we do anymore."

"Then be silent and let me find the way. I have been here only once and this world is always growing."

Dhozo quieted. Satisfied, Xartasia turned a slow circle, peering out at the vast, dark forest. Finally, she pointed.

"This way," she said.

Xartasia led them between the trees. There was no trail or road and the terrain was rough. Roots thicker than even Dhozo's body twined through the black soil. They flew over and walked under fallen leaves the size of houses.

"Was this forest here when you left Anzhotek?" Xartasia asked as Dhozo sliced his red laser through a tumbled branch covered in needles as long as Xartasia's wing.

"This?" Dhozo repeated. "No. When we closed the Anzhotek facility, there wasn't much left."

"But some."

"Some," the Glorious commander agreed. "Enough to–"

Dhozo's heavy boot came down on something hard, something other than the soft loam of Arborus. He shined his light across a road. It was badly cracked and had crumbled away to nothing in places.

Xartasia landed silently next to Dhozo. The road was made up of a million tiny tiles that threw back the light with a metallic gray sheen. Xartasia's knights landed beside her and they walked with the Devourers down the ancient roadway.

Not much had survived the eons and the encroaching forest of Anzhotek. There were some hollowed and cracked buildings, with windows like empty eye sockets. The structures were large, built to the Devourers' impressive scale, though it was difficult to make out the original details. Everything was covered in thick layers of dirt and moss and slimy, decaying leaves. But what Xartasia could see made her glance sidelong at Dhozo. The alien engineer swept his spotlight back and forth across the buildings.

The ancient city was beautiful in a strange, severe manner. The lines of the place, even broken and crooked and twisted by age, had a certain predatory grace to them that Xartasia hadn't noticed on her last visit. She had eyes only for the Waygates then, and the mysterious promises that the ageless technology held.

"No," Xartasia told Dhozo, who had turned down a wide, crumbling side road lined with long-broken houses. "This way."

They moved quickly down the broad main street, over a fallen branch that had splintered one of the empty buildings into smooth, steely fragments like thousands of fallen blades. Xartasia led the fairies and Devourers over a bridge. The passage beneath was long since gone, filled with dirt and twisting roots. On the far side were the crumpled remains of what appeared to be a security station.

Xartasia flew over the tumbled building and landed in the road beyond.

They made their way between huge warehouses, still standing despite the passage of ages. The doors were gone, but the buildings had been made to last. The walls were as thick as Xartasia was tall, tiled in some sort of high-impact ceramic but torn away in places by the encroaching jungle to expose the metallic mesh beneath.

Inside, illuminated by the Arcadians' directionless magical glow and more harshly by the Devourers' sweeping spotlights, were Waygates. Pieces of them, at least, dozens of disassembled segments. No two were quite alike. Some were longer or shorter arcs, all made up of a hundred different substances. Some glowed with a dim inner light, others were glass or metal or stone. A few had the geometric golden lines of circuitry, arcane runes or the organized and multi-colored dots of an electronic display.

The warehouses gave way suddenly to a clearing, some sort of plaza. It was circular, as wide across as a coreworld city block, and lined all around with Waygates. None of them had fallen. Every single one of the ancient gates stood straight and tall, towering even over Dhozo's indistinct head. From a distance, the Waygates were dark and blank, but as Xartasia and her company drew closer, all twenty-eight began to swirl and glow with blue radiance that cast no light across the plaza. Dhozo strode into the center of the circle.

"The Anzhotek prototype lab," he said in a low, hissing voice. "It's still here."

In Dhozo's own language, he commanded the rest of the team to spread out and began to collect information. Threads of glittering black nanites twisted and played over every surface, scanning and collating and transmitting data. Dhozo stood in the center of it all, the nexus of information.

The Devourer team was so brutal and terrible... it was difficult to remember sometimes that Dhozo and his alien colleagues were scientists. But it was that very skill which Xartasia required now.

Only the Waygates' creators could tell her if the great devices could do what she wished, what she *needed* them to. If the Devourers discovered here that they could not, everything – so much blood and suffering and horror – would be for nothing.

"What have you found?" Xartasia asked.

"Just composition and telemetry of the Projector systems so far. We're learning how the Projectors were developed here and how they work," Dhozo told her.

His head was bare as the nanite swarm worked. The alien engineer's gray face twitched and his eyes flicked back and forth as the swarm computer poured information into his brain.

"Is it what I need?" Xartasia's hands were clenched at her sides. Her light wavered.

Dhozo was quiet for a moment. "Orix is accessing the computer network. It's badly damaged. Only partial recovery..."

"Tell me," Xartasia said. She knew that she should give Dhozo and his team time, space to work, but now that the moment was upon her, Xartasia found that she could not wait. "The Waygates work on memory. Memory of a destination. Will they be able to use ours to alter time instead of distance?"

"Calculating," Dhozo growled. "I'm still sorting the data. There are partial schematics... This is interesting. Temporal stasis. Noted effect of Projector integration."

"Temporal?" Xartasia repeated. "To do with time. Tell me."

"A side effect of the Projector systems," Dhozo said. "That's why there is no time dilation or contraction when traveling inside the network."

"That gets me no closer to the White Kingdom!"

"That's what I said. Let us work, little queen," Dhozo said. He opened huge black eyes and fixed them on Xartasia. "This would be faster if we didn't need to repair the old systems and manual interfaces. Give me the access to observational impact abilities that you promised, and I could interface directly with the structure of the

Projectors... the Waygates... and tell you exactly what you want to know."

Xartasia drew herself up straight and shook her head. "No. Not yet, Commander Dhozo. You will have your magic and Waygates – your observational impact and Projectors – back only when the White Kingdom is mine once more."

The shadowy commander bared his sharp white teeth. But for the next seven hours, he worked in silence. The Devourers' nanite network fired information back and forth as Orix's team dissected the ancient computer network. Zhyress' group actually pulled apart several of the Waygates. Watching the great, glowing rings shiver and then their monstrous creators dissect each segment would have broken Xartasia's heart, but it had been broken a century ago. Still, her glass-armored knights were clearly uncomfortable again and sang softly mournful songs every time one of the Waygates crashed to the ground.

"We have it," Dhozo said at last.

Xartasia thought for a moment that she had imagined it, but the Devourer commander was gesturing her over.

"Tell me," she said.

"We abandoned the Projectors and all of the technology surrounding them because it had flaws," Dhozo explained. "That's why they're lost technology."

"To you," Xartasia said.

"To us," Dhozo agreed. "They don't operate on memory, exactly, but observation. Memory is data only for places you've been and can accurately recall. The ancient Glorious Empire used sensors to collect that data from distant locations and then to calibrate the Projectors. There was a problem, however. The observational effect caused time lapsing."

"Lapsing?" Xartasia asked.

Dhozo's dark nanite swarm had closed up over his head again, obscuring his face, but Xartasia did not need to see it to read the irritation in his posture. The fairy queen could read it, but didn't care. She had to know.

"Emissions – light, radiation, radio waves – can only travel at the speed of light," Dhozo said. "The worlds and stars we observed were hundreds or thousands of light-years away. Our observation of planets in another galaxy were already centuries old or more when they reached our instruments. So when we opened the Projectors based on that information, it opened a portal up to that particular time, hundreds or thousands or more years in the past."

"You stepped through the Waygates not only into the world you saw," Xartasia said, "but the *time* you saw."

Dhozo nodded.

"It scattered the fleet through space and time," he rumbled. "We never did find them all and that's why we stopped using the Projectors. The losses were unacceptable."

"But time..." Xartasia said. Her heart raced. "Our memories of the White Kingdom... We *can* use them to open Waygates to the time we knew. That we loved."

"Yes. But what you want is more complicated than that. Just like I warned you. Since you will be working at such a large scale from memory, not observation, the Projector will need to cross-reference a lot of minds to sift out errors. If there are problems in the destination index, the Projector will just error out and call for technicians again." Here, Dhozo's nanites thinned enough to show off a chilling, sharkish grin. "And I'm not ready to share with any other teams just yet. Not until you've taught me observational impact."

"What else?"

Dhozo's face vanished behind a veil of swirling black nanites again. "We can't do it here. These are prototype Projectors. They're not what you need."

"This is not the answer that I seek," Xartasia told him in a soft, dangerous voice. "If you cannot deliver what I require, commander, then you win nothing."

"Not *here*, little queen," Dhozo said in a growling rasp. "Not even in Mysarex, your own star system. But the Glorious fleet didn't step through the Waygates. We flew."

"Waygates large enough for starships to pass through?" Xartasia asked.

She narrowed violet eyes, thoughtful and curious. Done with their work for the moment, the Devourers were slowly gathering around their commander and his queen.

"There were... are two major nodes in the network," Dhozo said. "One on our homeworld in the core, where our species evolved, and the other on the galaxy's edge, where our fleet and listening posts were stationed. I've collated the data and corrected for galactic drift."

"Show me."

Dhozo waved his arms and a sheet of his nanites solidified into a screen. A map of the galaxy lit up across it. A star on the end of one curving arm was circled in red. Xartasia stepped closer and peered at the glowing label. She couldn't read it.

"Display the names you referenced from the Alliance computer systems," she told Dhozo.

The map flickered, rippling more like a sheet of shining fabric than any monitor Xartasia had ever seen, but the angular Glorious script was replaced by blockier Aver names. Dhozo pointed to the red spot on the galaxy's edge.

"From here, the rim Projector is closer," the Devourer said. "You bring enough memories of your beloved White Kingdom, enough to remember your entire home, and you'll have what you want."

"Closer," Xartasia repeated, "but not by much. The journey is still a long one."

"You can always stop," Dhozo suggested.

"Never." She turned to her knights. "Recall our champions and those they have found to the fleet. Our recruitment is done."

"Yes, a'shae!" Corrus answered.

"She has what she wanted now," Orix said. The young Devourer was standing very close. Xartasia could feel the heat of his swiftly burning metabolism baking off him. "We're done. Give us the magic you promised, aerad!"

Xartasia looked up from Corrus and pointed to the map. She did not actually touch the seething nanites.

"You are not done yet," she told the Devourers. "Your great old Waygate has not remained empty since you abandoned it. I will require one last thing of you."

"What?" Orix snarled.

"There is a long flight yet ahead of us. Take us there," Xartasia said. "Protect us on this final journey and then I will give you the magic that you want, to burn and destroy your enemies and to use the Waygates once again."

"What about Anzhotek?" Dhozo asked, gesturing with one huge black claw to the plaza. "We've collected every morsel of information from the lab systems."

"I have sent Syle to destroy Maeve's young kingdom, but we cannot risk that my cousin or anyone else may find what we have."

"Has your man reported in? If he's done, we don't need to worry about Maeve."

"Syle will send us no messages. He is not a common soldier or even a knight. Syle works in absolute silence. Any transmissions or messages run the risk of interception. I trust in his work, but I will risk no failure so far into this song. Are the fleet's lasers powerful enough to attack the surface?"

"Of course," Dhozo said.

Xartasia spread her wings to fly back up to the canopy. "Then burn Arborus to ash. Leave nothing to find."

[26]
SEARCH OUT

"Wisdom doesn't come from what happens to us, but what we do about it."

- DUAAL SINNAY (234 PA)

"Can you believe it?" Jaissa asked.

Gavriel looked over the top of a datadex and hoped that his wife could see the stern frown lines across his forehead. Yellow sunlight streamed in through the open curtains above the sink. Even after thirty-two years on Tynerion, Gavriel could never get used to the brilliant sun of his new homeworld.

"I believe," he growled, "that this wedding is going to cost us five years of my salary."

Jaissa scoffed. "Of your old Zeon salary, maybe. But Poes Nor University pays you ten times as much. Besides, we're not skimping on our only daughter's wedding."

"She may be our only daughter," Gavriel pointed out, "but this is her second wedding."

"The first one was just practice," Sarru said.

She came into the kitchen, high heels clicking on the tiled floor. She bent and kissed her father's thinning hair.

"Besides, that one didn't cost you a thing," Sarru said.

"Xiv took you for everything you had. That's why we're paying for this wedding."

Sarru made a face and turned to her mother. "Dad's getting grumpy in his old age, isn't he?"

"Yes, sweetheart," Jaissa agreed. "But he's allowed to. We're very exasperating people, after all."

Gavriel relented and smiled at his wife and daughter. "Fine. Get going before I change my mind and refuse to let either of you out of my sight. I don't care if you spend every cenmark I've ever made, as long as you're both happy."

"We are, love," Jaissa said.

She kissed Gavriel and grabbed her purse from the counter. Jaissa and Sarru waved and then went out the side door, the one that led to the little cobbled walkway and the road. Jaissa's car was in the garage, but Sarru preferred to drive. Her tiny sports flier was hardly a family car, Gavriel reflected, and if this marriage worked out, Sarru would need something a little bigger. Maybe as a wedding gift...

Gavriel thumbed his datadex over to mainstream access. Looking at a few options couldn't hurt. He was still pulling up the dealership's node when he heard the deafening squeal of tearing metal, the sharp shattering of glass and then the screams outside. Gavriel jumped to his feet and ran for the door. But by the time he reached the blood-spattered curb and shoved past his neighbors, it was far too late.

— • • • —

Writing speeches and giving them were entirely different things, Panna discovered. Her already towering respect for Maeve went up a few more notches as she washed her sweaty hands for the fifth time. She turned off the faucet and watched the last drops of water fall in a swift, fine spray under the influence of Hadra's high gravity. Panna reached out, but the towel was gone. She had already thrown it down the laundry chute two hand-washings ago. She sighed and wiped her dripping fingers on her shirt.

It was Sir Ballad's job to help Panna find their fellow Arcadians and bring them together, but she was the one who had to speak to them. Panna had tried a couple times to persuade Ballad to help out with the speeches. The young knight had been hand-picked by Maeve as Anthem's first squire, after all. But Panna knew the queen and the new kingdom better, Ballad argued. She never agreed, but the Prian fairy had been stubborn and refused to give ground.

The bathroom door – which had been stripped and repainted so many times that it looked as though it had some sort of disease – swung suddenly open and Ballad appeared in the mirror. Panna jumped, swearing.

"Get out of here!" she shouted.

But Ballad didn't move. "You're not doing anything. We need to talk."

"I could have been in the shower!"

"You weren't, though," Ballad said with that annoying and unarguable Prian pragmatism. "What *were* you doing?"

Panna mumbled a noncommittal answer, but followed Ballad back into the cheap motel room. She sat on the edge of one bed.

"How did it go down in Dark End?" Panna asked. That wasn't the district's real name, but that was more or less what the Hadrian Arcadians called it.

"Darkened?" Ballad asked, raising one wheat-colored eyebrow in obvious confusion.

"Dark End," Panna repeated, enunciating each word carefully. "Dark... End."

Ballad snorted. "That's not what it sounded like."

"What?" Panna crossed her arms. "As though you can speak. I can barely understand you through that stupid accent!"

"*My* accent?" Ballad asked, scowling. "You talk like you went to school on Tynerion!"

"I did!"

"That explains why your Arcadian is so bad. It's even worse than your Aver."

"What? No, it's not!" Panna said. She jumped up to her feet and felt heat in her cheeks. "I speak *perfect* Arcadian! It's not my fault you come from the back end of the galaxy."

"Back end of the galaxy...?" Ballad asked. His face was turning quite red, too. "Prianus is... alright, fine! Maybe it *is* a bit out of the way, but..."

He trailed off and then turned his back on Panna, glaring out the windows. She didn't sit down. Ballad might have given up, but Panna was still angry.

"I guess neither of us really sound like the old fairies, do we?" he said, not looking at Panna.

"No," she agreed reluctantly. "I guess not."

Panna's anger suddenly collapsed, giving way to a sharp-edged depression. She flopped back onto the bed. Hadra's gravity made it a harder flop than Panna intended and Ballad looked back at the thump. He sat on the other bed, angling himself so that his wings remained free. Flaunting them, she could not help thinking.

Arcadians – or *aerads*, as they had once been called – were children of the air. There had been four races of fairies in the White Kingdom, roughly corresponding to what the old civilizations of both rim and core considered to be the four elements: the dead but fiery pyrads, the amphibious nyads, the forest-dwelling dryads, and the white-winged aerads.

Not long into Panna's studies with Professor Xen – the memory of her teacher still made Panna's eyes sting – she was certain that this poetic delineation of the fairy species couldn't be the work of natural evolution. Someone must have *designed* the four fairy races. Panna considered the gods of her parents and even the coreworlder

Union of Light creator, but after many talks with Xen in the Poes Nor University cafeteria, that seemed unlikely.

If a god or gods had created all life, that would certainly explain the similarities Professor Xen had studied, like the common genes between the Lyrans and wolves found on many planets, as well as the presence of humans throughout the galaxy. A single creator or committee of them might have such a common and unified vision of life.

But what about the imperfections? The Mirran tendency toward high blood pressure and heart failure? The relatively weak Hadrian immune system? These were obvious results of adaptation to their planets, but poor ones that must have evolved side by side with the more useful traits.

Mirrans were fast and held most athletic records in the galaxy – with the notable exception of water sports, over which the Hyzaari appropriately claimed mastery – and their stripes had concealed them for generations from Mir's many predators. But evolving as prey animals had made them high-strung, nervous and edgy. Over seventy percent of humans with at least one Mirran grandparent suffered some sort of hypertensive condition. If a god had created the Mirrans, surely they would not have included such frailties. No, it was clearly the result of natural pressures. There was some sort of strange mix of intelligent design and natural evolution taking place in the galaxy.

Panna had to admit that Xen's opinions might have shaped her own. As a species, the Ixthians weren't generally great followers of the Union of Light. For the most part, it had been the human races who founded the religion.

Lyceum representatives from Ixth had approved the creation of a unified faith in those early days of the Central World Alliance, but more to put an end to the humans' incessant religious wars than any desire to adopt a god of their own. The Ixthians were gods unto themselves, Professor Xen was fond of saying. Their creations had no heart problems. Not, at least, that they couldn't fix in the next version.

So Xen ruled out a god creator. The professor had theorized a common ancestor for most life in the galaxy. Or at least a common *planet* of origin, a world on which the dominant life-form was bipedal, with a single head, two arms and two legs and an omnivorous diet. That planet had obviously had the insects and wolves from which Ixthians and Lyrans descended. Probably some sort of large primates, too, that eventually became the powerful Dailons. Xen had not been popular around campus with the other Ixthians for suggesting that their own species might not have been the dominant one on some ancient shared homeworld. Xen had been very brave, Panna always thought.

But Panna's own people, the Arcadians, did not seem to entirely conform to the rules of Professor Xen's theory. They were close to human in appearance and had a great many genes in common, but also shared partial redprints with several bird species. Panna had no access to dryad or nyad cells, but suspected they were equally specialized hybrids. Without a natural evolutionary divergence like that of the human species, the fairies likely couldn't have interbred.

Someone had probably designed the fairies not to breed, which would also have explained the incredibly low Arcadian birthrate and high cultural esteem placed on siblings. And it meant that the rumors that Cavain's black hair came from pyrad blood were highly suspect. Maeve might be disappointed, but Panna like to hope that when Cavain wiped out the pyrads ten thousand years ago, he at least wasn't killing his own people.

There was the Arcadian stellar system itself to consider, too. All five planets circled their sun, Aes, on a single perfect orbit. Each tilted at an exact seven-degree angle. Panna had run simulations in the Poes Nor lab over three hundred times. The chances of such a system occurring naturally were in excess of one in eight hundred trillion.

It wasn't impossible, but extremely unlikely – unless someone created it that way, created the Arcadian worlds and inhabitants like the Ixthians created new organs in their sealed ceramic vats.

What about the Waygates, ancient even beyond Arcadian reckoning? Gripper said the language one of them boomed across Pylos was similar to his own, that it was summoning its technicians. Its creators, the Devourers. What if the *Devourers* were that common ancestor to the coreworld races and creator of the Arcadians? Their observable biology certainly fit the profile Xen had laid out...

Panna realized Ballad was talking and probably had been for some time. His wings were alternately flexing, one after the other in agitation. Panna waved him off.

"Hold on, I need to write something down," she told Ballad.

The leather-clad young knight stopped speaking and cocked his head to one side, frowning.

"What?" he asked. "You weren't listening to a word I said!"

"No," Panna agreed as she reached over the edge of the bed. She found a datadex and rummaged through her backpack for a stylus. "Sorry."

Ballad slapped his hand down on the screen. "Panna, stop! Will you just listen to me for half a minute?"

"This is important!" Panna said, yanking the datadex out from under Ballad's fingers.

"So is what I'm trying to tell you! There's someone else–"

"It can wait!"

Ballad stood, throwing his hands into the air and stormed from the motel room.

Sweat dripped down into Logan's eyes. He ignored the salty sting and carefully slid the thin tweezers beneath the coils of green and black wires.

"Can you even see what you're doing, Hunter?" Gripper asked.

"No," Logan said. "You're not supposed to be here. Get back with the knights."

"You might need the extra hands. I'm not leaving."

Logan didn't spend energy on an answer. He held his breath and slid the tweezers delicately along the bottom of the timer casing, beneath the snaking twist of tangled wiring, until he felt the point impact something. There. More sweat rolled down the back of his neck, soaking his hair. The dim, hot red sun burned down on the damp skin, reflected and refracted by Kaellisem's glass towers.

Slowly, Logan worked the tweezers' prongs under the obstacle. The little tool slid in his grip and nearly fell into the opened bomb, right into the lumpy yellow-white bars of hand-packed nitrocycline. Logan squeezed and pried up the tiny piece of metal, tugging it gently free from the casing. The half-circle of copper was welded clumsily to a length of the green wire and Logan swiftly pressed the contact down onto the small battery gripped tightly in his illonium left hand.

"What did you do?" Gripper asked.

"Put the timer on its own circuit. We have about thirty seconds before the system shorts on the uncalibrated voltage."

"So we just need to get the nitrocycline out, right? That doesn't sound so bad."

"It's corrosive," Logan said. "Did you find the amylide?"

"No," Gripper told him. "I'm sorry. I never need it on the Blue Phoenix."

Logan nodded. "Fine."

He carefully passed the battery to Gripper and flexed his illonium hand three times. The joints didn't like the dry dust of Stray and the metal ground with grit. Well, it would have to be good enough. Logan held the cylindrical bomb steady in his right hand and reached inside with his left. There was a hiss and a pale, toxic-smelling thread of smoke rose as the nitrocycline seared the metal.

Carefully, Logan lifted one block of explosive free. The illonium covering his cybernetics was blackened and corroding.

Logan tasted blood. He was biting his tongue. Twenty percent of his melting hand was still agony. The nitrocycline seared his fingers like sticking his hand into molten steel. But the metal didn't sweat. It didn't bleed.

"Give me the bleach," Logan said.

Gripper nodded and held out a large ceramic mixing bowl and Logan quickly dropped the nitrocycline bar into the slippery, oily-looking liquid inside. The white explosive began to froth and then dissolve into the bleach.

Logan repeated the process for the rest of the nitrocycline, dropping the last block into the now muddy brown bleach just as the timer wire sparked. The detonator – a small ignition coil taken from a vehicle engine – popped and glowed orange for a moment, then went dark.

Gripper jumped to his feet and punched the air with one huge brown fist. "You did it, Hunter!"

Logan sat back on the sandy ground, sweat pouring down his back and blood filling his mouth.

"Give me the rest of the bleach," he said in a rough voice.

"Oh, shoot." Gripper stopped his victorious canter and grabbed the bleach bottle from next to his toolbox. "Yeah. Hold out that hand, Hunter."

Logan gratefully let Gripper douse his burning metal fingers. The bleach that ran over his corroded illonium hand dripped dark gray onto the sandy ground. When Gripper was sure that all of the corrosive nitrocycline had been neutralized, Logan pulled back and forced his right hand to unclench. The skin was slicked with sweat and his fingernails had carved red crescents into his palms. Logan inspected the damage to his other hand. The gray illonium was streaked in foul-smelling black burns. The metal was blistered and brittle, already cracking in places like seared skin.

A winged shadow fell over Gripper and Logan, growing until its owner landed. Sir Anthem's golden hair and glass armor gleamed under the morning sun. The knight looked down at Logan as blackened bleach dripped from the human's hand and the ruined illonium creaked in weak protest of its abuse.

"Is your job done?" Anthem asked.

"Yes," Logan answered. He spat red blood into the sand. "The bomb's been dismantled. I need a box or case to remove the parts. Something with no metal. One of the crates from the Blue Phoenix should do."

Anthem nodded and relayed the Prian's instructions to two of his knights in his own lyric language. Logan's Arcadian was improving, but it was still hard to follow the swift, liquid flow of Anthem's speech. Gripper poured distilled water over Logan's burned hand, rinsing away the bleach. Logan didn't let himself wince. The water wasn't cold, but it was painful on his exposed wiring.

Gripper bent down to examine Logan's cybernetics. "It doesn't look like much of the nitrocycline got inside. You ruined the plating and we need to replace it. All the seals around the fingers and wrist are shot, too."

"Nothing like this happened when you found the other bomb," Anthem said.

"The others weren't nitrocycline," Logan answered. He stood up and brushed the sand from his pants with one hand. "Our bomber is stepping up his game. That much nitrocycline would have taken out this tower and probably a few of its neighbors."

"And the sharp... sharpanel..." Anthem said, faltering. His Aver was improving, as well, but still imperfect. The knight sighed. "The broken glass would have hurt many more."

"But your knights found it first," Logan said. "The new patrol patterns are working."

Finding the second bomb – only a day after the theater explosion – had been sheer luck. Duaal had noticed the strange device while on a walk. The bomber seemed to know where Kaellisem's knights would be and when, making it all too easy to plant their explosives where they wouldn't be found until it was far too late. But Anthem's random reassignments and reordering of his knights had eliminated that advantage. Logan would have preferred to find out how the bomber knew in the first place, but...

"But we lack your experience in dealing with explosives," Sir Anthem said. "Thank you for responding so quickly."

Logan nodded. There weren't enough cops on Prianus to make up dedicated bomb response units, so all police there were trained in the basics of dealing with explosives. Logan's hand grated as the blackened illonium crumbled and pieces caught in the machinery inside. Suddenly, the red Stray dust didn't seem so bad. Nitrocycline presented a challenge even for experienced demolitions experts. The chemicals were expensive and the byproducts were incredibly toxic. Whoever made this device had probably carved twenty years off their lifespan.

It was getting worse. This was the second bomb Anthem and his knights had found in a week. The Gharib police had been by to collect their bribes but offered no help in dealing with the bombs. How long would Anthem's randomized patrols keep them ahead of the Kaellisem bomber?

Another Arcadian shadow raced over the city towers and the emptied street below. Anthem and the rest of his remaining knights dropped at once to one knee as Maeve landed. Logan followed suit, bowing his head as much to avoid looking at the fairy queen as out of respect. The throbbing, searing heat in his damaged illonium hand was nothing next to the feeling in his heart.

It's just a fluid pump, Logan told himself. *It doesn't feel anything.*

That was a lie. Logan's computerized heart hammered achingly behind his ribs as his eyes rose disobediently to Maeve. The fairy queen's black hair was damp and unbound, spilling like ink across her shoulders. One of the royal handmaidens landed with a puff of dust behind her sovereign. It was the smaller one, Dain, and the girl was panting hard with the effort of keeping up.

"Logan, what happened?" Maeve asked, voice sharp with fear.

"All is well, my queen," Anthem answered. "We found another bomb, but Coldhand has dealt with it."

"Is he hurt?"

Maeve ran to Logan before Anthem could answer and reached for the Prian's burnt left hand. Logan snatched it back and shook his head.

"Don't touch it," he said.

Maeve's hands remained extended. "Why not?"

"I'll burn you."

"It's fine," Gripper told Maeve. "The acid's all been neutralized."

Logan made a mental note to shoot the Arboran just as soon as Maeve wasn't looking.

Dain lunged at Maeve, but then seemed to think better of tackling her queen, even away from the perceived danger, and fell still. Maeve didn't seem to have noticed the girl at all. She took Logan's hand in both of hers. The ruined metal crumbled under her delicate touch. Logan didn't let himself wince as the raw sensory wiring was suddenly exposed to the hot, gritty air of Stray.

"Can you repair it?" Maeve asked Gripper. "Do you have the supplies?"

"Not on um... hand," the Arboran answered. "It's shielding. Illonium mostly only gets installed where there is going to be massive radiation or weapons' fire. But the Blue Phoenix uses phenno for radiation and we don't have any guns."

"How long will it take to get some?" Maeve asked.

Maeve's skin was smooth and warm and just slightly damp with sweat against Logan's hand. Or was that his imagination? There was no way that the crude cybernetic sensors could feel so much. Did he miss touching Maeve so much that he was making things up?

Yes.

"I'm not sure. Maybe a few days?" Gripper said. "I can message Unbreakers. I'm sure the Blues can get some."

Maeve raised her eyes to Logan's. "Does it hurt?"

"No," he lied.

She knew better. Maeve released his hand and glanced back over her wings to Dain and Anthem. The little queen straightened. Rust-colored dust clung to her pale dress like bloodstains.

"Anthem, please send one of your knights to see Vyron," Maeve said. "If they have what Gripper needs to make repairs, then I want it delivered to Kaellisem by evening."

Anthem saluted, but did not immediately dispatch one of the other fairies. Did he like seeing Logan Coldhand squirm? But the unfailingly regal prince consort was difficult to read.

"There may be a swifter solution, a'shae," he said.

"What is it?" Maeve asked.

Anthem gestured to the nearby street.

"Glass, my queen," he said. "Hyra is here in Kaellisem and his glass is as strong as illonium, I think. The casing of a hand does not look so different from a gauntlet."

Maeve shot a look at Gripper. "Would that work?"

"Maybe..." said the Arboran mechanic. "If we can make some changes to help it withstand impact a little better than the theater did. I need to clean out the broken illonium, but other than that, the damage seems pretty superficial. All Hunter needs is new plating. I don't see why it couldn't be glass."

Maeve turned back to Logan. "Would a hand of Arcadian glass be acceptable?"

"It might be better," he said. "The nitrocycline reacts particularly violently with metal. Glass should be a little more resilient."

"Then we will use the Bherrosi glass," Maeve decided. "It contains no metallic impurities."

Gripper cleared his throat. "And I'll order up some amylide, too. Let's not burn your hand off next time."

"Yes," Maeve agreed softly. She didn't meet Logan's eye. "I thank you for your bravery and skill, my hunter, but they are poor trade for your life."

The fairy queen turned quickly away and leapt gracefully up into the clear morning sky. Dain scrambled to follow, leaving Logan alone once more with Gripper and the knights. Anthem held his hand out to Logan.

"Let us get you to the glass-singers," he said.

Logan pushed himself to his feet without assistance. "I'm not much good to Maeve with a broken hand. Let's go."

[27]

THE WHITE KNIGHT

"We scream and shout not to change someone else's mind, but to change our own."

- PANNA SUL (234 PA)

Ballad didn't try to talk to Panna very much over the next week. Each worked alone to speak with the Arcadians of Hadra and convince them to join Queen Maeve in Kaellisem. For each fairy that agreed, they bought a starship ticket to Stray. But luckily for her dwindling funds, Panna didn't find many Arcadians on Hadra. The high gravity was hard on their wings and fragile bones. Fairies who could leave the planet had already done so. Unfortunately, those who remained behind were stubborn in their refusal to go except in the embrace of the Nameless. The gods had cast them down under Hadra's burning suns to die, they stated flatly. So die they would.

In two weeks of work in five different Hadrian cities, Panna and Ballad convinced only thirty-nine Arcadians to make the journey to Stray and Kaellisem. The strain was beginning to show. Panna slept badly, dreaming constantly of forgetting her own speeches in front of a much larger crowd than she ever managed to actually gather, all pointing and laughing at her lack of wings. And that was when she could sleep at all.

Sir Ballad slept face down in the cheap motel beds, snoring into a stained pillow with his wings flopped to either side. Panna tripped on them every time she got up to get a drink or use the bathroom. By the end of the month, she was seriously considering smothering the knight in his sleep.

During their short breakfasts together, Panna repeatedly tried to convince Ballad to wear his glass armor.

"No way," he answered each time. "I can't move in that stuff. Not in this gravity. Besides, I get enough *move along* talks from the cops here as it is. Can you imagine what they would think of a hawk in full armor flying down their streets?"

The one time his stubborn pride might have worked in Panna's favor, Ballad insisted on being practical. He wouldn't even carry the spear that was effectively an Arcadian knight's badge of office. Every morning, he slid his fibersteel boxer's bracelets into the pockets of his worn leather jacket, put on his sunglasses and left.

Panna was no knight. She didn't have the right to wear the glass armor, even if Hyra would agree to fit a suit for any fairy without wings. Instead, she had brought a large wallet of Arcadian glass in narrow strips. These small, glittering pieces of their heritage had inspired several Hadrian fairies to make the flight to Stray.

The little glass rectangles also served as samples when Panna had the chance to talk to local retailers. The planetary gravity made large windows difficult on Hadra and several manufacturers had expressed interest in the stronger Arcadian glass. Panna had no firm commitments or actual orders yet, but had spent an evening writing up and transmitting a proposal to manufacture a polarized version of Kaellisem's sole export. She had not yet received an answer from Duke Ferris.

One bright Hadrian afternoon, Panna finished giving her latest speech to a dozen dirty-faced Arcadians. Or tried to... As soon as

Panna reached the part of her story about surgically giving up her wings to go to school, half of the small crowd turned away, uninterested. The rest lost heart when told that they would be going to Stray, not back to their native planets on the galactic rim.

Panna quickly finished her speech and was unsurprised when only two of the fairies lingered to ask if she could spare any change. She dug the last white cenmark chips from her pockets and divided them between the pair. They thanked her in Arcadian and hurried away. On foot... They were too weak, too malnourished to fly in the high gravity.

Panna watched the other two fairies go and readjusted her sunglasses. She didn't like wearing them, but for anyone born without the Hadrian membrane over their eyes, they were a necessity. The darkened plastic gave the whole world a dim brownish tinge that made Panna want to take a janitorial nanite spray to everything she saw. She turned the other way to head out of the little side street and back to the motel, but another Arcadian stood in her way, his wings spread wide to block the sidewalk. Even through her glasses, the fans of white feathers were almost painfully bright in the Hadrian sunlight.

Panna raised her hand, half in greeting and half to block a little more light. For an irrational moment, she thought Sir Anthem had come to Hadra. The man before her wore a brilliantly shining suit of glass plate mail. But it wasn't the prince consort... This man was shorter than Sir Anthem and his braids were several shades paler. Almost white, though that might have been the effect of the glaring sunlight.

"Eru shen'ai?" he asked. *Why are you here?*

The newcomer's eyes were concealed behind a black scarf tied across his temples, but they seemed to be narrowed. Panna smiled her best, most diplomatic smile.

"Ai na Panna Sul," she introduced herself. *"D'hanni ai an Cerri Maeve."* I work for Queen Maeve.

At this, the glass-armored fairy's hands clenched into fists and Panna noticed the short, curved glass blades extending from the knuckles. Who was this man?

Panna squinted. His armor was not Kaellisem-made. The glass was utterly clear, like still water, and didn't have any of the veins or swirls of color that marked the glass forged on Stray. Could Hyra be making suits from the white Bherrosi sand? But Panna knew all of Sir Anthem's knights and she was quite sure she had never met this man before.

"En calla ma cerri. An na Xartasia!" the other Arcadian snarled. *There is only one queen. Her name is Xartasia!*

The White Queen's knight yanked something from the pale sash around his waist, a knife with a strangely long handle. It had a double-edged glass blade and the haft was made of some sort of dark metal or ceramic. The knight slashed at Panna's stomach. She was already staggering back, but the tip sliced through her shirt and into the unprotected flesh beneath. Blood poured down the front of Panna's pants, hot and wet and heavy. For a dizzy moment, she worried that she had wet herself.

This was going to be a short fight. Panna was no knight or any other kind of fighter. How could she stand her ground against the other Arcadian?

Panna threw herself at the man, but to one side. He spun to face her, slicing another bloody wound into Panna's inner arm as she brought it up. She felt soft cloth sliding through her fingers. Too fast...! Panna clutched at the scarf, yanking it clumsily from the knight's head. The fabric tangled with his braids, snaking free from Panna's grasp. But the scarf was no longer covering his eyes and the knight dropped his strange knife and clawed at his eyes, suddenly blinded by the dazzling sunlight.

Panna pressed her hands hard against her bleeding stomach and ran. Her pulse pounded in her ears, throbbing inside her eyes like some maddened creature struggling to free itself. Behind her, the armored Arcadian spread his wings and leapt into the air, but then landed again just a few steps away. The Hadrian gravity! Panna wanted to kiss the whole planet.

She stumbled out of the narrow side street, nearly overshooting the sidewalk and running into the wide main road. Several cars swerved and honked loudly. One cheap-looking flying sedan – null-inertia technology was very popular on Hadra – crunched into the shiny chrome bumper of the car in front of them. The driver leapt out, his face turning purple with fury.

"What the hells are you doing, girl?" he shouted at Panna. Then his white-membraned eyes dropped to her blood-covered hands. "Oh God, what happened?"

Panna looked back. The man in glass had recovered his weapon and ran after her, scattering pedestrians before him. Panna whirled back to the driver.

"Get me out of here!" she cried.

"Let me call you an ambulance–"

"Just get me out of here!" Panna interrupted with a gasp.

The Hadrian man nodded and yanked open the passenger door. By now, other cars were swerving around and sometimes over the stopped null-inertia sedan. Panna all but fell into the seat, slumping into an uncomfortable cushion of crinkling mycolar fast food envelopes and old drink boxes.

"Come on!" she shouted.

Xartasia's knight was closing fast. He vaulted acrobatically over the broad shoulder of a tall Hadrian father clutching his frightened daughter close. The Arcadian spread his wings again. He couldn't fly well in Hadra's unrelenting gravitation, but he would surely be able to make the jump onto the car. Then what? Pull Panna out and stab her? Throw her out into traffic? A red convertible with sweeping, stylish lines shrieked past. That would certainly do the job.

The sedan's driver finally clambered into his seat and slammed the door closed behind him. Had he seen the Arcadian man chasing her?

He must have, Panna decided, as the Hadrian grabbed the shift control and threw his vehicle into gear. The inexpensive null-field filmed the windows over with faintly orange light and the whole vehicle jolted up into the air. The engine whined in protest – Panna hazily wondered how long since it had been to a shop – and then rumbled. Panna's new best friend yanked his car back into the swift river of other vehicles, eliciting a raucous new chorus of honking and shouting.

But the Arcadian was too close. He vaulted up onto a corner news display, making the screen shudder, and then leapt onto the top of the car. Panna wondered who was screaming. Blood filled the hands still clutching at her stomach.

The Hadrian driver shouted and yanked the steering wheel as the glass blade scraped across the roof, shrieking against the metal. A blinking traffic signal spun past as the vehicle turned sharply and Panna squeezed her eyes shut. She was going to be sick and she was going to throw up her guts all over the dashboard. Ballad would have to finish this alone. She was going to die...

Xartasia's knight slid across the wildly spinning car, boots scrabbling for purchase on the roof. He staggered and then fell over the side, barely holding on by glass fingertips wedged into the top of Panna's door. They stared into each other's eyes for a fraction of a second before the wind caught the knight's wings and yanked him away. He smashed into the side of a building and fell out of sight. Panna slid down in the red-stained seat and swiftly lost the battle for consciousness.

"Does that hurt?"

"No."

Gripper looked over the magnifiers strapped awkwardly to his huge brown head. His long, drooping ears twitched.

"Glass isn't here anymore, Hunter."

"Yes... that hurts," Logan admitted.

"Good," said the Blue Phoenix's mechanic. Now Logan's mechanic, too. "That means the wiring is still intact and carrying a signal. But the insulation is a little uh... melted in spots, so we'll need to replace that with glass, too."

"Will it be flexible enough?" Logan asked as Gripper withdrew a small probe from between the bundled wires running through the U-shaped cradle of his wrist.

"Normally, no. That's one of the problems with glass insulation. By the time you nanostructure it small enough to bend, it gets toxic. That's why no one makes fiberglass anymore."

"Prianus does."

Gripper flushed. "Anyway... we've been working with the fairies here to make a better version; something about a coiled substructure instead of fiberwoven like hull plating. I'm not sure, but we'll be trying it out on your new hand."

"Have you told him the even better news?" Duaal asked.

The well-dressed captain stood across a nearby table from Hyra, who studied the datadex that Duaal brought with a scowl.

"No," Gripper answered. "It was *going* to be a surprise."

"Well, too late for that now," Duaal said cheerfully. "Those plans that Hyra's glaring at right now are from Xia. They're a little rough, she says. I wouldn't know."

"What are they for?" Logan asked.

"Nerve endings, more or less. If Hyra can pull it off, we will–"

"What is this *we*?" Hyra hissed in thickly accented Aver and his single wing twitched in agitation.

"Hyra will be able to use some of the metal-rich glass fibers like super-fine wires," Duaal went on smoothly. "Like nerves. It should return some of the feeling you've lost."

Logan blinked. "What?"

"Not all of it," Gripper added quickly. "Glass isn't skin. We can only give you about eighty-five percent sensitivity."

"It will take time," Hyra said, looking up from Xia's schematics. "Lots of little pieces. But I can make this in one week."

A week... After seven years of near numbness. One week more and Logan could feel again.

It wasn't so long to wait.

But how many bombs could be built in a week? There was more to do than just to find and defuse the explosives – and even that was threatening to overwhelm Anthem and his knights. It was Logan's job to find the one setting them.

There was too much work to be done. Logan shook his head.

"No," he told them. "I don't have time for that. Just get this thing sealed up again."

Gripper sighed and rolled his big brown eyes at Duaal. "See? That's why I wasn't going to tell him."

Duaal frowned.

"Are you sure about this, Logan?" he asked. "Just think how it will feel to hold Maeve with two working hands."

Logan tossed a canister of compressed air up to Gripper and he got to work cleaning and sterilizing the exposed cybernetics.

"I can't hold Maeve now," he answered. "And Anthem never will if someone kills her. Just get me back out there."

An Ixthian woman was standing over Panna when she woke. They were alone in a small, pale cubicle with a curtain instead of a door. The Ixthian was checking over something on the computer display at the end of the bed.

"You're awake," she said. "Good. I'm Doctor Xel. How are you feeling?"

Panna swallowed and thought about her answer.

"Thirsty," she decided. "And sort of weak. But otherwise alright. Can I have something to drink?"

Xel filled a cup from a small nearby sink. Panna drank it down in three huge gulps.

"You lost a lot of blood," the doctor said, then pursed her shiny lips. "We replaced it, but that very nearly killed you, Miss Sul."

Panna wondered for a moment what that meant, then blushed scarlet and held out her cup for more water.

"You tried to give me human blood?" she asked.

Xel nodded and refilled the plastic cup. "You really should wear a tag or something."

The doctor probably had some more to say – either a lecture on proper redprint identification or else on Panna's surgical alterations themselves – but a crash from outside the cubicle interrupted her.

"Get your bloody hands off me!" someone shouted. The loud voice had a thick Prian accent. "Where the hells is she? You said she was here!"

The curtain was suddenly torn aside and then Ballad was there, wings tangled in the fabric. A human hung from each of his arms. The first was an Axial or colonist in blue scrubs. He shouted for Ballad to leave, but was shockingly unsuccessful at actually forcing the smaller Arcadian to do so.

The second human was more grabbed by Ballad than the other way around. It was the Hadrian man whose car Panna had tried hard not to die in. His white eyes were wide as Ballad hauled him into the cubicle.

"I'm right here," Panna said.

Xel had closed a six-fingered hand on Ballad's shoulder and was preparing to help the orderly haul him away, but she quirked her antennae toward her patient. "You know him?"

"Yes, I do," Panna said. "We work together."

Ballad stopped struggling and the hospital staff let go of him. He even released the Hadrian, but Doctor Xel waited until she was sure that Ballad was no further danger before excusing herself and the orderly.

"Just press the call button if you need us," she told Panna.

"Thank you."

Panna sat up slowly, wincing in preparation for the pain in her stomach, but there wasn't any. She wished that she could check the wound, but unless she wanted to pull off her already rather skimpy paper gown in front of the two men, it would have to wait.

Ballad's sharp jaw was clenched so tightly that Panna worried about his teeth.

"You shouldn't have gone off on your own," he said. "You could have been killed! What the hells happened?"

"Wait, how did you find me here?" Panna asked. She intended to answer Ballad's questions, but she had a few of her own.

"He came looking for you," the Hadrian answered, speaking up for the first time since their abrupt entrance. "I was still answering questions with the police when he showed up. They can't find the guy. He got away. Sorry, I guess."

"You helped Ballad find me?" Panna smiled. "Thank you. Um, I'm sorry. I never got your name."

"Jacks," the wiry man said. He looked uncomfortably between Ballad and Panna. "If you don't need anything else from me..."

"No," Panna said. "Thanks."

Jacks quickly ducked out of the hospital cube. Panna smoothed the blanket over her lap and inspected her right arm, where Xartasia's knight had cut her. There was a pink line across the skin, but even that was faint. She didn't think that it would scar. The Ixthians did amazing work.

"Panna, what happened?" Ballad asked again. The young knight didn't sound angry this time. "Are you alright?"

"I'm fine. There was another knight. At least, I think that's what he was. He wore armor, but it wasn't like yours. His was like the old suits." Panna frowned and drained her water cup again. "No, it was definitely modified. But that glass didn't come from Kaellisem. I'm sure of that much."

Ballad refilled Panna's water and handed it back. "What did he do? Did he say anything?"

"Yes, actually," Panna said. "When I told him that I serve Queen Maeve, he answered that there was only one queen."

A deep scowl tugged at Ballad's lips. "Xartasia."

Panna nodded. "Then he attacked me. I pulled the scarf off his eyes and ran. Jacks got me away."

"And called the cops," Ballad said. "They brought the Ixthians."

Panna just couldn't resist anymore. She held up the blanket as a barrier and pulled aside the pale green gown to look at her stomach. The skin was a little red, but otherwise there was no sign of her struggle with the knight. Panna covered herself up again and found Ballad staring at her, eyebrows raised.

"I've never actually been to a real Ixthian medcenter," she said. "I was always careful to avoid them. I knew it wouldn't take long to realize that I wasn't human."

Ballad didn't seem to know what to say to that.

"What now?" he asked instead.

Panna pressed the nurse's call button. "We settle the bill and get back to work. Xartasia's got a knight on Hadra, too. We need to get to the Arcadians here before he does."

[28]
SHARP EDGES

"It is easy to kill a queen. To destroy her is something else entirely."

- SYLE LAMANNA (234 PA)

"I am so very sorry, Your Majesty," Duke Ferris said. "I have no idea how this is happening."

Maeve slammed her hands down on her desk. There were no desks in Arcadia, but she had grown accustomed to the coreworlder practice of using one. Her desk was one of the few things in the royal tower not made of glass. It was a flimsy thing, little more than two sheets of printed mycoboard with a piece of already scuffed and scratched steel bolted to the top. The desk was one of Xyn's and the scientist had been more than happy to give it away. It was cheaper than the disposal fee and easier than dumping it in the desert. The desk was a convenient place to keep things Maeve was working on and an uncomplaining victim of her frequent frustrations.

"That bomb could have killed Logan!" she said.

Verra winced, but Ferris' expression remained neutral. The old duke's already graying hair had gone entirely steely at the temples and Maeve almost felt guilty for yelling at him.

"That would have been regrettable," Ferris said. "What of your consort, Sir Anthem? Is he well?"

"He is fine," Maeve answered, refusing to rise to the bait.

She hammered her fist against the desk one more time for good measure and then resumed her angry pacing along the length of the study. Ferris tucked his hands into the gold-trimmed sleeves of his flowing robe and glanced sidelong at the open door, at the pair of glass-armored knights standing outside. Hannu listened with obvious interest. He blushed and hid behind one wing when he saw the two older Arcadians staring. On the other side, Syle's eyes remained fixed ahead. Maeve wondered if he was really ignoring the conversation or simply preserving his queen's fragile dignity.

"We must increase your security," Duke Ferris said, wrenching Maeve's attention back into the room. "We cannot risk any danger to you, my queen."

Maeve felt the insane urge to laugh at the stodgy old duke. She settled for a wry smirk.

"I am in no danger," Maeve said." It is not so difficult to get close to me that our bomber could not have done so at any time in the last weeks."

"Do they have some other aim?"

Maeve nodded. "Their target must be Kaellisem itself. Not the towers, but the dream. *Erritasia.*"

"*The dream of dreamers,*" Ferris said in Aver. "The spirit of Kaellisem. You believe that this bomber is trying to ruin our city?"

"How many fairies have left Kaellisem since the enassui? More than three hundred! When the people learn that this newest bomb contained nitrocycline, more will go. Those who know the word, at least. Killing me is little in the face of true destruction."

"A dead queen is still a queen," Ferris said quietly.

"But a queen who cannot protect her people will not be queen for long," Maeve finished. "My people will all leave, in time."

"Finding the bombs slows the process, I am sure, Your Majesty."

"But does not stop it!" Maeve kicked her desk and winced in pain. "And while I struggle to hold a single city together, Xartasia is still out there. I do not know if we have slowed her at all."

———— • • • ————

Panna threw her arm up over her eyes as they stepped out into the brilliant daylight. Ballad prodded her shoulder with one wing and handed her a pair of sunglasses. Panna accepted them gratefully.

"Where are we going?" she asked as Ballad struck a quick pace down the sidewalk.

He ignored a group of scowling Hadrians in dark suits.

"Motel," the young knight answered shortly. "And if you didn't like the one we had before, you'll love this place. We spent most of our money on your treatment."

"Ixthians are the best. You can tell by the bill."

Ballad smiled tightly. "If we're going to send anyone else back to Kaellisem, we need to save all the colour we can. That means we're sharing a room again."

Panna came to an awkward stop in front of a crowded cafeteria.

"What?" she asked.

"Unless you feel like sleeping on the street. I've had plenty of practice," Ballad said. He looked back over a leather-clad shoulder. "Want to give it a try?"

Panna hurried to catch up. "Nope, the motel will be fine. But not just yet. We need to go back down to Yebdemi. There are still a lot of Arcadians over there."

Ballad slowed again when Panna caught up, but the sweating young knight was glowering.

"You just got out of the hospital," he growled. "Xartasia's hawk stabbed you in Yebdemi!"

"He grazed me," Panna corrected.

"You nearly bled to death!"

He had a point and if the Ixthians were any less skilled doctors, Panna probably would not have been alive to admit it. Still, Panna didn't want to tell Ballad that he was right. She stopped at the street corner and ignored a shouted suggestion that *Hey Sweetie* should drop her fairy boy for a real man. Ballad stuck his thumb and last finger out at the car that shout had come from.

"Stop that, Sir Ballad," Panna said. She adjusted the sunglasses over her streaming eyes. "You're just giving him what he wants."

"He wants you," Ballad answered.

Panna flushed, but doubted he could see it through the blinding light. Out in the road, dual rows of tall orange barriers rose up and beeped insistently at the pedestrians. Panna jogged into the street, packed in close between much taller humans. Ballad swore under his breath and had to fly to catch up. He landed next to Panna when she reached the other side of the road. Ballad didn't apologize to the Hadrians his arrival displaced.

"Maybe we should rent a ride," Panna said. She looked around the light-washed city streets and pulled out her com. "I don't even know which way I'm going. How far away are we from Yebdemi?"

"Not sure," Ballad answered.

The fairy knight shoved his way back to the curb and scanned the busy road until he located a car with a glowing green taxi sign on top. The cab raced down the second story lane on its null-field, ignoring the pedestrians below. As it slowed for the next traffic signal, Ballad leapt into the air and rapped his knuckles against the window. Panna couldn't see the driver inside, but the cab lurched to one side.

Ballad pressed a small cenmark chip to the window and glared through the tinted glass. There was a short shouted exchange above Panna's head and then Ballad pulled the rear door open. He planted his feet inside and held his hand down toward the sidewalk.

"The plucked driver says he can't land here," Ballad said. "Give me your hand."

Panna reached up. Ballad grabbed her wrist and then pulled, lifting the wingless little Arcadian off her feet. Panna grunted as he heaved her up into their cab. It was hot inside and stank of sweat. Ballad followed her quickly inside, then shut the door behind him.

"That was more of a climb than I was hoping for," Ballad said. "Is everything still inside that's supposed to be?"

Panna touched her stomach. It ached faintly, but not enough to bother complaining about to the prickly Prian fairy. She nodded.

"Good," Ballad said. He tapped the thick glass barrier between the back of the cab and the front. "Yebdemi."

The Hadrian driver refused to budge until Ballad paid the entire fare up front. Even then, he muttered into his com the entire time. Panna didn't catch any of the words and wasn't sure she wanted to. Instead, she watched Ballad. The other Arcadian sat forward, uncomfortably hunched as his wings took up most of the seat with fluffy white.

"So where are you going today?" Panna asked Ballad. "Back to Dark End?"

"Yebdemi. If Xartasia sent a knight, you're going to need yours."

Caith waited for Maeve at the fountain. The glass sculpture of Cavain stood five times taller than any Arcadian and water cascaded from his upraised hands. What was that supposed to mean? It was the nyads who lived in the water, not Cavain's own species. Was the water some metaphor for the wellspring of peace and unity that his war had won? Or maybe Maeve was reading too much into it. Perhaps the fountain was intended only to be beautiful. It was that, at least.

Maeve landed beside her brother with a soft clink of glass. Caith wore the white robes of a Spire Adept, but they were sashed shut with a richly embroidered scarf of Cavainna red and gold. Whatever trade the royal princes and princesses took up, they always wore the family colors and

Maeve wondered why. Wasn't their black hair symbol enough? But she shook her head and hugged Caith. When Maeve released him, her brother frowned.

"What is wrong?" he asked. "You have been crying again."

Had she? Maeve wiped her face with her hands, but the glass of her gauntlets absorbed nothing and succeeded only in smearing the wetness across her skin. She shook her head. "Orthain was at Morningfire Court. It is hard to... Never mind. I am fine. Tamlin and Karrian await."

With obvious reluctance, Caith flew alongside his sister toward the Illisem Waygates. Despite the early hour, the capitol city was alive with people. The streets were full of nyads with their shining cerulean skin and the delicate gills draped between their shoulders, like tiny versions of their masters' wings. There were thousands of green-haired dryads, too. They tended the endless gardens of the White City, caring for the soft lawns, ordered orchards and flower-dotted hedges. Dryads and nyads both kept their heads down, focused on their work as their Arcadian overlords flew overhead.

Caith glided in close beside Maeve, his feathers brushing against her beating wings. He said nothing as they landed in the broad white-paved plaza in the city's heart. Thousands of Arcadians filled the ground and sky under the shifting shadows of King Illain's palace. The castle of glass rose on a steep green hill over them, the verdant slope crowned in a hundred glittering towers.

Maeve and Caith made their way to the foot of a great white staircase. Another knight with simpler armor than Maeve gestured the young prince and princess forward, past the lines of other fairies all waiting their turn to travel through the ring of glowing Waygates. He inclined his wings to Maeve and Caith.

"Highnesses," he said respectfully. "Where are you bound?"

"Orindell," Maeve told the knight. She gestured to her brother. "We are to relieve the Tamlin openers."

The Arcadian nodded and pointed to one of the Waygates. "The falcon gate is open to A'sai, princess."

Maeve thanked the knight. She and Caith flew up the graceful white ziggurat, ignoring the oversized stairs that ran up the center of each face. Only the dryads and nyads climbed those. They landed at the top, where another robe-clad Spire Adept waited. He paused for a moment and then nodded to Maeve.

"The way is clear," he announced. "Please pass through."

Maeve took Caith's hand. He didn't need her help, but she ached for contact with her brother. He squeezed her fingers gently and they stepped through the Waygate. Blue light shimmered around them and then faded, leaving them alone in another ivory plaza not unlike the one they had just left. There was no Waygate here, however. The great constructs worked in only one direction and required no receiving gate. In the center of this tiled plaza rose a transparent plinth with an intricate glass heron on top. There were so many of these reception sites all over the White Kingdom — each one bore some mark, some symbol to differentiate it from the other so that the Spire Adepts could remember them in detail. After all, without memory, the Waygates would not function.

Maeve had been to so many of these plazas with Caith that she suspected she knew every single one in Arcadia. She turned slowly, orienting herself. It was late in the afternoon on Orindell. To one side were the blue glass domes of A'sai, glowing in the golden afternoon light. That meant Tamlin was to the northwest. She gestured to Caith with one wing.

"This way," Maeve told him. "We can reach Tamlin in an hour if the wind is with us."

"Wait."

Maeve lowered her wings and turned to look at her brother.

"What is it? I thought you were in a hurry to reach Tamlin. You said that you would die if you could not see Karrian tonight." Maeve smiled at his youthful overstatement, but Caith didn't smile back.

"Maeve, I know your separation from Sir Orthain has been painful," Caith said. He touched gentle fingertips to Maeve's cheek. "Yes, I do miss Karrian, but I will remain with you. I would never leave you alone with your pain."

[29]

BITTER SALT

"We want glass to break. Anything we can see right through really should be fragile, shouldn't it? We prefer to think that obfuscation is stronger than transparency."

- XIA (234 PA)

Logan dismissed the knights with a wave of his new glass hand. The four Arcadians nodded and took to the air, leaving the Prian alone in the red-dusted Kaellisem street. Well, almost alone.

"Maybe you've scared the bomber off," Gripper suggested. "It's been days since any of the knights found something scary. Maybe whoever set them is gone."

Logan shook his head. He began walking down the road, hands in his pockets. The glass one still felt strange, light and cool even through the cloth of his pants. Worn servos and hinges were plainly visible through the transparent Bherrosi glass, a reinforced metal skeleton twined with wire nerves. The finger surfaces and the palm were subtly textured in minute scrollwork to make them viable gripping surfaces, just like the knights' gauntlets. Even so, Logan insisted on wearing his worn black leather half-glove over the glass.

The glove was familiar, comfortable. It was a pointless sentiment, Logan knew. But it just wasn't so simple to shut down his emotions. Not anymore.

"Why would they stop?" Logan asked. "We haven't caught them. We haven't even gotten close. No, it's something else."

"Like what?" Despite his longer legs, Gripper had to jog to keep up with Logan.

"They're changing tactics. The bombs we found, including the one that blew up the theater... They've been effective, but all home-made. Simple timers, no complex remote detonators. That means giving us time to find them. And we have, so our bomber is moving on to something else."

"Like what?" Gripper asked.

Maeve – *Queen* Maeve – speculated that the first bombing wasn't an attempt on her life. There were far easier ways to kill her than attacking the enassui theater and the largest gathering of Arcadians in recent history. But it was that very fact that made Maeve suspect the bomb was to shake faith in her rule, to convince the fairies that she couldn't keep them safe. To chase them away.

And that made sense. Maeve Cavainna was a perceptive woman, Logan admitted with painful pride, and he had to agree with her.

Logan stopped walking and looked back down the street to the red and gold royal spire. A winged shape stood on one of the delicate balconies. Was it Maeve...? He couldn't tell from this distance. Logan turned away.

A large group of Arcadians stood clustered around one of the larger buildings of Kaellisem, a dark brown dome swirled in rusty red: the food distribution center. Few fairies had money, but Maeve had no intention of letting them go hungry.

Panna had devised, planned and created the supply infrastructure, relying upon a system of digital ledgers and identifications to make sure no one took an unfair portion. There was even a weekly allowance for the occasional humans or other hungry coreworlders who came to Kaellisem in desperate search of food. It built good-will between the fairies and Alliance, Panna had said.

Duke Ferris required at least two knights to stand guard, to keep away any dangerous alien elements and prevent thefts. Panna had protested, of course. There were not enough knights to protect the sort of widespread distribution she envisioned. What Ferris wanted would require centralizing the process into a single center. That meant lines. That meant waiting and impatience. But in the end, Maeve had reluctantly sided with Duke Ferris. The safety of Kaellisem's citizens *had* to come first.

So the food lines became a part of life in Kaellisem. The options were limited – mostly flavored protein powders, basic grains and a few vegetables – but were still better and more generous than what the fairies were used to since the White Kingdom's fall. Generally, spirits were high in the lines and waiting Arcadians used the time to catch up with their neighbors. The knights inside the dome were rarely forced to involve themselves in any of these exchanges.

Logan and Gripper stopped walking as they neared the glass dome of the food distribution center. There was a group of fairies outside the door, not waiting in a line but together in a close pack. Logan began searching for some Alliance species, maybe a human or Dailon... There had been tensions between Vyron, Kessa and the Arcadians before everyone in Kaellisem became accustomed to the Dailon family.

But this looked nothing like those first encounters. The Arcadians had been afraid of Vyron and Kessa, so much larger than any of the fairies. What Logan saw in their faces now was not nervousness or even fear. It was anger. Logan signaled Gripper to stop. The Arboran did, following his friend's gaze.

"What's going on?" Gripper asked.

Logan didn't answer as he left Gripper at a safe distance and moved quietly closer to the group. They faced each other and did not notice the Prian's approach. His understanding of the Arcadian language was growing with each day in Kaellisem, but it was still hard to catch some of the quick, hissed words.

"How could she lie to us?" asked one woman with scars on her left cheek that looked like Lyran handiwork. *"She is our queen!"*

"Maybe it is not true," said a man standing beside her. Nervously, Logan thought.

"How could one woman be ra'ahadu?" asked another fairy. *"Even one of Cavain's daughters?"*

The first woman's wings rustled. *"Someone opened the Black Gate! We* sumanni'i *they died with the rest, but what if she escaped Tamlin?"*

"The queen is guilty," said a man with a bitter frown twisting his lips. *"Why else build all this? She is trying to* eru a'malla!"

"What if this is not amends...? If she is gathering the survivors of her destruction to deliver to the Devourers?"

"Queen Maeve slaughtered our people. She opened the Tamlin gate!" the scar-faced woman said, shaking her wings in rage.

Logan grabbed the Arcadian by the shoulder and yanked her around to face him. Her green-brown eyes widened and she gasped. The other fairies scattered with frightened, musical cries. Feathers filled the hot air.

"Where did you hear that?" Logan snarled.

The scarred fairy squirmed in his grasp, but she was tiny and no match for the Prian's strength.

"All know!" she cried in nearly unintelligible Aver.

"Who told you?" Logan asked.

"Some here," she answered in a hiss, pointing both wings to the glass food dome. "Long line and we talk!"

Hundreds of fairies passed through the food distribution center every day, most lingering for hours or more with nothing better to do than gossip. There was no way Logan could trace the origin of the information. He released the Arcadian woman, who staggered back and then leapt into the air, beating her wings frantically in her haste to get away.

Logan turned back to the banded glass dome. It was still mid-afternoon and the food center was crowded with hungry, waiting people. The Arcadians inside watched him with a mixture of fear and anger. An old fairy man near the doors squinted suspiciously at Logan.

It was enough to get the attention of the knights inside. Syle and Eranna pushed their way through the angrily murmuring crowd toward Logan. The sight of their glass armor and spears seemed to comfort the fairies, but there were still a great many glares leveled at Logan.

"What is going on, sir?" Eranna asked.

Logan held no official position in Maeve's court, but most of the knights showed him a certain deference.

"They're saying that Maeve was responsible for the fall," Logan told Eranna. Other than Anthem, the knights didn't know the truth about the Tamlin Waygate. No need to confirm the rumors. "I need to know who first said that."

The angry muttering rose again. The old fairy Logan had seen before shot out a withered, accusatory wing at him.

"The Gray Queen keeps company with a human bounty hunter," he said in Arcadian. *"She takes an alien to her bed. She spits on her own people. Maeve Cavainna destroyed the White Kingdom!"*

There were more shouts and loud songs in reply to this, some in agreement and others arguing, but Logan barely heard them. He grabbed the old man by the wing until the fairy grunted.

"Her lover?" Logan said back at the fairy in his own language – awkwardly, he had to admit. *"Her enarri? Maeve has taken her Arcadian king! For you!"*

"Hunter! No, stop it!" Gripper was in the door and shouting at Logan. "Let him go!"

Logan forced his glittering glass hand to unclench, dropping the old Arcadian man to the floor. The fairy panted, but wouldn't be so easily silenced.

"Her Arcadian king? You mean Anthem Calloren? Prince Anthem is a whore," he said. *"Xartasia's whore and brother to Devourers! Our queen and prince are traitors. Kaellisem is a lie!"*

A dented metal cup flew from somewhere in the crowd and hit the hysterical old fairy in the temple, opening a bleeding gash in his thin skin.

The violence erupted as suddenly and explosively as a volcano. There were suddenly dozens of Arcadians in the air, grabbing and striking at one another or simply trying to escape the glass dome. Eranna waded into the burgeoning riot, calling for calm. Syle gave Logan an even, golden-eyed look.

"Leave now," he told the Prian, loudly over the shrieking din but quite calmly. "You will only make things worse. Tell the queen and Sir Anthem what is happening here."

Something about the way Syle said that made Logan pause, but then Gripper was grabbing his arm and towing the human outside. Voices and the sounds of blows rang out from the dome. Something crashed inside, and someone screamed.

"What's going on in there?" Gripper asked as they ran down the road, back the way they had come.

Logan yanked the com from his belt and didn't stop running.

"Maeve?" he asked. "Maeve, are you there?"

"Logan?" Maeve answered. "What is wrong? Are you alright?"

"They know about the Tamlin gate, Maeve. I don't know how, but they know. Get knights to the food center now. The Arcadians are rioting."

"Where *are* they?" Panna asked.

"Gone," Ballad answered. He jumped down from the rooftop to land beside Panna. "It's not like any Arcadian on Hadra has a job to go to."

"They might."

Ballad had the same thought. "Like Anthem did, maybe? That's mostly nighttime work. It's the middle of the day."

"Sir Anthem worked days," Panna protested.

"Really? How do you know?" Ballad asked, frowning. The two Arcadians moved through the glaring light and down the road in search of their own kind. "He doesn't say a word about his prostitute days to us."

"Not to me, either. But why should he? It's between him and the queen. How do you even know about his old job?"

Ballad gave Panna a sidelong look. "Syle told me. I'm not sure who said it to him. Why? Who told you?"

"Xia," Panna said with a blush. "I guess there were some uh... health concerns."

Ballad scowled. "Anthem is a right hawk. I don't mind working with him, but I don't grasp at all why Maeve left Logan for him."

Panna blinked. How could he not understand? Rough as Ballad was, he was a royal knight. "If Queen Maeve is going to create a new kingdom, it's important that she has an Arcadian husband."

"Why?" Ballad asked.

"Why?" Panna repeated. "What do you mean, why? You can't have a monarchy without a royal line."

"There are orphans. Why not just adopt some fledglings?"

"The line of Cavain has ruled over our people – unbroken and undiminished – for ten thousand years," Panna said. "You can't just adopt new ones!"

"Even you say that Cavain was a tyrant," Ballad pointed out.

He was right about that. Panna's reverence for Arcadian history didn't mean she was stupid.

"That still doesn't invalidate his house's claim to the throne, Sir Ballad," she said. "Cavain a'Shae built the White Kingdom."

"Out of pyrad bones," Ballad answered. "And on the backs of dryad and nyad labourers."

Panna flushed again and wondered if the bright Hadrian sunlight blotted out the color in her cheeks. She was surprised that such a crass, rough young fairy would know enough about his race's history to even have an opinion. Panna had to admit – silently and only to herself – that she had misjudged him.

"Yes, but..." Panna stammered. "Well, it's not as if Logan Coldhand would have made a very good prince."

"Why not?" Ballad asked her. "Because he's human? Because he's Prian?"

"Well, yes. His devotion to Maeve is beyond question, but–"

"You're telling me," Ballad said with a slightly crooked grin that made him look even younger.

"–but he doesn't know very much about the Arcadian culture and history."

Now Ballad stopped in the middle of the sidewalk and looked at Panna with his brow furrowed under his short, sweaty blond hair.

"Anyone can learn that stuff," Ballad said.

"Like you have?"

"Logan taught me most of what I know," Ballad answered. "Back home – on Prianus, I mean – most of the older fairies don't think I'm much better than a human. They didn't spend time teaching me our history."

"How does Logan Coldhand know about Arcadian history and civics?"

"Does it matter?" Ballad asked. "He learned. Logan doesn't have to be Arcadian to love Maeve or to care about Kaellisem! Is it really better to have an Arcadian prince just because he's from one of our noble houses than a smart and devoted human?"

Panna walked faster. When Ballad put it that way, it did sound stupid. But lineage was important, wasn't it? Ten thousand years of history hung in the balance. Not an entirely spotless history, Panna admitted, but a proud and complex one on the verge of extinction. Surely that was worth protecting.

Ballad wasn't letting Panna off the hook that easily, though. The young knight glided a few steps and landed at her side again. A Lyran walking the opposite way growled low in his furry throat and Ballad growled right back. The effect would have been comical if Panna weren't so worried about the Lyran's claws. But he stomped past them with no further incident. Ballad gestured toward the retreating Lyran.

"Doesn't that bother you?" he asked.

"No," Panna lied. "I'm used to it."

"Really? And it doesn't bother you that you had to cut off your wings to attend an Alliance college?"

Panna snapped her mouth closed so fast that she bit her tongue. "Ouch! Fine, yes! Of course it bothers me, Sir Ballad. I... I hate it."

"We all hate how the Alliance treats us. But you're not doing any better, are you?"

Panna glared at him and tasted blood in her mouth. "What the empty pit of the Nameless' heart is that supposed to mean?"

"What does Logan have to cut off before he can love Maeve?"

Panna had no answer. She walked on, keeping her head down, but her eyes still streamed in the glaring sunlight. Where were the Arcadians? She had only been in the hospital a day.

She and Ballad spent the rest of the day searching Yebdemi, but found no other fairies. Panna pointed out one of the stout buildings where several Arcadians had said they lived. With a grunt, Ballad launched himself up against the heavy gravity and scrabbled over the roof's edge. A moment later, his face reappeared above.

"You'd better get up here," he said in a choked voice.

"Why?" Panna asked. "What's wrong?"

"They're all dead."

Panna climbed awkwardly up the fire escape ladder, kicking a window hard enough to make the apartment's occupant – a barely-dressed Hadrian man – shout at her through the glass. Panna told him to go back inside and call the police. The man grumbled and told her that he sure as hells would, but two minutes later, Panna wished that she hadn't said anything.

Ballad grabbed Panna's wrist and helped haul her up onto the apartment roof. The flat, sun-scarred roof was covered in blood. It was dark and dried, but the stuff was everywhere. There were four contorted Arcadian bodies stiffening under Hadra's relentless twin suns. Their wings had been slashed, keeping them helpless on the ground. Panna covered her mouth with her hand and crept closer. Tiny green ants crawled all over cloudy eyes and into open mouths. Panna turned away, retching. It was a good thing she had skipped breakfast.

"Oh gods," she gasped. "What... what happened?"

"They must have died fast," Ballad said. "Look, they're all sitting around this bag here."

Panna made herself turn back toward the bodies. Ballad was right. Death had splayed their thin limbs across the hot concrete, but all four Arcadians were more or less circled around a mycolar bag of bread. It was open and dried crumbs stuck in the darkened blood. For all the gore, they had been murdered quickly, attacked in the middle of a meal and unable to defend themselves. Or to make much noise, Panna guessed, remembering the unpleasant Hadrian below – all she had done was kick his window.

Ballad crouched beside one of the bodies and reached slowly toward the man's bloated, blood-smeared face. The throat beneath had been opened with a long, deep gash. Panna recognized him. He was one of the men who had asked Panna for money just before Xartasia's knight assaulted her. He must have bought the bread. She choked back a terrified sob.

"Don't..." Panna told Ballad, who froze. "Don't touch him. The police are on their way. We shouldn't be here when they arrive."

"Why not?" Ballad asked.

"We can't get caught here. This isn't murder under Alliance law because they're not citizens, but there will be an investigation and the cops will make at least a token attempt to catch someone. We don't want to be their prime suspects."

Ballad cursed under his breath and stepped back. He helped Panna make her way down the ladder – more carefully this time – and back to the ground. As casually as they could, they crossed the street and walked away. It was several minutes before a shiny white squad car came gliding down the road and parked in front of the building they had just left. A Hadrian officer climbed out, talking on his com. Ballad took Panna's arm gently.

"That guy at the window got a good look at you," he told Panna. "Let's get out of here."

Panna nodded and followed Ballad. When they had put a few blocks between themselves and the crime scene, they heard sirens, but only faintly. Panna paid a few white cenmark chips and they rode a crowded bus the rest of the way back to their motel room.

"What do you think happened?" Panna asked quietly once they were back inside. She didn't really think that Ballad would have an answer, but she had to talk about what they had seen.

"They were killed," Ballad said in a flat tone that Panna usually only heard from Logan Coldhand. He shrugged out of his leather jacket and threw it over the corner of his bed.

"But why? And how? None of them were shot. Those were blade wounds. If they're going to murder some Arcadians, wouldn't most coreworlders just... just shoot them?" Panna dropped heavily onto her bed, tired of fighting Hadra's gravity.

"Plenty of people still use nanoknives," Ballad told her. "They're cheaper and easier to get than guns. They don't use ammunition, slugs or batteries. Maybe that's–"

Ballad fell suddenly silent and there was a thump from somewhere outside. Panna frowned at the young knight as his eyes went wide. Ballad leapt onto Panna, tackling the girl down to the rough beige motel room carpet just as broken glass filled the air. A winged shape hurtled through the hole where the window had been.

Panna could see only a shoulder and a single arm past Ballad's wings, but her blood went cold. Plates of glass encircled pristine white scarves beneath and crystal-armored fingers wrapped around the glittering gray haft of a strange, long knife. Panna had a sudden, icy certainty that this was the weapon responsible for those slashed wings.

"Did you kill those people?" Panna shouted at the half-hidden white knight. "They didn't even go to Queen Maeve! They didn't do *anything!*"

"My queen has what she needs," the knight answered. "Now she flies on black wings to the Tower. Her business here is done."

"What?" Panna gasped. "The... the Nnyth Tower?"

The glittering arm was swinging the glass knife down at her and Ballad sprang to his feet to meet the blow. His own spear leaned in the corner, but it might as well have been light-years away. By the time he reached it, Panna would be dead. But Ballad grabbed the other knight's wrist in one hand and jabbed with his other fist. The boxer's bracelets – when had he put those on? – rang on the glass armor, but it took far more than a punch to shatter Arcadian glass.

Panna rolled out of the way, doing her best to avoid the sharp glass that littered the motel room. Ballad grunted and swore as he wrestled with their attacker. Panna saw him do something complicated with the other Arcadian's wrist and the knife was almost out of the knight's hand when it... changed.

The slick gray metal elongated, tripling and then quadrupling its length. It moved with the fluid ripple of nanite reconstruction, but faster than any kind of nanomechanical technology Panna had ever seen before. The white knight swung his spear, forcing Ballad to release his hold and leap back.

Panna heaved herself to her feet. She fought terror and Hadra's gravity for each step to where Ballad's spear leaned against the wall. She grabbed the weapon and shouted.

"Ballad!"

The Prian fairy turned toward her as Panna threw his spear, but she had miscalculated the gravity again and it fell short. She also miscalculated that Xartasia's killer might have heard her shout as well as Ballad did. His spear flicked out and slashed down Ballad's arm as he reached out. The gray haft swept around in a tight half circle and knocked his legs out from under him. The other knight reversed his grip on his spear and pointed the blood-smeared blade down at Ballad.

Panna screamed and yanked the lamp off the motel dresser. She flung it as hard as she could at Xartasia's killer. It shattered against his glass armor and sprayed the floor in more broken fragments. The knight glanced up at Panna for just a moment, but it was long enough for Ballad to wrap his fingers around one of the porcelain shards and stab it into the gap between his attacker's boots and greaves. The broken edge slashed through white scarves and freed a spray of bright blood.

Xartasia's pale knight hissed in pain and kicked out, but Ballad wrapped himself around the other man's ankles and spilled him to the floor with a swift jerk. Without his armor to weigh him down in Hadra's gravity, Ballad was the first back on his feet. He grabbed the white knight's long hair and rammed his knee into the other man's face. Blood ran from his nose and Ballad tried again, but the other Arcadian brought his arms up. The kick rang off glass.

The other knight grabbed his spear from the floor and surged up again. He slashed another bloody line through Ballad's shirt and into his chest. The Prian leapt back as the blade lashed out again. Panna threw herself to the floor. Where was Ballad's spear? There, under her bed. She squirmed her way across the floor, feeling glass and broken pottery slice through her shirt.

Ballad jumped to one side as Xartasia's knight lunged at him. His glass spear sliced into the wall just beside the broken window, yellow mycofoam insulation blooming around the blade. Ballad lunged at the knight, throwing a flurry of punches that rang off the plates of glass armor, but which forced him back, to release his grip on the gray spear.

"You fight like a dryad," spat the strange fairy. "You are no match for a knight of Arcadia."

"I'm more a knight than you are, hawk," Ballad answered with a roguish grin only somewhat undermined by the red blood staining his teeth.

Ballad threw himself at the other knight, kicking and punching. Panna couldn't see anything through the storm of red-spotted white wings. Her sweaty fingers slid off the haft of Ballad's spear. Panna bit her lips and grabbed it again, yanking it out from under the bed.

She jumped to her feet, spear in hand, just as the white knight threw himself back toward the window and the wall where his own weapon was still impaled. Ballad grabbed for the other man, his bloody fingers leaving streaks like red paint across the glass armor. The knight ignored Ballad and grabbed his spear, yanking the gray haft free.

"Ballad!" Panna threw the spear once more.

This time, she didn't miss.

Ballad seized the weapon out of the air. His opponent was still wrestling with his own spear and Ballad slashed out at the white knight's wing, spattering the feathers in gore. Xartasia's man sang out as he finally wrenched his spear free and brought it around on Ballad. But the other man was too close and he couldn't retract his spear quickly enough. Ballad slammed a kick into his chest and the knight toppled backward out of the broken window. The knight fought to spread his wings, but the injured one would not hold his weight. The limb snapped and folded, tumbling the white knight down into the street.

It wasn't a very long fall, but in the high Hadrian gravity, it was far enough.

"Are you alright?" Ballad asked Panna.

"Am *I* okay? You idiot," Panna gasped.

She wrenched her eyes from the dead knight below. She wished they had been able to question him. She looked up at Ballad. He was bleeding from a dozen messy wounds.

"We have to get out of here," Panna said.

"Yeah, the police will never let us out of this one," Ballad agreed. "And we need to tell Queen Maeve what he said about the Tower."

That wasn't what Panna meant at all.

"And we will," she told Ballad. "But I hope you liked Doctor Xel. We're going to see her first."

[30]

KNOWN

"A new name can't change a man's stripes."

- MIRRAN SAYING

At first, the riots couldn't gain much momentum. It was hard to kindle anger with Queen Maeve in the very place she gave away food. For those first hours, there were only a few minor injuries.

Until the prince consort arrived. When Anthem heard Logan's news, he immediately took wing with all nearby knights and made his way to the scene. But he was even less welcome than Logan had been and Anthem swiftly retreated, chased by screams of *whore* and *traitor*.

With Logan's help – riots were commonplace on Prianus and he had some experience with them – Anthem directed his forces from a distance. Within the hour, they had dispersed the crowd and sent everyone home. Logan didn't like working alongside Anthem, but if he could give up being with Maeve in the name of Kaellisem, Logan would force himself to be professional with his replacement.

The sullen peace did not last long. Word of Maeve's role in the White Kingdom's fall spread quickly. The next morning, there were three fights in the food lines between Maeve's supporters and those shouting for her blood. Knights stepped in each time, but by noon, there were screaming matches and worse breaking out all across Kaellisem. The sky was full of angry, self-righteous and frightened fairies.

"This is even worse than the theater bombing!" Duaal said as he paced across the Blue Phoenix's mess.

They had relocated the queen and her tiny royal court back to the ship for her safety. At the last report, there were over a thousand Arcadians in the street and sky surrounding her red and gold tower.

"Arcadian lives were lost during the enassui," Anthem pointed out. "There have been injuries today, but none have died."

"So far," Duaal said. "But that will change. There's a mob of over a thousand fairies out there, all screaming for revenge."

"Duaal!" Xia gasped. She gestured subtly to Maeve, who sat at the table with her face in her hands.

"It is not as if I do not know," the queen said.

She wasn't wearing the glass circlet that Duaal had designed for her and several strands of white stood out in Maeve's midnight hair that had not been there a month ago.

"And for what we're trying to do here, for keeping the Arcadians away from Xartasia, this is worse!" Duaal said. "How can we keep Kaellisem together now? And how the hells did they find out about Tamlin?"

"We're the only ones who know, right?" Gripper asked. "I mean originally."

"Panna does, as well," Duke Ferris said. The old fairy nobleman glared suspiciously around at the coreworlders.

"Sprite's out on Hadra!" Gripper objected. "She couldn't have done this!"

"Then perhaps Panna told someone before she left," Ferris said. "Who then told another...?"

"That could be true of anyone in this room," Logan said.

"Did any of you speak of this?" Anthem asked.

Duaal shook his head. So did Xia. Gripper did so more slowly.

"Just to Glass," he said. "And she sort of um... knows."

Logan looked at the two Arcadian men. "What about you?"

Duke Ferris' lined face was a mask of indignation.

"I would never," he said. "It was *I* who advised Queen Maeve to keep the secret of the Tamlin Waygate! If I wished it known, all I had to do was remain silent."

That made sense, but Logan wasn't done. "Building Kaellisem on Stray meant leaving your injured daughter back on Sunjarrah. That would be difficult for any father."

Ferris' cheeks turned red. "How dare you? *Ella esu cerri vae!*"

I am loyal to the queen, Logan translated the angry shout. He was inclined to believe the old nobleman. Ferris was stubbornly honorable and Logan doubted that he would risk putting Maeve or Kaellisem in danger.

Anthem had been quiet. Logan studied him. There was a purple bruise on his temple where one of the rioting fairies had thrown a rock at the prince consort. He still wore his glass armor and carried his spear. Anthem *was* Xartasia's lover... or had been a century before. What if his heart and loyalty still belonged to her?

"No," Sir Anthem said at last. "I do not think I have spoken to anyone on the matter. I have not thought much about it, in truth."

Maeve raised her face. Her eyes were rimmed in red.

"Not thought much about it?" she asked in a loud, raw voice. "I killed our people, Anthem! And you just forget...?"

"I did not say that."

Maeve jumped up to her feet, wings and arms wrapped around herself.

"Who first told Kaellisem about Tamlin is not to blame in this," she said. "The fault is mine. The deed is my own and even now, I am not done destroying Arcadia! Is it not enough that entire worlds are left shattered? Now the knowledge will break apart Kaellisem, too. And without Kaellisem, Xartasia wins."

"We've got to get the information under control," Xia said. "Gossip has vectors, just like any other pathogen. We can probably project–"

"Too many people already know," Duaal interrupted. "We could contain the borders of Kaellisem, couldn't we? No one here has any real weapons except the knights. We could keep the Arcadians from leaving."

"No, absolutely not!" Duke Ferris said. "We are not turning the knights on their own people!"

"And it would not work, anyway," Anthem agreed. "We lack the numbers to enforce such a border, even if we left the queen entirely unprotected–"

"Which we are *not* doing," Logan said.

Anthem nodded. "Agreed."

"Um, can't we just tell everyone that it's not true?" Gripper asked plaintively.

"No. No more lies. I refuse to deceive–" Maeve began in a hard voice. One of her young handmaidens, Dain, came scampering into the mess and whispered to the queen. Maeve frowned. "Now? Dain, the people of Kaellisem are rioting."

"I told her that you were too busy," Dain said. "But Panna swears that her news is important."

With a sigh, Maeve rose, took the com that Dain held out and stepped out into the corridor. Logan caught just a glimpse of the queen's furrowed brow before she turned away and her wings hid her face from view. Anthem came to stand beside Logan.

"Do you think that you can find the one who betrayed Maeve's secret?" asked the prince consort.

Logan found himself glaring at the too-handsome fairy knight and reminding himself to be professional.

"The queen said that's not important," Logan said.

"But it may be the one who created the bombs," Anthem said. "Someone is trying to destroy Maeve and her kingdom. With this, they might have finally succeeded."

A sudden fury blazed inside Logan and he grabbed the front of Anthem's armor. Glass screeched against glass until Logan's fingers caught the edge of Anthem's breastplate and he yanked the smaller man up to eye level. Duke Ferris yelped indignantly and demanded that Logan put the prince down this minute. Gripper's hands flew to his mouth.

"No one will destroy Maeve," Logan said. "No one! And if you *ever* say something like that to her, I'll break your wings. You're her prince, Anthem. Act like it!"

"Logan!" Duaal shouted. "For the love of God, let him go!"

"Why?" Logan asked, not looking at Duaal. His eyes remained fixed on Anthem's deep blue-black ones. The knight stared back, unflinching. For all his tiny size and light, fragile anatomy, Anthem had guts. The servos inside Logan's glass hand strained visibly as his grip tightened.

"Look, I don't like it, either," Duaal said. "But Anthem's right. That knight on Sunjarrah and his pet Devourer, the police interference there and here on Stray, the bombs... Somehow this has managed to be so much worse. I didn't think there was anything in the worlds that could get the Arcadians to stand up and fight. Now we have it and... and it's horrible. They're fighting each other. They're fighting us. Anthem just said what we're all thinking."

"And what is that?" Logan asked.

"That we may have just lost this whole thing," Xia answered softly. "The only ground we held over Xartasia was being able to tell the Arcadians that Maeve had a more legitimate claim to the throne than someone who allied with the Devourers. But now they know Maeve's just as bad."

"Maeve made a mistake," Logan snarled. "Xartasia *knows* what she's doing!"

"That is small comfort to the people of Kaellisem," Anthem told the Prian. "The White Kingdom is fallen, they have grieved for a hundred years and now they finally have someone to blame."

"It's not–"

Maeve strode back into the room and everyone fell silent. She glanced at Logan and he replaced Anthem on the fibersteel floor. A bit sheepishly, the Prian had to admit. But Maeve no longer hugged her wings around herself. She raised her sharp chin and Logan knew he would be proud of whatever she did next. Maeve handed her com back to Dain, who accepted it with a bob of her head.

"Panna and Ballad have news," Maeve said. "Their recruitment efforts on Hadra have not been very successful, but they encountered one of Xartasia's knights."

She raised her hand to forestall any questions.

"He is dead. Ballad protected Panna admirably... She was most emphatic on that matter. But before he died, Xartasia's knight told them something. My cousin has the Arcadians she needs, it seems. Her work there is done. Panna believes that her recruiters are now killing any of those who did not join Xartasia."

"But why?" Gripper asked in a tiny voice. "Why would she ever do that?"

"Perhaps out of bloody and petty vengeance. Perhaps to keep them away from us," Maeve said. "From me."

"So that's it?" Duaal kicked the couch and then slumped down onto it. "We've lost and Xartasia wins?"

Logan glanced back at Anthem, but it was impossible to read the knight's expression. Not because it was stony, but because there were too many obvious feelings warring for control. Anger and despair, hope and joy all rippling across Anthem's fine features like waves across the sand.

"No," Maeve said. "We are not finished just yet! That knight told Panna that in order for Xartasia to execute her unknown plan, she has taken her people and Devourers to the Tower."

"Tower?" Xia repeated. "What tower?"

"You mean the Nnyth Tower?" Gripper asked. "The star wasps? Where you got the phenno?"

Maeve nodded once. "That was Panna's conclusion, as well."

"The Nnyth..." Ferris said. The duke had sat down again, rather pointedly with his back to Logan. The old fairy never liked Logan and he had just proved himself to be the brutish, dangerous animal Ferris always thought him. "You served at the Waygates, Majesty. That is known to all now. Then you know the Nnyth's wisdom in those mysteries."

"The Nnyth taught the first Spire Adepts," Maeve said. "And it was from them that the Arcadians learned to use the Waygates."

"Yes, a'shae," Ferris agreed, nodding. "None know the Waygates better. And Xartasia used a Waygate on Prianus to summon those Devourers that fly with her now, you told us. Perhaps she intends to bring more into the galaxy."

"But why go to the Nnyth for that?" Gripper asked. "Aren't there a bunch of Waygates left in the White Kingdom? She could use any of them."

"And that doesn't explain what she needs all the Arcadians for," Xia said. "You told us no one understands the Waygates better, but that's not true. As far as we know, the Devourers built them in the first place. So they would know the most about the gates, right? What could Xartasia ask the Nnyth that the Devourers wouldn't know more about?"

"I do not know," Ferris admitted.

"It's a long flight all the way out to the galactic rim," Logan said. "That's not a journey anyone would want to make unless absolutely necessary. Whatever Xartasia's up to next, she's got to be very sure that it's going to work. Everything she's done up until now has been to make this move."

"How can you know that?" Ferris asked, finally looking at Logan again.

"Logan is right," Anthem said. "Titania... Xartasia... is a clever and careful woman. She will not cast a hundred stones and just hope that one strikes her target. The Nnyth are the most ancient and powerful race of the galaxy – perhaps excepting the Devourers, but I know little of them – but even the Jinn cannot claim them as friends. Even in the days of the White Kingdom, we did not simply arrive unannounced at the Nnyth Tower."

Maeve nodded. "Now we must go to the Nnyth and warn them. We must ask them if they understand Xartasia's plan and stop it, if we can. Space is vast and dark on the edge of the galaxy. The Blue Phoenix has reached the Nnyth Tower once before."

"When we first brought back the phenno for Xyn," Duaal said. He smiled sadly at Maeve. "That was your first time on the Phoenix. Tiberius hired you as a guide."

Maeve smiled, too. It was a raw, painful thing and tears filled her eyes at the memory. Logan felt it, too. Tiberius Myles had been a good man. He deserved better than to be killed by Gavriel... but he had fallen fighting Duaal's tormentor, fighting for the boy who had been Tiberius' son in all but name. That, at least, was right.

"We'll need to pick up a few things from Unbreakers to make the flight," Duaal said. "The Tower is a long way, even from Stray. But we can refuel in Gharib and be in the black inside a day. From there, it should take about a month to get out to the Rynn system on the rim."

"I can probably shave off a few days if we push the engines a little," Gripper added. "We just need enough food to make the trip."

Everyone looked at Maeve.

"There may be words traded with the Nnyth," Duke Ferris said. "Who shall serve as your emissary? Who will be your voice, a'shae?"

Maeve paused and Logan recognized the calculating look in her gray eyes. After a moment, she inclined her head to the duke.

"If you will agree, Your Grace," Maeve said, "then I would like you to stand for me."

Ferris' wings rustled and he beamed with pride. "Of course, my queen. It would be my greatest honor."

"Wait, why aren't you coming out to the Tower with us, Glass?" Gripper asked.

"Our queen has responsibilities in Kaellisem," Anthem said. He turned toward her. "What of the riots rising in the city? There has already been blood and it is only a matter of time until lives are lost. What do you want us to do, Maeve?"

"They are already surrounding my tower, demanding answers," Maeve said. "Gather the rest of Kaellisem there. The theater is in ruins, but I must speak to my people."

"What's the point?" Duaal asked. He shook his head. "What do you think you can tell them now that will make the slightest bit of difference?"

"It will be done," Anthem said, saluting Maeve with a long wing and ignoring Duaal's objections. He took out his com and began relaying orders to his knights.

"Maeve, you're just torturing yourself," Duaal told her. "Let this simmer down."

"Have you not always told me how much appearances matter?" Maeve asked with another small, sad smile that made Logan's heart ache. "A queen is more than the crown she wears or even the blood in her veins. I am no queen without my kingdom. I cannot ignore what they need, Duaal."

"No, I guess not."

Maeve returned her attention to Ferris. "I have recalled Ballad and Panna from Hadra. Their work on that world is done, such as it has been. I will assign the pair to you. Ballad has proved himself a more than capable knight. He will protect you. Panna is intelligent, insightful and organized. She will be an excellent administrator. They should be back on Stray soon."

Duke Ferris' eyebrows crept fractionally up his weathered face – he didn't like Ballad much more than he did Logan – but he simply inclined his head. "Yes, Your Majesty. As you wish. I will prepare myself for the journey."

Ferris turned and left. Duaal, Gripper and Xia scattered to begin preparations to get the Blue Phoenix into the black, leaving Logan alone with Maeve. And Dain and Anthem. The little handmaiden was helping Sir Anthem count out how many Arcadians each of his knights needed to collect. Neither one paid much attention to the queen and the bounty hunter for now.

"Logan?" Maeve asked.

"Yes, a'shae?" Logan answered.

Maeve winced. "I would like you to go with the Blue Phoenix."

Logan's mechanical heart felt like it was made of lead, but he made himself bow. He had no wings to give the proper obeisance.

"If that's what you want," Logan answered.

"You are not going to ask me why?" Maeve asked.

"Does it matter?" Logan asked her with a shrug. "I'll do whatever you need me to. Always."

"What happens here in Kaellisem will be for the Arcadians, to help and serve them," Maeve said. "But flying out to the Tower, that may save or damn many more lives than that. I need you there. No one in the worlds is stronger than you."

"You are," Logan said before he could stop himself.

Maeve's cheeks burned with color and Logan turned away and left the mess before the urge to hold her overwhelmed him. He felt Maeve's eyes on him as he went.

"Yes, Sir Anthem," Syle said into his com. "Of course. I will bring them at once."

The yellow-eyed knight keyed off the device and slid it back into the sash tied around the waist of his armor. He returned his attention to the scene below.

A dozen or so Arcadians stood together, back to back and their wings overlapping in fragile feathered shields. They were loyalists, those who either didn't believe what the rest of Kaellisem said about the queen or – for reasons that eluded Syle – did not loathe her for it.

But a larger group of Arcadians surrounded them, shouting and closing slowly in. Most of the aggressors were unarmed, but a few had taken up stones or shards of blackened glass – pieces of the ruined theater. The disastrous enassui had become a symbol across Kaellisem of Queen Maeve's failure, a sign that the gods themselves decried her reign.

A pair of Gharib police cars circled high over the crowd of Arcadians and then raced off back toward their city without landing. Who had called them? Syle suspected the Dailon man, Vyron, or maybe his wife. They insisted on taking an interest in things that had nothing to do with them.

But it didn't matter anymore. Things were moving too fast. The Gharib police wouldn't risk involvement unless things spilled out of Kaellisem. Syle doubted that would happen... the fairies were leaving, abandoning Queen Maeve in droves. Kaellisem would cannibalize itself within a week, leaving Maeve Cavainna alone and helpless to make any move against Xartasia.

Syle smiled. It had been almost too easy. A single piece of information whispered into a few pointed ears had done a far better job than weeks of bombs. For all of the work that Syle had put into a variety of interesting devices, those had failed to topple Kaellisem.

Sir Anthem Calloren and Logan Coldhand had proved entirely too clever for Syle's taste. He assumed that the two men's rivalry for Maeve's affection would distract them more than enough for Syle to finish his work, but both proved more dedicated to their duties – or maybe to the queen herself – than that.

Syle considered ignoring Anthem's orders. It was a good time to leave Kaellisem. His work was done, after all. The other knights would notice his absence, of course, but Syle would be long gone by then. He had money enough for a fast ship off Stray and with so many Arcadians on the planet these days. No one would notice the comings and goings of one more.

But Syle was a professional. There was no name for his profession, but he took pride in his work. Surely the White Queen herself would have delicately applauded Syle's success.

It was a pity that she would never know the intricate details. By necessity, Syle operated in absolute silence, never once calling back to Xartasia to report his progress. Such long-range communications were logged and recorded at any terminal. Messy. And by the time Syle could tell his queen of his deeds in person, it would be far too late. The story would mean nothing.

The regret tasted bitter in Syle's mouth, but perhaps it was for the best that Xartasia would never know what had passed in Kaellisem. The White Queen's heart broke the day her kingdom fell, and she didn't know that Anthem Calloren had survived the destruction. But it was best that Xartasia never discovered how he had betrayed her.

Syle loved his queen. He would spare her any pain.

Below, one of the frightened loyalists finally broke from the ring and darted into the air, trying to escape, but three others leapt and tackled the woman swiftly back to the sandy ground. A low moan went up from the loyalists and then a louder, high-pitched note from the rest of the Arcadians. One of them brandished his sharp, crooked spike of black glass and Syle's smile became a wolfish grin.

Let Maeve bring her failing people together for more lies. Let her make her empty promises. Let her drive the final spear through her own kingdom.

Syle whistled a sharp note and spread his wings. He dove down into the center of the crowd. Red Stray sunlight shone blindingly off his glass armor. Syle raised his spear and sang in a loud voice.

"Queen Maeve calls you to her! She has something to say."

[31]
HEAR THEM

"It's often not important what you do, but what you *won't* do."

- VYRON FETHRU (234 PA)

Maeve flew down from the hovering Blue Phoenix to her tower as her knights struggled to keep the growing crowd at bay. Even over the roar of the cargo freighter's engines, she could hear their cries and angry songs.

Inside, the gold-streaked crystal walls rang with voices. Maeve wanted to cover her ears, but Verra was working urgently on the queen's windblown black hair. She made herself sit patiently as the girl labored. Dain approached with a properly somber gray and red gown, like smoke and flame swirling together. Delicate coal-black embroidery curled around the edges. It was not a new addition to the royal wardrobe, but Maeve had never worn it before. She sighed and let her handmaidens dress her.

When Verra was done, she took the glass crown that Duaal had designed and pinned it into the queen's dark curls. Maeve inspected the effect in a mirror, but she barely recognized the woman staring back at her. When had her hair gotten so long? How old were those lines at the corners of her eyes? The streaks of white at her temples? She was only two hundred years old…

Maeve rose and made herself smile at Dain and Verra. The two girls were annoying at best, and more often unwelcome chaperones. But they were only trying to do their jobs.

"Have you heard what they say in Kaellisem?" Maeve asked.

"About you, Majesty?" Verra asked.

Maeve nodded and the two Arcadian girls traded a look. Dain looked down at the polished glass floor and said nothing.

"Yes," Verra finally admitted.

"And what do you think? Do you believe them?"

"It does not matter what we think, Your Majesty," Verra told the queen. "We serve the crown."

Their loyalty was unshakable. It was reassuring, yes, but Maeve frowned at the girls. "It matters if it is true. A queen must be worthy of her crown. If that were not so, we would all serve Xartasia now."

"Yes, a'shae," Verra answered at once.

Maeve's frown melted away. Dain and Verra were just children. In a better world, they wouldn't have to worry about such things. The royal tower thrummed with the sound of the crowd outside as though caught up in an endless roll of thunder.

Maeve knelt – eliciting a gasp from Dain as the skirts of her new gown caught under her knees – and held out her arms to both girls. The two handmaidens hesitated and then ran to the queen. Maeve hugged them both close. Dain was crying and Verra shivered despite Stray's heat. They were frightened. If Kaellisem fell now, what would happen to these sweet, irritating girls? Their wings trembled against Maeve.

"Remain inside until this is done," she told Verra and Dain. "Sir Anthem's knights will not let anything happen to you. You will be safe here."

Dain sobbed something that Maeve couldn't quite make out, but then Verra took the younger girl's hand and pulled her back.

Maeve went to the doors. They swung open on smooth glass hinges and she stepped onto the balcony overlooking the sunset spires of Kaellisem.

The roar was deafening. The streets and skies of Kaellisem were a sea of white wings and loud, furious voices.

Most of Maeve's small court stood arrayed along the balcony's curved edge. Ferris stood to one side, with Duaal on the other. Sir Anthem and Logan had taken up the forward positions, facing the chorus of angry and spiteful songs. Three thousand Arcadians stood in the street below, hands and wings raised. More were in the air, circling the tower like a storm and blotting out the red light of the setting sun. The rest of Anthem's royal knights stood on other balconies and roofs and windows, all half-crouched and holding spears at the ready.

Maeve stepped out through the flickering sunset shadows. A bottle arced from somewhere up in the swirling cyclone of angry fairies and smashed into the glass floor at her feet. The sick-sweet smell of narcohol suddenly flooded her senses. How long since her last drink? Prianus? Before that? Maeve could no longer remember.

"Make sure everyone can hear me," she told Duaal.

The mage nodded.

Logan and Anthem drew back as Maeve came to stand between them. The fairy queen held up her hands. She remembered Gavriel standing just here, in front of the crooked black cathedral that once rose up from the desert sand. The very same sands that now made up the red and golden tower where Maeve stood. She took a deep breath of the hot air.

"Kaellisem!" she said.

Maeve knew that Duaal's spell would carry her words through the whole city. Her voice echoed off the crystal towers and filled the sandy streets. There was an answering roar from the crowd so full of rage that Maeve took an involuntary step back from the edge of the balcony. Her heart pounded hammer blows against her ribs.

"I hear you!" Maeve said. Why hadn't she asked Panna to write this for her? "I hear your voices, your anger. You feel betrayed! And you are not wrong."

Duke Ferris shot Maeve a look, but she ignored him. This was more important than politics. She had to try to win back Kaellisem's trust. The cost no longer mattered.

"You know what happened at Tamlin," Maeve said. "You do not need to hear the song again. We have sung it for a hundred years. But you deserve to hear that I... I am sorry I did not sing my own part for you. What you have heard of me, of Tamlin, is true. I went to the Waygate there alone, while my brother spell-singer remained back in the city with his lover. I attempted to open the Tamlin gate and my failure called out to the Devourers. It was an accident... but it was mine.

"Kaellisem is small and it is fragile, and I feared that it would shatter if you knew what I had done. A kingdom – even one as tiny as Kaellisem – belongs not to its queen, but to its people. This city is yours. You built all of this and it belongs to you! I hear your voices, your anger and your demands. And I will listen. I belong to you, too. I have always belonged to you. So if you no longer wish me here, I will go. I am leaving Stray!"

Now Duke Ferris was striding toward her, shouting something that Maeve couldn't hear. Sir Anthem grabbed the duke's arm and hauled him back. Maeve felt Logan's eyes on her, as cold as ice in the heat of the desert. She grabbed her crown and yanked. It came free with a few strands of black hair still tangled around the glass. Maeve held it aloft.

"News has just reached us that Xartasia is bound for the Nnyth Tower," she said. "We do not know what she intends there, but I will go with Captain Sinnay to warn the Nnyth and find out. I may not be worthy to lead, but I will still serve my people! It is not my right to ask your forgiveness, Kaellisem, and so I go now to repent some small measure of my crimes!"

Maeve looked at Anthem and then at Logan, then stepped back. There was no applause – only silence. The storm of white wings above circled once more and then broke apart. Hundreds of Arcadians scattered like dandelion puffs, flying away through the rising darkness. The only sounds were fading wingbeats and footsteps as everyone in Kaellisem turned away.

"What have you done?" Duke Ferris all but screamed. Anthem held him fast. "You are our queen!"

"A queen serves her people," Maeve answered. "And the people have made it very clear that they no longer want me. I am leaving."

Maeve gestured to Anthem, who finally released Ferris and the old nobleman fell to his knees. "No, my queen! We need you!"

"Ferris, you and Panna truly ruled Kaellisem," Maeve told him. "And now I place the two of you in charge of the city's care. You will need Panna, Your Grace, and Sir Ballad will protect you."

"But... I..."

Maeve had never seen Ferris speechless before. She offered her free hand to him. Ferris took it and rose. Maeve held out her crown.

"Keep this safe," she said. "I may not be worthy of it, but it is a powerful symbol nonetheless."

Ferris accepted the crown with shaking hands. One by one, the glass-armored knights landed along the edge of the tower balcony. Eranna wept openly. All nineteen fell to one knee around Maeve. Nineteen? There should have been twenty... But Maeve didn't have time to recount. Anthem knelt, too.

"Our loyalty is to you, a'shae," he told her. "It always has been. Command us and we will obey."

"Stay here in Kaellisem," Maeve said. "There are still dangers in Gharib. Protect the city as you always have."

"Yes, a'shae," the knights answered together.

They rose and flew off into Kaellisem. Except for Anthem, who remained on one knee. Duaal raised a dark brow and looked significantly at the remaining fairy knight.

"What are you still doing here?" Duaal asked.

"With your permission, Captain Sinnay," Anthem said, "I will go with you to the Nnyth Tower."

"Permission denied," Duaal answered. "Didn't Maeve just give you an order? And didn't you just promise to keep obeying her?"

"And as a knight, I am bound to do so." Anthem rose and turned to Maeve. He took her hands in his. "But as your consort, my queen, I am sworn to remain by your side. Besides, I am no more popular in Kaellisem than you are right now."

Maeve stared. Of all the possible outcomes of her decision, this one had never occurred to her.

"Anthem, you do not need to do this," she said.

"I believe in the dream of Kaellisem," the knight told her. "But there are things I believe in more. You. Titania. If you go to face her, then I will be with you when you do."

Maeve held Anthem's glass-gloved hands and nodded slowly. "Fly with us, then."

Duaal pulled out his com. "Gripper, get two extra rooms ready. Maeve and Anthem are coming with us. Get your big brown butt moving! The Tower isn't getting any closer on its own."

Maeve removed her hands from Anthem's and turned away. She had to collect her armor – she would need it before this was done, Maeve was sure. Logan Coldhand already stood at the door, blue eyes unreadable.

There was no moon that night and all of Kaellisem sank swiftly into darkness. The city was quiet, strangely subdued in the wake of the queen's announcement. A few fairies moved slowly through the sky and the streets, drifting like snowflakes. They sang softly, if at all. They had what they wanted. They had exiled their own queen for her crimes...

Syle flew low on silent wings, searching through the darkness. His armor was already gone, an unwanted glittering skin peeled away and left not far away from the golden royal tower. The spy and saboteur still carried his spear, however. He would need that.

Maeve Cavainna was leaving Kaellisem. She was going to the Tower in pursuit of the White Queen herself. Even if the new kingdom failed now, Maeve was still a danger to Xartasia. Syle hissed an oath to himself as the cooling desert wind ruffled his feathers. He should have seen this coming, should have known Maeve would fight to the last breath. Even without Kaellisem, the queen would never give up.

There... Out beyond Kaellisem's glittering edge, the ugly, bulky silhouette loomed up suddenly from the night. The cargo ship was graceless and thorny as a demon. Every piece of ceramic and fiber-steel glistened with the faintly iridescent gleam of phenno. Syle landed quietly on the packed red sand next to the Blue Phoenix and began searching for a way inside.

[32]
ONCE AND NEVER

"Life owes you nothing. It's life. It's already given you more than anyone else ever will."

- KESSA FETHRU (233 MA)

There wasn't much to collect from Maeve's tower. Her glass armor, some clothes and a couple of other personal effects, but she gathered them all up in a single trip and then made her way discreetly to the Blue Phoenix to join the rest of the expedition. The tower would belong to Duke Ferris now, if he wanted to use it. Dain and Verra were still there and were welcome to remain. The girls had asked to come along with Maeve, but didn't put up much of a fight when she told them *no*. It would be a long and dangerous journey. Dain and Verra did not really want to go. They just didn't want to abandon Maeve.

It was strange to be back in her own bunkroom. Alone. No one watching, no one trying to brush her hair or get her signature on a datadex. She had left detailed instructions for Duke Ferris, but Panna would be far more useful to him. She and Ballad should be back on Stray a day after the Blue Phoenix was scheduled to leave.

Maeve felt a little guilty about being grateful for that. She didn't want to face Panna or explain to the young anthropologist why she had to leave Kaellisem.

Maeve added a few favorite dresses to her old wardrobe, but left the rest empty. The bunk's sheets were neat and clean and white. Someone had laundered them since Maeve left and she ran her fingers over the inexpensive cloth. Gripper, she guessed. There was no dust in her room, although Stray was covered in the stuff. That had probably been Gripper, too, or maybe Xia. Maeve just could not imagine Duaal cleaning rooms.

All of Maeve's needles and narcohol bottles were gone, too. Had she done that herself? Maeve couldn't remember. It seemed like a lifetime since she had stayed here on the Blue Phoenix. The little quarters should have felt cramped, she supposed. They were much smaller than any of the rooms in her glass tower and there was only the single scratched porthole window. It was pointed away from Kaellisem and looked out only across empty sand and desert. If Maeve pressed herself against the wall on the left side, she could *just* make out the edge of Gharib.

But the room didn't feel small... Maeve changed into a pair of her old spacer's pants and a backless shirt from her little closet. The flowing dresses and scarves that made up an Arcadian queen's wardrobe were impractical on a starship full of moving parts and sharp metal edges. She tied her black hair up into a tail and inspected the results. Sloppy. Dain would have been aghast, but Maeve found that she didn't mind. She pushed a few stray strands of black hair behind her ears as the door chimed.

"It is open," Maeve answered. "Come in."

Gripper ducked to poke his head inside. "The Blues are here to make their last delivery. I thought you might like to say hello."

"Yes, thank you."

Maeve turned away from the mirror and then followed Gripper through the Blue Phoenix. The hold was full of crates and piles of parts tangled up in orange cargo nets. Duaal and Logan placed a final pallet of boxes against the cargo bay's rear wall. Both of the men were stripped to the waist and sweating in the Stray heat.

As promised, Vyron and Kessa were there. The Dailons stood beside Xia, who held Baliend with a smile curling her silver lips. The baby burbled at Xia and reached for her antennae.

Maeve stopped at the bottom of the stairs and took in the scene. It should have been a happy one. Just like old times, before Kaellisem and Xartasia. The Phoenix getting ready to fly away again, off into the black. Better than old times, in fact – Logan was helping them, working alongside Duaal instead of hunting Maeve across the galaxy, hounding their every step. But Maeve didn't smile. Her blood ran cold through her body, freezing her to the spot.

This was *not* old times. This was no cargo run, just trying to get a load of apples from Koji to Axis before they rotted. Everything they did now was dreadfully important. Tiberius was gone. Xartasia and the Devourers were out there. Arcadians were dead and, if any of Maeve's unpleasant guesses were right, many millions more lives would follow into the Nameless' unwelcoming embrace.

Kessa looked up from her son's face and ran to Maeve. She flung strong arms around the much smaller woman.

"Duaal says you're going out to Nnyth space. Do you really think you'll find out what Xartasia wants out there?" Kessa asked.

"I do not know," Maeve said. "But we know where she is going, if not why. We will find Xartasia, one way or another."

"You're very brave." Kessa told her. The Dailon mother kissed the top of Maeve's head. "Thank you."

Maeve couldn't help the brief smile that crossed her face.

"What do we owe you for all of this?" she asked, gesturing to the crates and barrels. "They have not yet cut off access to what passes for the Kaellisem royal treasury."

"Don't worry about it," Vyron answered. "You wouldn't believe what Xyn and I are making off distributing the Arcadian glass. It's a damned good thing, too. Xyn's phenno redprint is starting to break down and we're having trouble getting a viable batch. Without the glass, Unbreakers would be eating sand by now. I don't suppose you can bring us a fresh genetic sample while you're out at the Tower?"

Maeve blinked and wasn't sure how to answer that. Kessa glared daggers at her husband, who just shrugged and held up his long-fingered blue hands.

"What?" he asked. "You can't blame me for trying. I'm a businessman."

Duaal leapt down from the now-secured tower of crates, Logan thumping more heavily to the deckplates behind him. The Hyzaari mage raked fingers through his dark, sweaty hair.

"Well, that about does it," he announced. "Gripper, are all the new filters loaded?"

"All in, captain. We had a break in one of the central ducts, but I've got it all under control now."

Duaal nodded to Maeve. "Your Majesty, we're ready to go. Just say the word."

She began to nod, but then looked around the hold. "Where is Sir Anthem?"

"Oh," Duaal said nonchalantly. "I sent him into Gharib to get us a new duonetic converter."

"What is that?" Maeve asked.

Duaal shrugged. "No idea. But it should keep Anthem busy for the rest of the day. He can barely say *duonetic*."

"Because you made it up," Xia said. She ruffled Baliend's hair. "Anthem is still trying to learn Aver, Duaal. That was cruel."

"Yeah, probably. So let's get up into the black before he figures that out," Duaal said.

He turned toward the stairs that led up to the rest of the Blue Phoenix. Maeve stood in his way and did not move.

"Not until you call Anthem and get him back to the ship," she told Duaal. "And apologize!"

"Seriously?" the mage asked.

"No more games," Maeve said. "Too many lives are at stake."

At least Duaal had the grace to look chagrinned. He nodded and took out his com. He made his farewells to Kessa and Vyron, then vanished up in the direction of the Blue Phoenix's cockpit. Xia reluctantly returned Baliend to his parents and escorted them from the ship. Maeve looked up at Gripper.

"Is there anything that I can do to help here?" she asked.

"Don't think so, Glass. We've got everything pretty much ready to go."

The young Arboran engineer looked and sounded quite certain. They were flying a long, long way into terrible danger, but Gripper showed no signs of sharing the fear that clenched Maeve's stomach.

"It's good to have you back, Glass," he said. "I'm really sorry for how it happened, but it's still good. Do you need anything?"

"No," Maeve answered. "I still remember where everything is."

"Make sure Silver closes up the lock when she gets back inside," he called down.

Maeve promised that she would and Gripper reached up to the edge of the catwalk, then swung himself up onto the next level. She noted with regret that Logan had pulled his shirt back on, but he said nothing as Maeve and Xia waited at the airlock for Anthem.

The knight arrived from Gharib a half hour later. Anthem made no comment on Duaal's deception, but secured himself along with the rest of the crew for takeoff. He sat awkwardly next to Maeve, leaning forward in a pointless attempt to make room for his wings. They ended up draped and twisted uncomfortably over the back of the seat, tangled with his queen's.

Maeve braced herself for a rough takeoff, but Duaal piloted the Blue Phoenix smoothly up off of Stray and then out into the darkness beyond the planet's atmosphere. After only a few minutes, thin clouds gave way to stars and then they lengthened into the multi-colored streaks of superluminal flight.

Duaal came back down into the combined mess and lounge. He had replaced his shirt, as well.

"And that's it," he said. "We're on our way to the Rynn system. We don't have an accurate travel estimate, but it will take us somewhere around twenty-eight days," he said. "The charts out beyond Stray aren't very precise and God knows the last time anyone bothered updating them. We'll need to make some stops to check our bearing and make sure we're not going to smash into some comet no one knows about."

"What do we do now?" Anthem asked.

"Uh, mostly we wait," Gripper answered. "We wait a long time and try not to go crazy wondering what's going to happen when we finally reach the Tower."

Their cold, tiny corner of the Hrana's hold had cost Panna every cenmark of their remaining money. Not just the money Maeve had given them, but Panna's own savings, too. The Hrana's captain must have sensed their desperation and hurry. Ballad's poker face wasn't very good and Panna doubted hers was much better. The money didn't matter anymore, but Panna couldn't help glaring a bit at the dark-haired freighter captain as they climbed out of the Hrana and back into Stray's familiar dry, dusty heat. At least the gravity was better than on Hadra. Ballad didn't stick his thumb and finger out at the man and Panna was rather proud of the young knight. He was actually learning some restraint.

It was midafternoon in Kharnig and the fat, dim sun beat mercilessly down onto the craggy red-brown city. The heat was almost as bad as Hadra. Ballad jumped down from the airlock, balancing his small bag of belongings on his shoulder.

"He could have at least dropped us off in Gharib," Ballad said. "We're on the other side of Stray."

"Not quite, but almost," Panna said. She checked a datadex. The mainstream signal was weak, but it was there. She called up a map. "We're only about seven hundred miles from Gharib, actually. We can probably get Captain Sinnay to pick us up."

Panna put the datadex away in her satchel and then retrieved the com from her pocket. A sudden gust of wind whirled her hair and filled her mouth with sand. Ballad shot out a wing to shield her, but too late. Panna pushed her hair back into place and spat out muddy dust.

"Well, thanks anyway," she told Ballad.

That was almost chivalrous and Panna thought it was kind of sweet. Which annoyed her. So Panna turned on her com and called Duaal, but there was no answer. She frowned.

"That's strange," Panna said. "Duaal always answers his com. You would think he was waiting for a boy to call him back, he's always so eager."

"Try Logan."

"You do it. That man still scares me."

"You've faced down Devourers and Xartasia's butchers, Panna," he said. "But you're afraid of Logan Coldhand?"

"Hells yes. Please just call him?"

Ballad reached into his leather jacket for his com. His brow and the back of his sunburnt neck were already beaded with sweat. "As you command, my lady."

Panna blushed. Ballad smirked and chose Logan's name from a list on the display. The channel chirped several times, but no one answered. Now Ballad frowned, too. Panna tried Xia next, but still no answer. Not even Anthem picked up. Panna considered calling Duke Ferris, but though the old fairy carried a com – Maeve had insisted on it and Ferris reluctantly agreed – he had no idea how to use the coreworld device.

Instead, she called Kessa Fethru. The channel toned and Panna was about to close it when someone finally picked up.

"Hello?" came Kessa's voice.

The Dailon sounded harried and tired. Even more than usual. Panna knew Baliend could be a handful, but this was strange.

"Kessa, it's Panna," she said. "Uh... Is everything alright? I can't get ahold of anyone."

"Panna?" Kessa asked. There was noise in the background that didn't sound like Baliend crying. "Oh, thank God! Finally... Where the hells have you been? The Hadrian fairies have been here for a week!"

"We had trouble finding a ship on Hadra that was coming back here. Where's Captain Sinnay? Ballad and I are in Kharnig and we need a lift to Kaellisem."

There was a long pause.

"The Blue Phoenix is gone," Kessa said at last. "Maeve and the rest are on their way to the Nnyth Tower."

Ballad listened over Panna's shoulder.

"What?" he asked.

"You didn't know?" Kessa asked. "They went there on information you brought."

"Maeve left?" Panna repeated. "She's gone? Then who's running Kaellisem?"

"You and Duke Ferris, according to Maeve," Kessa said. "You'd better get here now. He needs your help."

"With what?" Panna asked.

"If we don't get the water distribution under control, there are going to be more riots."

"Riots?" Panna repeated. "What's going on in Kaellisem? Wait, tell me when I get there. Can Xyn or Vyron send a ship to Kharnig? Tell Duke Ferris I'll be there as soon as I can."

"Have you ever dealt with the Nnyth?" Xia asked. "Either of you?"

Anthem shook his head.

"No," he answered. "Our contact with the Nnyth was always handled by the royal family and the Ivory Spire. Even then, it was infrequent."

Everyone looked at Maeve. She held up her hands. "I was a long way from the throne and important royal matters. I trained as a knight because I needed a profession. I am sure Titania dealt with them. But not me."

"What about when you collected the phenno?" Gripper asked. "That was a couple of years before I got here. Did you talk to the wasps then?"

"We only encountered one Nnyth on that trip," Duaal answered. "And we... fought. Maeve tried to talk then, but it didn't seem to go very well."

"No," Maeve agreed. "Even at the height of the White Kingdom, the Arcadians did not travel often to the Tower."

"Do you think Xartasia has an invitation?" Logan asked. "If the Nnyth are that secluded and dangerous, what is she risking?"

"Perhaps very little," Anthem said. The knight spoke slowly, as though reluctant. "Titania was the king's daughter. I know that she had visited the Tower at least twice before the fall."

"And you never went with her?" Duaal asked him. "Weren't you two pretty much engaged?"

"We had traded our oathsongs," Anthem said. "But no... I never accompanied Titania."

Maeve rubbed her temple and reached for a bowl in the middle of the table. Her fingers brushed the edge, but she couldn't quite manage to reach. Gripper pushed it closer. Maeve thanked him, refilled her plate and then stared down at the limp pile of lettuce and apples. Why had she taken more? She wasn't even hungry.

When dinner was over – no one had much more appetite than Maeve – Gripper collected all of the dishes and set to work cleaning them. One by one, they all left the mess in silence.

Maeve went back to her room and sat on the edge of her bunk, wondering what she was going to do once they reached the Tower. It had seemed like such a good idea back in Kaellisem, leaving her city and her angry people on a quest of redemption. Finding Xartasia and stopping her... That was the whole point of this, after all. It had been from the beginning.

Not for the first time, Maeve's gut knotted with guilt. Everything she had done really *was* a gamble against Xartasia. It wasn't about helping or restoring hope to the Arcadians. Maeve was using them, just like her cousin.

Am I any better than Xartasia at all? I manipulated my own people just to fight her... And I do not even know why!

But how could Maeve turn back now...? Her friends and her people had all sacrificed too much to give up. Arcadians were dead. Anthem had sided against his own enarri. Maeve had given up her own beloved hunter. It *had* to be for something. Didn't it?

Maeve covered her face with her hands and prayed to the gods for the strength to make it through the next four weeks.

Logan had leaned a roll of packing mats against one corner of the Blue Phoenix hold. He threw a short, fast flurry of low punches at the cylinder of rough fabric. He stepped back, looking down at his mismatched hands. The cool, sterile recycled ship air stung across his abraded knuckles. Logan had tape, of course. No self-respecting boxer went anywhere without it. Gloves, too, that protected the all too delicate skin and bones. Xia probably had something helpful in the medbay, too.

But his glass left hand remained stubbornly unblemished by its punishment. Logan slammed his right hand into the mats again. It left a smear of red.

"Ballad told me once that you shared a teacher," Anthem said from behind him.

Logan turned to look at the fairy knight. "After a fashion. Jocasta – Ballad's teacher – and I both studied at Vorus' palaestrum. We all learned lowland boxing. Other styles, too, but lowland is Vorus' specialty."

"Ballad has spoken well of Arctan Vorus."

Anthem stepped around a pile of crates. He wasn't wearing his armor. In fact, the fairy barely wore anything at all – just a nearly sheer skirt tied around his narrow hips. Logan wiped the back of his bloody hand on his pants. It was virtually impossible not to feel like a dirty peasant in the prince consort's graceful presence. Logan was painfully aware of how much better a match Anthem Calloren was for Maeve.

"Really?" Logan asked. "I was under the impression Arcadians didn't think much of boxers."

"We are not well built for it," Anthem admitted. He flexed his white wings. "We lack the physical power of the coreworld species. Ballad, however, seems to make it work."

"It's not all about strength."

Anthem nodded. "It is not. At least, not strength of arms. There is a resilience of spirit and passion that makes Ballad an excellent knight."

"He's a good hawk. What do you want, Anthem?" Logan asked.

Anthem blinked his deep, dark blue eyes slowly and waited a long moment before answering. He held out his hands. They were large and long-fingered for an Arcadian, but much smaller than Logan's mismatched ones.

"I have enemies enough in Kaellisem and in the woman I once loved more than life," Anthem said. "I do not wish you as another one, Logan. You are a good man and a skilled warrior. I know what Duke Ferris thinks of you, but I do not share that opinion. You have conducted yourself with honor and a... sort of grace. I would prefer to be friends–"

Logan's jaw clenched.

"–but if we cannot, then we should at least not be enemies."

"What do you want from me?" Logan asked. "I haven't gotten in your way, Anthem. Not with your knights, and not with Maeve. I've kept my distance. Out of respect for her, not you. There's no hawk to hood here. There's nothing that needs to change."

The handsome fairy's brow furrowed, but not deeply. He didn't look upset at Logan's words, just... confused.

"Things will change," Anthem said. "And when they do, know that my hands are extended in friendship."

Logan looked down again at Sir Anthem's outstretched hands. He had made something of a study of Arcadian traditions and this was not one of them. Logan raised an eyebrow at the smaller man.

"Just one hand," he said after a moment. "You only shake with one. Two hands looks like you're begging."

Anthem nodded and pulled back his left hand, leaving the right out to Logan. The Prian hunter turned back to the rolls of mats.

"Unless you want to spar a match against me," Logan said, "go away. Go take care of Maeve. She's been having a hard time."

"You noticed."

It wasn't a question.

"Yes. I noticed," Logan said. He punched at the makeshift bag. "There are no knights on the Blue Phoenix for you to order around, Anthem. You only have one other job. Maeve is hurting. Go to her."

Anthem's shadow didn't move for several minutes, but Logan kept his back resolutely turned and worked the rolled-up mat until blood ran down his right arm. Finally, the slender winged shadow retreated and left Logan alone.

[33]
HE SAID

"Better dead than grounded."

- TIBERIUS MYLES (232 PA)

Duaal Sinnay stepped out onto the white sand. Salty seawater streamed from his braids and down his muscular bronze back. He tucked the board under one arm and jogged up the beach to where his friends waited. They all applauded and cheered. When he reached the shade of the collapsible filter, Duaal bowed.

"Thank you, thank you," he said, grinning. His perfect white teeth flashed. "Well, don't stop clapping."

"Great curl," Haan congratulated. "It's choppy as hells out there, Du. I can't believe you pulled that off."

Haan gestured out to the aquamarine ocean. Hyzaar's largest moon, Beven, hung huge and pale in the sky, outshining even the suns. In just three more days, Beven's orbit would bring it closer than any moon in the Alliance. The seas would become a tidal riot, churned by Beven's gravity into an impassable twist of foaming waves. And then it would be time for the Beven Races, the most dangerous aquatic competition anywhere in the galaxy. There would be swimming, boat and board races of all kinds across Hyzaar. The winners wouldn't have to buy their own drinks for the rest of the year and never go to bed alone, except maybe out of sheer exhaustion. But then, Beven winners didn't get tired.

Haan draped a long bronzed arm around Duaal's neck. Shaala was on Duaal's other side, fingers already hooked into the waist of his trunks. She kissed his ear, pausing to nibble a little.

"So are you signed up yet?" Haan asked, trailing his finger up Duaal's spine.

"Signed up? For what?" Duaal asked, feigning innocence.

Haan laughed. So did everyone else.

"For the races! When are you finally going to enter?" Haan asked.

"Oh," Duaal said dismissively. "Those. I'd forgotten all about them."

He hadn't, of course. His friends — hells, his parents, too, and all their friends — told Duaal every year that he should enter. He grinned at Haan and Shaala.

"Tell you what," he told them. "Why don't you two show me what victory is going to taste like tonight and I'll sign up in the morning."

Shaala giggled and Haan nodded gravely.

"Let's get you back to my place," he said.

Haan took Duaal's hand and winked. Shaala held Duaal's other hand and waved back to their friends as they swiftly retreated up the beach, followed by whistles and 'phin-calls.

Duaal whispered some suggestions to Haan on where they might start and it began before they made it to his apartment. Duaal enjoyed an audience. Haan flushed, sending Shaala off into more gales of laughter. But Haan did exactly as Duaal told him to. They always did. Duaal didn't need to win a single Beven race. Why risk losing when he already had exactly what he wanted?

———— ● ● ● ————

The days passed in tense, worried bursts on the Blue Phoenix. The whole ship was as taut as a guitar string. There were several minor injuries as people moved too fast, incautious and distracted. Xia tended each one with a silver scowl and terse advice.

The ship didn't escape unscathed, either. Few starships were made for the long flight out to the galaxy's edge and the Phoenix wasn't one of them. By the end of the second week, Gripper had already run through most of his replacement parts and complained loudly about it at dinner.

Meals were a problem, too. Xia promised that she had properly calculated their daily caloric needs, even factoring in the addition of Anthem. But they were going through their food faster than expected. If they were going to make it back from the Tower, Xia argued, then everyone on the Blue Phoenix had to cut their daily intake by fifteen percent. No one bothered to point out to her that a return journey might never happen.

Duaal found Maeve pacing down in the hold again. As supplies dwindled, there was more and more room there. At least they had one increasing resource, Duaal reflected sourly.

As usual, Sir Anthem Calloren stood nearby, watching the little black-haired queen. She looked strange without her crown, Duaal realized. He had gotten rather used to seeing her in it.

Logan and Gripper were in the cargo hold, too, working in the hanging garden planters. The dangling crates of dirt were the Blue Phoenix's only source of fresh produce. Xia must have been lonely, too – she had one of the medical supply boxes laid open and was counting out emergency oxygen canisters and plastic bags of keline inside. The computer inventory was doubtlessly up to date, but she dutifully marked everything down on a datadex anyway.

Duaal leaned against the stairs. The old fibersteel creaked.

"Have you got a minute?" he asked Maeve.

She paused in her pacing. "What is it?"

"Are you alright? Never mind. Of course you're not. Nothing's gone at all according to plan. That's sort of what I wanted to come and tell you."

Maeve had started moving again, but now she stopped. Duaal sat down on one of the steps and laced his fingers under his chin.

"Something's been weighing on me," he admitted. "And I want to apologize. To you, Maeve."

"For how you have treated me since you were a little boy?" she asked, hands on her hips. She brushed a hand across her eyes. They were red and bloodshot. She sighed. "Forgive me, please. I am tired. You and I have not always had an easy relationship, Duaal, but that was more my fault than yours. I was bitter and broken. That is no fault of yours."

"Not really, no. But I still did my part being a little brat," Duaal agreed with a smirk. "Sorry. Still, that's not what I wanted to say. This is... a lot more serious."

"What?" Maeve asked.

"It's about Prianus," Duaal said. He had been thinking about it for weeks, long before Panna's news, and before Maeve's decision to leave Kaellisem. Everyone else in the hold had stopped what they were doing to watch Duaal. He rolled his eyes and raised his voice.

"Alright, since you're all going to listen anyway, I guess everyone deserves to hear it," Duaal announced, then looked over at Anthem. "Except you, maybe. But you're not leaving Maeve alone, are you?"

"Not yet, no," Anthem said.

"I really could have left you on Stray. You have Maeve to thank for this chance to die on the edge of nowhere," he told the knight, who nodded gravely.

Duaal turned his attention back to Maeve. "Alright. It's about Prianus and what I did there, banishing Xartasia and the Devourers. Hells, I shouldn't even use the word *banished* at all!"

Duaal ran fingers through his hair and then stared down at his hands. They were shaking.

"I... I'm saying that it's my fault that Xartasia's still around. If I had just done my job better, this could have been over months ago. I'm sorry, Maeve. I'm so sorry for all of this."

He heard light footsteps and looked up to find Maeve standing in front of him with a small smile on her face. "This is not your fault, Duaal. You bought us valuable time on Prianus. We would not have survived against the Devourers. They would have swarmed all across Prianus. Billions would have died. You did what none of us could."

There were slow nods all around the cargo bay. Duaal frowned at Maeve.

"But you've talked about Tamlin," he said. "When you closed the Waygate there, the Devourers vanished from Arcadia, right?"

"Yes," Maeve admitted. "That is true. Though I admit that I still do not know where they went or by what mechanism they were recalled."

Gripper hung from a support and scratched his chin.

"Remember what the Pylos Waygate said?" he asked. "It called for technicians because something had gone wrong."

"The opening spell had been interrupted," Maeve said. "It was the same in Tamlin. I did not know the spell as well as I hoped and I faltered."

"When you closed it, you probably fixed the problem, as far as the Waygate was concerned. No need for technicians," Gripper said. "So it sent them back."

"But I didn't *close* the Waygate." Duaal laced his fingers together in his lap and sighed. "I used it. Maeve and Xartasia were wrestling for control. I just seized some of the Waygate's power to move them, to send them away. It wasn't the same thing, I guess."

Anthem stared at Duaal.

"You seized some of the Waygate's power?" he repeated, clearly stunned. "While another sang the spells? How?"

"Duaal has a far deeper and more intuitive grasp of magic than we do," Maeve told her consort. She made a looping gesture with her hands. "He knows some of our battlefield charms, but he does not need the songs. He understands the underlying mechanics well enough to use them in ways we cannot, though Panna could better explain why. She has an impressive theory about how and why our spell-songs work."

"It seems to be correct," Duaal said. "What she taught us makes it possible for me to do the magic I do. But it wasn't enough to truly get rid of Xartasia. Look, I don't apologize much, Maeve. Don't lose sight of this rare chance."

"You saved us all, Duaal," the Arcadian queen said stubbornly. "What is happening now is Xartasia's fault, not yours."

"How can *you* say that?" Duaal asked in a loud voice. Something inside him ached. "You spent a century blaming yourself for the fall of Arcadia and finding weird ways to kill yourself to make up for it."

"And Titania forgave me for what I had done. As you ask me to do now," Maeve said. "But her forgiveness meant nothing, in the end. Not because she is herself a monster, but because the fault was never mine. Some of the responsibility, yes... Most of it, in truth. But not the *fault*. That belongs to the Devourers. They killed my people and destroyed my world."

Duaal considered that. Could Maeve be right? All this wasn't his fault?

The idea was appealing, of course, and Duaal's admittedly inflated but often fragile ego seized on the chance to escape blame. But was it *true*? Maeve had no reason to lie to him. She was right. Duaal and Maeve never had what anyone could call a close relationship. She wasn't looking to do him any favors. So why did Duaal still doubt her?

Duaal closed his eyes. What... what would Tiberius say? Did it matter? The old Prian was dead. Tears stung behind Duaal's lids. But he knew. He knew what Tiberius would tell him.

That was a damned fine piece of work, boy. Stop smirking and get up to the cockpit. Do your job.

He opened his eyes and stood, clapping his hands against his thighs as he rose.

"You're right," he said, ostensibly to Maeve and the rest of the Blue Phoenix crew. "I'd better get back up front. It's about time for another sub-SL check. If we're going to die horribly, then Xartasia will just have to do it herself. Some uncharted asteroid's not going to finish the job for her."

Duaal made his way up the stairs, through the mess and up to the cockpit. The tiny room full of dials, monitors and control panels glowed in green, yellow and red. He paused at the pilot's seat. He could have repaired the multitude of talon gashes in the chair or the cracks in the controls left by Tiberius' frustrated fists, but he never had. He never would, Duaal realized.

He sat in the captain's old chair and checked the navigational computer. Just twelve more days and they would reach the Rynn system and the Nnyth Tower. Duaal reached for the superluminal engine controls.

———— ● ● ● ————

Gripper inspected the air filter. It wasn't just dirty – it was broken.

What was going on? What could possibly be damaging so many pieces in the ventilation system? The Blue Phoenix had picked up a couple of rats before, even a chuulo one time. The rodents chewed up wires and seals, gummed up filters with their droppings, but nothing like this. Gripper frowned.

"Hunter, can you hand me my soldering stuff?" he asked.

Logan sat on the end of the workbench. Right in the spot that Maeve liked to perch. The human reached behind him and handed Gripper a bent soldering iron and a spool of wire. Gripper took them and got to work. He felt Logan watching him.

"When's the last time you talked to Xia?" the Prian finally asked.

Gripper thought for a moment. "This morning, at breakfast. She needed me to look at the locks in the medbay. One of them was broken. You know, a lot of things are breaking on the Blue Phoenix."

"It wasn't that long ago that you kept track of everything she did. And got in her way to give her flowers."

Gripper laughed. "Yeah."

"What happened?"

"What do you mean?"

"Why aren't you... falling all over yourself to get her attention anymore?"

The Arboran finally looked up from his work and found Logan watching him intently. Those pale blue eyes were still more than a little unsettling. When they weren't as cold as ice, their intensity seemed to burn like that Talon laser he carried. Gripper set down the solder and leaned against the workbench.

"I... guess it was watching you and Glass," he answered slowly. "Everything you two have been through."

Logan's jaw set. "We showed you just how fragile and painful love is."

"No. Well, maybe a little." Gripper pointed at the glass-armored cybernetic hand now clenched around the edge of his workbench. "Glass can be fragile and sharp... Or it can be really, really strong. Yours is strong, Hunter. It is. You have to watch Glass and Spear together all the time. She's nearly died and so have you, sometimes because of one another. But you still love each other."

Gripper could hear Logan's teeth grinding and winced.

"You do," the mechanic told him firmly. "I'm not dumb, Hunter. I know you don't want to, but you still love Glass. And she loves you, too, even if she can't say or do anything about it."

"What does that have to do with Xia?" Logan asked.

"It's just different with her. With us. What you and Glass do for each other... You let her go, Hunter. You hated it, but when she had to become queen, you let her go to Anthem. It tortures you every single day, but you've never tried to stop them. Not like Shimmer and I have. We interfered because we're Glass' friends. And yours. But you love her, so you weren't stupid like us."

Gripper examined the broken filter and then looked back down at Logan.

"But it's not like that with me and Silver. I like her. She's pretty and smart and I want her to be proud of me. But I'm not proud *for* her like you are for Glass. You don't love Glass just because she's beautiful and makes you feel good. You love Maeve for all that she *is*, including being an Arcadian queen, even if it takes her away from you."

Logan couldn't seem to meet Gripper's eye. The bounty hunter stared at the floor instead so intently that it was a wonder the fiber-steel didn't melt.

"I just don't love Silver like that," Gripper told him. "And if what you're going through is what real love is like, I think I'll happily wait until I'm a lot older to go find it."

"Wise decision," Logan said. "But you may not get to choose."

Gripper nodded and picked up his soldering iron, then got back to work fixing the filter. He had no more replacements... This one had to hold up until they reached the Tower and that was still five days away. Gripper crossed his fingers that the filter was still repairable. Xartasia and the Devourers awaited them at the Tower, along with all the Nnyth. Gripper wondered if any of them were going to live long enough to worry about the future, but he said nothing. Sometimes being a good friend meant shutting up.

/ # [34]

THE SONG AND THE BLADE

"No one can survive on honor alone."

- ANTHEM CALLOREN (234 PA)

Maeve sat alone in the dark. Well, not actually alone and it wasn't actually all that dark... She heard Anthem breathing and the soft, near-silent sounds of cloth against skin as he shifted his weight. But she kept her eyes squeezed tightly shut. She didn't want to look at him. If she could just pretend that he was not there, that... that...

But it was useless. Maeve opened her gray eyes. Anthem sat at her desk, reading over a datadex with an expression of intense concentration on his handsome face. His lips moved as he sounded out the Aver. It was rather cute, Maeve decided, but she still could not bring herself to be moved. Anthem was strong and sweet and brave and a perfect consort, but Maeve could not love him. She had tried but all she felt was an empty, painful pit where her heart should be. With every passing day, it grew harder to care if Xartasia ravaged the entire galaxy. What did it matter anymore?

Maeve stood and went to her closet, wondering if there was a forgotten bottle of narcohol, some needle tucked away into her old clothes... There was a sound and Maeve glanced back at Anthem, but he was still focused on his datadex. The noise came again, so quiet that she almost couldn't make it out.

Not noise, but music. The soft, thrumming notes of a guitar.

Logan.

Maeve's heart pounded. She couldn't remember the last time she heard the Prian play. Sunjarrah, that night under the stars on Maeve's first night as queen? She checked the time. It was late, long after midnight by the Blue Phoenix's clock.

Maeve darted another look at Anthem, but he didn't seem to hear the music. Silently, she slipped from her room and out into the corridor.

The music was louder outside – still quiet in deference to the late hour, but Maeve could make out the notes now and the strong, smooth sound of Logan's voice singing. She crept through the Blue Phoenix, down the hall to the hold. The bounty hunter sat on top of one of the plastic water barrels, his battered guitar across his lap. The sunlights over Gripper's hanging garden glittered off Logan's glass hand as he played. His eyes were closed in concentration, lips forming the words he sang with precise care.

"En ai enarra,
Eru lua'vi a arna..."

Maeve knew those words. An Arcadian oathsong. She slipped over the railing and glided down into the hold. Logan heard her landing behind him and looked up, fingers frozen on the strings of his guitar.

"Do not stop," she said softly.

Logan didn't look at her, but every muscle in his back tensed at the sound of her voice.

"I was only practicing," he said. "I don't know the last line. No one in Kaellisem would teach a human. I overheard the rest."

Maeve stepped closer, remaining hidden behind her hunter.

"Ae lua'vi a arna delassua," she sang, careful to articulate each of the vowel-heavy Arcadian words.

Logan's fingers moved along the guitar's scarred neck, playing back the notes until he knew them. The sound echoed through the cargo hold.

"En ai enarra," Logan sang.
"Eru lua'vi a arna,
Ae lua'vi a arna delassua."

Perfect... The song pulsed through Maeve's entire being. The cold, empty place inside of her echoed with the sound of Logan's voice. Her hands were moving of their own volition, sliding around her hunter and up to his chest. Through his shirt, she felt the hard, knotted scar over his heart.

"Maeve..." Logan said in a thick voice. He pressed his cold glass hand over both of hers and bowed his head. "I love you. I need you. Not to have, not to keep to myself... Just to live. I want you to know that it's enough that you were ever a part of my life. The best part... I want to give you my oathsong, even if you can never sing it back to me..."

Maeve laid her head against his back. Logan was trembling and she could hear his mechanical heart beating so fast. She remembered now why she fought Xartasia. How could she have forgotten, even for a moment? Maeve kissed Logan's back and his cybernetic fingers tightened convulsively over hers, beyond Logan's control. It hurt. Maeve closed her eyes. She should go back to her room, back to Anthem and her duty...

"Play it again," she told Logan. "Play the song."

Slowly, he removed his hand from hers. It fell once again to the guitar strings and he began to play the rising scale of notes. Maeve took a shuddering breath.

"To you I give my love," she sang to Logan in his own tongue. "My heart and life, the heart and life we share."

The last note cut off.

"No, Maeve. Don't–" Logan said.

Maeve pulled her hunter down from his seat and around to face her. There were unshed tears in his pale eyes.

"I need you," Maeve told Logan, using his own words. "You have sung your heart to me, my hunter, and I have given mine in answer. I love you and I can love no other. You give me reason to sing and to fight on, Logan. I need you."

The guitar fell from Logan's fingers and crashed to the fibersteel floor. He grabbed Maeve and pulled her crushingly close. Through her own tears, Maeve managed to find Logan's lips and press hers against them. Too hard... She tasted salt and blood. That was how her hunter always tasted. *Her* hunter. Logan was hers, sworn by oathsong, and she was his.

Maeve grabbed Logan's pants as his strong hands went to her shirt, tearing fabric in his desperation. Clothes fell away and Maeve sang out in visceral relief at the sweat-slicked feel of skin on skin. Relief, need and longing churned through her. Logan lifted Maeve, held her against the wall of the hold and then that cold, empty place inside her was full of blazing love and light.

Syle crouched in the dirty darkness at the intersection of two large air shafts. The ventilation systems gave him access to every corner of the Blue Phoenix, as well as carrying sounds to him from all over the ship.

He had been waiting and listening for weeks, stealing food and water as he needed it. But Sir Anthem was never far away from his queen. Syle was good, but not good enough to fight the paramount knight to get to her. Not unless Anthem was distracted...

Maeve's voice echoed through the airshafts, musical and sharp in her passion. Finally. Syle had begun to wonder if Sir Anthem's charms would ever win out against the Maeve's ridiculous affection for her human bounty hunter.

Syle spared a small, thin smile for Anthem Calloren. He hoped that the knight was enjoying his conquest of the queen. It would be the last thing he ever did.

Syle wormed his way through the ventilation. His wings ached, cramped and sore from too many days without room to stretch, but he barely noticed. It was finally time for Maeve Cavainna to die. The rest of the Blue Phoenix crew would follow her into the Nameless' embrace, but Syle had to begin with the Gray Queen. Maeve was the greatest danger to Xartasia. Syle kicked his way through another air filter, dragging his spear behind him over the textured fibersteel. To judge by Maeve's ringing cries, she was down in the cargo bay...

Why were Anthem and Maeve in the bay? Syle stopped at the vent cover. His fingernails still hadn't healed from prying up other such barriers all over the Blue Phoenix. Syle squinted through the mesh. He could just make out the narrow corridor that led out onto the cargo bay catwalk below. He placed his elbows against the cover and pushed. The metal squealed – not loud enough to be heard over Maeve's voice, he was sure – and then dropped to the floor.

Syle slid out of the ventilation duct and dropped to the ground. He pulled his spear down and crept toward the hold. The hallway glowed dimly with blue nightlights.

"I do not think that they wish to be disturbed," said a quiet voice from behind Syle.

Xartasia's spy and saboteur whirled. Anthem Calloren stood in the dim azure light, dressed for sleep but carrying his spear. The ribbons rippled in the breeze flowing unimpeded through the open vent above him. Syle stared.

"Anthem?" he hissed. "If Maeve is not with you, then who...?"

"I told her before," Anthem said. "I know she loves Logan Cold-hand. I thought that perhaps we could love one another, but we cannot give hearts that are no longer our own. Maeve should have gone to him months ago. She needs her hunter. No one can survive on honor alone."

Syle fell into a low crouch, his spear held close and his wings curled. He whirled and sprinted toward the cargo hold, for Maeve. He would kill the queen and her human lover... Anthem was on him in a second, as silent as falling snow. Syle cried out once as the blade of Anthem's spear slid between his ribs. The knight clapped his hand over Syle's mouth even as blood poured from between his fingers.

"Go now, Syle," Anthem said sadly. "You will not be alone in the dark for long."

[35]
THE TOWER

"Life is only as precious as what we will die for."

- NNYTH AGREEMENT (2,401 MA)

Three hours had passed since Duaal's surprisingly smooth drop out of superluminal flight. Logan stood next to Maeve at one of the viewports in the mess. She stared out through the thick glassteel with an intent look on her beautiful face that made the hunter want to sweep her up into his arms. Logan settled for a small kiss on the soft skin of her neck. It was like silk against his lips.

"Hey, Logan," Duaal's said over the Blue Phoenix com. "Get up here. This place is even worse than I remember. I'm going to need a hand."

Logan kissed Maeve again, then made his way in the direction of the cockpit. Anthem sat at the table, reading. He glanced up at Logan as the Prian passed, but said nothing. In fact, everyone else on the Blue Phoenix had left both Maeve and Logan largely alone. Anthem had been quiet and even stopped his incessant hovering. Logan wondered if the knight was avoiding him and decided that he didn't really care. He had Maeve. Nothing else mattered.

Up in the cockpit, Duaal tightly gripped the control yoke with white knuckles. Logan looked at the main display. It was easy to see why Duaal wanted a hand, even a glass one. The Rynn system was like nothing Logan had ever seen before. It was small by Alliance standards and ancient, located far away from the hot, dense pack of younger stars in the galactic heart. Logan squinted. They weren't far away, but he could barely make out the star at the system's center. It was a pale, flickering blue-gray spot only barely visible against the deeper darkness of space: a neutron star, the core of a larger dead star that had collapsed violently under its own weight to the size of a single city.

There were two other stars in the Rynn system – a pair of tiny, dim brown dwarves too distant in their slow and wide orbit to make out with the naked eye. But there were no planets... not anymore. They would have been destroyed when the system primary blew off its outer layers of volatile gas and then the massive radiation burst of the star's implosion. All that remained now were billions of tons of rock and ice, millions of asteroids twisted by the neutron star's intense and unpredictable gravity to form several convoluted belts.

Logan slid into the copilot's seat. Duaal didn't dare look up.

"Can you fly through this?" the young captain asked.

"Yes."

Duaal gratefully turned over control to the copilot's station with the flip of a switch.

"Great," he said. "I need to find the Tower. It's been a while since we were here and it isn't exactly stationary. It doesn't even follow a real orbit."

Logan tipped the Blue Phoenix up onto the relatively vertical axis to glide alongside a roiling cluster of small, rough black stones torn free by the collision of two larger asteroids. The debris glinted in the Blue Phoenix's running lights as though faceted.

"Are the sensors working in this?" Logan asked. "There's a lot of material out there."

"They're working fine," Duaal said. "But the Tower is stone, just like the asteroids. The Nnyth chew up rock and then secrete it to build their hive. The Tower is made of the same stuff as the rest of this mess, so the sensors can't differentiate."

"What about size?"

"I'm showing several large bodies in the system. It could be any one of them. We're going to have to get close enough to use our eyes." Duaal shook his head and scanned the sensor readout again. "You know, I seem to recall the Tower being a lot bigger than any of the asteroids, this giant sort of ring-shaped thing. But I was just a kid the last time. Everything probably looked bigger... Maybe the Nnyth are smaller than I remember, too."

"I've seen Tiberius' original data. Not likely."

"Great," Duaal said sourly. "You're a real beacon of light in dark times, Logan."

Logan didn't answer. A pair of huge, pyramidal chunks of stone tumbled slowly ahead. He pushed down on the controls and slid the Blue Phoenix beneath the obstacles while Duaal consulted his readouts and adjusted their course.

"We can try this one," Duaal said, pointing to a large blotch on one screen.

Logan glanced at it. "The one in grid seven is closer."

"Yeah," Duaal agreed. "But look at how much other stuff is in that grid, Logan. That's going to be some tough flying."

"But odds are better that one of those massive signatures is the Tower," Logan said.

"Shouldn't we rule out the easy ones first?"

Logan gave Duaal a pointed look and the young mage grinned.

"You're absolutely right," he said. "Why stick to the easy stuff? We're trying to save the whole damned galaxy!"

That wasn't what Logan had suggested, but it was close enough and Duaal punched in their new course. Without slowing, the Blue Phoenix pivoted and changed direction. They looped up over the pair of pyramid-shaped stones and into a glittering patch of darkness that reminded Logan disconcertingly of the Devourers' nanite swarms. The asteroids were too many and too close for the pale radiance of the neutron star to penetrate. The only light was that of other, brighter but far more distant stars flashing off tumbling and turning faces of the celestial stone.

The Blue Phoenix flew slowly through the asteroid field. Even with both Duaal watching the monitors closely and Logan making myriad minute corrections, a dozen or more skull-sized black asteroids smashed into the Blue Phoenix's hull. Duaal winced visibly.

"You know, I've been working really hard on my flying," he said. "A little more of this and no one is going to believe it."

"I'm flying," Logan pointed out.

"You're Prian and I've seen your ships. They're not exactly delicate machines."

"And the Blue Phoenix is delicate...?"

Duaal laughed shortly. "Nope. But her captain sure can be."

Logan arced the Blue Phoenix up over a huge, flat slab of stone almost twice the old freighter's size. Logan glanced down at the asteroid.

"What's the chemical breakdown of this system?" he asked.

"Not sure," Duaal answered. "Nitrogen, carbon and nickel, I guess. All the usual stuff. Probably some iron and heavier elements from when that star blew."

Logan pointed to a long, thin spar of dark stone.

"Those things don't look like any asteroids in the Prian system," he said. "These seem almost crystalline. They're structured."

"You're right." Duaal looked up from the computers at Logan. "I don't remember any asteroids like this last time."

Stone floated and tumbled slowly all around the Blue Phoenix, impacting the fibersteel hull with ringing thuds. What the hells was going on? Asteroid fields – even those surrounding unstable stars like Rynn – were usually thinly populated and rather staid areas, full of silently and smoothly gliding stone and metal that contently circled its parent star. This was too crowded and too chaotic to be normal in a stellar system so old.

"What is happening up here?" Maeve asked, suddenly standing in the cockpit's door.

Duaal jumped.

"God, Maeve," he gasped, but didn't look up at the fairy. "Don't do that!"

"Why are we hitting so many asteroids?" she asked.

"I don't think they're asteroids, dove," Logan told her.

"Then what are–?"

Maeve fell silent as they reached the center of the astroid field, the large body that the Blue Phoenix's sensors had picked up. Her gray eyes widened and one hand flew to her mouth.

They had finally reached the Tower. A hundred or more shattered pieces of the great star-hive floated crooked orbits around a single broken crescent of dark, faceted-looking stone. The ruins of the Nnyth's home tumbled slowly through space.

"What in the hells?" Duaal asked, gasping. "What happened here?"

"The Tower's gravity is pulling the debris back in," Logan said. "We're exposed out here. We need to move back."

Duaal nodded. "Whatever did this could still be out there."

"Wait!" Maeve said. "No, take us into what remains of the Tower. There are openings large enough to fly the Blue Phoenix inside."

"What?" Duaal asked. "Why?"

"We need to find out what happened here. Perhaps some of the Nnyth yet live. We came to warn them..."

"It's too late for that, dove," Logan said. "You know who did this – Xartasia and her Devourers."

Maeve stared at the Tower, dark and broken. "But we still need to discover *why*, enarri. Why was Xartasia here? And why did she attack the Tower?"

"I'm more worried about *how* she did it," Duaal pointed out. "Maeve, she could still be here!"

"Is that not what we wanted?" the fairy asked. "To finally catch Xartasia? We have followed my cousin since this began! Now we have some slim chance to find out what she wanted here. Take us to the Tower. Please, Duaal."

The Hyzaari captain looked at Logan, waiting for him to argue with Maeve. But Logan said nothing. Maeve was right. Duaal drew a deep, hissing breath.

"As you command, my queen," he said.

Duaal toggled control back to his own station and flew toward the ruins of the Tower.

As the huge gray crescent eclipsed their vision, Maeve wormed her hand into Logan's. He squeezed her fingers gently and wanted to reassure her, but had no idea what to say. What did she hope? That the Nnyth lived? Dead star wasps posed no danger to the Blue Phoenix or anyone else, but they couldn't answer questions, either. And whatever Logan thought of the Nnyth and their secretive, defensive isolation, he didn't particularly want the species wiped out.

Did Maeve hope to find Xartasia still haunting the ruins of the shattered Tower? Or that the White Queen was already gone, her terrible work here done? Logan didn't hope either way. He simply sat, waiting.

Duaal carefully circled the shattered Tower. The Blue Phoenix glided along the outer edge of the crescent. Duaal swore once as a huge segment of gray and black stone suddenly shuddered and tore free from the ruined hive. Logan watched the massive thing spin slowly through the cold void. Smaller pieces – smaller, though each was still larger than his Raptor had been – fractured and then broke away. The loss of mass slightly changed the vast stone's spin toward the Blue Phoenix. Logan leaned forward. There was something inside the rock...

"Do you see that?" he asked Maeve.

Logan pointed. The interior of the broken stone – easily larger and longer than a CWAAF starcruiser – wasn't black or gray, but a pale pink like the inside of a seashell. As Logan and Maeve stared, a subtle blue shimmer rippled over the rose-colored surface. Logan knew that pale light. He had seen it back on his own homeworld, in the mountains above Pylos.

"A... Waygate?" Maeve asked.

"A piece of one," Logan said.

The Blue Phoenix flew around the huge floating stone and the glowing pink inner surface vanished from view. Duaal wiped the back of his hand across his forehead.

"You keep telling us what great Waygate experts the Nnyth are," Duaal said. "Makes sense that they would have one of their own."

"But I have never seen one so huge," Maeve said. She traced a circle in the air over Logan's shoulder. "A ring. A great ring in the stars. The whole Tower is a Waygate!"

Logan looked up at her. "At least, it used to be."

They were flying low and close along the faceted surface of the Tower. The ring's shattered edge suddenly loomed up ahead, as sharp and dark as obsidian. Maeve and Duaal were silent. Logan felt the Arcadian queen's breath against the back of his neck as she leaned close, staring through the viewport. Logan switched on the sensor panel to his right, but there was no sign of any other ships. Not that he could find, at any rate...

But even snapped in half, the Tower was beyond huge. There were vast pentagonal openings into the ring's surface, wide tunnels into darkness more than large enough for a starship to land inside. Surrounded by the stone and metal of the Nnyth hive, what chance did the Blue Phoenix's outdated sensor system have of picking them out...? Xartasia and her whole army could be anywhere out there, hiding among the destruction.

A dark, streamlined shape streaked through the flickering and inconstant starlight, right at the Blue Phoenix. Duaal shouted and jerked the controls, but not fast enough. The thing landed on the old freighter's conical nose. A large, sleek silhouette crawled up the front of the Blue Phoenix until it was looking into the cockpit.

It was a Nnyth. The star wasp was the size of a small fighter. The weight of its own black and red-striped exoskeleton would have killed it on the surface of any planet, collapsing under the gravity. But out here in the void, it moved with a fluid, alien grace. Almost... One of the shiny black legs – longer than Logan was tall – ended abruptly at the first joint. Dark ichor leaked slowly from the wound and beaded into glistening spheres that froze and floated away into the darkness of space.

The Nnyth tilted its triangular head one way and then the other, peering into the Blue Phoenix. Colors swirled across the compound eyes, reminding Logan at once of an Ixthian. But while Xia's eyes changed color, they only ever showed a single hue. The eyes staring at them now were a swirling mosaic of bright, sunny yellow, blue and orange and a deep violet so dark that it was nearly black but for the nearly ultraviolet glow.

But below those eyes were the Nnyth's mandibles – blade-like black hooks longer than Logan's arm and barbed all along the inner curve with spines that could tear fibersteel apart as easily a paper. The Nnyth's mandibles worked open and shut as it studied the Blue Phoenix.

Finally, the colorful eyes fixed on Maeve. She gripped the back of Logan's chair so tight that he could hear the plastihide creaking. The huge wasp lowered its head and slowly unfurled long, translucent wings. It spread them wide and then swept them back... Just like the Arcadians did to their queen. The Nnyth was bowing.

Both Duaal and Logan stared at Maeve. Her gray eyes were wide and she inclined her head in reply. There was no room to move her wings, but the Nnyth seemed to understand. It raised its own wings and caught the wild stellar winds, soaring out ahead of the Blue Phoenix and then turned back toward the ship again.

"I think we are supposed to follow," Maeve said.

Duaal let out an explosive breath.

"The worst part is," the mage told no one in particular, "this isn't even the weirdest thing that's happened to me in the last year."

Duaal flew the Blue Phoenix after the injured Nnyth, following. The wasp led them over the Tower's sharp, shattered end and along the crescent's inside surface. Logan saw many more of the five-sided tunnels, but most were blocked by silvery stone rubble. Cracks ran down the length of the sundered ring's curve, some so wide that a much larger ship than the Blue Phoenix could have landed easily inside.

And deep inside the broken Tower, pale light flickered fitfully. Not with the steady heartbeat throb of the Pylos Waygate, Logan thought, but lights on the verge of burning out.

Closer to the Tower now, there were more Nnyth. The striped star wasps crouched on the facets of the Tower's surface, their long wings shining in the starlight. There were hundreds of them, but still fewer of them than Logan had expected. Shouldn't there have been thousands, tens of thousands of Nnyth? Where were the rest?

Their guide led the Blue Phoenix to one of the openings in the Tower's curved side. The tunnel had been huge to begin with, more than large enough for a ship, but now a jagged crack tore it wide and the stone yawed open like a monstrous mouth. The Nnyth vanished inside and Duaal looked to Maeve.

"This *could* be a trap," the young captain said. "Xartasia and her whole army of fairies and Devourers could be in there, just waiting to tear us apart."

"I know," Maeve answered. She put her hand on Logan's shoulder. He pressed his glass one over it. She drew a deep breath. "We have come all this way to find Xartasia. If this is her trap, then let us spring it."

"That sounds brave and all, Maeve," Duaal said, "but we don't have a single weapon on this ship. If Xartasia is here, then what?"

"Then be ready to fly," Maeve said.

Duaal gave her a lopsided smile. "Same as usual. Got it. Logan, keep an eye on the proximeters. I don't want to run into anything down there."

"I will," Logan answered.

Duaal nodded and then flipped on the internal com. "Attention, everyone. The Nnyth appear to be inviting us into the Tower and Queen Maeve has kindly accepted. Keep your eyes open and your weapons close. We have no idea what's waiting for us in there."

He released the com button and pressed the control yoke gently forward. The Blue Phoenix glided down into the Tower.

[36]
TIME AND TRUTH

"A queen armed with truth needs no spear."

- TITANIA CAVAINNA (234 PA)

The Blue Phoenix descended into the darkness. Maeve could make no sense of the numbers and vectors that Logan read off to Duaal, but the young mage nodded at each one and made tiny corrections to their course. The Blue Phoenix's lights played off the tunnel's flat side and the ragged edges of cracked and torn stone. A few Nnyth crawled and flew along the passage's sides.

Unable to help with the navigation, Maeve studied the wasps instead. Like their guide, most of them seemed to be injured. Their wings were torn and limbs were missing. Several had lost eyes or antennae. All of the Nnyth watched the ship pass with huge multi-colored eyes.

The tunnel ended suddenly and Maeve's stomach lurched. The Blue Phoenix was in a large chamber, one so vast that the ship's bright dorsal spotlights couldn't reach the side... Ceiling, in truth. There was gravity inside the huge cavern. Not strong, but enough to tug against the artificial network inside the Blue Phoenix.

Duaal rotated the ship to align with the local gravity. Maeve pressed her hand to her mouth and stared around. The Nnyth that they followed had landed on the only thing that Maeve could see – a pentagonal pillar of stone rising from the darkness far below.

"Can we land on that?" she asked, pointing.

"I... think so," Duaal said. "It looks just big enough for the Blue Phoenix. Is there anything else out there?"

Logan scanned the readouts. "More Nnyth. About two hundred of them. But that's all I can see."

"Two hundred is more than enough to kill us if we set foot out there," Duaal said.

"Two hundred is more than enough to kill us inside the Blue Phoenix, too," Maeve pointed out. "Is there atmosphere?"

"A little," Duaal answered. "It's pretty thin, but there's enough oxygen for us to breathe. Xia might have her own opinion, though."

Maeve wiped sweat-damp hands on the thighs of her pants. "Let us discover what the Nnyth want, then."

Logan followed Maeve out of the cockpit as Duaal set the Blue Phoenix down on the black stone pillar. Anthem, Gripper and Xia waited in the mess. They all stood.

"What's going on?" Gripper asked. "Are we inside the Tower?"

Maeve nodded. "Yes. It is broken... There is no sign of Xartasia, but that may mean nothing. The surviving Nnyth seem to want something of us. They have brought us to a place to land. We will go to meet them. Be careful – there is little gravity or air outside."

"I'll get the emergency canisters," Xia said.

"We'll meet you down in the hold," Logan told her.

Anthem was already wearing his glass armor and held his spear at his side. He fell into step behind Maeve and Logan as they made their way down into the Blue Phoenix's hold. It wasn't hot or even particularly warm on the ship, but there were beads of sweat along the knight's hairline. Maeve had not spoken with Anthem since she and Logan had exchanged their oathsongs. Teasing but genuinely pleased comments and smiles from Gripper and Duaal led Maeve to believe that the entire ship had overheard the aftermath, if not the songs themselves. Maeve blushed.

They reached the nearly empty hold just as the Blue Phoenix jolted gently underfoot. Duaal had landed. He jogged down into the cargo bay a moment later, coattails flapping, followed swiftly by Xia. She held six small yellow canisters and handed them out.

"There's about an hour of extra air in each of these," she told everyone.

"Thanks," Duaal said. "But if Xartasia's got something sneaky up her dress sleeve here, I suspect air is going to be the least of our worries."

"Better not to have to worry about it at all," Xia answered.

Maeve tucked the extra air into a pocket of her pants and went to the airlock controls. She was no expert in coreworld technology, but the door was simple enough. Her hands hovered over the red-lit button. Maeve looked at her friends.

"None of you need to go with me," she told them. "This journey was my decision and is my responsibility."

"You're not going alone," Logan said.

Maeve smiled. She did not expect her enarri to let her face the Nnyth on her own. But she waited for the rest. Sir Anthem stepped wordlessly toward the airlock. Duaal held out gloved hands in a helpless gesture.

"I promised you my ship, Maeve," he said. "Until this is done, we're all yours."

Xia and Gripper nodded. Maeve pressed the airlock button. The inner doors slid open and they stepped through. Duaal pressed the next large, glowing rectangular button and the doors closed again. There was a hiss and then the outer door slid to the side. Thin, damp air filled the airlock and Maeve felt dizzy. Gripper had to lean against the side of the airlock until he adjusted. And then, one by one, they stepped out into the Tower.

Duaal was right. The stone column was barely large enough for the Blue Phoenix to land on top of. At the back of the ship, they stood right next to a deadly plunge down into utter darkness. Lights studded the vessel, but none of them did much to illuminate the shadows.

Maeve took a step, spread her wings and leapt easily into the air. Duaal shouted for her not to go far and then broke into a fit of coughing. The air was thin, but the Tower's gravity was even weaker and Maeve beat her wings slowly, hovering above the Blue Phoenix. She searched the inky shadows for the Nnyth who had brought them, but there was no sign of the great wasp.

"Now what?" Duaal asked when he had recovered his breath.

"Now we speak," answered a hundred voices. Each one was just a fluttering, rasping whisper – but together, they became a hissing thunder that made Maeve want to clap her hands over her ears.

A pale blue glow rose from far, far below and filled the chamber with light. It wasn't as large as Maeve had supposed. The ceiling was far above, yes, but the walls were much closer than she originally guessed. It was not so much a chamber as a vast shaft.

And it was full of Nnyth. Two hundred star wasps clung to the vertical walls, overlapping one another until the whole thing was a cathedral of long diaphanous wings and graceful striped bodies, studded all over by the whirling rainbows of Nnyth eyes. Antennae waved like grass in the wind.

"What happened to the Tower?" Maeve asked, gasping to catch breath enough for the question.

"Titania came here," said the whispering, shouting answer. The Nnyth spoke together, in perfect unison. Each single voice was soft, but together, they were a storm.

"Is Titania here still?" Anthem asked. His question was raw and desperate.

"Titania came here," the Nnyth said again. "She came with the First, the eldest of this galaxy. They call themselves Glorious, but you call them the Devourers. The first life known in these worlds, the firstborn who left the galaxy behind."

"How the hells do you know so much about the Devourers?" Duaal asked. "We've tried our best, but all we have are guesses."

"Our individual lifespans are not as long as those of the aerads," the Nnyth said together. "But the memory of the Tower is ancient. Together, we *remember*."

"A hive mind," Xia breathed. Her short antennae twitched.

"As you and your kind have long since forgotten, little cousin. The Ixthian passion for life, for the perfection of their families and worlds is no mystery to us. You were once a part of the Tower. You knew the thoughts and needs of one as those of all. The health of one was the health of all."

Maeve beat her wings slowly. It didn't take much to remain aloft in the Tower's low gravity, even in the thin air.

"Xartasia," she said. "Please, can you tell us why she was here? Were there Arcadians with her, too?"

"Yes, many," the Nnyth answered. "Xartasia and the First came with ships full of aerads."

"What did she want?" Maeve asked.

A rattling, hissing sound echoed through the ruins of the Tower. "At the heart of the Tower is a Waygate. The largest of the Waygates, built by the First to carry their ships out of this galaxy in search of food. Only the greatest gates would serve her purpose and Titania demanded its use."

"Did you let her?"

There was another great hiss like thousand warning snakes.

"No," said the Nnyth.

Maeve waited, then asked, "What did she want with it? There are a hundred Waygates across the White Kingdom. What need did she have for yours?"

"Was it a matter of size?" Logan asked, raising his voice to the Nnyth. "We interrupted her work on Pylos. Did she summon more

Devourers? With a Waygate this size, she could have summoned entire ships. A fleet of Devourers."

Maeve's blood ran as cold as ice. If Logan was right, there was nothing that they could do. With an army of Devourers behind her, Xartasia would destroy the entire galaxy. Even if the Alliance rose up against her now, it would be far too late.

"Is... is that what happened here?" Maeve asked. "Did Xartasia summon the Devourers and then destroy the Tower?"

"No," the Nnyth whispered. "Xartasia did not break the Tower. We did. We would not let Titania take the Waygate."

"*You* did this?" Duaal said loudly. "We could barely get samples from the Pylos Waygate! It sat through a million years of quakes in the mountains. How did you crack yours in half?"

Hundreds of multicolored eyes fixed on the young Hyzaari man. "Power is as creative or destructive as its wielder. What burns in the heart of stars exists within us all to summon forth. You know this, Duaal Sinnay. You have felt it."

"How do you know my name?" Duaal asked. "How do you know about any of us? Hells, how do you speak such good Aver?"

"The Tower remembers," buzzed and hissed the Nnyth. "We remember what has happened, what will happen... And what might have happened. The Tower stands high above time and space. We see far."

"But why did you destroy the Tower?" Maeve asked. She didn't understand. "What could Xartasia possibly have asked that would make you destroy your own home rather than give it over to her?"

"She wishes the return of the White Kingdom. She would tear time apart," said hundreds of dry voices in perfect unison. "Titania would unmake history."

"What?" Maeve landed on the sharp nose of the Blue Phoenix and stared into the impossible column of Nnyth. "How?"

"Through the Waygate. Like all the First's greatest creations, the Waygates depend upon thought and memory. We taught your Ivory

Spire to hold in thought the place they wished to go, to open your Waygates to those locations. Titania would open our Waygate to another *time*."

"That's what she wanted the Arcadians for," Logan said. "Why she didn't want anyone born after the fall. She needs the old fairies' memories of the White Kingdom. Her own memory isn't enough. It's too unreliable. She needs as many witnesses as she can get."

"Yes," whispered the Nnyth. "From the First, she has learned the secrets of the Waygate, secrets not even known to the Tower. From the aerads, she has gathered the memories of thousands to build her new kingdom of brittle sorrows and glass. And from us, she intended to take the greatest Waygate in the stars."

"But why did you not let her use it?" Maeve asked. "If all that Xartasia wants is to go back to Arcadia with her people, let her!"

"She does not simply want to return," came the echoing answer.

"The kingdom would still fall," Xia said. "She wouldn't want to live through that again."

"Titania would turn the power of the Waygate not in but *out*, all across the galaxy," the Nnyth said. "Further, if she can reach. She would unmake all that has happened since before Arcadia's fall to prevent it. And then she would reforge time anew, in the form of *her* choosing."

Maeve's head was light, spinning, but it wasn't from the lack of air. "But that is more than a hundred years! Trillions of lives have been born and ended across dozens of planets in that time. What happens to them?"

"They will never have been," the Nnyth said in rustling agreement. "Some variation, some similarity will be born, but those lives which exist now will end."

Gripper, who had been silently wringing his hands through the whole eerie conversation suddenly burst out. "But... but that's not fair! She can't just wipe out a hundred years of life because she's homesick!"

The Nnyth fixed their eyes on the Arboran now, all rippling with deep blues and reds.

"Her world is lost, Anandrou," the wasps said. "The destruction we have wreaked on the Tower can never be repaired. The Waygate was the heart of the Tower. Without it, we cannot summon new air, new food. We are dying. We know the pain that Titania feels. And you will know it, too."

"Wait, what?" Gripper asked. He scrambled to the edge of the pentagonal pillar and stared out at the gathered Nnyth. "What does that mean?"

"Weh-Weh has met the same fate as the White Kingdom," they answered. "Titania and the First flew there to find lost knowledge of the Waygates' most secret workings. When their research was done, they consumed all living there and burned the rest."

"A... All?" Gripper gasped. "All of them? They're *all* dead?"

"Yes. You are the last of your people, Anandrou."

Gripper fell to his knees on the gray stone and wailed in heart-broken agony. Logan put his hand on the Arboran's huge shoulder and said nothing.

"Why?" Gripper cried. "If she just wants to go home, then why is Xartasia doing all these horrible things?"

"These horrors mean nothing to her. If she succeeds, then the last hundred years will be destroyed," hissed the Nnyth all around. "None of it will have happened."

Maeve remembered what Xartasia had told her back in Pylos, as Gavriel tortured her. *Be at peace, cousin. Soon, none of this will matter.* She had thought that Xartasia only meant that Maeve would soon be dead, but the older princess was being more literal than that.

Maeve jumped down from the Blue Phoenix and went to stand beside Gripper. The huge alien's whole body shook as he sobbed for his lost home.

"I am so sorry," she told him, then raised her eyes to look at the Nnyth. The great wasps were dying, she realized. That was why the air was so thin. They were running out. How much of it were they wasting talking to Maeve and her friends? "But you destroyed your Waygate before Xartasia could use it. You said that your gate would do what she needed. You have stopped her. Is this not done?"

"No," the Nnyth answered. "Only the most powerful Waygates are capable of a gate inversion. One of those was here, the largest gate ever built by the First. But there is another. We have denied her the Tower, and so that is where Xartasia is bound now."

Anthem finally spoke. He gripped his spear so hard that the glass of his gauntlet cut into the weapon's carbonide haft. "Where is she going?"

"Kahazzek," the Nnyth whispered. The star wasps' voices were quieter now, Maeve thought. Was that fear? Reverence? "The original homeworld of the First, the seed of all life in the galaxy. Where they built the most powerful Waygate to take their people away into the stars. The world you call Axis."

"Axis?" Maeve repeated. "She is taking the Devourers and the Arcadians to the capital of the Alliance?"

"There's a Waygate on Axis?" Logan asked. "Where? Axis is the most heavily populated planet in the CWA. Are you saying there's a Waygate there that no one noticed?"

"Humans have lived on Kahazzek for millions of years," said the Nnyth. "But long before that, it belonged to the First. Humans have buried the old world under uncounted tons of metal and concrete, but the seeds of life remain there, on a mountain at the shore of the sea that birthed the first life."

"The surface," Logan said, nodding slowly. "The actual surface of Axis. There may be sun- and starlight on Level One, but the Axis' real surface is Level Ten. It's been sealed off for centuries."

"But that's not going to mean very much to Xartasia," Duaal said. "Not with her Devourers. They'll cut a path for her right down to the surface of Axis and then Xartasia can take her Arcadians to this Waygate."

"And a hundred years or more are just gone," Xia finished. "Trillions of lives are erased."

"Wait, how is any of that going to help her?" Duaal asked. "If she uses the Waygate not to go back through time, but to turn *back* time, isn't the same thing just going to happen again? The fall of the White Kingdom, the Arcadian refugees? All of it?"

"The Waygates are anchors in time," the Nnyth told him. "That is why your chronologists did not find the time dilation in superluminal travel that they expected. That is the effect of the First's great engineering. And it will preserve Titania's memories of what has been. With that knowledge and the Kahazzek Waygate's power, it will be simple to reforge the last hundred years to fit her own desires. It will take only thought, a wish."

The Tower full of slowly dying insects rustled like a great tree in the autumn wind. Gripper turned his huge, tear-streaked face up toward Maeve.

"But... but we can stop Xartasia, right?" he asked. "We can keep her from hurting anyone else, can't we? Now that we know where she's going and what she's doing...?"

Maeve didn't know how to answer that, but everyone else was looking at her.

"When did Xartasia leave?" she asked the Nnyth. "Can we catch up to my cousin?"

"Thirteen days ago," whispered the Nnyth. "Her ships are of the First's design and their speed is far greater than yours. Titania and her army will reach Axis in eight more days."

Gripper whimpered like a wounded child. "Eight days? We can't even get back to Stray that fast, to say nothing of Axis."

"What about a message?" Xia asked. "Could we at least warn the Alliance?"

"Any transmissions would take almost two weeks to get to the core from here," Logan answered. "And that's assuming that anyone would listen to it."

"What about Arcadia?" Gripper asked desperately. "There are Waygates there! Can't we just use one of them? There must be *something* we can do!"

"Our worlds are on the other side of the galaxy," Anthem said, shaking his head. The beads woven into his golden braids clattered against his armor. "It would take the Blue Phoenix over a month to reach Arcadian space."

Maeve bit her lip so hard that she tasted blood and turned back to the Nnyth. "What of your Waygate? Can it not be repaired?"

"The machines built by the First are ancient and strong," the Nnyth answered. "It required powerful magics to break the Tower and our hive will never be whole again."

Duaal stepped to the edge of the pillar beside Maeve and then... off. Maeve shouted and reached for him, but the young mage stood quite steadily on the empty air. The Tower's gravity was weak, but not *that* weak. Duaal should have plummeted into the deep darkness, but he did not.

"You're right," he told the Nnyth. "Even broken, this Waygate is powerful. I can feel it."

"Yes." The Nnyth's rasping, dead-leaf voices echoed through the Tower. "You can."

"I can use it, can't I?" Duaal asked, raising his face to the Nnyth. "All of those broken and frayed edges... There's still enough of the Waygate's power for me to grab onto. You can't use it anymore and neither could the Arcadians or the Jinn. But I can."

"Yes."

The blue glow from so far below flickered like firelight.

Duaal pivoted on nothing and looked back at Maeve, who still stood staring from the stone. He grinned. "I can do this. I can take you to Axis, Maeve. I can drop us right in front of the Lyceum, if that's what you want."

Maeve began to nod, but Logan grabbed her shoulder. He shook his head.

"There are only six of us," he said. "Xartasia has an army. She'll cut right through us and we won't even have slowed her down. We need your Arcadians, Maeve. We need to go back to Kaellisem."

"But Xartasia is flying to Axis!" Maeve protested.

"Flight time from Stray to Axis is between five and nine days," Logan pointed out. "Depending upon the ship. If we move quickly, we can still beat Xartasia to Axis."

"There are only nineteen knights in Kaellisem," Anthem said.

"Nineteen...?" Maeve asked. "But I thought that we had twenty knights."

"Nineteen, a'shae," Anthem repeated firmly. "More than there have been in a long time, but still far from an army. We cannot hope to match Xartasia with such small numbers."

"The Arcadians back in Kaellisem know next to nothing about combat," Xia said. "They're no army. That's why we've needed the CWAAF since the beginning."

"We don't have the Alliance army. We have Arcadians." Logan looked at Duaal. "But maybe we can use one to get the other. Can you get us back to Stray?"

"Inside five minutes," the mage answered confidently.

"One last thing," Logan said and raised his glittering glass hand to the Nnyth. "I need one of your dead."

"Logan!" Maeve gasped.

What could her enarri have in mind? She knew that Logan was clever, an intuitive and skilled hunter, but...

Two Nnyth unfurled their long, delicate wings and then glided silently to the Blue Phoenix. Between them, they carried a striped, curled shape. A dead Nnyth. They set it down gently on the stone pillar and then flew off once more, into the darkness.

Logan ran his fingers over the Nnyth's black and russet-striped skin. One of the legs was shorter than the others, black ichor hardening over the stump that remained. Maeve wiped her eyes. When Logan lifted his hand, it shone with a faintly iridescent wetness.

"Phenno," Gripper said. "You want fresh phenno? Why, Hunter? Are we going to be flying into another star?"

"No. We don't need phenno. But we do need money."

"Money?" Maeve asked, frowning. "We have money."

"Not in the amounts we'll need. We need to get thousands of Arcadians to Axis inside eight days. For that, we need the biggest and fastest ships on Stray. Xyn's redprint is breaking down. We can buy a lot of captains for the cost of a fresh source. Help me get this loaded into the hold, Gripper. And then it's time to go back to Kael-lisem and your people, Maeve."

She nodded. Gripper and Logan wrapped the dead Nnyth in its own limp wings and carried it carefully to the airlock. Xia followed. Duaal stepped back onto the stone. He bowed once to the dying Nnyth.

"It'll be easier to move us all if we're inside the Blue Phoenix," he said.

"I will be there in a moment," Maeve answered.

Duaal nodded and vanished into the ship. Maeve looked up into the dimming light of the Tower.

"I thank you," she told the remaining Nnyth. "You have given so much to protect life and time. I do not know that I could sacrifice what you have."

"You have given much," the star wasps whispered. "And you will give up more, Maeve Cavainna, before this is done. Fly now. Time grows short."

Maeve turned away and made her way to the airlock. When she reached the door, she glanced back. Anthem still stood on the black and gray stone, holding his spear tightly.

"Did you speak with Titania?" His question was meant for the Nnyth... Maeve didn't think she was supposed to hear Anthem ask. "As you did to us?"

"Yes."

"Has she... Does she have a new enarri?"

"She remembers you, Sir Anthem Calloren. And she misses you every day."

Anthem's wings sagged and he shook his head, confused. But without another word, he returned to the Blue Phoenix. He paused in the airlock, looking at Maeve with such pain in his dark eyes that she couldn't hold his gaze. She pressed the glowing airlock controls and the door slid shut. Maeve squinted out through the window, but the Tower had gone entirely dark outside and she saw nothing.

And then everything blazed with blue light.

[37]

THE CALL

"You can't always wait for the weapons you need. Fight with the ones you have."

– LOGAN CENTRA (234 PA)

Ballad swooped over the blasted ruins of the theater, scanning the blackened ground. It had been over a week since the last riots in Kaellisem and even those had been small ones, resulting in little more than a couple of bruises. But the glass hunters were still a problem. Arcadian glass remained more or less unique to Kaellisem and even the twisted shards left behind after the enassui bombing were worth some money. Not much, but enough to lure scavengers that sometimes snuck in from Gharib to hunt for loose shards.

Ballad was from Prianus and he didn't resent the coreworlders for trying to earn a bit of color. But the sorts of folk who were desperate enough to search the sands for a few lumps of glass were sometimes the same ones who might be more than happy to knife an Arcadian and it was Ballad's job to protect the citizens of Kaellisem. With Sir Anthem gone, Ballad was in command of the remaining knights.

He whistled sharply to Suvaen. The other knight wheeled with Ballad, up and then around the dagger-like remains of the royal box. They flew a last circuit, but it was too hot out even for the glass hunters and Ballad led Suvaen back toward Kaellisem.

For such a dim sun, Ballad never ceased to be amazed at how effectively it could bake Stray's surface. Prianus' primary had to be three times brighter, but Ballad couldn't remember *ever* being warm in Pylos. On Stray, though, several other knights – including Suvaen – had adopted his short Prian haircut. The long, flowing Arcadian styles just weren't practical in the hot desert. Especially in the wearable prism that was their glass armor.

A sudden wind whipped up a funnel of sand and Ballad threw his weight back, cupping his wings to come to an abrupt stop before he plunged headlong into the whipping grit. A sandstorm...? Ballad grabbed for his com to warn Panna, but the cloud of sand was too small for a storm. He waved to Suvaen and the two of them landed, pulling scarves up over their mouths. It had been weeks since any sort of attack on Kaellisem, but they had never caught the elusive bomber... Maybe this was some new sort of menace.

The red and orange sand settled, suddenly revealing the large, spiny shape of the Blue Phoenix squatting in the desert dust. Frost crackled along its dented fibersteel hull and steamed in the desert heat. Ballad pulled off his sunglasses and stared. Surely this was... what? A trick?

The Blue Phoenix wasn't supposed to be back in Kaellisem for another month or more. If it returned at all from the confrontation with Xartasia. And why hadn't they seen the freighter's approach? Surely Maeve would have told Panna if she was back in the Bannon system. And then Panna would have told Ballad... She was actually talking to him now. *To* him instead of down to him. She was almost bearable.

The Blue Phoenix's fibersteel cargo ramp hissed and ground, lowering down into the sand. Duaal Sinnay stood at the top, his back turned to Ballad and Suvaen. The Hyzaari captain's hands were spread in a gesture of humility that was anything but.

"Ha!" he said. "I guess there's a *new* Waygate expert. Not even the Nnyth could have used a broken Waygate to move an entire ship halfway across the galaxy!"

Ballad had no idea what Duaal was talking about, but he told Suvaen to stay put and ran up the ramp. Queen Maeve, Logan Coldhand, Sir Anthem Calloren and the rest stood in the Blue Phoenix's hold, all gathered around a large plastic crate. Other than Duaal's swaggering confidence, the air was more like that of a funeral than a celebration. Logan was the first one to catch sight of Ballad and raised his translucent glass hand in a short greeting.

"What the hells happened?" Ballad asked. "Is it over? Did you stop Xartasia?"

"No, not yet," Maeve answered. "Xartasia was not there. She is bound for Axis and we must get there before she does. I need to speak with Panna and Duke Ferris."

"Vyron and Xyn, too," Logan added. He stood next to the queen, Ballad noted, not Sir Anthem.

"Yes, sir," Ballad said and hurried away to do as he was asked.

A half hour later, they were all gathered in the Blue Phoenix hold. Maeve would have liked to meet in her glass tower – she missed it far more than expected – but she would have been noticed moving through Kaellisem. Not yet.

Instead, Panna and Duke Ferris had joined Ballad on the ship, followed a bit later by Vyron and his family. The last to arrive was Xyn. The Ixthian scientist waddled into the Blue Phoenix with a suspicious look on his silver face.

"You're back early," he grumped.

"We're fine, Xyn," Xia said. "Thanks for asking."

Maeve stood next to Gripper and touched his thick arm gently. He wasn't fine, but there was still work to be done. The big Arboran looked down at her with red-rimmed eyes. He was tired. They all were... Reluctantly, Maeve returned her attention to the council she had called. She had refused to answer Panna's many questions until everyone was assembled. There was too much to say, to do, and too little time. They had one chance.

"We must act quickly," Maeve said when Xyn and Xia finished squabbling. She heard the hard tone of her own voice. "Xartasia intends to unmake all the years of history since the White Kingdom's fall. To do this, she took her Arcadians and Devourers to the Tower. The Nnyth destroyed their own hive to prevent her from taking it, so Xartasia left. She goes now to the Devourers' homeworld, Axis, and will arrive in eight days."

"Hold on," Panna said. "What? Can Xartasia do that? Just delete more than a century of life?"

"The Nnyth believe so," Maeve answered. "And fear the results enough to destroy their own home and condemn themselves to a slow death."

"So what do we do about it?" Ballad asked.

"Xartasia needs to get down to the surface of Axis," Logan said. "To find a special Waygate there. We're going to fight her for it."

"How?" Ferris asked like an accusation. "How can we challenge Xartasia with a handful of knights?"

"We get CWAAF to back us," Logan answered.

Now everyone was staring at him, including Maeve.

"Logan, we spent months trying to rouse the Alliance to action," she reminded him. "With no success. They simply did not believe the threat that my cousin poses to the galaxy. How do you propose to convince them now?"

"By making a threat of our own," Logan answered.

Panna's eyes went wide. "Threaten the Alliance? Have you lost your mind?"

"We take every willing Arcadian to Axis and we gather them for a fight. We make it public and we make it loud. That will *force* the Alliance to respond. Xartasia is out of the way, working in relative secret. We won't."

"CWAAF won't just let you amass an army – even a small one – on their capital planet," Duaal said, dark brow furrowed. "They'll respond in numbers."

"That's the point, isn't it?" Ballad asked, giving Logan a look of admiration. "It's a trick."

"Yes. And a dangerous one," Logan admitted. "We want to get the Alliance ready to fight by threatening them ourselves, but we don't want to give them enough time to actually start a war with us. If we fight on Level One, we should have a CWAAF response within an hour. A major mobilization within three."

"We have a date for Xartasia's arrival, but no time or location," Maeve said. "We will be guessing where to make our stand."

"And if our guess is incorrect, if we give the Alliance too much time to focus on us," Anthem added, "Arcadians will die."

"Or at least spend their lives in prison," Panna said.

"But if we do not do this, you will never have been born," Maeve told the girl. She looked around the hold. "Most of you were born less than a century ago. You can let your world be cut out of time or you can die trying to save it."

"But what about you?" Panna asked softly. "You and Sir Anthem and Duke Ferris? Almost half of us are older than a hundred years. Do you think they really want to risk their lives? How many of them would be just as happy to throw away the last century? It's been horrible for them. For you."

"I... have made my mistakes," Maeve said. "And the losses have been staggering. But there are billions of humans, Dailons, Ixthians and Lyrans here in the core. Trillions of lives in the last hundred years. I cannot just let Xartasia unmake them."

"Yes, my queen," Anthem agreed, nodding.

Duke Ferris stood very still, his hands tucked into the flowing sleeves of his robes.

"Xartasia would restore the White Kingdom to all its glory, a'shae," he said. "That is no small dream. Millions died at its destruction, and now even the Nnyth Tower is falling."

"Surely you will not condemn the entire population of the CWA for that," Maeve said.

For all his blustering pomposity and strict adherence to Arcadian tradition, Duke Ferris had always been loyal to his queen. It never occurred to Maeve that he might not back her now.

"My daughter is in an Alliance prison," Ferris said, "for no crime greater than not having a home. We left her behind on Sunjarrah, my queen. I have not forgotten. Unmaking these last hundred years would be a blessing to her."

Maeve had forgotten all about Ferris' daughter... She swallowed against a suddenly painful feeling in her throat. Duke Ferris turned on his heels and stalked to the cargo ramp, then spread his wings and leapt into the pale blue-green sky. In a moment, he was gone. Panna sighed and rubbed her eyes.

"I'm sorry," she apologized. "He's been like that ever since I got back from Hadra."

"Ferris is not wrong," Maeve said. "Not so wrong as I would like. Xartasia's plan is not quite the evil that we long suspected. But it must be stopped..."

"You're going to need a lot of Arcadians to pull this off." Vyron stood behind Kessa, his large blue hands on his wife's shoulders and black eyes on Maeve. "And you won't get their help if Kaellisem agrees with Ferris."

"Vyron's right. We need at least a thousand fairies if we're going to get the Alliance to take us seriously," Logan said. "Dove, I know you're sick of speeches, but I think you'd better give one more. We can't let the gossip get ahead of us on this one. Public sentiment is too much against us."

Maeve closed her eyes and then nodded. "One more, yes. I can do this one last time."

Kessa raised the one hand that wasn't curled around Baliend.

"What do you need us to do?" she asked. "Not go to Axis, I hope. I believe with all my heart in what you're doing, Maeve, but Vy and I can't go back. We went through too much to get off that planet."

"No," Logan answered. "Xyn, we have something for you."

The bounty hunter pulled up the lid of the crate they had gathered around. Inside lay the curled, striped shape of the dead Nnyth. Xyn gasped and pressed six-fingered hands to his chest.

"A Nnyth!" he said unnecessarily. "A whole Nnyth! Not just the skin that Tiberius brought me."

"This is worth something to you," Logan prompted. "And to the ship captains you supply?"

"Oh yes! With this, I don't have to clone phenno. I can study and recreate the actual glands that secrete the protein." Xyn clasped his hands over his heart as though he were looking at a particularly adorable child. "No more telomeric degradation, no transcription errors. Hells, I might even be able to produce a skin layer for ships that secretes its own phennomethylln."

"Ew," Gripper said.

Xia put one hand on the other Ixthian's elbow. Her eyes were a serious sapphire color.

"Treat these remains with respect," she told Xyn. "The Nnyth are our cousins and they gave a lot to help us."

Xyn gave her a sidelong look and seemed as though he might protest, but he only nodded. "I will."

"Good," Logan said. "Xyn, we need you to charter ships. Enough to get a thousand or more Arcadians to Axis within eight days. You can use whatever remains of the royal treasury–"

"About five thousand cenmarks," Panna supplied.

"Is that all?" Ballad asked, frowning.

"Glass production declined steeply with all the riots," she said. "We're still trying to get it back up."

"–and promise whatever colour you need to from the profits of the phenno sales or the phenno itself," Logan went on. "Whatever it takes to get as many of the fastest ships on Stray to fly Arcadians onto Axis."

"Can't Duaal just... magic us all to Axis?" Ballad asked.

"Not unless you've got a Waygate hidden in that jacket," Duaal answered. "I can control the power, not generate it. We need ships."

Xyn's eyes turned scarlet. "Look, I know we've had a good partnership, but passage for a thousand fairies...!"

"You'll be compensated," Logan said. "Either by the Alliance or by us after this is all done."

"And if you die?" Xyn asked.

"Then we have failed and you will never have been born at all," Maeve told the Ixthian scientist. "Or at least, this conversation will never have happened."

"Vyron will help you negotiate the best rates," Logan said. "He's a good salesman. And then your part in this is finished, Xyn. All you have to do is get rich and hope that we preserve the past."

"How soon do you want to leave?" Vyron asked.

"Tomorrow morning," Logan answered.

Vyron whistled and pulled a com from his pocket. "I better get to work, then."

Maeve spent most of the afternoon letting Caith try in vain to talk her out of her pain. Orthain was a good man and a good knight, yes, but there were hundreds of those in the White Kingdom. She was a princess, niece to the king himself, Caith reminded Maeve. She would find love again. And in the meantime, they had each other.

So Maeve had smiled at her brother in the flickering light of the Tamlin Waygate before pleading hunger and flying alone into the city.

She swooped between the sapphire towers and domes that looked like ice. Other Arcadians landed, spread their white wings in respect and let the princess pass. Maeve ignored them...

Most of them, at least. A man in blue-edged glass armor flew past, with silver beads braided into his long gold hair. He did not land or step aside like the others. The knight was flying in a swift, straight line in the direction of the Waygate Maeve had just left. He passed so close to Maeve that his wings tangled with hers and both knights crashed to the ground, scattering a group of dryads working in the orchard below.

When the world stopped spinning, Maeve jumped to her feet.

"Watch where you are flying!" she shouted at the other knight. "You could have killed us both!"

It was an exaggeration, of course, but Maeve was in a foul mood. The man with the silver beads in his hair sat up slowly, holding one hand to his shoulder. For the first time, Maeve noted his red-rimmed eyes and the shining wet streaks down his cheeks. Maeve frowned. She was sure that she recognized the other Arcadian, but could not place him. The knight didn't rise.

"I am sorry, princess," he apologized. "I did not see you."

Maeve scrubbed at the grassy green streaking her armor with one hand. "That much is clear. Where are you going in such a hurry?"

"The Waygate. I want only to get out of Tamlin. Away from..."

The knight's face went red and he didn't finish the sentence. Finally, Maeve recognized him.

"Sir Anthem Calloren," she said, half to herself, and then cocked her head in thought. "Princess Titania is in Tamlin tonight, is she not?"

"Yes," Anthem said. The red in his cheeks darkened to a deep, angry purple and he spat his answer bitterly. "She is. Titania is at the temple of Erris, praying for the health of her father, the king."

Maeve wanted to ask what could have infuriated the elder knight so badly, but she didn't dare... That was between Princess Titania and her consort. Maeve offered her hand to Anthem. He took it reluctantly and stood. Maeve wondered if he saw how bloodshot her eyes were, too.

"Your sorrows will not remain in Tamlin after you have gone," she suggested delicately. "I thought to leave mine in the White City, but they follow me wherever I fly."

Anthem sighed and picked up his spear from the ground. "You are right, princess."

"I am bound for the Starflower," Maeve said, naming Tamlin's famous restaurant. Now that she thought about it, she actually was hungry. "It has been a long day. Do you want to come with me?"

Anthem nodded. "It would be my pleasure, princess."

"Maeve," she told him.

The handsome knight gave her a small smile.

"Maeve," he repeated.

— ● ● ● —

Maeve spent the next hours trying to listen as Panna updated her on what had happened in Kaellisem over the last three weeks, but worrying about money and politics felt so... so pointless when held up against the impossibility of trying to stop Xartasia and her army from unmaking more than a century of lives. Finally, Maeve raised her hand.

"Enough," she said and stood. "Panna, you have been more than capable of handling Kaellisem in my absence. I trust that you have done right and from here, it no longer matters. All that is important now is convincing as many Arcadians as I can to fly with us to Axis."

"But..." Panna glanced at the datadex in her hands. "There's a whole city of your people out there. They need food and shelter and medicine every day..."

"And they have you to take care of that," Maeve told the girl. "I've never done more than approve your ideas. This city is *your* creation, Panna, and that of Duke Ferris. For me, Kaellisem is a tool.

A way to thwart Xartasia, to take Arcadians away from her. But to you, it has always been so much more. You know our people. You know the knights that protect Kaellisem. I cannot even remember their names."

Maeve shook her head and combed her fingers through her white-streaked black hair. They were still in the Blue Phoenix mess. At Anthem's insistence, the queen would return to Kaellisem only once to make her final speech. Maeve went to the sink and picked up the single bowl and spoon inside.

"Do you want me to work on your speech for tonight?" Panna asked uncertainly.

"No," Maeve told her. "Tonight, I will say my own words. My last words, perhaps. I will plead our case to Kaellisem plainly."

"What do you want me to do, then?"

Maeve washed the spoon and smiled at her inverted reflection inside its curve. "Whatever you wish, Panna. The world we know may end in eight days. Is there something you wish to do before it is gone?"

By the time Maeve finished cleaning the bowl and spoon, Panna was already gone.

Both Logan and Anthem were too well known and too little liked in Kaellisem, so the task of gathering the remaining Arcadians fell to the small group of remaining knights.

Ballad had just returned to the Blue Phoenix to report that only about fifteen hundred Arcadians had agreed to let Queen Maeve address them one final time. Less than half Kaellisem's remaining population, Ballad informed them unhappily. The rest wanted nothing to do with their monarch.

"We might be able to convince some more with colour or extra food," Ballad suggested, but Anthem shook his head.

"Anyone who requires such bribery simply to listen to a speech will not be of help," he said.

"Those aren't the people who will be willing to risk their lives against Xartasia and CWAAF," Logan agreed.

Ballad's sunburnt brow furrowed as he thought about that, but Panna swept down the stairs, grabbed the young knight and pulled him into a long, deep kiss. Ballad didn't seem to know where to put his hands and his face went even redder.

"But I thought you didn't even like me–" he began.

"Well, you're wrong," Panna interrupted, tugging Ballad toward the airlock. "As usual."

The two young Arcadians vanished quickly in the direction of Kaellisem's crystal towers. Anthem watched them go with a small smile on his lips.

"We will see them tonight, I think," he said. "But not before."

"Probably not."

Anthem turned to Logan, the strange, sad smile still on his lips. "I can finish arranging this evening, if there is somewhere else you would like to be, as well."

"You mean with Maeve," Logan said.

"I do."

Logan narrowed his eyes at Anthem. "You're encouraging me to go right now to the woman who is supposed to be *your* enarri?"

"Maeve has loved you since long before I ever met her," Anthem said. "Perhaps in another life, Maeve and I... But we have only one life, one heart, and she has given hers to you completely."

"You're not angry that she and I..."

Logan hesitated, not quite sure how to end the sentence. But Anthem shook his head.

"Syle was hiding on the Blue Phoenix," he said. "He belonged to Xartasia, never to us. He intended to assassinate Maeve. He bombed the enassui, I think, and made the other explosives that you disarmed."

"If he worked for Xartasia, then he would have known about Maeve and the Tamlin Waygate. He must have let it slip when he was working the food lines, starting the riots."

"Yes," Anthem agreed. "I believe so, too."

"What happened to Syle?"

"He is dead."

"You killed him?" Logan asked. "Why didn't you call me?"

"What you were doing at that moment was far more important," Anthem said. He actually smiled, the first real smile Logan thought he had ever seen on the serious knight's handsome face. Not a bitter or sad look. "And loud enough to cover the sounds of our battle, brief as it was."

Logan felt something hot on his cheeks and realized that he was probably blushing.

"Sorry," he said curtly.

Anthem's smile fell away. "No, I am sorry. Syle was my knight. I should have seen his treachery. I did not until it was too late."

"Maeve is still alive," Logan said.

"But Syle did a great deal of damage." Anthem's dark blue eyes seemed old and tired. "If he had not attacked the enassui, if he had not turned Kaellisem against the queen…"

"I should have found Syle, too."

"He was a knight. He knew everything that you and I did. It was all too easy to maneuver around us. There is blame enough to keep us debating until long after Xartasia lands on Axis, but it no longer matters. What is done is done."

"Not if Xartasia has her way."

"My beloved is a strong and clever woman," Anthem said. "For all that Titania has done, what she intends to do, I cannot help but admire her. She is still wrong – terribly wrong – but my enarri is a great queen."

Logan couldn't bring himself to agree, but he extended his left hand to Anthem. The knight took it and glass rang against glass.

The two men held each other's gaze for a moment and then both turned away, nothing left to be said.

Both Anthem and Panna had argued her choice of venue. But if this was to be her final act as queen of Kaellisem, Maeve would do it her own way. She stood on the uneven remains of the stage. For the first time since her coronation, she wore her armor. But not her crown... That symbol remained in Duke Ferris' keeping.

The theater was a blasted, nightmare landscape of twisted black glass. Arcadians stood among the sharp, frozen shadows in clusters, none of them approaching the stage too closely. Was it Maeve they feared? Or something else? There were more than the seventeen hundred fairies that Ballad had promised, maybe drawn by some morbid curiosity. But not many more. There were still less than two thousand Arcadians willing to listen to Maeve speak. How many would do what she asked?

"How many ships did you manage to get?" Duaal asked Vyron, standing to one side of the stage. A dry wind stirred his dark hair.

Vyron looked across the ruined theater. "More than you're going to need, I think."

"Where's Xyn?"

"Back at Unbreakers," Vyron answered. "Gleefully dissecting the Nnyth you brought him. Xia's with him, looking over his shoulder with her eyes turning red. What happened? I didn't think Xia had any particular feelings about the Nnyth."

"You had to be there, I think," Duaal said, then turned to Maeve. "Are you ready for this?"

"No," she told him. "But there is not time for me to get ready. We must leave by dawn."

Logan and Sir Anthem walked silently on either side as Maeve strode to the center of the stage. Her glass armor was an unfamiliar weight and she felt strangely graceless lumbering around in it. Had it truly been so long since she was a knight, since she had worn a suit like this every day? Maeve took her spear from Logan.

"Kaellisem!" she called.

Or tried to. Maeve stammered. She was shaking and the plates of her armor shivered against one another like wind chimes. In the last year, she had given as many speeches as any Alliance politician, and even grown used to it. But this was different. She would ask her own people to risk their lives for the Alliance that had never, ever protected them... Maeve closed her eyes and fought for breath.

"Kaellisem!" she cried again. "We have been to the Tower and found it fallen! It was not by Xartasia's hand, but the Nnyth themselves who sundered their own home to prevent the White Queen from using it. They knew what Xartasia plans, and have told us. She flies now to the center of the galaxy, to Axis, to unmake all that has happened since I went to Tamlin. To restore the White Kingdom. To save our homeworlds."

There were a thousand cries and sharp, shocked notes from the crowd at this. Not displeased, but clear, happy songs that Maeve had not heard for a long time. She hated herself as she raised her spear like a banner.

"But to do this, Xartasia must destroy over a hundred years of history," Maeve shouted over the noise. "The coreworlders do not live as long as we do! Trillions have been born and lived since the fall of the White Kingdom. Xartasia will sacrifice their lives, their history to save our own.

"The Central World Alliance has been no friend to Arcadia, it is true, but they are a young empire. The White Kingdom stood for ten thousand years! Next to us, the people of the Alliance are but children. Children can be cruel. They can be heartless. But they are *innocent*, Kaellisem. I come before you tonight not as your queen, but as a knight. We have witnessed true destruction, true loss and pain! Anslin Sky-Knight charges all warriors to fight such enemies.

"I will go to Axis. Not to face Xartasia – she has numbers beyond ours, and the Devourers held in thrall – but to the CWA itself. We will stand before the Alliance and challenge them to battle. We go ourselves as bait, as cause to rally their army, so that they will be ready when Xartasia comes to Axis."

Another sound rose from the theater, no longer pleased but cries of disbelief and dismay. The Arcadians pulled back from the stage, cringing. Maeve longed to tell them not to be afraid, to retract the words that she had already spoken... but there was no going back now.

What has been can never be again.

"It will be dangerous, I know. Many of us will die," Maeve told her people, struggling with the words and to fight back tears.

She recognized Duke Ferris in the crowd. The old nobleman stood at the base of a blasted tower, a blackened stump of shattered glass, with angry eyes and clenched jaw. But he was there. He was listening. Maeve brought her spear down on the uneven stage. The charred glass cracked with a sharp, hollow noise like a gunshot.

"We may die," Maeve said. "Or at least spend the rest of our lives in Alliance prisons. And you know that itself is nothing less than a death sentence! Ever since the fall of the White Kingdom, we have waited to die, for the Nameless to finish her work. But now we have the chance to die *for* something.

"I know what it is I ask of you, Kaellisem! But I know that it is in you to give! When I came here, when I called to you, I did so with the sole intent to stop Xartasia. That was my only plan, my only desire. But you have built an entire city of sunset glass, of fire given form unlike anything even the pyrads ever dreamed to build!"

Maeve swept her spear in a wide arc to gesture out across the broken theater. "We will rouse the Alliance to battle. They may kill us, or Xartasia's army may, but we will fall defending life and light. We are Arcadian! The gods made us to sing the new songs, to dance those steps never danced before. They made us to live and to die as they cannot. What has been can never be again. Xartasia has forgotten that. She would sing the old songs again. She would tear apart all that is new, turn back time and unmake all!

"It is our responsibility, our destiny, our right and our pride to stop her, to forge ahead and never to look back!"

Maeve raised her spear and sang out a single high, pure note. There were no more words. What else could she say? She had asked her people to die so that others could live, to throw themselves at the CWAAF in the mad hope that when Xartasia came, the Alliance would be ready for war. It was not even a hopeless battle. It was pure sacrifice of blood for the future of a galaxy that despised and dismissed them.

Logan was the first to take up Maeve's note, an octave lower. And then Anthem sang, too, clean and clear as glass. Another voice joined the three, high and tremulous. It was Duke Ferris, his face raised to the darkening sky and tears streaming down his withered old cheeks. One by one and then hundreds of voices joined, a single thrumming, resonating note.

Maeve stared out across the shattered glass theater. Hundreds of Arcadians were turning away, so many leaving and returning to their safe home and filling the night with retreating white wings.

But more stayed.

[38]
EIGHT DAYS

"Do not weep for my death. I fly into the light while my enemies
hide in the dark."

- SUVAEN DAMMAR (234 PA)

Logan selected the fastest starships that Vyron had hired for the
flight. The Dailon was right – there were far more ships willing to
ferry Arcadians for a drum of Xyn's new phenno than fairies willing
to die for the Alliance. Panna's final count was nine hundred and
twenty-seven volunteers, including all of Anthem's knights, herself
and the crew of the Blue Phoenix. Less than a quarter of Kaellisem.

Maeve argued with both Duke Ferris and Panna. Someone had
to manage the city. More than three thousand Arcadians remained
in Kaellisem. But both just shook their heads. Thanks to Panna's
planning, everyone should have food and water enough for the next
month. She bribed the Gharib police extravagantly to check in from
time to time with the understanding that there would be more color
later if the fairies remained safe and well.

"I'm not sure where we'll get the money," Panna said with a wry
smile. "But if we don't stop Xartasia on Axis, it's not like they'll be

sniffing around after their cenmarks. If Captain Janse even exists, Kaellisem won't."

"Captain?" Maeve asked.

"She got promoted while you were gone."

An hour before dawn, twenty-eight ships lifted off from Gharib's dusty landing crescent. They flew in a crooked diamond across the dim pewter moon and then were gone.

"They're gone?" Kessa asked.

Vyron nodded. "They left this morning."

"Did you get them a good deal on the ships?"

"Of course, Kes."

Breakfast sat untouched on the kitchen table. In the corner of the kitchen, Baliend had found a spoon and merrily banged on one of his overturned pots. The baby boy burbled happily. Kessa looked at her son and husband.

"Without them, we wouldn't have... any of this," she told Vyron. "If Xartasia changes time and saves Arcadia, Maeve will never have come to Axis. She'll still be in the White Kingdom. Logan won't be fighting with her that day. I'll be alone. The Sisterhood will catch me. They'll kill me and Baliend."

"I'll still be with the Steelskins," Vyron agreed quietly. "Probably dead in the next few years, if not already."

Kessa took Vyron's large, strong blue hands in hers. He raised his black eyes and closed his fingers around his wife's. They leaned across the table until their foreheads touched. Long black hair fell down around Kessa's shoulders and she took a deep breath. Baliend squealed in delight and hurled his spoon across the kitchen.

"Father of all life," Kessa prayed aloud. "God of all the worlds. Please watch over our friends. They need your help. We all do."

————●——●——●————

Hyra went to the glass forge early. The tent was long since gone, replaced by a wide, gently spiraling hall with windows that looked out across Kaellisem. The city glowed red and copper and gold with the first light of dawn. White-winged shapes stirred in windows and the smell of cooking bread and petrimeat drifted into the warming morning.

Hyra called out for Lorren, but the younger glass-smith did not answer. Hyra stumped down the glittering pink corridor, searching and twitching his single wing in irritation. Where was that girl? But Hyra found only a couple of confused apprentices in the drawing room and a startled pigeon in the central forge chamber. The gray and brown bird burst into the air with a flurry of tiny wings and vanished through one of the arched windows. Something small and white drifted down to the floor at Hyra's feet. Not a loose feather, he realized, but a scrap of paper.

Hyra, the note read.

I have gone with the queen. We have built such beauty here. I cannot stand by while Xartasia tears it all apart.

- Lorren

The little idiot...! Hyra had forbidden Lorren to attend Maeve's speech. Lorren was three hundred years old, but still only half of the senior glass-singer's age. Hyra did his best to watch out for the girl and was afraid that there would be more riots following whatever the Gray Queen had to say. But Lorren had gone anyway. Hyra read the note twice and then crumpled it in his hand.

"Fallo!" he called. "Anallia!"

The two apprentices landed a moment later, still scrubbing the sleep from their eyes. Anallia had cut her white-blonde hair short, Hyra noted with exasperation. Ever since Sir Ballad's return, the style had grown in popularity. Hyra stabbed his wing at the younger Arcadians.

"We are down a voice," he said. "You two will do Lorren's work until she gets back from Axis."

"Lorren went with the queen?" Fallo asked. "But they are saying she will not return..."

Hyra grabbed the apprentice's pointed ear between his thumb and forefinger, making him screech.

"Lorren *is* coming back," Hyra said. "And you two are doing her work until she does."

Malla ignored another catcall from the Gunju Prince's crew. One day on the ship and she had already been in two minor brawls and fended off a Dailon who was far too curious about what a bird-back might be like in his bunk. Even if Malla wanted one last toss before she died, it would not have been with a huge, strange blue alien.

She pushed the door control with the side of one wing and went into the bunk she shared with Eranna and three other Arcadians. The room was designed for two.

Eranna sat on the edge of the upper bunk. Malla handed one of the trays to the other knight. Eranna took it with a small nod.

"Thanks," she said.

Malla accidently stepped on someone's wing as she climbed up to sit beside Eranna.

"Sorry," she said.

There was a grunt from somewhere below. Eranna unwrapped a fork and began picking at the pink-brown mass of what appeared to be some sort of... sausage?

She made a face.

"If I had known that saving the galaxy would involve food like this," Eranna said, "I might have stayed in Kaellisem."

"As though we ate better there," Malla answered with a snort. "Without dryads to do our farming, we rely on Cyrus and the other agriworlds just as much as the rest of the Alliance does."

Eranna speared a crumbling cube of processed green vegetable. "We are knights. Even if Arcadians ever become farmers, it will not be you and I who take up spades."

"Hannu talked about it sometimes, you know," Malla said. She suddenly wasn't very hungry anymore and handed her dinner tray down to one of the other fairies. "Even before we left Sunjarrah to follow Queen Maeve. There was so much open grassland there. It wouldn't have taken much to fly out past where any of the Mirrans could find us and start a little farm. Just enough to feed a couple of us."

"Your brother wanted to be a farmer?" Eranna asked when she had chewed and swallowed. "But he was a knight. It is the highest calling the gods can bestow."

Malla looked down at her hands. Without her glass gauntlets, they looked small and fragile.

"Maybe. But Hannu and I didn't become knights because the gods called us or even because Queen Maeve did. Hells, we tried to join Xartasia first, but she wouldn't take us. We were too young. All we wanted was a home. A real home."

"Why are you flying to Axis to die, then?" Eranna asked.

"Because my brother is dead," Malla said. "Hannu died at the enassui with a piece of glass as long as my arm through his guts. Xia came, but it was too late and Hannu died. Without him, I don't care about a home anymore. So I may as well die for someone else's."

Stars streaked past outside the O'Collin's viewports. There were more of the elongated rainbow lights outside now, as the ship raced toward the galactic core. Four more days and the O'Collin would land on Axis with the Blue Phoenix and the rest of Queen Maeve's tiny army.

Dellan held Gael's hands gently. Gael's eyes were closed and his lips moved silently. Even after all these months, the withdrawals were bad. Dellan had found Gael in Gharib twice, trying in broken Aver to buy more Deep from the suspicious coreworlders. Dellan had managed to get Gael back to Kaellisem before anything terrible happened, but his friend was always so quiet afterward.

Just like he was now. Dellan squeezed Gael's hands firmly until the other Arcadian finally opened his eyes. The right one was still cloudy, despite Xia's best efforts to repair the damage. She offered to send away for a cloned replacement, but Gael always refused.

"Where are your thoughts?" Dellan asked.

"Here," Gael said.

"Why do you seem so sad? Are you afraid to die?"

Gael shook his head. "I have been waiting to die since our home fell, my friend. I do not fear the Nameless."

"What is it, then?"

Gael touched his fingertips against Dellan's cheek. They were cool and shook slightly.

"You," Gael said.

"Me?"

"I worry for you," Gael told him. "Why are *you* here? You loved Kaellisem, my friend."

"Queen Maeve asked us to come. After all she has done for us, how could I stay behind?"

Gael's pale lips turned up into a thin smile. "After what she did for me, you mean. She saved me, not you."

"By so doing," Dellan said, ducking his head, "our queen saved me, too."

Gael leaned against Dellan and rested his head on the other man's shoulder. "You are not really here for Queen Maeve. I know you better than that."

Dellan didn't answer. He wrapped his wing around Gael's shoulder. The O'Collin was a Glawn ship. Glaw was a cold, dark world of tunnels and ice. It was probably too cool for Gael. The thin fairy smiled again.

"Thank you, Dellan," Gael said, "for being here with me at the end of everything."

"Always."

Duke Ferris Verridian looked up at his reflection in the computer monitor, studying his hair. It was more gray than golden now. Ferris was younger than King Illain had been when he died, but looked far more ancient.

"New Hennor prison com system," said a recorded voice with the distinctive Mirran burr. "Please clearly state the number of the prisoner you would like to contact."

"One-three-seven-two-eight-eight-nine," Ferris recited. He had the number written down, of course, but he didn't need to look at it. The duke had memorized it long ago.

The Sunjarrah parliamentary crest remained on the screen, an emerald-green tree studded with silver stars. Ferris waited. Finally, the automated voice spoke again.

"The New Hennor penal system regrets to inform you that prisoner 137-288-9 is deceased," it said. "Time of death was 11.28.234 PA, 02:52 local time. Please submit any further comments or questions concerning this inmate to Warden Junmorro. Would you like to be transferred to their office now?"

"No," Ferris whispered. "Thank you."

He pressed a glowing button and the com monitor flickered, then went dark.

Ferris cried for a long time. Il'mani had been a baby when the White Kingdom fell. He remembered cradling the infant girl to his chest as he flew. Ferris had clutched at Shae's hand, too, but the Devourers pulled her away with black chains that sprouted hooks all along their lengths even as she screamed and bled into the grass. But his wife had not screamed in pain, only for Ferris to fly, to take their daughter and get away... She had been so brave.

Il'mani was too young to remember her mother or the White Kingdom. She would never see them now, not unless Xartasia managed to reforge time. Then Ferris would stand in Aes' warm golden light again. With his family.

But... but the queen – the true queen, the Gray Queen – was right. The White Kingdom was dead and gone. Like his wife and his daughter. The All-Singer gave life and the Nameless took it away. Ferris loved his family and his kingdom, but they were lost to him. He could miss them – and would every day for the rest of his life – but he could never, ever hold them again.

Gripper sat in the corner of the darkened engine room. There were twenty-three Arcadians staying in the hold of the Blue Phoenix. Several of them had volunteered to care for Gripper's garden. It was the least they could do, they said, in return for the honor of flying in the same ship as Queen Maeve. Gripper let them. He just didn't feel like taking care of the plants anymore.

The young Arboran wrapped long arms around his knees and buried his face into his furry forearms. He didn't realize that there was anyone else in the engine room until soft feathers brushed his skin. Gripper looked up as Maeve sat down beside him.

"Logan is worried about you," she said. "He told me that you did not want to talk."

Gripper wiped his nose on an oil-stained rag. "It's not his fault. Hunter just doesn't understand. He tried, though."

Out of the corner of one eye, Gripper saw Maeve smile.

"I never thought that you and Logan would be friends. You two have nothing in common."

"That's not true. We both like you, Glass."

"That is not the sole basis of your friendship."

"No," Gripper agreed. "I guess not."

They sat together in silence for a long time. The Blue Phoenix's engines – blissfully ignorant of everything wrong in the huge galaxy – churned and chugged loudly. The null-inertia field generator hummed like a huge insect, audible even through seven layers of shielding and insulation. Air rushed and rattled through ducting, through the lopsided old pyramid of the gas exchanger and then out again.

The water and waste systems were a level down from the engine room, through a hatch and then down a narrow ladder that Gripper seldom bothered with. But he heard them working, too. There was the high-pitched groan of the pump seal, the one that was always breaking. Gripper must have welded it shut again dozens of times since Tiberius first hired him.

"Those things I saw down on the surface of Arborus," Gripper said slowly, "those really were Waygates. Prototypes, I guess. And that person I followed through one, to Kahl... Do you think that was Xartasia?"

"Yes," Maeve said. "I can think of no one else who might have business on your world."

"If the old sycona tree hadn't been sick, if it hadn't fallen, I never would have been there. I never would have followed her through the gate. I wouldn't be here."

Maeve chewed her lower lip and said nothing. Gripper's vision blurred with tears again. They stung on his cheeks and splashed to the stained engine room floor.

"I guess Arborus was in this galaxy," Gripper said in a choked voice. "Maybe... maybe out on the rim somewhere. It would be a really long flight to get home, but we've been out to the Tower.

Flying to Arborus probably wouldn't be too hard compared to that. But there's no point anymore, is there? Everyone is dead. Eaten. Just like Arcadia."

"Yes."

Gripper grabbed Maeve's tiny shoulders. How could she stand it? Knowing that no matter what she did, how far or fast she flew, no matter how many things she fixed or charts she looked at, there was nothing to go home to? Here and now... that was all Maeve had left. It was all Gripper had, too.

"And... and we're related to those monsters?" he asked. "I am?"

"Yes. But you are not alone," Maeve answered. "Xia believes that the humans are close relatives to the Devourers, as well. Not direct descendants, as the Arborans are... were. But yes, life born of the same genetic seeds and shaped by similar forces. She calls it convergent evolution."

"You mean that if species like the Axials and Mirrans and Prians keep evolving, they will end up like the Devourers?" Gripper asked, horrified.

"Perhaps," Maeve said. "Xia says that the galaxy is not the same as it was when the Devourers ruled it. And the people are different. They may breed different traits."

Maeve pointed to her own chest.

"The Arcadians, too, are made from the same genes, Xia tells me. That is why we look more or less human. To coreworlder eyes, at least. The Devourers designed us to look this way. We have probably evolved a little in the last few million years, but she suspects that we were quite recognizable to our creators. Just as they could not have failed to note the similarities between the Arborans and themselves."

Gripper wiped his eyes and stared at Maeve. "You mean that when they ate Arcadians and Arborans, the Devourers *know* they're eating their own creations and relatives?"

"Yes. On Prianus, too, when they faced the human police."

"How can they do this?" Gripper asked desperately, shaking the little fairy woman. "How can they do this to us?"

"They are hungry. You have calculated the energy needs of their nanite swarms," Maeve said. "Most life in the galaxy sprang from the seed they left behind. We all have it in ourselves to become just like the Devourers."

Gripper cried. He didn't care why anymore. Why the Devourers left the galaxy, why they came back just to kill and consume their own descendants. Arborus... Weh-Weh... was gone.

Gripper wished Maeve didn't understand, that he could just cry all alone in the engine room. But she did understand. Gripper wept great hiccuping sobs into Maeve's white wings and she held him awkwardly, but had no comfort to give.

Panna stood at the railing of the catwalk. Ballad was just behind her, his hands on her waist and his wings wrapped around them both. She could still see down into the cargo hold, but her peripheral vision was full of white feathers. Panna smelled the leather of Ballad's jacket. The glass armor was an honor, he said, but too stiff and clunky to wear around the overcrowded Blue Phoenix. Panna felt Ballad's warm breath on the back of her neck.

"Hard to believe that in four more days, none of this may exist anymore," he said.

The Arcadians down below didn't seem to notice them, or at least were too busy with their own thoughts and errands to pay the knight and the wingless girl any mind. Panna brushed the back of one hand against Ballad's wing.

"We won't be here to notice anything wrong," she said, shaking her head. "Neither of us would have been born if the White Kingdom never fell."

Ballad tightened his arms around Panna.

"Maybe there would be some variation," he suggested. "Both of our parents are older than the part of history that Xartasia wants to chop out, yeah?"

"Yes, but would those people be us?" Panna wondered. "I would still have wings. You would never have been a knight."

"How do you know?" Ballad asked. "I'm a damned good knight."

"The best, if you ask me. But Avadain isn't a noble name," Panna said. "You don't have any house colors. There's no way you would be a knight."

"I would still find you."

Panna laughed and turned to face the Prian fairy. "One unimportant girl somewhere in a kingdom that spanned five planets?"

"Five planets?" Ballad asked. "Damn. I didn't know Arcadia was so big."

Panna smiled ruefully. "I don't think your chances of finding me would be very good."

"I could do it."

"Even if you could, I wouldn't be me," Panna said. "If I was born at all, I wouldn't be the same woman you know. If Xartasia does this, she'll erase our whole existence. That's the point."

Ballad kissed her fiercely.

"Fine," the young knight growled against her lips. "But I would try. Maybe I'd fail, but I'm not giving up without a fight. Let Xartasia ruin and reset the last century. I'll fight her all over again."

"You may be the most stubborn man I've ever met," Panna said.

Ballad grinned and she yanked him down the corridor toward the bunks. He elbowed the door controls and pulled her into the room. Panna grabbed him with her own stubborn ferocity.

"Whatever else happens," she whispered, "I'm glad I met you, Ballad Avadain."

Duaal sat in the cockpit. One of his legs hung over the arm of the pilot's chair. He scanned idly over the instrumentation, but everything was running smoothly. After their long flight to the Tower, the jump to Axis seemed almost... routine. How many times had he and Tiberius made this same flight? Duaal ran his hand over the worn armrest of the pilot's chair and missed the grumpy old Prian.

There was a soft knock at the cockpit door. Duaal didn't look up.

"Three days," he said. "We'll be landing in three more days."

Duaal announced their updated arrival time every morning and evening, but it didn't stop the curious Arcadians from asking. They were all counting down their remaining hours, Duaal supposed.

Imminent death or incarceration had an odd effect on people.

"I know," Xia said from the door. "I heard you this morning."

Duaal looked up. "Sorry. I thought you were one of the fairies."

"Can I come in?"

"Sure."

Xia sat down in the copilot's chair. It was strange to see anyone there besides Logan. Duaal giggled to himself. It was even stranger to think of being used to Logan Coldhand. But the truth was that Duaal liked having the Prian hunter on his ship. And not just because of the view when Logan left the showers.

"What's so funny?" Xia asked.

"Nothing," Duaal said with a wave of his hand. "Just thinking about boys. Since Maeve is back in the bunk with Logan, you don't think that Anthem would be interested, do you?"

"Anthem?" Xia repeated, blinking her colorful compound eyes. "Anthem Calloren? He doesn't seem like your type."

"Why not?"

"Anthem's a good man. He's gentle and polite. You don't usually go for that type."

Duaal laughed again, a little louder this time.

"I suppose not. But you changed my taste more than a bit," he said and then gave Xia a more serious look. "Thanks for that."

The Ixthian smiled and curled her short antennae. "It was my pleasure."

"I hope you mean that."

Xia nodded and then paused before speaking again.

"Three more days?" she asked.

"Yeah."

"Are the other ships keeping up?"

"The O'Collin had some kind of pump failure, but they're back on schedule," Duaal answered. "The Zhan and the Starfire are both claiming fuel issues. But I bet my nonexistent pay that they're just trying for some more money. The Xol-tan is having computer problems and they're running about an hour behind."

"I wonder if that hour will get them killed or save their lives," Xia said.

Her eyes were a deep, dark blue that Duaal did not often see. He put a hand on her knee.

"You don't need to do this," Duaal said. "You could have stayed in Kaellisem. Hells, they probably could have used your help. You're the only doctor in the whole city."

"If Xartasia pulls this off, Kaellisem will never have existed. I might not, either. There are billions of people living now that–"

"But *you* don't need to do this," Duaal said. "One Ixthian medic isn't exactly going to get CWAAF riled up and out into the field. You know that."

"I do," Xia answered. She sat back in Duaal's old seat and stared out at the rainbow stars. "I thought about staying. Kessa offered me their spare room. I almost accepted."

"Why didn't you?"

Xia turned to look at Duaal. "You're not leaving after the Arcadians get off the Blue Phoenix, are you? You're going with them to face the Alliance and fight Xartasia."

"Of course."

"Why?"

Duaal opened his mouth to answer, but couldn't find the words. How could he *not* fight? It wasn't just his own life that would be unwoven like cheap cloth, but the lives of billions. No matter how petty and selfish Duaal was at times, what kind of man would he be if he just... let that happen?

Xia was still watching him. She put her feet against the bottom of the console and wrapped her arms around her knees.

"I know," she said. "Me, too. I don't know what the future may hold, but..."

Duaal nodded "But we're not about to let Xartasia take away our right to that future."

"Even if that means prison or death?"

"Well, you know me," Duaal said. He picked an imaginary speck of dust from his red velvet sleeve. "I don't do anything halfway. If the world's going to end, I don't just want front-row seats. I want to be up on stage."

Logan stroked Maeve's hair. There were more white strands in the black now, forming silvery streaks at both her temples. Far more eloquent marks of her queenship, Logan thought, than her glass crown had ever been. Maeve's gray eyes fluttered open.

"How long?" she asked.

"Twenty-seven hours until we reach the edge of Axial space," Logan answered. "Three hours more until we get to the planet."

Maeve brushed her fingers against Logan's stubble-roughened cheek.

"One more day," she said. "Only one more."

Logan caught Maeve's hand and kissed it. "I would rather have one day with you than my whole life without you."

Maeve smiled, but the queen's gray eyes shone with tears. The only light was the shifting, multi-hued radiance of the stars racing by outside the Blue Phoenix. Spots of color played across Maeve's graceful, naked body like dancing butterflies.

"Is this truly the only way?" Maeve asked. It wasn't the first time and Logan wished he could give her a different answer.

"We can face Xartasia directly," he told her. "But she's got better numbers and we're barely armed. The Devourers will massacre your people, dove. And that doesn't even take into account any of her own people that are in fighting shape. We know she has some. Remember Calathan."

"I do." Maeve sighed and pulled herself into Logan's lap. Neither of them wore anything but starlight. "I do not fear death, enarri."

"I know, dove." Logan kissed her and traced her delicate spine with one hand. "You're afraid for the Arcadians we're bringing with us. This shouldn't be their fight."

"But it is." Maeve bowed her head and placed her small hands over the twisted scar in the center of his chest. "It is your fight and ours. It is the entire galaxy's fight. We must convince the Alliance of that, even if it costs us our lives."

Logan kissed Maeve again. He didn't want to die, not when life felt like this – his heart racing in his chest, his whole body aflame with desire, when it tasted like Maeve's lips against his. A year ago, he would not have given death a second thought. When life meant nothing, neither did death.

But now life was full of tears and longing, fears and joys. Now that Logan didn't want to die, he probably would. Maeve may not have feared death... But Logan Coldhand finally did.

"I don't ever want to leave you again," he told Maeve. "Never. I love you."

"And I love you, my hunter," she said. "I will never give you up again. I will give my life, but never you."

———————•—•—•———————

Anthem Calloren knelt alone in the darkness. Tomorrow, the Blue Phoenix would reach Axis. Tomorrow, so would Xartasia.

Titania, my love.

My enarri.

My enemy.

A single lock of black hair lay curled in his hands.

● ● ●

Smoke rose up from the White City. Queen Titania Cavainna pointed a single pale finger at the black plumes. The knights closest to the throne flinched visibly. Their glass armor was smeared in ash and darkening red blood.

"How have they breached the imperial city?" Queen Titania asked in a ringing voice. "Have you lost control of the Waygates?"

"No, my queen," Sir Syle said. "But the dryads know the land better than our knights. They march even now on the city's heart."

"What of the west shore?"

"The nyads are massing in the river," Syle told her. "We cannot fight them at that depth."

The fairy queen rose suddenly from her birchwood throne. Her red-trimmed golden armor glowed like flame. Aes' bright light smoldered in her glass crown and violet eyes.

"Cavain's empire has endured for ten thousand years," she declared. "The dryads and nyads will not tear down our towers! They will die on our spears and blades. I will finish what divine Cavain began. These sons of stone and daughters of water will join the pyrads in death. The White Kingdom will belong to the aerads alone! We are the only Arcadians. This is our world and we will not give it up!"

Syle rose with a shout and banged his spear against the white flagstones. A hundred thousand knights echoed his drumbeat, filling Illisem with thunder. Titania seized her spear, trimmed all along its length with red ribbons that made the weapon look like it was dripping with blood.

She raised the spear over her head. A hot, smoky wind lashed her long hair into twisting streamers just like the smoke. The dryads had numbers and knew the land, but only Arcadians had armor and weapons stronger than wood. The nyads could not hide in their rivers and lakes forever. When they emerged, they would find the Arcadians waiting with sharp glass.

Tears burned like acid in Titania's eyes. Anthem Calloren's rebellion would follow him into death. The queen of Arcadia had already killed her enarri's new lover and her brother, slain Maeve and Caith with her own hands. Thieves and rebels and traitors all... Now Titania would finish the job. They would die. She would reduce the White Kingdom to ashes, if she had to, but those ashes would be hers.

Queen Titania spread her wings and leapt up into the air, leading her people to war.

[39]
AXIS

"Welcome back to Axis. Our home away from scattered homes."

- TIBERIUS MYLES (232 PA)

Commander Kharos jumped down from the CWAAF shuttle before the bullet-shaped landing craft had even shut down its engines. A private jogged across the empty street toward him. The young Axial streamed sweat in his green body armor. He jerked to a halt and saluted.

"What's the situation?" Kharos asked. Behind him, the rest of Ground Team 288 poured out of the shuttle.

"We've got about a thousand Arcadians gathered in thela sector. There are a few CWA citizens with them – an Ixthian, a couple of humans – and some other huge thing we've never seen before."

Commander Kharos shouldered his laser rifle. "Hmm. Hostages maybe. Are the Arcadians armed?"

"Some of them, sir," the ensign said. "Less than five percent, we count. Isn't Central kind of overreacting?"

"We'll find out. What do they want?"

"We were hoping you could tell us, sir."

"Did you clear the streets?"

"No, sir," said the ensign. "They did."

Kharos nodded. He raised his hand to the rest of his team. They jogged together down the road. Axis' bright sun gleamed brilliantly from the graceful glass and steel of starscrapers. The street running between them was eerily empty. But not quiet – the pale blue afternoon sky was full of stars and a mechanical flock of fighters and helicopters.

A glowing yellow wireframe lit up across Kharos' display from the computer in his helmet and projected across his polycarbonate visor. A blinking arrow pointed the way to thela sector. Kharos and his team turned between a pair of needle-shaped business spires, their boots pounding against the white concrete sidewalk. There were delicate-looking green and pink bushes planted to either side that did little to disguise the huge vents in the ground that funneled processed air up to Level One. The shrubbery rippled in the artificial breeze.

The corporate starscrapers parted almost suddenly as Kharos followed the glowing arrows on his display overlay and he found himself running through the lavender shadows of expensive condominiums and penthouses. Arrows flashed and they came around another corner. Thela sector. That was not what the locals called it, of course. A tall, thick wall ran along the road's far side and the tall steel gate stood open. Kharos could just make out black blastphalt beyond. Haven Field, the only private landing field in this part of Level One, Kharos' computer informed him.

There were the Arcadians. The road was full of them. Hundreds of the alien fairies stood in rows, filling six lanes with small bodies and white wings. It was difficult to count them through the overlapping feathers, but Kharos' computer was making quick work of the task, picking out targets in the crowd and marking them with green crosshairs. The targeting computer recognized the other CWAAF transponders and superimposed red silhouettes over each of the other soldiers to prohibit friendly fire. There were two thousand, four hundred and thirty-eight Alliance soldiers surrounding thela sector, according to the readout that popped up at the corner of Kharos' vision. More than twice as many as there were Arcadians in the large road. He swiped the information away with a flick of his gloved hand.

The ensign had been right... Only a handful of the fairies were armed. Even fewer wore armor – suits of plastic or glass platemail that Kharos had never seen before. No matter. Commander Kharos keyed up the audio controls and switched over to general broadcast.

"Attention. This is an illegal assembly," Kharos announced. His voice echoed inside his own helmet and boomed from the circling aircraft. "Surrender yourselves and we can end this now, before anyone gets hurt."

One of the Arcadians stepped out of the crowd. Kharos magnified his view. She was a tiny thing, with white-streaked black hair that didn't seem in keeping with her pretty, youthful face. She wore more of the strange glass armor and carried a spear. A larger group followed a step behind. One of them was another Arcadian. This one was a man, also armored, with long hair worn in braids that fell nearly to his waist.

There were some humans, too: a Hyzaari kid, a slender blonde girl and a much larger man, probably from Cyrus or Prianus. There was something terribly wrong with his left arm. Below the elbow, it was ghostly transparent and threw a halo of rainbows onto the road at his feet. Kharos spotted the Ixthian that the ensign mentioned, too – a woman carrying a white satchel over one shoulder marked with a medic's quartered circle.

The last member of the strange group moved down the road reluctantly and nervously, but looked like nothing Kharos had ever seen before. He – the creature seemed to be male – was even taller than the Hadrian commander and nearly twice as wide. The alien monster wore oversized pants and a shirt stretched tight across his massive shoulders. Where his skin showed, it was a rough-looking brown just a few shades lighter than Kharos' own – except for the creature's thick forearms, which were covered in a shaggy coat of green fur. He had long ears and a wide mouth that sagged into a frown at the corners.

"My God," Kharos gasped. He was still broadcasting. The words echoed across thela sector.

The black-haired Arcadian woman raised her spear. Kharos and a thousand other soldiers snapped their weapons up and aimed at her, but she did not seem fazed. White ribbons streamed from the fairy's upraised weapon. A white flag, maybe? Was she surrendering? Kharos closed back down to a private band and told the rest of his team to keep sights on the Arcadian. He lowered his own rifle and strode cautiously closer.

She stood in the center of the street. Processed air rumbled up from deeper within Axis's massive superstructure, stirring the Arcadian woman's dark hair around her shoulders.

"Is this your surrender, miss?" Kharos asked.

"No," she said. Her voice was heavy but musical. "I am afraid I cannot. Not yet."

"Who are you?" Kharos asked. "What are you doing here? Is this some sort of protest?"

That seemed unlikely. The Lyceum was almost halfway across Axis. Why would these Arcadians be protesting thousands of miles away from the legislature? The tiny winged woman shook her head and then glanced back at the Hyzaari boy in the elaborate clothes. He nodded.

"My name is Maeve Cavainna. I am queen of these people," she said. "We are here to fight, but not against the Alliance."

She hadn't raised her voice, as far as Kharos could tell, but the sound of it suddenly surrounded him and seemed to fill the whole city block. There were shouts and shocked cries. Several CWAAF soldiers looked up, searching for the source of the voice they all heard so clearly. The Hyzaari kid just smirked. Kharos snapped his rifle up to point at the boy.

"Whatever it is you're doing, stop it," Kharos ordered.

The boy's mouth set into a grim line, but he did nothing. The Arcadian – Maeve – took a half step closer, still holding her spear aloft like a banner. Kharos swung his gun toward her. She stopped.

"Something terrible is coming," Maeve said. She glanced at the name and rank stamped into the plates of his green armor. "Commander Kharos, Xartasia is on her way to Axis and she brings the Devourers. There is a Waygate far below us, commander, on your planet's surface. If Xartasia reaches it, she will unmake you all."

Kharos stared. Was the fairy girl insane?

He spoke into his helmet com. "Carson, you and Sanders get on the line with sector police. Find out what they know about this."

"Yes, sir," Carson answered.

Maeve watched Kharos and he held out his hand.

"Hand over the spear, Miss Cavainna," he instructed. "You and all your friends are coming with us."

Maeve stepped back, an unhappy expression on her face, and Kharos raised his rifle again. The armored fairy man spread his wings and whipped his own spear to one side. The human with the strange hand – it seemed to be glass as well, Kharos thought – drew his big, ugly laser pistol from a hip holster in a blur of motion.

A warning light blinked in the corner of Kharos' display as two thousand guns aimed at Maeve and her little band. Kharos was in the line of fire. He pulled back, bracing his rifle against his shoulder. The big ogre thing flinched and then glared at Kharos.

"Please stop!" he shouted in a shockingly boyish voice. "Xartasia is coming! She's already wiped out Arborus. She'll turn your entire planet into a ruin and then just erase you!"

"Easy there, big guy," Kharos said. "Nothing like that is going to happen. There doesn't have to be any bloodshed if you and your friends just put down your weapons. Hold it!"

This last was directed at another Arcadian man. He appeared to be wearing black scarves and strips of leather under his glass armor and had been side-stepping his way slowly around Kharos. The fairy scowled and made a gesture with the hand not holding a spear that Kharos assumed was supposed to be obscene.

"We cannot stand down," Maeve said with terrible finality. "Xartasia must not reach Level Ten. You will be ready to do battle with her, Commander Kharos, one way or another."

The Arcadian woman spun her spear and leveled it at Kharos. He hooked his finger over the trigger of his sleek silver rifle.

"Don't do this, Miss Cavainna," Kharos told her. To his surprise, he found that he meant it. She was obviously suicidal, but Kharos didn't want to kill the strange fairy woman. "Everything will be fine if you all just come with me."

Maeve didn't answer. Instead, she shared a lingering glance with the human man by her side. His pale blue eyes were hard, but he nodded once. One thousand Arcadians murmured musically, but didn't run or fly away. Largely unarmed and unarmored, they stood their ground as CWAAF soldiers inched closer, lasers held ready to burn them down where they stood. Some of the Arcadians held hands or embraced each other. An old fairy man was down on one knee in the road, apparently praying.

What the hells were they doing? Kharos could not guess, but it was not his job to question. His orders were to round up the Arcadians and get them off Level One.

Did these fairies actually believe the lunatic things their queen said? Were they willing to die for her...?

"Get down on the ground," Kharos instructed on the broadcast channel. His order echoed through the street. "Hands and wings above your heads."

"Stand fast!" Maeve said. Her voice shook, but carried somehow to every single ear. "Fight to your last. We need every moment that our blood may buy."

The Hyzaari boy nodded grimly. His hands closed at his sides and then opened again, red-gold fire burning impossibly between his fingers. The blond Prian with the glass hand trained his laser on Kharos.

"Hurt Maeve," he said in a flat voice, "and you die first."

The other man's eyes were as cold as polar ice. Sweat beaded on the back of Kharos' neck and rolled down his spine, tickling under the layer of body armor. The warm, refined Level One air was taut with impending violence. A squadron of CWAAF fighters hovered overhead, ready to fly down any escaping fairies. It would be a bloodbath. The Arcadians were only committing elaborate suicide.

Kharos would have to act quickly. If he could take the Arcadian queen down, the rest might lose their nerve and let themselves just be arrested. But as soon as he moved, the three men would be on him. Kharos was certain that his body armor could easily withstand a broad swing from the Arcadian's spear, but a good thrust could probably punch between the reinforced plates. And that laser pistol in the Prian's hand might have been ugly, but it looked powerful. There was no way it would miss at this range.

"Aim for the entourage," Kharos instructed his team from the privacy of his own helmet. "I need that blond knight and the Prian down before Maeve hits the pavement."

"With pleasure, sir," Sanders said into his ear.

A green pinpoint of light appeared on Kharos' display and lit up in the center of the armored Arcadian male's glass-helmeted head. Sanders was an ass, but he was the best shot on Kharos' team. The virtual sight – invisible to anyone not wearing a CWAAF display – didn't waver. Somewhere in the distance, there was a deep booming sound. Kharos ignored it.

"On three," he told his team. "One, two–"

A red bar flashed insistently across Kharos' display. Incoming transmission. Urgent.

"Hold!" he barked, then swiped up the message with one glove.

"What the hells–?" Sanders shouted, loud enough to be heard outside his armor.

Maeve exchanged a wide-eyed look with her Prian.

"All teams, we've got an incursion in orlon sector of Level One!" a dispatcher shouted over the com channel. Not the same one who had called Kharos out to Haven Field. "Thena sector... another one – no, two – in cyron sector...! We've got one coming into thela, too!"

Thela sector? That was where Kharos and his team were now. He looked up, jerking his weapon with him. All he could see at first were fighter jets and helicopters circling wildly as they received the same broadcast. And then something boomed, shaking the ground and making sensors bleat inside the soldier's armor. A ship plummeted toward Axis. It was long, angular and absolutely black, like a tear right through the star-studded sky of Level One. But the blade-shaped ship streamed black smoke as it fell.

"Xartasia," Maeve said. She stared at the ship, too. "My cousin is here."

Kharos looked down at the fairy woman. She was only barely more than half his height.

"Is that what you were so afraid of?" Kharos asked. He pointed. "That ship is crashing. Look at the smoke!"

"That isn't smoke," the Prian said grimly.

Suddenly, the gray-black cloud changed. Kharos never figured out how exactly to describe it. The smoke went somehow... rigid. In an instant, it changed from a dark gas to something terribly solid, still spreading out through the clear, starry blue Axis sky. And then it split open like a monstrous black flower.

"What in the three hundred hells is that?" Kharos asked.

"A Devourer ship," the Prian answered.

Lines of darkness vomited out from the ship. The sinuous black filaments must have been halfway across thela sector, but Kharos couldn't stop staring. They twisted, writhing like impossibly huge snakes, and then speared toward the ground. Something dark rose from Axis' surface – real smoke this time. A moan loud rose from the street full of fairies and the soldiers surrounding them shifted their weight uncomfortably.

"Thela sector teams!" a dispatcher shouted into Kharos' ear, the same woman who had given him the first order to apprehend the Arcadians. "Does anyone have eyes on that... thing?"

"This is Sky Team 713," answered another voice. A pair of the fighters above had turned on their tails and soared off in the direction of the black ship. "We're approaching now..."

"We have civilian calls coming in all across the board," said the dispatcher. Commander Kharos heard more voices shouting in the background. "Local law enforcement is trying to get close, but that thing has punched right through the upstructure and down into Level Two."

The pair of CWAAF fighters were quickly dwindling specks in the azure sky, but one of the huge black tentacles was all too visible as it darted toward them. Something that big should *not* move so fast. The slithering spar of darkness slashed through the air and impacted. The two jet fighters exploded into shrapnel and momentary balls of red flame. Then there was only more smoke billowing into the sky, obscuring the silvery twinkle of the stars.

"Our enemy is here," said a quiet voice. It was Maeve Cavainna, the tiny fairy queen. She was in a low crouch, her wings spread and her spear clutched tightly. "You can waste your time trying to arrest us, Commander Kharos, or we can fight them together."

"Damn it," Kharos said. He switched his suit mic back to broadcast. "All teams, we're moving in on that landed ship. Arcadians, I can't spare the soldiers to detain you. If you're smart, you'll get the hells out of here."

"With all due respect, sir... What the hells?" Sanders asked over the team com channel. Kharos saw the lieutenant's targeting sight still centered on the armored Arcadian man. "We can't just let them go! These bird-backs aren't supposed to be here!"

Sirens sounded out across Level One. Kharos turned to Sanders, grabbing the younger soldier by the front of his green armor.

"That thing just swatted two of our fighters out of the sky like flies," Kharos shouted at him, not bothering with the microphone. "We've got bigger problems than a few fairies. Now move!"

"What about us?" asked the blond girl that Kharos had noticed earlier. "We want to help!"

"Axis is an Alliance world," Kharos said. "And we're the Central World Alliance Armed Forces. It's our job to protect this planet and that's what we're going to do. You just stay out of our way!"

Kharos clenched his gauntleted fist, sending the *move out* order to two thousand men. He turned on his booted heels and ran for the shuttle. The bladed black shadows spread like a storm across Axis' bright sky.

[40]

THE DEVOURERS

"Death is just your body running out of ammunition. So slam in a fresh battery and keep fighting!"

- VICTOR KHAROS (234 PA)

A squadron of shining silver Alliance fighters screamed through Axis' atmosphere toward the great black Glorious warship. Bizax hung suspended at the core, his nanite swarm linked out to the warship's weapons and sensors. The massive black ship was just an extension of his armor, a huge and devastating extension torn from the corpses of Alliance space stations, ships and fringe colonies, deconstructed and reconstructed by nanites to serve this purpose: to feed its Glorious masters.

Bizax's swarm raked the starry skies of Kahazzek – or Axis, as its new inhabitants called it, according to Xartasia – with huge midnight tentacles longer and thicker around than the buildings below. The approaching Alliance fighters broke formation and fired a wide spread of red lasers. Bizax saw it all without eyes, visual data transmitted directly from hundreds of thousands of sensors straight into his implanted computer. The defensive subroutines reacted at once, pulling the nanite armor into a glassy obsidian shield that refracted the lasers. And then Bizax sent the ravenous nanomachines after the Alliance pilots.

A tower of nanites split as it missed a starfighter, hooked around and lashed out at the retreating craft. It seized one wing, slicing into the quickly crumbling fibersteel, and then tore through the ship in search of meat. The pilot ejected as his fighter collapsed into fragments. He fell through the air for a moment before a twisting spear of nanites tore the human in half. The swarm pulled both pilot and ship apart and drew the dissolving matter back into Bizax's ship.

Another squadron of CWAAF fighters wheeled and swooped in for another pass, strafing Bizax's ship with another energy weapon: electromagnetic pulses. A wide grin split Bizax's gray face. These primitive evolutionary accidents were trying to disable the Glorious nanites with EMPs. They weren't the first species to try such tactics, but even the microscopic machines of the Glorious were hardened against all radiation. The Alliance's swift response was unexpected and useless, but it whetted the appetite.

The CWAAF ground forces massed on the surface of Level One. Lasers flashed far below Bizax, lending his black nanite swarm a hellish crimson glow. Bizax's ship compensated instantly, hardening the underside of the hull against the assault. The Alliance concentrated their fire on the front of Bizax's ship, trying in vain to overwhelm the black armor. Heat rose from the Glorious ship's hull in shimmering waves.

"Commander Dhozo," Bizax reported. His swarm transmitted the words across Axis. "I have encountered resistance."

Resistance wasn't part of the plan. There were only fifteen of the Glorious, each in the center of their own huge and hungry ship, all across Axis. The approach had been flawlessly silent, every Alliance spaceship and satellite transmission countered and jammed. The Glorious ships consumed the signals as greedily as flesh and metal. The unsuspecting population should have collapsed into panic and fear, just like millions of planets before them. An organized defense – however futile – was unexpected.

"Resistance?" Dhozo asked. "Details."

"Several thousand armed beings have amassed in my sector," Bizax said. "They're armed with lasers and EMPs."

"Can they damage you?"

Bizax hesitated.

"These are better prepared than the humans on Prianus," he admitted. "And there are many more. My swarm reads just over two thousand meat, three hundred ships and vehicles. Enough to overwhelm personal armor..."

A pair of Alliance starships lifted off from a walled landing field. Bizax slashed them from the air with an arcing blade of nanites two hundred feet long. The serrated black blade sawed through the hull and then slithered like shadowy roots through the terrible gashes, tearing the ship apart from within. But as Bizax consumed the two ships, one of the CWAAF fighter teams raced along his hull, raining down concussion missiles. Impacts rippled through Bizax's great nanite swarm, absorbing the explosions with minimal loss of materials. But there *was* loss...

The warship shuddered around its Glorious master.

"And perhaps a ship," Bizax admitted.

"Tarno, you're closest to Bizax's location," Dhozo ordered. The commander's voice fed directly into their brains. "Move in to reinforce him. Rhozan and Jahav, prepare to follow."

"Yes, sir," came the hissing, growling replies.

"Our primary infiltration has met little resistance," Dhozo said. "Continue the surface assaults. Destroy and consume everything in your path. The Glorious have waited long enough. Eat well."

"We've got to go, dove," Logan said. "Maeve, come on!"

He grabbed her wrist and pulled her away. Every nerve in her body sang to fly, to fight back against the Devourers. But Logan was right. The black ship sitting at the center of dozens of raking, blade-tipped tentacles and red laser beams was not the reason they had come to Axis.

"Yes. We must reach the Waygate before Xartasia does," Maeve agreed reluctantly. She turned to her people. "Find shelter now, my brave Arcadians! You have done what I asked of you and more! We have given the Alliance some chance against our enemy, however small."

She gestured behind her with one wing, up toward the Alliance fighters circling the Devourer ship, raining ordinance down on it. Flames bloomed and then were swiftly swallowed in black storms of nanites. The two thousand CWAAF soldiers that had surrounded Maeve and her Arcadians just minutes before were all shouting and scrambling to move in on the new threat. Transports swooped out of the sky and skidded across the road. Armored men and women leapt inside before they even landed, team leaders gesturing urgently to pilots in the direction of the spreading jet-black storm of the Devourer warship.

Maeve looked at her knights. Ballad and Anthem crouched low, spears gripped tightly as they stared after the scrambling Alliance warriors. Even during the fall of Arcadia, they had never faced such monstrous horrors. But each of Maeve's knights was ready to fight for Axis. She waved Panna over.

"Take our people and find somewhere safe," Maeve instructed over the noise of engines and boots on the pavement. "I wish to see no more Arcadian blood today. Duaal, we must reach Axis' surface quickly."

"Way ahead of you, Your Majesty," Duaal said. He grinned and jerked his thumb back at Haven Field. "Remember those ventilation pipes that went down to the illegal landing fields? The ones that Tiberius wouldn't let me fly?"

"Let's go," Logan said.

"There's no time like the present," Duaal agreed.

"Yes, there is!" Gripper said. His voice cracked with stark terror. "There's later! It's just like the present only... you know, later!"

Maeve laid a hand on Gripper's elbow, as high up his long arms as she could reach. "We must go."

There was no more time. Maeve glanced back once at her gathered people, but Panna was already shouting and organizing them much more efficiently than she ever could. Duke Ferris stood at her side. He scowled at the wingless girl, but didn't argue with her. Sir Anthem caught Maeve's eye and saluted, one wing folded across his chest. The other knights repeated the gesture.

"We are with you, my queen," Anthem said. "To whatever end awaits us."

Maeve saluted in reply. They ran back across the road, through Haven Field's gate to where the Blue Phoenix squatted on a gray blastphalt strip. Duaal opened the ship's cargo ramp with a wave of his hand and sprinted up the steps to the main corridor. Logan was right behind Duaal, taking the stairs two at a time. Maeve flew up to the catwalk and followed them while Anthem arranged the knights in the Blue Phoenix's cargo bay.

Duaal jumped into the old pilot's chair. "Let's fly!"

Logan buckled himself securely into the copilot's seat and then toggled control of the Blue Phoenix to his station.

"This isn't a game, Duaal. Sit down and strap in," he said. "Just give me the location of those vents."

"What? Oh, come on!"

"Now!"

The Blue Phoenix rose, angling up into the crowded sky. The Devourer ship hung in the air above them like an inky hurricane. Its massive swarm blotted out the sun. The smoky clouds solidified into immense chains and ropy limbs, snatching ships out of the air and punching through formations of Alliance soldiers.

Maeve clung to the door frame, spreading her wings for balance as Logan banked the Blue Phoenix sharply. Her wings banged into the walls and Maeve staggered. Logan rolled the ship away from a tentacle as big around as a building, but a long, jet-black offshoot barb knocked the old freighter into a spiral. Logan fought to steady the Blue Phoenix.

Outside, Commander Kharos' soldiers fired up at the Devourer warship in regimented groups, coordinating their blasts against the boiling banks of dark armor. The Alliance had called out heavier weapons, too – laser canons and huge null-field rail guns, but they had little effect. The ordered fire was too predictable, too easy for the Devourers' computers to forecast and block. The hungry black warship didn't form lasers of its own, instead sending a black cloud of nanites into the streets that dissolved soldiers like acid. The CWAAF fighters above had switched from EMPs to lasers and null-field cannons, but their perfectly executed strafing runs met the same impenetrable defense.

Something flickered in the corner of Maeve's vision. She leaned over Logan's shoulder and squinted through the Blue Phoenix's old glassteel viewports. A monstrous black shadow loomed up on the horizon, long and predatory. Another Devourer ship was closing in on Kharos' position.

"Logan!" Maeve gasped, pointing.

"Damn it," he growled. "Duaal, I need the ship's com."

Duaal threw the switch to turn on the Blue Phoenix's intercom. "You're on."

"Gripper, I need you to do something. Those Alliance troops are wasting time they don't have," Logan said. A broken piece of fiber-steel cracked against the Blue Phoenix's hull and then bounced away before a glittering whip of black snatched it from the air. "Can you get into the military mainstream? Send them everything we learned about the Devourer's nanite armor and how to fight it."

"They wouldn't listen to us on Mir, Hunter. I don't think they're going to now," Gripper said.

"Then tell the computer you're a general or something!"

The curving rope of nanites finished its metal meal and then shot through the smoky air toward the Blue Phoenix again. Logan dove under it and between a pair of starscrapers. Debris rattled on the hull as the Devourer's huge tentacle slammed into and then through the building. Concrete, glass and thrashing bodies flew in every direction. The black swarm plucked struggling coreworlders from the wreckage and tore them to bloody rags. Maeve felt ill.

"Here!" Duaal said. His voice was strained and he stabbed one finger at a scuffed display. "We need to get down this vent!"

Maeve was Arcadian, born to fly, but even her stomach flipped as Logan banked sharply around a huge, shining pyramid of glass and steel, rolled the Blue Phoenix and then angled the nose down toward the ground. They plunged through the shadows between starscrapers, straight down through one of the layered skyways that connected Axis' levels. Null-inertia vehicles blared their horns and swerved around the starship diving between them.

A bridge suddenly rose up in front of them. Duaal gasped and Logan yanked the controls, jerking the Blue Phoenix to the side. He angled around the bridge and gaping pedestrians clutching the rails, then dropped again.

"There!" Duaal shouted.

Steam and swirling gasses billowed from a circular opening in the floor of Level Two. Logan nodded. His glass hand left dents in the yoke as he arced the Blue Phoenix up over control and security pylons, and then plunged down into the ventilation shaft. Darkness swallowed the Blue Phoenix.

Panna could still taste Ballad's kiss on her lips. *Be careful, dove,* he had told her. She really hoped that was still an option.

With Duke Ferris' help, Panna managed to get the other Arcadians back into Haven Field. Logan had paid the Lyran manager a fortune in phenno and now a pair of wolfin technicians slammed the gates shut behind the retreating fairies as the street outside filled with running, screaming people. Panna didn't have the heart to tell the techs that their gate wouldn't help at all, but she grabbed the sleeve of the nearest Lyran.

"We need one of your hangars," she told him. Panna shouted to make herself heard over the noise. "The biggest and strongest that you've got."

"Yeah, yeah," the jumpsuited Lyran answered. "Hangar A. It's over there."

He pointed distractedly to a huge hemispherical building on the other side of the main runway. Panna nodded.

"Gather everyone you can and get in there with us!" she said.

"What?" the tech asked. "Why? CWAAF is out there, lady. We'll be fine."

"The Alliance has no idea what they're facing out there," Panna said. "Those are the Devourers, the aliens who destroyed the White Kingdom and Arborus. And this is their homeworld!"

A vast black shadow fell over Haven Field as the Devourer ship rose up, tentacles spreading like colossal snakes preparing to strike. The Lyran stared.

"Arianna won't like that," he whimpered.

"But she'll like being torn apart and eaten alive even less. So get everyone into that hangar!" Panna shouted to the tech. "And bring your welding gear. We're sealing ourselves in until this is over... one way or another."

———— ● ● ● ————

"Where the hells are the ships?" Kharos bellowed into his com. "We need bigger guns!"

Military lasers were exempt from the sound generator laws, but the explosions of missiles and the shriek of tortured metal as the alien ship tore starscrapers apart into shrapnel more than made up for that. Even through his helmet's filters, the cacophony of battle was deafening.

"The defense fleet is mobilizing now. Estimated arrival in seven minutes," came the barely audible response.

"We're not going to last seven minutes!" Kharos shouted.

"I'm sorry, sir! Those things are all over Axis and most sectors weren't as prepared as yours."

So far, Kharos and his soldiers had managed to contain the vast black ship inside thela sector, but the ship itself seemed invulnerable. The dark clouds that swathed the vessel hardened into glossy black shields under laserfire and CWAAF had yet to score anything like a critical blow. The dispatcher was right. It was the same all across Axis and the body count was rising swiftly. But not as high as it could have already been... It was lucky that Kharos had such a large force already assembled when the aliens attacked, able to get eyes and sensors on the threat and send information back to Central Command.

No. Not luck – the so-called Arcadian queen had known. She had lured CWAAF to arms.

A huge, glittering black spike plunged down from the sky and slammed deep into the side of an already buckling starscraper. The sharp limb spun like a drill into the building's side. Humans and Ixthians in expensive suits streamed from inside, many bleeding, and ran screaming toward the CWAAF soldiers.

The black spike – easily twice as long as Kharos was tall – fired out streamers of smoky darkness at the fleeing civilians. A pair of the shadowy tendrils seized a Mirran around the neck and waist. They began pulling the shrieking woman back. Kharos shouted an order and Ground Team 288 opened fire on the long black spine. They raked laserfire across the tendrils holding the Mirran woman. There didn't seem to be anything solid enough to damage, but the tentacles dropped their prisoner and snaked instead toward Kharos and his team.

"Shit!" he shouted. "Concentrate fire!"

Lasers burned through the air and into the black needle, but the thing's dark surface coalesced into smooth, glossy black armor.

A flagged report flashed up on Kharos' display. He almost waved it aside, but something there grabbed his attention. Targeting information, but not the sort of strike orders that the commander had ever seen before. It was a report from Central, stripped down to its essential information: these Devourers' ships and armor were made up of nanites controlled by a central computer, which could be confused by randomized and rapid fire. Enough unpredictable shots could open gaps in the otherwise impenetrable defenses.

"What the hells?" Kharos growled.

He didn't recognize the name tagged on the report – Admiral Anandrou Gripper – but it was *something*. Kharos snapped orders to the rest of Team 288. They spread out their fire across the black spike's glossy surface. The nanites swirled like oil, struggling to be everywhere at once, to predict the suddenly erratic laserfire. Kharos held the trigger down on his rifle and cut a wild zig-zagging pattern across the uneven armor. The lashing tentacles withdrew, retreating to cover the weapon's main body, but there weren't enough. Team 288 sliced the massive, writhing harpoon into several large chunks that fell to the ground in a seething, half-liquid form that burned deep into the concrete before finally going still.

"Spread out your fire!" Kharos ordered into his com. "Teams one through sixteen, randomize your attack patterns. Teams seventeen through twenty-five, take out any targets you can find!"

The unit commanders relayed orders to ground and air forces. Concentrated laser beams diverged and spread out over the ship.

CWAAF fighterss fanned out, ignoring their automated targeting systems. Razor-edged limbs whipped up from the huge black ship, cleaving a fighter in two before its ruptured engines exploded.

But the remaining Alliance fighters loosed their payload as they streaked past. The storm cloud of nanites condensed into a shield here and another there. Missiles exploded harmlessly against the slick black plates, but others flew into the cloud to detonate on the hull, scorching the metal. The giant blade of the Devourer battleship began to list and sag, red and orange flames blazing from inside like divine fire.

Cheers broke across all thela sector, ringing in Kharos' helmet com. He raised an armored fist and shouted, but there was another voice in his ear, almost drowned out by the elation of victory.

"What was that, Central?" Kharos asked. He muted the connection to the rest of thela sector. "Come again."

"You've got more hostiles incoming on your position. There are three more of those things flying into thela sector now!"

Kharos lifted his helmeted head skyward. The gathering clouds were turning stormy and dark overhead. No, not clouds... Devourer swarms. Even the sun vanished behind them, sinking the surface of Axis into artificial night.

Maintenance lamps glowed along the narrow shaft, but pipes and walkways blurred past faster than the lights could reveal them. The Blue Phoenix' artificial gravity yanked against the planet's and the ship lurched as Logan lifted it to clear a conduit jutting out across the disused shaft and then, just as quickly, he shoved the pointed nose down to avoid a cluster of broken pipes. Water streamed from them, out into the apparently bottomless shaft, and splashed off the ship as they hurtled straight down into the planet. Maeve's stomach clenched.

"Oh yeah!" Duaal shouted, a wild grin on his face. His hands raced over the computer controls, bringing up a rapid succession of layered plans and route information. Despite the grin, sweat poured down the young captain's dark skin. "Take this right... No, not that one... This one!"

Maeve wished she could share in Duaal's exhilaration. She had every confidence in Logan's piloting, but her thoughts were with the thousands dying up on the surface of Axis so far above. And on the trillions who would never live if Xartasia succeeded.

"Hurry, Logan," she said.

Her hunter nodded. He reached out and slammed the throttle down flat. The sub-light engines roared, shaking the Blue Phoenix like a trembling child.

Captain Soval leaned forward in his seat as his enemy came into view. The CWAS Stalwart's tactical displays had already acquired their target, but actually seeing it was something else entirely. A storm cloud hovered malevolently over thela sector. Dark, thick columns of glittering darkness stretched between the cloud and the surface like funnel clouds. Soval stared in disbelief as one of them touched a starscraper. The glass and alloy turned gray, and then cracks shot across the entire surface. The huge building crumbled under its own weight. Dust hurtled into the air, but the black cloud seemed to drink it up. It only grew darker and larger. Red lasers shot through the blackness like bloody lightning.

Somewhere in the middle of that mire was a ship, one of four now pouring lasers and alien weapons down onto Level One. And somewhere out there were seven other CWAAF cruisers, but Soval couldn't see any of them through the black Devourer storm.

"All gunners acknowledge new targeting instructions," Captain Soval said into the shipwide com. "Focus fire on the starboard side!

Concentrate the nanite shield there. All fighter groups launch and come around for an attack run on the port flank at my command."

One of the huge clouds turned toward the CWAAF starcruiser, flattening into a rectangle of armor and weapons twice the size of the huge Alliance battleship. Drifting black tentacles, vaster even than the starscrapers they tore apart, withdrew into the cloud as it lifted away from the surface to meet the Stalwart. Soval gripped the controls of the command chair. The ship vibrated as laser cannons and batteries of guns fired. The nanite cloud darkened into glossy patches of armor to intercept the beams and rounds.

"Gunnery crews two, four and six – cover our fighters!" Soval ordered.

Enormous barbed whips slashed at the squadrons of CWAAF fighters as they arced around to the black ship's far side. Lasers strobed, targeting the limbs and forcing them to contract into reflective shields. The fighter wing streaked past the tentacles, but the cloud was reacting to the Stalwart now. Billions of balefully glittering nanites gathered into massive spears that lanced out at the Alliance battleship.

"Brace for impact!" Soval shouted.

Proximity sensors counted down rapidly, but Soval couldn't tear his eyes from the viewports and the hard black lines streaking toward the ship. They struck hard, throwing the captain from his seat. Soval hauled himself to his feet as the scream of sundering fiber-steel filled the Stalwart and a warning klaxon blared.

"Gunnery crews five and seven, shoot those things the hells off us!" Soval ordered. "All other gunners, keep firing. Lieutenant Karn, you're clear to make your attack run!"

The smaller Alliance interceptors descended on the Devourer ship, firing missiles on the unprotected port side. The nanite spears puncturing the Stalwart thinned and then retracted, joining the shields that protected their ship. The black cloud shrank in on itself and Soval thought he could see the vessel itself now.

The Stalwarts' artillery batteries hammered the Devourer ship as it shifted resources to defend against the CWAAF fighters, and even the alien vessel itself seemed to be shrinking inside the nanite cloud. Soval called for confirmation. The Devourer ship was consuming itself, cannibalizing its own superstructure to feed the dark swarm. The Stalwart rocked from a flailing tentacle blow and then the limb dissolved as a spread of missiles attacked random points along its vast length. Flames vomited out from ragged holes in the ship's armor and the alien ship began to drop.

Police spacecraft swooped in, firing hundreds of grapple cables into the falling warship's sides to keep it from tumbling devastatingly to the city-world below. Its descent slowed and then halted.

"What is that?" Soval asked. He pointed out the viewport.

A slick black substance raced up the grapple lines. Nanites. The police interceptors jerked sharply. One by one, the Devourer vessel pulled them in. The shrinking cloud reached up as they drew close and then swelled as it swallowed the police fighters.

"Tell the police to cut those grapple lines immediately!" Soval barked. "Gunnery crews, recommence fire. We'll have to let it fall! Coms, talk to those cops! Tell them to evacuate the crash zone!"

"Sir, there's no way they can move that many people–"

"Just get them out of there!"

Logan raced the Blue Phoenix through the tunnels of Axis at full speed, scraping noisily past jutting obstacles. Constellations of red and amber lights lit up across the controls. Maeve heard a few oaths from the Arcadian knights in the hold echo up the corridor. There were louder ones from Duaal.

"Hey, that's my ship!" the Hyzaari captain shouted.

"What are those?" Maeve asked, pointing to the lights flashing across the cockpit.

"Proximity sensors," Duaal said. He followed it up with some of Tiberius' favorite curses.

Logan remained silent, his jaw clenched and icy eyes fixed on the darkness ahead. Other close scrapes had already smashed out exterior running lights and snapped off sensor spars, but the Prian didn't flinch.

The shaft ahead bent sharply as it neared a sprawling factory district. Maeve clutched at the back of Logan's chair, struggling to keep her feet as he pulled up on the yoke. The heavy aft of the ship bounced off the tunnel as it abruptly changed directions. The Blue Phoenix fell sickeningly down the ventilation shaft and then shot out of the open tunnel into the leveled old factory of the illegal landing field. The cargo freighter bounded across the cracked blast-phalt once and then came to a skidding halt.

"This is as far down as we can fly," Logan announced.

"Thank God," Duaal said.

Maeve sprinted back down to the hold before the Blue Phoenix had stopped rocking. There were illegal landing fields as far down as Level Seven, she recalled. Which meant that there was still a long way to go before reaching the surface and Xartasia's Waygate.

Anthem already had the knights up on their feet. They checked their weapons and tightened the knotted cords of their glass armor. Maeve leapt from the catwalk and glided to the floor of the cargo bay. Anthem handed over her spear with a short nod. He raised one wing and formed the knights up behind Maeve. She clutched her spear nervously.

Heavier footsteps announced the arrival of the rest and Maeve turned to find Logan, Duaal, Xia and Gripper all hurrying down the stairs.

"Now we must fly into battle," Maeve said. "Gripper, Xia, you have already done more than I could ever ask. You have been better friends than I have deserved. You are not warriors and you need come no further."

Xia adjusted the strap of her medical bag to make sure that it was clear of her laser pistol. "You said you're going into battle. That means people are going to get hurt. You'll need a doctor."

Maeve looked up at Gripper, the huge alien that had become the little brother she lost so long ago. He wrapped his arms around himself, rocking back and forth on callused feet.

"Maybe we'll all die trying to stop Xartasia, Glass," Gripper said. "Maybe I'll never even be born. If this is all we have left, then I just want to be with my friends at the end. I'm coming with you."

"Your knights stand ready, a'shae," Anthem said.

Maeve nodded without trusting herself to speak. Glass armor chimed as her gathered warriors stood at attention. Duaal pounded the button and the cargo ramp lowered. The landing field outside held only a couple of ships and a dozen people milling around near them. Maeve wondered if they knew anything about the war raging high above. A lean Lyran stalked across the blastphalt toward them.

"What kind of landing was that?" he barked. "Who the hells are you people? Your ship is leaking all over my field!"

"I am sure that we can work out some sort of–" Anthem began.

Logan strode past him and launched his glass fist into the Lyran's snout. Blood spurted and the Lyran fell back. He cupped his hands over his nose and curled into a whimpering ball on the blastphalt.

Maeve turned toward her tiny army. "We must find the Waygate before Xartasia. Somehow."

"Maeve, I think I can feel the gate," Duaal said. He squinted his eyes and cocked his head, trying to focus on a sense that relied on neither sight nor hearing. "I'm the greatest expert on the Waygates in the galaxy, remember?"

"How far away are we?" Xia asked. "Axis is a big planet, even this far down."

"We'll need a car," Duaal answered, eyes still closed. "We're four or more sectors away and several levels too high."

Logan knelt over the fallen Lyran and pulled a keycard from the man's pocket.

"Which one is yours?" he asked.

"Get bit!" the Lyran snarled weakly.

Logan brandished his glass fist again and the Lyran whimpered. "The... the red Gallex behind the office."

Maeve thanked the Lyran, but he didn't seem to be listening to her. She sighed. If any of them managed to survive the next few hours, Maeve hoped they could return and make amends, but she was not optimistic. She turned to Duaal.

"Show us the way," Maeve said.

Logan drove the dented red Gallex around the corner. Gripper, Xia and Duaal jumped inside. Maeve and the rest of the Arcadians spread their wings and leapt into the air, beating their wings hard to keep up as Logan raced down the dirty streets of Level Seven.

Captain Soval ordered the Stalwart back, circling in a holding pattern with the Starfire and the Shimako. He hated to give ground, but the fleet needed time to rearm and refuel. They had destroyed three of the monstrous black ships, but their missiles and ammunition were down to critical levels and Central Command just notified them of five more Devourers closing in on thela sector. Two other CWAAF battleships and their fighters had taken down another one in carce sector, but the Thalion, the Vanguard and the Vanoran Pride had been destroyed.

The Vanguard still smoldered down below, the remaining black Devourer ship crawling all over it even now, tearing the Alliance battleship into pieces and rebuilding itself from the corpse before Soval's eyes. Kharos' ground teams poured across the blasted cityscape to suppress the downed alien ships, but they were taxed to the limit and too far away from the Vanguard.

"Hold your fire and conserve power as long as you can," Soval commanded.

Outside, the ominous black cloud rolled over the remains of the Vanguard and Soval had to suppress the urge to call down to the hangar deck for yet another status check. The Devourer's ship had already restored thirty percent of its lost mass. The air around it shimmered with heat and toxic gasses, by-products of rapid metal processing. Black nanites billowed out like an inky fog bank and then the ship was in the air again. Dark patches solidified across the surface of the Devourer's craft.

"Sir," a young Lyran lieutenant called out. "They're targeting the Starfire!"

In the blink of an eye, ten tons of glittering black nanites had assembled themselves into a battery of laser cannons and molten red destruction lanced out at the Starfire. The CWAAF ship shook as the Devourer lasers boiled away ablative armor and found the vulnerable points beneath.

The CWAS Shimako swept around in a tight arc, but couldn't bring enough weapons to bear in time. The eerie alien vessel was on the Starfire like a pouncing cat and wrapping huge appendages around the other ship. Crushing and consuming it.

"All stations fire, random targets," Soval said. "We're out of time! Launch whatever fighters we've got!"

The Stalwart circled the huge alien vessel, gun batteries roaring to life and adding their deadly energy to the already superheated air. Alliance fighters hurtled from the hangar bay and began their bombing run along the enemy ship. The Devourer's lasers pivoted impossibly fast and raked all down the Stalwart's port side. Captain Soval called for a damage report.

"Main engines damaged. Gun batteries one, two, seven, eight, and ten are nonoperational."

"Captain Soval!" a woman at the helm called out. "The enemy ship is on a collision course!"

The Starfire fell in huge, flaming pieces across Level One and the black ship hurled itself at the Stalwart. The angular ship's prow opened like a giant's mouth, complete with teeth the size of fighter jets.

"Full reverse!" Soval shouted.

The Stalwart fired massive thrusters, shattering glass for a mile across the city below, but too slow. The enormous black warship swept through the storm of laser beams and null-inertia rounds. The nanite cloud deflected everything the damaged cruiser could throw at it. The fighters were still making their first pass, firing the last of their missiles in an effort to stop the alien vessel. Soval was dimly aware of someone telling him that the Shimako was firing all weapons, but it was too late.

The dark nanite cloud reared up until Soval could see nothing but darkness outside the forward viewports. And then monstrous teeth came down, shearing through the middle of the Stalwart.

Something slammed through the viewports and glassteel shattered into a thousand sharp splinters. Black nanite tendrils crawled through the widening cracks, splitting into smaller tentacles and then fanning out. Soldiers scrambled for the bridge hatchway, but hooks and blades sank into their flesh and dragged the screaming crew from the shattered bridge.

Soval tore his sidearm from its holster and leapt to his feet. He braced his laser pistol with both hands and held down the trigger, bellowing his defiance. The Stalwart's captain was still screaming when the nanite blade cut both legs out from under him. Horrified, Soval watched his own severed limbs bounce and roll across his bridge. Alien smoke wrapped around them, dissolving flesh and muscle and bone. Eating them.

The black cloud descended on Soval and the universe exploded into raw red pain.

"Report."

"We have encountered much heavier resistance than expected, Commander Dhozo. Bizax, Chovvad, Rhozan and Jarhav are dead. I have received no transmissions from Silex or Ulazzar. Tekker has engaged three of the damaged Alliance vessels, but has sustained heavy damage."

"Cannibalize Tekker's ship," Dhozo said. "All remaining units, converge on Tarno's position and hold the Alliance there. We have reached the planet's surface. Soon, this will be over and then we will never be hungry again."

[41]

KAHAZZEK

"Life is worth dying for."

- XIA (234 PA)

With the rest of the Glorious assaulting Kahazzek far above, Dhozo and Xartasia met little resistance as they moved down toward the planet's long-buried surface. While the sky of Axis burned with nanites and lasers, they landed in an unremarkable stolen Starwind bulk freighter. The ship was slow and unwieldy, inferior in every respect to the Devourers' but for its anonymity.

And its size. The hauler was large enough to move twelve thousand of Xartasia's aerads, if not in comfort. But as their queen reminded them, pain meant nothing. Soon, none of it would ever have happened.

As soon as they set down on a Starwind manufacturing block on Level Six, private security tried to stop the unwelcome *bird-backs*. The Starwind guards protecting their factory were numerous, but poorly prepared for what faced them now.

Dhozo, Orix and Zhyress fed well, and now reaching Kahazzek's surface was a simple matter of their nanite swarms eating their way through the artificial upper crust of the ancient homeworld. Twelve thousand aerads flew down behind them, a blizzard of wings that sang their victory over the world that had rejected them.

Level Ten of Axis was a tangle of darkened streets, full of trash and humans that came closer when they saw the Arcadians – easy pickings – then fled screaming into the shadows when they caught sight of Dhozo. The Glorious engineer ignored them and consulted his cross-referenced maps. He pointed to a dark, dilapidated motel. Most of the windows were already broken, but a handful of frightened faces peeked out from behind the shattered, dusty glass.

"This is the thinnest spot near the old Projector," Dhozo said. "Cut through here."

Xartasia's fairies filled the filthy street, standing wing to wing, but they found the room to flinch back as Orix and Zhyress tore the building and its inhabitants apart to carry out Dhozo's order.

Duaal led the way, following some sense that Logan did not understand. He pointed to one road and then another. They raced down spiraling ramps that led further into the ancient megatropolis. They were on Level Eight now, searching for a route down that wasn't collapsed or closed off for repairs.

Logan turned their stolen car down another ramp. There were glowing barriers set up on this one, too, warning of some far-future resurfacing endeavor. Logan drove over the warning lights. Gripper looked back once, but didn't complain. The red Gallex bumped and shuddered along the uneven road. It really did need work... Sparks flew and metal squealed in protest as the road scraped along the car's undercarriage.

Logan spared a glance up at Anthem. The knights flew a mobile perimeter around Maeve, soaring above and laboring to keep pace with the car.

What would Anthem do when they confronted Xartasia? Could he bring himself to fight or kill the woman he still loved? If their positions were reversed, could Logan do the same to Maeve...? He didn't think so. It might damn him and a hundred years of history, but without Maeve none of that had any meaning at all.

The descent ramp finally let out into the dark, filthy streets of Level Nine. A group of even more dented cars raced past, ignoring the red-lit traffic signal. Duaal told Logan to keep going straight, but then waved his hand.

"Stop!" Duaal shouted. "Stop here!"

Logan hit the brakes and then jumped out of the car, pocketing the keycard. Chances were slim that he would have much use for it later, but Logan Coldhand always planned ahead. He whistled to Maeve and the Arcadian queen landed, surrounded by her knights in glass.

"This is it," Duaal said. "Now we just need to find a way down through to the surface."

"Gripper?" Maeve asked.

The Arboran pulled out his computer and shook it a few times. "Mainstream signal is pretty weak down here. Give me a minute..."

"We may not have it," Maeve said. "Please, work quickly!"

Gripper chewed his lip and didn't waste energy on an answer. He turned the computer this way and that, then pointed off down the street.

"This way, I think," Gripper told Maeve. "There should be an access shaft... According to the mainstream, it's left over from some old construction."

"Move," Logan said.

They sprinted the direction Gripper had pointed and finally found the pitted metal hatch half-buried by trash and generations of lumapaint gang tags. Logan and Gripper strained to lift the metal door, but if it were that easy, the hatch would have been pried up long ago.

Logan waved everyone back and set his Talon-9 on a continuous beam. He drained half of a battery cutting through the thick metal, and then Ballad and Anthem grabbed the still-glowing edges of the hatch in their gauntleted hands, heaving it free. There was a ladder built into the side and Logan began climbing.

It was a long descent down through the metal that made up the floor of Level Nine. Every level of Axis felt huge and stable, a world unto itself. But they kept moving down deeper and deeper. How long would it take to reach the surface? Would Xartasia already be done by the time Logan finally felt dirt beneath his feet? A war raged up on Level One, but down here, it was impossible to tell.

They climbed through abandoned maintenance ducts, tunnels full of pipes and wires and ancient, darkened computer terminals. Stinking, slimy things grew in the darkness that didn't invite closer inspection. The Arcadian knights hummed uncomfortably, unable to use their wings in the tight confines, but not one of them complained.

Finally, Gripper curled his blunt claws around a cover painted over in peeling yellow warnings and lifted the heavy grate out of the way. Duaal crawled to the edge and peered over into the pitch-black emptiness.

"We have to get down there," he said. The mage's voice echoed faintly.

Logan cracked a chemical light in his glass hand and dropped it. The pale green rod tumbled for several seconds and then stopped. It glowed like a tiny wound in the absolute darkness.

"That's too far to jump. We need to fly," Logan said. "And watch your footing when you land. I'm not sure what's down there."

A pair of fairy knights took Xia by each arm and flew her down. The rest helped those without wings, one by one. Six of the Arcadians labored to deliver Gripper down to Axis' dark surface. But Duaal simply stepped out and drifted as gracefully as if he had his own wings.

Logan drew his Talon-9 and a flashlight, holding it parallel to the barrel and sweeping the narrow yellow beam over Axis' long-abandoned ground. Maeve and a few of the fairy knights sang brief charms that conjured a pale, sourceless illumination.

Whatever the Devourers' ancient homeworld had been – jungle or grassy plains or mountains like Logan's own planet – there was little left of it now. The ground beneath Logan's feet was barren, stripped gray dirt and stone utterly devoid of life. Was it the Axials who had done this? Or the Devourers before them? Logan turned a searching circle, peering through the darkness.

"Which way?" he asked.

Duaal pointed into the deep, shapeless shadows and Anthem gestured with his wings, giving the knights the signal to move out. Logan followed, keeping close to Maeve. He felt their time ticking by, counted out by the mechanical metronome of his heart. Was Xartasia still on Level One with the Devourers? Or was she already down here on the surface? Logan found himself staring uselessly up at the distant floor of Level Nine as he wondered.

"Stop," Logan said just loud enough to be heard over the sounds of their footsteps and wingbeats.

Anthem whistled softly and the Arcadian knights extinguished their lights. Maeve leaned close to Logan.

"What is it?" she asked.

Logan pointed.

There was a large, ragged hole torn or melted through the floor of Axis overhead. The opening let in a weak but broad shaft of light from Level Nine. But that wasn't what had arrested Logan's attention – even the faint light sparkled off glass and lit white wings. Dozens of armored Arcadians perched in the shadow of a fibersteel stanchion so vast that several shining Level One starscrapers could have fit comfortably inside. They crouched among heaps of rubble and bare gray stone. At the edges of the rainbow reflections was a dark blot of swirling darkness. A Devourer.

"Duaal?" Logan asked.

"That's the way we need to go," the mage whispered.

"Xartasia is not with them," Maeve said.

"This can't represent her entire force. She recruited thousands of Arcadians for their memories. This is just her vanguard," Logan agreed. He looked down at Maeve. "We need to get you and Duaal through to the Waygate. If this thing has already begun, only you two have any idea how to stop it. We cut through as fast as we can and we don't stop."

"Can't we just go around?" Gripper asked.

Logan shook his head. "Not without losing time we don't have. They're covering Xartasia, which means she's nearby. By the time we avoid this group, she could be done unmaking half of Alliance history."

"Those knights outnumber us three to one," Xia gestured to the flat, dry ground. "And they'll see us coming."

"No," Duaal said. "They won't. Is everyone ready?"

The young mage didn't wait for anyone to answer. Duaal fell to one knee and slapped both palms into the cracked ground. Dust rippled and then rose up in a tidal wave, racing through the shadows toward Xartasia's waiting knights. Logan sprinted behind the moving wall of dust.

"Go!" he shouted.

Maeve beat her wings and leapt into the air. Ballad and Anthem flew at her side, the rest of the knights arrayed around their queen. Duaal, Xia and Gripper ran as the dirt billowed before them.

What lay beneath wasn't entirely flat. There were large, geometric shapes scattered across the ground. Squares and rectangles, but circles and large tetrahedrons, too. The tops of buildings, Logan realized. They were running over the ancient, buried remains of the Devourers' city.

And then there were other shapes moving through the dust – Arcadians jostling and struggling to rise above the rolling brown-gray cloud. Logan held down the Talon-9's trigger and raked the dirty darkness with the molten red laser beam. Xartasia's knights were armored and even helmeted in glass, but their wings were spread wide as they readied to fly. Logan caught eight of the Arcadians in his burst. The laser sheared through their wings and set feathers on fire. Crimson light splashed off the glass as it passed over their armor and the other Arcadians quickly scattered away from the bloody red light.

Anthem and his knights pounced on Xartasia's surprised forces as they struggled to get off the ground. Spears flicked out and rang against each other or shrieked off plate armor as they circled and climbed. Each knight sought the higher position in the air to make diving strikes on the gaps in armor at neck or wing.

A pair of Xartasia's knights dove at Logan. He fired up at them, but the laser flashed off glass armor. One beam found a gap under a shoulder plate and the knight spun off into the deep shadows, but the other kicked at Logan from the air, catching him in the chest. Logan staggered and barely managed to pull his feet back beneath him before the knight thrust his spear at the scar Hallax had left years ago.

Logan grabbed the blade in his glass hand and yanked as hard as he could. The fairy knight struggled to retain control of his spear, beating his wings hard and kicking up a cloud of dry gray dust. As he tried to wrest the spear out of Logan's hand, the Prian hunter brought up his Talon and fired through the fairy knight's unprotected throat. The Arcadian fell limp to the dry ground and blood turned the dry ground to dark, sticky mud.

Arcadian bodies littered the cracked ground. Several of Xartasia's knights had Anthem surrounded in a cage of glass spears. The handsome knight dove and wheeled with shocking skill, actually landing for a moment on one of his attackers' backs. The added weight buckled the woman's wings and sent her tumbling to the ground. Anthem leapt free and rose steeply into the shadows.

It was difficult to make out who was who in the flurry of wings... Logan wasn't sure if they were winning or not. He fired once at one of the banking knights chasing Anthem, burning through feathers and wings.

Xia shot at a pair of Arcadians who had driven Eranna down to the ground and pried at her armor with their spears. The Ixthian landed only a glancing hit that scattered across their glass armor, but both fairies vanished into the high shadows again. Xia knelt next to Eranna, spraying chemical cauterizers into several deep, bloody gashes. The young knight groaned and stood, leaning on her spear and dove back into the fray. Gripper loped through the dirt and darkness toward another fallen knight, scooped up the bloody fairy and carried him back to Xia.

Another trio of knights circled and dove at Logan. He shot one in the wing and then under the arm as she fought to regain altitude, but Logan couldn't get a good angle and his laser just glanced off the other two's armor. He threw himself to one side as they closed, but there was no cover in the flat expanse of the buried city. With a musical war cry, Maeve fell on one of the other fairies, burying her spear to the fluttering ribbons between the glass plates. She leapt free as fire blossomed around the last knight. It washed over the attacking Arcadian, incinerating wings and glass. The dead knight fell to the ground in a sizzling heap.

Duaal winked at Logan. But then his smile slid away and the mage flung a lightning bolt off into the darkness. The Devourer slid through the shadows, nanite armor reaching out. A tentacle of inky metal lashed and caught one of the Kaellisem knights around the ankle. He shrieked in pain as the nanites ate through his glass armor and into the flesh beneath. One of Xartasia's fairies drove her spear through his back and bright blood splashed inside his glass armor, dripping down the transparent plates. The cloud of nanites yanked him down to the ground, where the Devourer began to eat.

"Get off of him!" Duaal shouted.

A crackling fork of lightning flashed blue-white through the mechanical swarm. The nanites contracted into a slick black shell over the Devourer's body. It was a female, Logan saw. Much bigger than any woman he had ever seen before, but this alien's waist was narrow and her hips wider. Logan trained his Talon-9 on her and fired rapidly. The black swarm hardened against the assault. It was hard to vary his targets in this darkness without simply missing them.

"Can you do something about her armor?" Logan asked.

"I'm thinking!" Duaal shouted.

Fire and lightning blazed over the alien's ebony nanite shield. Pieces of glass and debris levitated and hurled themselves at the Devourer as though fired from a cannon. The Devourer crouched, reducing her profile and both energy and missiles broke over the hardened surface.

Logan pointed his laser at the ceiling. The glowing indicator set into the grip showed red, already flashing in warning. He squeezed the release and slid in another battery from his dwindling supply. Logan aimed high above the Devourer again and held down his Talon's trigger, pouring energy into the thick, aging alloy far above. Sparks turned into molten droplets and then larger pieces began to fall like glowing rain. Logan moved the beam in a careful circle, trying to carve out a large enough chunk. It was up to Duaal to keep the Devourer busy.

Duaal saw what Logan had in mind, but it would take some time. Time that was now the mage's job to buy.

Without the Prian hunter and his Talon-9, the Devourer woman took the offensive again. She lashed out with blades and tearing hooks. Duaal blasted them back with fire, lightning and barriers of brittle solidified air. He tried to reach into her nervous system and wrap his will around some vital blood vessel, but Duaal didn't know enough about Devourer anatomy.

The Devourer snatched a knight – Duaal wasn't sure if it was one of Maeve's or Xartasia's – from the air and tore the screaming fairy in half. White teeth flashed in the darkness.

Did these creatures ever stop eating? No, Duaal supposed. Glass crunched and vanished into the nanite swarm. With her energy renewed, the Devourer's black armor was reforming into some kind of red-glowing laser weapon.

"Logan," Duaal shouted. "It's got to be now!"

The circle of molten metal above closed and a massive plug of the Level Ten ceiling crashed down onto the Devourer. Tentacles spasmed and then fell in long lines of black dust. The power indicator on Logan's laser flashed red, and cracks radiated out from the fallen slab of fibersteel.

"Duaal!" Maeve landed hard on the crumbling ground. Several of her long pinions were charred black. "We need you!"

Several of Xartasia's Arcadians weren't carrying spears. Instead, they hurled fire and lightning. Mages. Ballad folded his wings and arrowed at one of them, but the Arcadian sang a song that Duaal knew all too well. Ballad shouted out as agony suddenly racked his nerves. Anthem reached out for the thrashing, falling fairy, but another one of Xartasia's knights slashed a bloody wound through Anthem's wing, forcing the knight down.

Duaal gathered himself and leapt, leaving the ground far below. Logan was already slamming a fresh battery into his Talon-9 and Maeve covered him with her red-stained glass spear. At the apex of his leap, Duaal hung in the air for an impossibly long moment, over the heads of the flying knights. With a smirk and a thought, he extinguished the other mages' flames and sent their lightning to ground harmlessly on the huge metal stanchion. Duaal pushed the air out below him in a billowing cloud, clearing a path through the jockeying Arcadians and landed in the middle of the spell-singers.

Trained in the same rote spells that Xartasia had taught Gavriel, the Arcadians rained fire and electricity on Duaal. But he knew those songs, recognized them from the first notes. It was a simple matter to slip aside or counter them. His nerves itched as the fairies tried to kindle agony in his body.

"Oh, no," Duaal said. "I don't think so."

The Hyzaari mage swept his arm in a broad circle, pointing at one Arcadian after the other. He reached into their brains, dilating a single blood vessel and sending a sudden rush of blood too hard, too fast. One by one, Xartasia's spell-singers dropped unconscious to Axis' cracked gray surface.

"I hope you all saw that," Duaal said.

But none of his friends seemed to have appreciated Duaal's cleverness. Maeve's dwindling knights were still badly outnumbered. Logan had acquired an Arcadian spear and fought back to back with Ballad, who had shaken off the effects of the spell and recovered his feet. Xia knelt over Anthem Calloren, hastily sealing the hole in the delicate membrane of his right wing while the knight grimaced in pain.

"Duaal!" Logan shouted. "You and Maeve have to keep moving. Go! Get out of here!"

Maeve opened her mouth to argue, but instead, she grabbed Logan by the front of his bloody shirt and pulled the hunter into a short, fierce kiss. Then, with a keening note of anguish, she flew toward Duaal.

"Which way?" Maeve asked over the screams and crash of glass on glass. "Where is the Waygate?"

"This way!" Duaal said.

He ran along the flat, packed ground in Maeve's shadow as she flew, following him. There was a crackling sound off to Duaal's left. The huge pieces of Level Ten's metal ceiling still glowed sullenly around the melted edges where Logan had burned it free of Level Nine, but the ten-ton slab of fibersteel was *moving*.

The metal turned duller, lighter and crumbled like chalk. Black fog rose up from the collapsing metal and Duaal threw himself backward as the Devourer stood up. Patches of slick black clung to her body here and there, tending to wounds. Smoky tendrils floated out cautiously. The Devourer was taking no chances. Duaal knotted his fingers and hurled lightning. The nanite cloud opaqued against the crackling bolt, but did not waver.

Maeve banked and circled back, but Duaal waved her off.

"No!" he shouted. "Keep flying, Maeve!"

The little queen's jaw set and she rose once more into the darkness. In a moment, Maeve was gone. Duaal threw himself high over the Devourer and landed out of reach of its tentacles again. She turned and advanced once more. Could he simply knock the alien killer unconscious as he had the Arcadians? No, he just didn't know enough about her anatomy.

A huge black scythe suddenly formed in the Devourer's hands and slashed out at Duaal. It whistled through the stale air, driving him back. Nanites swirled and formed a laser cannon that glowed with hellish light and Duaal heaved a buried piece of ancient wall up from the ground just in time to be blasted apart into blackened rubble. The burning chips of something like concrete pelted Duaal and he had to shield his eyes from the smoke.

He coughed. Where was the Devourer?

A dark spike as big around as his thigh shot out from the smoke and dust, spearing Duaal through the stomach. The mage gasped and blood poured across the ground. The spear of nanites changed form inside him, dividing and curving into hooks, and then tore free again. Shiny wet shapes looped around the barbed nanites. His intestines...

Duaal smelled the hot copper tang and the acrid scents of blood and acid leaking from his torn stomach. All the strength went out of his legs and he fell down to his knees. The Devourer stalked toward Duaal through the smoke and shadows, moving confidently now.

Tendrils of smoke flowed along the cluttered ground, seeking the splattered gore. Duaal felt a tugging from somewhere deep inside and he realized that his guts were still attached inside of him. The Devourer was eating him alive.

Pain boiled through Duaal, but he silenced his searing nerves with a thought. Her nanites condensed and clung to the Devourer's body like an oily garment. She held Duaal's viscera in her hand, chewing on the end with relish while his blood ran down her chin. The Devourer smiled with her mouth full of sharp white teeth as she ate him.

Tearing me into pieces while I watch, Duaal thought. *But aren't we all just pieces...? Swarms of molecules? Particles held together by electrons and atomic bonds?*

Duaal smiled right back into the face of the feasting Devourer as he dissolved those bonds. Her molecules, free of the forces that bound them into proteins and tissue, blew away in a fine red-black mist. The young mage fell onto his back in the dust and stared up at the shadowed underside of Axis.

Xia ran toward him, skidding to a stop beside her captain with eyes blazing red. He winked at her.

"Tell me... you saw that," Duaal said before darkness took him.

[42]

WHAT HAS BEEN

"It's not until we face death that we truly live."

- DUAAL SINNAY (234 PA)

Logan didn't remember when he lost the spear. He lifted his glass arm and parried a thrust upward. The blade missed his heart, but the point stabbed through the muscle of his shoulder. He gripped the haft to keep the Arcadian from ripping through to his neck and kicked out. His legs were longer than the knight's and Logan's kick landed solidly against his groin. Xartasia's fairy fell back, staggered but protected by his armor. Logan yanked the spear blade from his shoulder, but the bloody glass slipped through his fingers and fell. As the knight reached out to recover his weapon, Logan grabbed his glass helmet and twisted with all his strength. Something in the Arcadian's neck cracked and he fell to the ground.

Logan staggered away, ejecting the spent battery of his Talon-9, and slid in his last one. Anthem wasn't far away and the knight's armor was streaked with even more scarlet than the usual Cavainna colors.

"How many made it?" Logan asked.

Anthem's expression was sad. "Seven. Only four still fit to fight, including myself."

He swept his wing across the underground plain. None of the glass sparkled anymore. It was all covered with blood and dust and mud. Bodies lay strewn through the dirt.

"What about the Devourer?" Logan asked.

Ballad landed hard. He was limping badly and a cut on his scalp sheeted blood down the side of the young fairy's face.

"Duaal got it," Ballad said. "But it got him."

He pointed through the shadows to where Xia knelt in the mud. The Ixthian doctor had her medical bag open and worked frantically, wrist deep in Duaal's abdominal cavity. Not far away, Gripper pulled on his long ears. Big, glistening tears rolled down his dusty cheeks. Xia didn't look up.

"Don't stand there staring," she told him. "Make Duaal's sacrifice worth something. Keep moving!"

"Silver..." Gripper said, but the Ixthian shook her head and the young Arboran turned away.

Dhozo stood at the edge of the crowd. The aerads gathered around the ancient Projector in widening concentric circles, all kneeling in the blasted dust of eons. Years and disuse had buried the Waygate, of course, but Dhozo and Orix made short work of the layered dirt and stone, even the ancient metal and ceramics of their own long-lost cities. Within minutes, they had blasted a deep crater into Axis' surface. And at the center of it stood the Waygate.

It was here on Kahazzek, the Glorious homeworld, that Dhozo's species had built the first fully functioning device. From here, they had swarmed out into the galaxy, past the furthest colonies, taking what they needed from the worlds they found and built the greatest empire that had ever existed. Glorious.

Xartasia had frowned at Dhozo as he and Orix had demolished their own history to reach the Waygate. The little aerad queen had no appreciation for history's proper place. She wallowed in her past instead of using it.

Now the Projector rose up on its white ziggurat, a multi-colored ring on top that shone with blue light like hot, low-burning flames. More than ten thousand Arcadians swayed in ordered, widening circles around the towering stepped pyramid, all singing together as their queen stood before the first Waygate.

Dhozo had long since turned off his swarm's translation of the triumphant song. It was almost over now.

The Waygate pulsed with azure light as it sorted through the jumbled memories of the gathered Arcadians. Next to Dhozo, Orix paced like a caged beast. The closest ranks of fairies hesitated, their song turning sour as they recoiled from the angry young Devourer. One of Xartasia's knights warned Orix back in lyric Arcadian, but the Glorious tech snarled at him.

"Orix..." Dhozo warned.

"No!" Orix snarled. "No! Your precious little slave queen is down there, doing just what she's wanted all along. And she's given us *nothing*, commander!"

"Enough. We wait, Orix."

"We've waited enough!"

"Age flavors the meat," Dhozo said in their own language. The nanites didn't translate for the aerad knight still pointing his spear at Orix. "You've yet to learn focus, lieutenant."

"And your focus got Tarno and Bizax killed! Your own people are fighting up there," Orix shouted. "For what?"

"Xartasia's work down here is delicate," Dhozo told him. "Easily interrupted. That's *our* technology she's using."

"How long will you wait?" Orix asked. "Until she's knifed you in the back like she did to that old human man? No, I'm not waiting anymore!"

Another knight was approaching, drawn by the angry voices. Her spear was leveled at the two Glorious and Orix whirled, easily swatting the glass blade aside. The first knight hissed something in Arcadian and slashed out with his own weapon, gouging a faintly glittering line into Orix's black armor.

Orix roared in rage. His nanite swarm swirled around his huge hands, coalescing into a pair of glowing red lasers. He raked the beam over one of the knights. The glass armor dispersed the worst of the laser – until it reached his face. The aerad had no time to scream before the lasers boiled through his skull. Orix's nanites re-formed into barbed black chains that lashed out, wrapping around the other Arcadian.

A third fairy knight was flying toward Orix, spear outthrust and glowing blue in the Waygate's light, but a razor-bladed line of his nanites slid behind the knee of her armor and blood spattered the ground.

"Orix!" Dhozo growled.

The other Devourer had already torn the feathered wings from the grounded knight's back. The aerad's armor dripped with blood and he screamed in pain. Orix's swarm curled in around the fairy, devouring flesh and bone and glass within swift heartbeats. Dhozo bounded forward, his own nanite swarm forming a long, saw-edge blade that extended from his right hand. He sliced through the hook-covered black chains that held the remaining knight bloodily captive. Dhozo's sword sheared through the nanites, but they didn't require a physical connection to Orix to carry out his commands and the midnight chains tightened around Xartasia's knight.

"Let them go," Dhozo ordered.

Orix's expression was invisible behind the smoky cloud of his armor, but Dhozo heard the rage in his voice.

"No!" Orix roared.

Dhozo leapt on him, pinning Orix's thrashing limbs with barbs and blades. The other Devourer howled deafeningly and thrashed against Dhozo. Orix wrenched himself off of a black spike driven through his shoulder, tearing bone and muscle. Orix's stormy black armor drew together and lashed out at his superior.

"Command override," Dhozo said.

The nanites halted their attack, swirled like leaves in the wind and then abandoned Orix entirely. They floated gently to Dhozo and joined his own swarm, leaving Orix naked and bleeding on the ground.

Dhozo flexed his expanded nanite swarm and then tore into his lieutenant. The Arcadian knights scrambled back as bone snapped and flesh tore, but not a single drop of blood spilled into the dirt.

With his meal done, Dhozo straightened up. Xartasia's knights remained gathered around him, all gripping spears tightly. Dhozo turned away, ignoring them. He magnified his view of Xartasia. The White Queen stood in the circle of the glowing Waygate, her arms thrown wide as though to welcome a lover. Blue light rippled like water over her, but turning a poisonous-looking indigo at the edges.

Orix was right. Dhozo hadn't killed the young tech because he was wrong... The Glorious *had* waited long enough. Now it was time for Dhozo to take what he needed from Xartasia. And with the rest of his squadron dead or fighting far away, the knowledge would be his alone. Only Dhozo would have the power to use the Projectors. He could open the way to every edible world, every time, and he would have the best of every meal.

And Xartasia was going to be the first course. Dhozo strode past the knights and toward the White Queen.

A winged shape shot like glittering white laserfire high over the torn crater of the Waygate, black hair streaming behind her. The song wavered as the Arcadians filling the artificial valley gasped. It was the other princess, Maeve Cavainna, dressed in gleaming glass armor and clutching a spear. She soared through the shadows in the direction of the white pyramid and the Waygate on top. Xartasia didn't move, but stood unflinching in the Projector's shifting glow.

Dhozo brought his arm up, aiming a rapidly assembling particle beam at Maeve, but several more armored Arcadians poured over the crater's edge, followed closely by a blond human.

They all charged at Dhozo. Power signatures identified a hand-held energy weapon and cybernetic body parts. One of the degenerates of Anzhotek cowered behind the human. Dhozo was unsure how one of them had escaped the burning of their planet, but his lips curled in a snarl and the Glorious commander promised himself that none of those disgusting herbivores would survive.

"Gripper, go help Maeve!" the human shouted. "Get her to the Waygate!"

The Arboran nodded and ran, scrambling away as the human covered him. Xartasia's knights launched themselves into the air, spears flashing and wings filling the air with feathers. The human raised his laser and fired at the aerads fanning out to surround him.

Dhozo's computer monitored every position, feeding the data directly into his thoughts. He saw everything and his swarm reacted immediately to the laser, forming a reflective barrier to minimize the loss of nanites, but the human shifted his aim and fired again. Dhozo's computer analyzed the shots and found no pattern. His armor swirled in confusion.

But Dhozo had just commandeered Orix's entire nanite complement. The random shots might have been enough to overwhelm a confused single swarm, but the resources of two was more than equal to the task. Dhozo coalesced a thick but flexible layer of black armor against his skin, but there were more than enough nanites left to attack. He raked at the human with huge serrated claws. The man threw himself back and Dhozo sent barbed spikes darting out from the cloud after him. One of them slashed a deep, bloody wound across the human's thigh.

Dhozo's swarm showed him two aerads breaking off the fight against Xartasia's knights. They attacked from above, spears thrust out toward Dhozo, but they were slow-moving and easily predicted.

Nanites deflected the attacks and lashed out in response, forming the swarm into a seething urchin of thrusting spines.

One of the aerads – a male with frayed golden braids – jumped away, but the other wasn't fast enough. Dhozo knocked her clattering to the ground. She raised her voice in an urgent song and flame roared up between them. Dhozo smothered the fire with his swarm, devouring the flammable oxygen, then poured nanites between the glass plates of her armor, eating the flesh inside.

The human male rushed in again, firing his random shots into Dhozo's doubled-up swarm. The shots were wild, but they didn't miss. Dhozo charged at the blond man. His armor extended into a bladed spike longer than the human was tall. Dhozo shifted to bring the most heavily armored parts of his body into their attacks and slashed his blade in a flat arc.

Another Arcadian had joined the remaining knight, this one younger than the first and wearing black leather beneath his glass armor. The aerad in black jabbed his spear into Dhozo's shoulder. His nanites swarmed up the glass and carbide haft, devouring the minerals, but the sudden thickening of his armor around the joint pulled Dhozo's attacking blade to one side. The gleaming obsidian edge threw sparks from the side of an ancient building and Dhozo's swarm yanked the spear from the younger Arcadian's grasp. The fairy grinned and jumped back, raising balled fists covered across the knuckles with gray strips of fibersteel.

The human with the cybernetics fired several shots into Dhozo's swarm and the older aerad stabbed his spear at the Devourer's neck. Dhozo melted back, extending arms that bristled with sharp, hooked blades to slash at both aerads. The one in black raised his forearms and fists to parry the blows, even as Dhozo's nanites left brittle, cloudy streaks in his glass armor. The force of Dhozo's blows drove the knight down to one knee on the ground, but before the Glorious commander could complete his kill, the human stepped in his way.

His primitive laser raked the uneven ground on high output. It drained the power quickly, but the crumbling floor of ancient walls and roofs disintegrated and one of Dhozo's legs punched through, catching in the hole.

Dhozo growled and pulled his swarm into tentacles that heaved him up out of the ragged gap. One of them swept the human's feet out from beneath him and then shoved him into the hole he had just created. The long-haired aerad leapt at Dhozo, whirling his spear and carving glittering grooves into his armored skin. Dhozo swiped with a huge claw and snapped the weapon in half. Broken pieces fell into the dust as the aerad in black grabbed the human's hand and hauled him up out of the ground. All three spun to face Dhozo again.

"You hungry, hawk?" the young Arcadian asked.

"Always," Dhozo snarled.

The trio of smaller aliens surrounded him, jabbing and slashing and firing. The aerad in black ran at Dhozo, leaping into the air and beating his wings hard to throw punches and jabs at the Devourer's face. With each blow, Dhozo's nanites stripped away more of the glass and fibersteel armoring his hands until blood streamed down the aerad's arms, but the little winged slave wouldn't stop. A punch shattered Dhozo's nose and red ran down his face, into his mouth. The Devourer tasted his own blood and his stomach growled. He licked his lips.

Dhozo grabbed the Arcadian boy, growing twisted claws that bit deeply into the fairy's flesh. Dhozo opened his mouth. He was going to bite the aerad's head off, glass helm and all.

"Logan!" the aerad gasped. "Now would be good!"

The human aimed his ineffectual laser and fired a single shot into Dhozo's open mouth, through his skull and into his brain. His swarm's computer superimposed medical readouts and triage information onto Dhozo's optical centers, clinically notifying its master that he was dead.

<hr>

Ballad fell to his knees, blood pouring from his lacerated arms and hands. Anthem took Eranna's spear from the bloodstained ground as Logan helped Ballad to his feet. The Prian fairy wrapped ribbons from Anthem's shattered spear over his wounded knuckles. Logan raised his Talon-9 and checked the battery. The power was low, but there were a few shots left.

"Can you still fight?" Logan asked.

Anthem and Ballad nodded grimly.

[43]

MAY NEVER BE AGAIN

"There is nothing left now but to end this song and begin anew."

- TITANIA CAVAINNA (234 PA)

Maeve dove between a pair of Xartasia's knights. The two fairies wheeled after her, but Allados fell on them from above, clearing the way for his queen. Maeve heard him scream once as the other Arcadians turned on him. With tears in her eyes, she folded her wings close against her back and plummeted at the Waygate.

"Xartasia!" Maeve shouted.

Thousands of Arcadians knelt below, their heads bowed and wings outstretched as they sang, remembering the White Kingdom as it was. As it would be again. Maeve called out to Xartasia once more, but if her cousin could hear her at all, she didn't look up.

The White Queen – she was a true queen, regal and powerful in a way that Maeve had never managed – stood in the center of the Waygate, awash with writhing blue and violet light so intense that it left spots swimming across Maeve's vision. She was sure that the visible light was only a tiny part of the energy that blazed through the Waygate.

Xartasia's ink-black hair and flowing white gown swirled around her, whipped by the forces she had sung into existence. She raised one perfect hand and thousands of Arcadians sang together. The Waygate rang like a struck bell.

Maeve dove at the other queen, throwing all of her weight and momentum behind her spear in a deadly pinpoint of glass. Would killing Xartasia be enough to stop this? Maeve prayed.

But she slammed into something above the Waygate, an invisible wall of force as hard as any fibersteel bulkhead, and fell. Maeve landed painfully on one of the huge white steps below her radiant cousin. With a groan, Maeve hauled herself to her feet and pushed, but could not take even a single step closer.

"Xartasia!" Maeve called out. "Cousin, stop! The Alliance will be here soon. This is over!"

Finally, Xartasia glanced down imperiously from the Waygate. Her eyes danced with the brilliant indigo light and her crown rose like a circlet of blue-burning blades from the darkness of her hair.

"I can see it all," Xartasia answered in a voice that barely reached Maeve's ears. It was soft and secretive. Reverent. "I can see the White Kingdom again. I can see my father. I can see all I have lost…"

"Xartasia, no!" Maeve shouted. "Do not do this! You cannot just obliterate a hundred years, a trillion lives! We do not have the right to unmake their existences!"

"But they will not suffer," Xartasia said. "None of us will suffer, Maeve. All will be as it should have been. I will fix it all. There is nothing left now but to end this song and begin anew. I will see you again in our home."

Maeve sang a wordless note of anguish and flung herself against Xartasia's barrier again, but to no avail. She may as well have been trying to cut through the Waygate itself with a feather. Above her, Xartasia closed her eyes and spread her arms as though welcoming an embrace. All around her, the Waygate filled the darkness with twisting violet radiance. The Arcadians' song rose, thundering in Maeve's ears.

Someone called her name... Logan had pushed his way through the throng of singing, swaying Arcadians. His Talon-9 was still in his hand, the barrel steaming slightly in the stale air of Axis' long-dark surface.

Gripper was a step ahead and charged desperately at Xartasia, but he slammed into the same barrier that had stopped Maeve. He shouted in frustration. Ballad soared out of the darkness toward the White Queen, but could approach no closer than Gripper. Logan aimed his Talon and fired. The laser beam just refracted harmlessly, as though off Arcadian glass. He glanced down at the weapon and then holstered it.

Something was happening. All around them, Axis shimmered and wavered like reflections on the surface of the sea. Cold numbness seeped through Maeve's body, a sort of non-sensation that she couldn't describe except as... as though reality were fading away, a strange sense of distance from her own body. As though time and reality were draining away like blood from a wound.

A wound in time, Maeve thought, *and we are bleeding out.*

The Waygate blazed, pulsed and flared in a nova of cold indigo fire. Another Arcadian dove from the writhing purple shadows to land beside Maeve.

Anthem. The knight's armor shone like iridescent flame.

"Titania," he said. There was a century of pain and joy in that single word.

Xartasia's bright violet eyes flew open and she stared.

"Anthem...?"

The knight didn't try to hammer or fight his way to the burning Waygate. He stood in the shimmering final twilight, staring up at Xartasia.

"I lived, my enarri," he said. "And I thought of you every day."

"No... No, you died on Illisem," Xartasia answered. She took a faltering step toward the stairs. "Anthem..."

"I am here." He held out his arms. "But I cannot come to you, Titania. Not while you are doing this."

Xartasia drew herself up. "Anthem, my enarri... All that I have done, I did in your memory... I must do this...!"

"Titania, my love," Anthem said. "If today is truly to be the end of this chapter of history, let me hold you just once more before it closes."

Xartasia's violet eyes were wide and shining. She took one trembling step and then another toward Anthem, leapt and spread her wings. The White Queen fell into Anthem's embrace and he folded his wings around her, love and pain warring across his face.

The knight closed one gauntlet into a fist and slammed it hard into Xartasia's temple. She went limp in his arms, blood trickling from her midnight hair. Her glass crown fell to the ground, rolled once along its rim and then clattered into the dust.

"I am sorry, my enarri," Anthem said. "But I love you more than your pain."

The gathered Arcadians moaned as Xartasia fell. Their nexus was gone, the mind that connected theirs to the Waygate. First one and then hundreds of fairies jumped to their feet, filling the struggling shadows with a storm of wings. But the uncontrolled Waygate seared with bruised purple light, gashed through the middle with bloody red. Gripper grabbed Maeve's shoulder.

"She didn't close the Waygate!" he shouted. "If we don't get that thing under control, it's going to call the Devourers again, just like on Orindell and Prianus!"

"Duaal–" Maeve began.

"Is not here," Anthem finished. The knight lifted Xartasia's limp body into his arms. "You are the only one left who knows how to control a Waygate, Maeve. Go!"

"No!" Maeve said.

Her failure on Tamlin had started this whole thing, begun over one hundred years of pain and death that left her people homeless, that orphaned Gripper, that killed Tiberius and countless others.

"There's no one else, dove," Logan told her. "Close that thing!"

Maeve hated it, but he was right. Maeve leapt into the air. There were Arcadians everywhere, scattering into the darkness with the fall of their queen. Feathers flickered through red and purple light. The Waygate toned thunderously.

"*Szo ghemma b'ho leng. Hotek mev khavvna tek vommen.*"

Xartasia's barrier was gone now and Maeve landed hard on the slick white of the Waygate. She threw her arm across her face as the light blazed. All she had to do was sing the closure spell and then the whole system would shut down. The Devourers probably had some simpler, faster way to interface with their ancient technology, but Maeve had no way to ask them for help.

Maeve closed her eyes. Spots of light wavered behind her lids, but she didn't need to see. Just to concentrate. She had to get the spell right this time. Just close the Waygate and this would be over. All of this pain and loss and destruction would finally end. Maeve drew a deep breath that tasted of wet earth and feathers and blood. She found the words and opened her mouth to sing...

But Xartasia's song, her spell sang through the Waygate. The spell was out of control, but it wasn't dead.

I can see it, Xartasia had said.

And Maeve could see it, too. All of it. The violet light that filled the Waygate washed over her now, the filaments of time and energy Xartasia had spread like a spider's web or nervous system across the entire galaxy, across a hundred years.

A trillion lives poured into Maeve's mind through the Waygate, uncountable moments and trillions of possibilities. Everything that had happened in one hundred years. Everything that *might* have happened. The White Kingdom of Arcadia restored, never fallen. A shining jewel of glass that never faded...

But more. So much more. Maeve felt it all around her, through her – infinite threads of lives and moments not tangled in time, but a precise and intricate tapestry in a trillion breath-taking, luminous colors. It rippled against Maeve's inspection.

"Glass!" Gripper shouted. "Close the Waygate!"

Maeve heard him. Not with her ears... her blood pounded and Maeve was drowning in the dull red roar. But she knew her friend was speaking. She saw it, felt the moment like a tiny, delicate living thing in her hand. Every single moment of Gripper's life, from the tiny Arboran's first infant scream, his first steps to that moment he climbed the sick old sycona tree, when it crashed to the ground and he chased Xartasia through the ancient Waygate...

Maeve reached out and brushed her thoughts lightly across the tapestry. There were dark threads, pain and loss sewn through the boundless beauty. Maeve plucked at a single one and all of time shuddered at her touch.

"I can see it," she said. "I can see it all. And I... I can change it..."

"What are you doing?" Gripper cried.

"It does not have to be like this," Maeve told her friend. "You do not have to be alone out here. I can send you home. You will never come here."

"What?" Gripper's eyes were huge and he took an involuntary step closer to the burning Waygate. "I... You can... I could go back to Arborus? But everyone there is dead, Glass."

"I can fix it. I can change time..." Maeve whispered.

She could. It would take only a touch, not the crude hammer that Xartasia would have used. Maeve didn't have to change all of time, just... just a few moments...

Ballad landed on the white stairs. "Maeve, this is exactly what we came to stop Xartasia from doing. Shut down the Waygate!"

"No," Maeve said. "I do not have to change everything. I will not unmake anyone's lives... But there have been so very many painful, terrible moments. So many have died! The Alliance fights even now to contain the last of the Devourers on Level One. They will win their battle, but at such cost...! Tens of thousands are dead, dying!"

Maeve reached out one trembling hand. She could touch them, trillions of lives, so many points of pain. With just a tiny nudge, she could fix them all. So many other lives, so many possibilities...

Tiberius alive. Alive.

Gripper perched in a healthy sycona tree, never falling. Living a long life on green Arborus.

Xia married to Xen, with an adorable brood of healthy, well-bred silver children.

Gavriel on Tynerion, a teacher of philosophy once more.

Duaal under the bright sun and approving smiles of his own people.

Logan in his worn blue police uniform, holding his wife and son.

"Maeve, stop this!" Anthem said from the dark, distant ground.

She looked at the knight. "But I can send you through the same Waygate as Titania, Anthem. You never have to be separated from your love!"

"I am with her now." Anthem brushed Xartasia's black hair back from her face. "Perhaps she will hate me when she wakes, but at least I have held my enarri one last time."

"Tiberius does not have to die," Maeve said, turning to Gripper. "Duaal does not have to be taken from Hyzaar. He does not have to die here! Ferris' daughter and Ballad's sister... They can live! Xia will never be taken by pirates. I can fix it, all of it! You can finally go home, Gripper. It is the only thing you have ever wanted."

"No, Maeve," the Arboran answered. "I... I just want you to close the Waygate and come down from there. I just want this to be over. We can't play with time. You have to stop."

Logan had climbed the stairs, pushing past Ballad. The Prian bounty hunter was a silhouette, a shadow in the brilliant Waygate light... Except for his left hand. The brilliance broke into a hundred rainbows against the glass.

"Maeve," Logan said. "Close it."

"I can give you back your hand," she told him desperately. Why could they not see? All she wanted to do was make things better, just a few small fixes to time so that those she loved didn't have to suffer. "Hallax's sword will miss its mark. Reginald will live. You will keep your heart, Logan. I can save you..."

The wild storm of possibilities whipped around them. Winds of a hundred worlds tore at his clothes and hair. There was rain and snow, lightning in slashed fragments and sunshine lit the Waygate as Maeve reached through time. Silver moonlight and the flashing green and red of the Prian police car lights. Just the lightest touch and Logan would be whole again. Maeve could give him that with just a wish...

"What use do I have for a heart except to give it to you?" Logan asked. He held his glass hand out to Maeve. "If that Emberguard didn't take my hand, I would still be a cop on Prianus. I never would have become a bounty hunter. I never would have met you."

"I have hurt you," Maeve said.

"Yes," Logan agreed. "But pain shapes us, Maeve."

"It breaks us!" she wept. "Look what it did to Titania, to me... To you, my enarri."

"It makes us who we are. That's why we came here, dove, why so many people have died today. To defend the right to bear our scars. I wouldn't change a moment of my life, no matter how painful, if it meant I never met you."

Logan still held his gun in his right hand, the Talon-9 that had been at the center of their chase, their hunt for one another for so long. Tears shone in his hard blue eyes. But there were so many lives in Maeve's hands, so many terrible losses and moments of unbearable pain. They drowned Maeve in more tears than Logan could ever shed.

How could she turn her back on such suffering?

"I love you," Maeve whispered. "I only want to help."

"I only want you."

Her hunter raised the gun, aiming at Maeve. Logan would kill her and suffer another terrible scar rather than live his whole life without her. His hands were steady even as tears streamed down his cheeks. Logan Coldhand would kill the woman he loved to save that love... and the worlds. His scars were still raw, painful. They would never stop hurting. But they made him strong, too.

"We have been through so much," Maeve said.

"But it brought us here," Logan answered.

Maeve took Logan's glass hand and pulled him into the center of the storm, into the Waygate. The wind and storms of a thousand worlds whipped them as Maeve stood on her toes and kissed her enarri.

There was pain, yes, as his cybernetic fingers clutched too hard at her arm, but the pleasure of his touch outshone it all. Her hunter was right. There was no pleasure, no *life* without pain. Taking away the pain was just as terrible as anything Xartasia had tried to do. Even the dead had lived. Too short a time for too many of them, but those lives were their own. Maeve could not take them away.

She drew another deep breath and let go. Maeve sang Caith's song carefully and perfectly, singing the first Waygate to sleep again with Logan's arms around her. At last, the purple light faded and darkness fell once more beneath Axis.

REFORGED

"Those who truly want change must be the first to make it."

Aes was bright and golden in the sky of Illisem. Maeve stood with Xia and Gripper at the edge of the bright green grass. Without the dryads to tend it, the vast lawns of the royal court had become overgrown and wild in the last hundred years. It was time the Arcadians learned to care for their own homeworld again.

Wind rippled through the grass and hissed gently like waves against the shore. Broken glass towers rose up all around them, the shattered crystal ruins of the ancient White Kingdom that glittered in a dozen colors. Lorren and Hyra were training new glass-singers every day, but it would take a long time to repair the damage. Even Arcadian glass was not impervious to the years or the tenacious march of life. Vines and creepers grew over the broken city in delicate nets of green leaves and pale pink flowers. Blue and purple veilwings darted between the blossoms, ignoring the larger creatures entirely. Arcadia had belonged to the animals and insects for a century, after all, and these survivors of the White Kingdom feared nothing.

Duaal limped through the grass. After two surgeries, a new cloned liver, kidney and about ten feet of replacement intestines, the young mage was finally walking again. He came to stand beside Maeve in the green shade of the old willow tree. Like Gripper and Xia, Duaal was barefoot and dressed only in a simple white robe. He looked at Maeve.

"You know," he said, "it's a damned good thing you were at that Waygate instead of me, Maeve. All of time at my fingertips... The chance to have Tiberius back. I don't know if I could have resisted that kind of temptation."

"I did not. Not alone," Maeve told him.

"Are you ready for this?" Duaal asked.

"Yes," she answered. "I am. Are you?"

Duaal laughed in reply. Maeve turned to Xia and Gripper. They nodded.

Together, the four made their way slowly down the path. It was nearly invisible through the wild grass, little more than a scattering of weathered white stones jutting up from the emerald green like old bones. Wynerian and Orindell were huge, gleaming silver crescents in Illisem's clear blue sky.

They passed silently under the glass ruins of the west gate. Only one of the pillars still stood, a swirling sculpture of Anslin saluting the brilliant golden sun. His spear was gone, but the guardian god faced outward, his remaining wing stretching out high even over Gripper's head.

On the other side, Cavain's statue had been destroyed. All that remained were a pair of melted, blackened lumps. An aspen tree had sprouted between the pieces, pale roots wrapped around the misshapen glass and pulling them inexorably down into the dirt. In another ten years, they would vanish entirely.

Maeve, Xia, Gripper and Duaal stepped through the gate.

They had rebuilt the birchwood thrones. The pale wood rose up from wild green grass, delicate and beautiful and scarred black in places where the Devourers had come too close to the trees. Lorren had done her best to plane the burnt spots from the wood, but there was no place in Arcadia not scarred by the fall.

Maeve made her way toward the twin thrones. The glass gallery surrounding the royal court was long gone, but the overgrown field was full of Arcadians. Thousands of them. Some were from Kaellisem, others from Titania's army, but many more were from neither side of the brief and terrible Arcadian civil war. Just fairies happy to be home again.

Panna sat in the queen's throne, Ballad seated by her side. She wore an Arcadian gown of flowing pale green and her golden hair hung in burnished curls around her shoulders. The glass crown on her brow was as bright as a star. There had been arguments about it, of course.

"I'm not a Cavainna!" Panna had said.

"Cavain was a warlord," Maeve reminded her. "You know that. He wiped out the pyrads to build his empire. I killed even more dryads, nyads and aerads when I opened up the Tamlin Waygate. Titania tried to unmake trillions more. The Cavainna line had its chance and it is time for someone else to rule."

Now Maeve swept her wing across her chest in salute to the new queen and king. Even on the throne, Ballad refused to abandon his black leather jacket. Duke Ferris stood behind his new monarchs, managing to look both astonished and disapproving.

Ballad stood and returned Maeve's salute.

"Who stands for these three?" he asked in his Prian accent and Maeve thought she actually saw Duke Ferris flinch.

Maeve smirked to herself as she folded her wings back. "Queen Panna Sul and King Ballad Avadain, I am Vael Maeve Cavainna and I stand for my friends. They have fought through fire and darkness for life and light. They are brave and noble men and women."

Panna rose, too, and came to stand beside her king. She looked nervous. "Have they stood vigil through a day and night?"

"They have, You Majesties," Maeve answered. "They have made themselves ready."

"Well, that makes three of us," Ballad muttered. Duke Ferris spluttered and the new king raised his voice. "Stand forward, Duaal Sinnay, Anandrou Gripper and Xia."

All three approached the thrones and then sank to one knee. Duaal winked at the Arcadian rulers. Panna blushed, but touched her hand to Duaal's shoulder. This was usually done with a wingtip, but Panna had her scars, too, and used what she had. She moved down the line, brushing trembling fingertips to Xia and Gripper's bowed necks.

"In ten thousand years, we have knighted only our own people," Ballad said, his accented voice ringing out across the crowd. "It is long past due. These three have proven that one does not need wings to reach great heights! For all you have done, for all you have given, rise now as knights of Arcadia. It is our greatest and deepest honor to have you."

A musical cheer rose from the crowd. Grinning, Duaal was the first to stand and raise his hands to the assembled Arcadians. The fairies roared. Xia and Gripper more slowly followed suit, but there were shy smiles on both of their faces, too. Gripper hugged Maeve.

"I'm a knight," he said dumbly. "Just like you, Glass! I... I need a new name now!"

Maeve laughed and embraced her awe-struck friend, but Panna wasn't done yet. The young queen waited a moment and then spoke again.

"Maeve, will you please help Sir Anthem?" she asked.

Maeve nodded and flew to where Anthem waited in the shifting shade of a rippling blue tent. Titania stood between Anthem and Logan. Both men held laser and spear ready. The renegade queen was dressed in a simple, somber gray dress with illonium manacles around her wrists and ankles. Her violet eyes never left Anthem's face.

"It is time," Maeve said simply.

Anthem nodded. He took Titania by the arm and guided her to a spot before the thrones. Maeve and Logan walked behind the pair, watchful and cautious.

Titania stood before Ballad and Panna, head bowed. The king's eyes were Prian-hard and he held his own spear tightly.

"Kneel," he said.

Titania did as Ballad commanded, her chains clattering. Logan's Talon-9 remained trained on her, and so did the point of Anthem's spear.

"It wasn't easy to extradite you from the Alliance," Panna told Titania. "You've committed a great many crimes against the Central World Alliance. But I managed to convince the Lyceum that your transgressions against the White Kingdom predated their charges and we had the right to try and punish you."

"Yes," Titania agreed.

Ballad spoke in a voice full of tightly controlled violence. "I'm in favor of executing you for everything you've done, princess. It's the least you deserve for the lives you've taken and destroyed."

On her knees before the thrones, Titania closed her violet eyes. "All I have done, I did for love."

"I know," Ballad said. "And in her last act as queen, Maeve interceded on your behalf. She didn't want her last order or our first to be yet another death. Stand, Titania."

Maeve and Logan stepped back. The Prian holstered his gun as Titania rose, finally looking up at Panna and Ballad with confusion in her twilight eyes. The crowd waited in hushed apprehension.

"What's done is done. Despite your best efforts, we can't undo the harm you've done," Ballad said. "So you will spend the rest of your life in service to the galaxy you tried to destroy. You will begin by helping the Nnyth rebuild their Tower and, if possible, mending the Waygate they sundered to keep from you. And then you will return to the White Kingdom and serve in the rebuilding here. This is your sentence."

Titania's glorious violet eyes were full of tears. "What? But I..."

"Sir Anthem," Ballad said.

The knight saluted. If the sudden rise of his one-time subordinate bothered Anthem, it didn't show.

"Yes, my king?" he asked.

"Titania is powerful and dangerous. She will require a close eye. At all times and for the rest of her days, you will watch over her. If she strays from her sentence, if the princess ever brings harm instead of help, Sir Anthem, kill her."

"It's a difficult task, we know," Panna said. She held out the key to Titania's chains. "But you have shown your strength, Sir Anthem, and Ballad assures me that you are equal to all we ask."

"I... Thank you, Your Majesties," Anthem answered in a thick, choked voice.

He unlocked the chains and took Titania's hand, though he still held his spear close and ready. The knight and the princess took to the sky and soared toward the ruins of the imperial city. Maeve saw silver streaking both of their cheeks as they flew close enough that their wingtips brushed.

"Logan," Ballad said.

The Prian had been watching Anthem and Titania, too, but now he turned to face the Arcadian king and knelt. Ballad laughed and gestured for Logan to rise.

"No, don't you dare," he said. "Without you and Maeve, none of us would be here. You've saved us all, my friend. The only reason we haven't knighted you, too, is that the Alliance doesn't want their bounty hunters to swear allegiance to some other government."

"So that will just have to wait until the White Kingdom joins the CWA," Panna finished. "But I don't think that will take long. With the Waygates out on Prianus and Axis, travel and trade between our worlds will be a lot easier... Once we train up some more people to use them."

"Until they unearth more Waygates on the other coreworlds, Prianus will be second only to Axis in importance," Ballad added, smirking at Logan. "Our black-sky little planet is about to become a major player on the galactic stage. Who could ever have guessed?"

Logan nodded, but still said nothing. Maeve stood silently beside him. Panna lifted her chin and smiled at them both.

"Logan, you were born under the name Centra, but you've said yourself that man died years ago on Prianus with an Emberguard's sword through his heart," Panna said in a stately, measured voice. "And so you took the name Coldhand for the hunter you became. But that is no longer who you are. You have saved more lives than you ever hunted."

Maeve turned to Logan and took his hands in hers. Glass and warm, slightly sweat-damp skin. Her heart pounded inside her and she could barely speak.

"Will you take one final name, enarri?" she asked him. "Will you accept mine? Will you be my husband?"

Logan's pale eyes widened and he pulled her close.

"Yes," he answered. "With all my heart."

Ballad shouted a cheer and Panna raised her hands to address the throng of Arcadians.

"Then by the power given to me by Maeve herself, I name you Logan Cavainna, and welcome you to the House of Cavain. The first human ever to join an Arcadian house!" Panna called triumphantly. "My teacher, Xen, always said that we were all of one people. We are all descended from the Devourers, those that the Nnyth call the First. But that is only blood that binds us. Here today, with this first marriage of Arcadian and human, we *choose* to be a single people. Maeve, Logan, seal the bond between your hearts and our people."

Maeve pulled Logan's face down and kissed him, to the tidal roar of Arcadia's song.

Hours later, Aes had set and the rebuilding glass city glowed with colorful light. The feasting and celebration would continue late into the night. Duke Ferris had arranged most of it, but both Panna and Ballad had added their own touches and heavy Lyran hunt metal could be heard thumping loudly through the air.

Maeve and Logan Cavainna walked slowly together through the empty city streets and stopped in the middle of a cracked, grassy plaza. There were Waygates set all around the edge. Even now, they swirled with shifting, slumbering blue light. Logan's glass hand was cold against Maeve's skin.

"Xia offered to replace them both," he said. "The hand and my heart. When she was redprinting Duaal's new liver. I could get them replaced easily."

"But you would not," Maeve answered with a smile. She knew better. "They are a part of you now. Like your new name."

"Gripper thinks it's silly. If I needed a new last name, he told me, I should have chosen something more descriptive. He's in favor of *Hunter*, of course."

"Naturally," Maeve said. She laughed and the soft sound echoed through the empty plaza. "I wonder what name he will choose for himself."

Logan shrugged. "I'm not sure. He and Xia are working with his redprint. They're hoping to create more Arborans. Xia and Gripper may actually have children together after all."

Maeve smiled again. She and Logan stood together in the center of the broken old tiles and overgrown statues, holding one another and looking up into the darkened sky. The stars of the galactic core were a gossamer silver bridal train overhead. Beyond them, there was the endless darkness.

"The Devourers are still out there," Logan said. "Dhozo and his people were just one engineering team. The rest of their fleets are somewhere in the universe. They're hungry and now they know we're here."

"They may come back someday," Maeve agreed. "This galaxy is their home."

"It's our home, too."

"Yes. Scarred though it is," Maeve said, placing her hand over Logan's mechanical heart. "It is ours. We will always love it, and we will always fight for it."

For more books by
Erica Lindquist & Aron Christensen,
visit us at **LLStories.com**